ALSO BY MIKE BOND

FREEDOM

"A simply riveting and deftly crafted read from an author with a genuine flair for narrative driven storytelling and an impressive attention to historical detail." – *Midwest Book Review*

"A memorable read." – *St. Louis Dispatch*

"Firmly rooted in fact and history . . . highly readable." – *The Daily News*

"A testament to the effect the politics and moral revolution have had on America, how what happened then created what we are now." – *The Miami Times*

"Each of these characters could carry a novel on his or her own, but Bond has done a fine job of telling all of their stories." – *Arizona Daily Sun*

"Truly beautiful writing . . . a 1960s Coming of Age Masterpiece." – *Bookbites*

"Bitterly nostalgic, romantic, a little heartbreaking and surprisingly edifying." – *The Daily Californian*

"Although Freedom can stand on its own, readers may find themselves eager for the next book in the series" – *Booktrib*

"Mixing adventure and thrills . . . an excellent sequel which provides an interesting glimpse at part of our American story." *Netgalley*

AMERICA

"*America* is a Coming-of-Age Masterpiece" – *St. Louis Post-Dispatch*

"*America* is an extraordinary and deftly crafted novel that combines interesting characters within the context of an historically detailed background... an inherently entertaining... fascinating read from cover to cover... highly recommended." – *Midwest Book Review*

"An adventure through America's rich and compelling history... a provocative and engaging read." – *Movies, Shows, & Books*

"Mike Bond has done it again, focusing his formidable talents on yet another genre: the historical novel." – *The Daily News*

"*America* brings to mind classic coming-of-age masterpieces such as "*Look Homeward, Angel*" by Thomas Wolfe." – *BookTrib*

"The characters are so vivid and alive, you think you're reading about old friends and recalling fond memories of youth." – *The Times-News Online*

"An involving, thoughtful tale that explores America's tectonic shifts leading to Vietnam." – *Kirkus*

"What I like most about this book it was personal, it had emotions, it had fear, and I learned many things... This book is a winner because it introduces our tumultuous history with characters we can identify with, admire and root for." – *Goodreads*

"If you love the history of the US then this one might be for you." – *Crossroad Reviews*

"I was intrigued and engrossed the entire time... a vivid world for the reader to get caught up in. – *Books and More*

"The most beautiful prose I have ever read... The author does not tell how others should think, but the beautiful story will help others to think. Each new book from Mike Bond seems to become better." – *NetGalley*

"I recommend this book to fans of historical fiction, coming of age stories, and readers who enjoy reading about the 1960s in America." – *A Dream Within A Dream*

"We wonder if the youth of today will have to fight the same fights for the same rights all over again. It would behoove them to read this book." – *Arizona Daily Star*

SNOW

"A captivating story of three friends on opposing sides of a betrayal... Bond tells his story in a crisp, propulsive prose that darts from sentence to sentence... He also has a sharp ear for dialogue and a knack for character development... Themes of the destructiveness of greed, both private and corporate; the sacredness of nature; and the primeval ways of mankind lend weight to a well-paced tale with intricate storylines." – *Kirkus*

"An action-packed adventure, but also a morality tale of what happens when two men who should know better get entangled in a crime from which they can't escape. " –*Denver Post*

"More than just a thriller, *Snow* lights up the complexities of American culture, the tensions of morality and obligation and the human search for love and freedom, all of which makes it clear Bond is a masterful storyteller." –*Sacramento Bee*

"A complex inter play of fascinating characters." –*Culture Buzz*

"Exploring the psyche and the depths of human reasoning and drive, *Snow* is a captivating story." –*BookTrib*

"An action-packed thriller that wouldn't let go. The heart-pounding scenes kept me on the edge of my seat." –*Goodreads*

"A simple story at its heart that warps into a splendid morality tale." –*Providence Sunday Journal*

ASSASSINS

"An exhilarating spy novel that offers equal amounts of ingenuity and intrigue." – *Kirkus*

"Bond is one of America's best thriller writers ... You need to get this book... It's an eye-opener, a page-turner... very strongly based in reality." – *Culture Buzz*

"An epic spy story... Bond often writes with a staccato beat, in sentence fragments with the effect of bullet fire. His dialogue is sharp and his description of combat is tactical and detached, professional as a soldier's debriefing. Yet this terseness is rife with tension and feeling... A cohesive and compelling story of political intrigue, religious fanaticism, love, brotherhood and the ultimate pursuit of peace." – *Honolulu Star Advertiser*

"Packs one thrilling punch after the other... A first-rate thriller." – *Book Chase*

"Powerful, true to life, and explosive ... A story that could be ripped right out of the headlines." – *Just Reviews*

"Riveting, thrilling... so realistic and fast-paced that the reader felt as if they were actually there. " – *NetGalley*

"The action is outstanding and realistic. The suspense flows from page to page... The background is provided by recent events we have all lived through. The flow of the writing is almost musical as romance and horrors share equal billing... I wish everyone could read and understand this book." – *Goodreads*

"Assassins" starts out as a conventional book and then changes into a poem of pain, anger, and tragic existence...What sets this book apart from other thrillers by more famous authors is the deep character study of the protagonist. He is a patriot and does his work from that place. But the toll it takes on him can only be supported by a man of Herculean moral strength. – *Vine Voice*

SAVING PARADISE
Pono Hawkins Book 1

"Bond is one of the 21 Century's most exciting authors... An action- packed, must read novel ... taking readers behind the alluring façade of Hawaii's pristine beaches and tourist traps into a festering underworld of murder, intrigue and corruption." – *Washington Times*

"A complex, entertaining ... lusciously convoluted story." – *Kirkus*

"Highly recommended." – *Midwest Book Review*

"A rousing crime thriller – but it is so much more... a highly atmospheric thriller focusing on a side of Hawaiian life that tourists seldom see." – *Book Chase*

"An intersection of fiction and real life." – *Hawaii Public Radio*

"An absolute page-turner." – *Ecotopia Radio*

"An unusual thriller and a must-read." – *Fresh Fiction*

"A complex murder mystery about political and corporate greed and corruption... Bond's vivid descriptions of Hawaii bring *Saving Paradise* vibrantly to life." – *Book Reviews and More*

"*Saving Paradise* will change you... It will call into question what little you really know, what people want you to believe you know and then hit you with a deep wave of dangerous truths." – *Where Truth Meets Fiction*

KILLING MAINE
Pono Hawkins Book 2

FIRST PRIZE FOR FICTION, 2016, *New England Book Festival* : "A gripping tale of murders, manhunts and other crimes set amidst today's dirty politics and corporate graft, an unforgettable hero facing enormous dangers as he tries to save a friend, protect the women he loves, and defend a beautiful, endangered place."

"Another terrifically entertaining read from a master of the storytelling craft... A work of compelling fiction... Very highly recommended." – *Midwest Book Review*

"Quite a ride for those who love good crime thrillers... I can 't recommend this one strongly enough." – *Book Chase*

"Bond returns with another winner in *Killing Maine*. Bond's ability to infuse his real-world experiences into a fast-paced story is unequaled." – *Culture Buzz*

"A twisting mystery with enough suspicious characters and red herrings to keep you guessing. It's also a dire warning about the power of big industry and a commentary on our modern ecological responsibilities. A great read for the socially and environmentally conscious mystery lover." – *Honolulu Star-Advertiser*

"Sucks in the reader and makes it difficult to put the book down until the very last page... A winner of a thriller." – *Mystery Maven*

"Another stellar ride from Bond; checking out Pono's first adventure isn't a prerequisite, but this will make readers want to." – *Kirkus*

GOODBYE PARIS
Pono Hawkins Book 3

"There's tension, turmoil and drama on every page that's hot enough to singe your fingers." – *New York Times* Bestseller, Steve Berry

"A rip-roaring page-turner , edgy and brilliantly realistic." – *Culture Buzz*

"Exhilarating ." – *Kirkus*

"Another non-stop thriller of a novel by a master of the genre." – *Midwest Book Review*

"A stunning thriller, entrancing love story and exciting account of anti-terror operations." – *BookTrib*

"Doesn't stop until it has delivered every possible ounce of intelligent excitement." – *Miami Times*

"Fast and twisty, and you don't know how it's going to end." – *Arizona Sun*

"Mike Bond is my favorite author... and his books are nothing short of works of art... I could not put this book down once I started reading it." – *Goodreads*

"A great book with normal special forces action and thrills, but what makes it great is the integration of Islamic terrorism." – *Basingtone Reviews*

"An action-packed story culminates in an exciting ending." – *The Bookworm*

"Thrills... crisp writing and intelligence." – *St. Louis Today*

THE LAST SAVANNA

FIRST PRIZE FOR FICTION, 2016, *Los Angeles Book Festival* : "One of the best books yet on Africa, a stunning tale of love and loss amid a magnificent wilderness and its myriad animals, and a deadly manhunt through savage jungles, steep mountains and fierce deserts as an SAS commando tries to save the elephants, the woman he loves and the soul of Africa itself."

"A gripping thriller." – *Liverpool Daily Post (UK)*

"One of the most realistic portrayals of Africa yet… Dynamic, heart -breaking and timely to current events … a must-read." – *Yahoo Reviews*

"Sheer intensity, depicting the immense, arid land and never-ending scenes… but it's the volatile nature of nature itself that gives the story its greatest distinction." – *Kirkus*

"One of the most darkly beautiful books you will ever read." – *WordDreams*

"Exciting, action-packed … A nightmarish vision of Africa." – *Manchester Evening News (UK)*

"A powerful love story set in the savage jungles and deserts of East Africa." – *Daily Examiner (UK)*

"The central figure is not human; it is the barren, terrifying landscape of Northern Kenya and the deadly creatures who inhabit it." – *Daily Telegraph (UK)*

"An entrancing, terrifying vision of Africa." – *BBC*

"The action is exciting, and a surprise awaits over each new page." – *NetGalley*

HOLY WAR

"Action-filled thriller. " – *Manchester Evening News (UK)*

"This suspense-laden novel has a never-ending sense of impending doom… An unyielding tension leaves a lasting impression." – *Kirkus*

"A profound tale of war … Impossible to stop reading. " – *British Armed Forces Broadcasting*

"A terrific book … The smells, taste, noise, dust, and fear are communicated so clearly." – *Great Book Escapes*

"A super charged thriller … A story to chill and haunt you." – *Peterborough Evening Telegraph (UK)*

"A tale of fear , hatred, revenge, and desire, flicking between bloody Beirut and the lesser battles of London and Paris." – *Evening Herald (UK)*

"If you are looking to get a driver's seat look at the landscape of modern conflict, holy wars, and the Middle East then this is the perfect book to do so." – *Masterful Book Reviews*

"A gripping tale of passion, hostage- taking and war, set against a war- ravaged Beirut." – *Evening News (UK)*

"A stunning novel of love and loss, good and evil, of real people who live in our hearts after the last page is done…Unusual and profound. " – *Greater London Radio*

HOUSE OF JAGUAR

"A riveting thriller of murder, politics, and lies. " – *London Broadcasting*

"Tough and tense thriller." – *Manchester Evening News (UK)*

"A high-octane story rife with action, from U.S. streets to Guatemalan jungles." – *Kirkus*

"A terrifying depiction of one man's battle against the CIA and Latin American death squads." – *BBC*

"Vicious thriller of drugs and revolution in the wilds of Guatemala." – *Liverpool Daily Post (UK)*

"With detailed descriptions of actual jungle battles and manhunts, vanishing rain forests and the ferocity of guerrilla war, *House of Jaguar* also reveals the CIA's role in both death squads and drug running, twin scourges of Central America. " – *Newton Chronicle (UK)*

"Grips the reader from the very first page. An ideal thriller for the beach, but be prepared to be there when the sun goes down." – *Herald Express (UK)*

TIBETAN CROSS

"Bond's deft thriller will reinforce your worst fears… A taut, tense tale of pursuit through exotic and unsavory locales. " – *Publishers Weekly*

"Grips the reader from the very first chapter until the climactic ending." – *UPI*

"One of the most exciting in recent fiction… An astonishing thriller." – *San Francisco Examiner*

"A tautly written study of one man's descent into living hell… a mood of near claustrophobic intensity." – *Spokane Chronicle*

"It *is* a thriller … Incredible, but also believable." – *Associated Press*

"A thriller that everyone should go out and buy right away. The writing is wonderful throughout… Bond working that fatalistic margin where life and death are one and the existential reality leaves one caring only to survive." – *Sunday Oregonian*

"Murderous intensity ... A tense and graphically written story." – *Richmond Times*

"The most jaundiced adventure fan will be held by *Tibetan Cross*." – *Sacramento Bee*

"Grips the reader from the opening chapter and never lets go." – *Miami Herald*

THE DRUM THAT BEATS WITHIN US
Poetry

"Passionately felt emotional connections, particularly to Western landscapes and Native American culture... compellingly linking the great cycles of stars with little, common lives... to create a powerful sense of loss... a muscular poignancy." – *Kirkus*

"The poetry is sometimes raw, painful, exquisite but there is always the sense that it was written from the heart." – *LibraryThing*

"A collection of poetry that explores the elements of nature, what nature can provide, what nature can take away, and how humans are connected to it all." – *Book Review Bin*

"An exploration of self and nature... that asks us to look at our environment through the eyes of animals... and the poetry that has been with us since the dawn of time... comforting, challenging, and thought provoking." – *Bound2Books*

"His poetry courses, rhythmic and true through his works. His words serve as an important alarm for readers to wake from their contented slumber of self-absorbed thought and notice the changes around them. Eye-opening and a joy to read, the master of the existential thriller can add another winning title to his accolades." – *BookTrib*

"The language is beautiful, heartbreaking, romantic, sad, savvy, and nostalgic all at once. From longer poems to very short, thought-provoking poems, the lines of each take the reader to a world the poet has experienced or given much thought to. Truly beautiful." – *Goodreads*

"This is such a beautiful book of poetry ... the imagery is vibrant, devastating, and haunting... A thoroughly modern 21st century collection that revisits and revises classic themes. Highly recommended." – *NetGalley*

"The poems are beautiful and range from the long lyrical expressions of love and nature to the brief expressions of a moments insight into a sudden feeling, expressed with a few words that capture the moment and the feeling perfectly. " – *Metapsychology Reviews*

"*The Drum That Beats Within Us* presents us with a world gone awry, a world in which the warrior poet has fought, and a world in which only love survives." – *Vine Reviews*

REVOLUTION

to
David

"Those who make peaceful revolution impossible
will make violent revolution inevitable."
— *John F. Kennedy*

"Most men and women will grow up to love their servitude
and will never dream of revolution."
— *Aldous Huxley*

Meet the new boss,
same as the old boss.
— *The Who*

When the music's over,
turn out the lights.
— *The Doors*

MIKE BOND

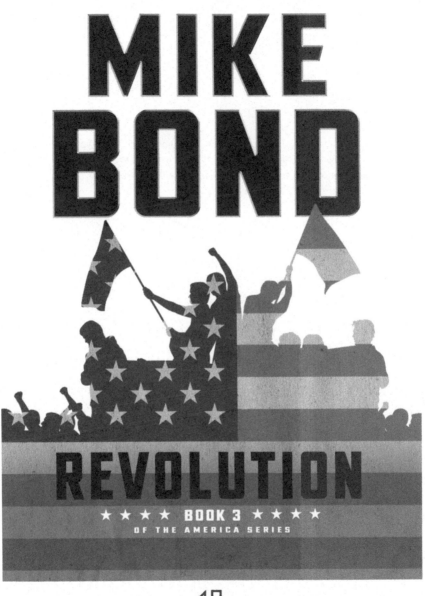

REVOLUTION

★ ★ ★ ★ ★ BOOK 3 ★ ★ ★ ★ ★
OF THE AMERICA SERIES

BIG CITY PRESS

Published in the United States by Big City Press, New York.

ISBN PAPERBACK: 978-1-949751-27-7

ISBN EBOOK: 978-1-949751-28-4

ISBN AUDIOBOOK: 978-1-949751-29-1

PUBLISHER'S CATALOGING-IN-PUBLICATION DATA

Names: Bond, Mike, author.

Title: America : volume 3 / Mike Bond.

Series: America.

Description: New York, NY: Big City Press, 2022.

Identifiers: ISBN: 9781949751277 (pbk.) | 9781949751284 (ebook)

Subjects: LCSH Friendship--Fiction. | United States--History--1961-1969--Fiction. | United States--Social conditions--1960-1980--Fiction. | United States--Social life and customs--1945-1970--Fiction. | United States--History--20th century--Fiction. | Bildungsroman. | BISAC FICTION / General | FICTION / Historical / General | FICTION / Coming of Age

Classification: LCC PS3619.O54 A64 v.3 | DDC 813.6--dc23

1

TET

THREE SAMPANS piled high with long canvas bundles slid out of the darkness of the Perfume River and vanished into the Bach Dang mist. Standing on the riverbank by the sports complex, Troy joyfully inhaled the river's musky rotten fertile dampness of fish and sewage and mud and almonds and bougainvillea, listened happily to the city quieting into night, its putt-putting scooters, grumbling buses and bedlam voices easing into silence, St. Xavier's melancholy bell tolling midnight through the thickening fog.

Su Li was here and the war faraway, nearly illusion, *Hué eternal,* the spirit of humanity, too ancient and sacred to harm. Even in the World Wars they didn't bomb the cathedrals. Nonetheless in the morning he'd tell the ARVN commander, Colonel Trang, that Bach Dang needed more Marines. Just to keep it this quiet. Apart from the war.

Severe yet friendly, Colonel Trang was short, round-faced, slightly bent forward. He had a frequent smile, a mix of gracious courtesy and natural good nature. He seemed to understand right away where you were coming from, and smiling in a kindly fashion, nodding, arms crossed, he would wait for you to get to your point.

Troy wondered as he crossed Tran Cao Vanh Street and nodded to the sentries as he entered the MACV compound gate, did Colonel Trang know about Su Li?

In his squad's main room a woman was screaming on the TV. Guys were laughing, drinking beer and smoking cigars, *Don't go around tonight* on somebody's Sanyo, *Well it's bound to take your life... Hope you are quite prepared to die...*

He climbed the wooden stairs to his room. His roommate had pulled a week in Saigon and Troy was happy for the solitude, in his warm bunk in the narrow little room in the far sleepy din of radios and songs, loving the drift into sleep and thinking of Su Li.

HE WOKE UNEASY from a dream of superstition and sorrow, sat up rubbing sleep from his face and wondered what was wrong. Barefoot on the cool floorboards he pulled on his pants and checked his rifle and the three spare clips and two grenades beside it.

The city was quiet. *Dead of night.* Why call it that?

A rocket screamed into the courtyard and blew, shrapnel ripping through the compound walls. He hit the floor, rolled up, snatched his gun and ammo and yanked on a grenade vest as another rocket howled and knocked him down. He grabbed his boots, jammed the mattress against the outside wall and ran to his battle station on the northwest wall facing the Citadel. Flares flashed through the sky, rifles and machine guns were firing from the gate. Another AB-40 rocket smashed into the courtyard, men screaming. Three shadows flitted across the street below; he fired too late.

"They're hitting the front gate," someone yelled. He ran for it, his untied boots flapping, in the horrible wail and spatter of bullets, and took cover with other Marines behind the compound wall, jumped up to fire at the incoming tracers from a machine gun in the street. The machine gun stumbled, stopped, then suddenly blasted at him knocking stone chunks from the wall, other Marines firing back at it and a barefoot Marine with a blooper dropped two grenades on it. When the grenades blew, Troy ran with others up the street leaping flare-lit bodies and rubble and downed branches and crippled cars, green tracers leaping at them from everywhere, there was no cover but the corners of houses and tree trunks and cars and any indent in the terrain they could find as they pushed foot by foot toward Le Loi Street, dead Marines littering the road.

Sheltered by two Ontos anti-tank vehicles they fought their way up Le Loi Street, VC hammering them with converging machine guns from streetside trenches, from windows and roofs, Marines falling, others running for the fallen only to fall too, the survivors piling the wounded on the Ontos, a Marine sobbing and holding his torn belly as he died, a buddy trying to staunch his wound as bullets snapped around them.

Gasping, screaming, dazed, breathless, heart pounding with fear and danger, Troy tried to see everywhere as he was running, crouching, crawling, rolled on his back to change clips and ran forward, firing again.

At An Cuu Bridge he led a fire team around the abutments into a hail of machine gun bullets and rockets, dead Marines clumped on the pavement. A mortar hit twenty feet ahead with a hail of shrapnel and ripping girders, two Marines falling, metal screaming as the bridge began to drop into the river. He dashed from one pylon to the next, bullets zipping, the bridge still shivering from the hit, and another mortar whispered down hitting the river with a great *oomph*.

Fearing a bullet through his helmet he inched his head round the pylon. From the far bank green tracers were converging on them, a constant *rat-ta-tat* of death against the girders, a wall of bullets they could not push through. On the river below the Citadel, Chez Henri was burning.

They were naked here. Through the hiss and crack of bullets Marines were trying to protect each other. From the stilt houses all up and down the far bank of the river and from the streets beyond green tracers were focused on them; they couldn't go forward but to stay here was to die.

He dashed to the next pylon. Bullets yanked at his sleeve and knocked the rifle from his hand, one smacked into his head and he knew he was dead but could not find the hole in his head, only a long gash across his temple. Fearing the flashing and crashing booming noises, he rolled on his side grasping for his rifle that seemed both protection and danger. It was smashed at the breech; he dragged himself to a dead Marine, grabbed his gun and three clips slippery with warm blood.

Five Marines ran across the bridge, two falling halfway, three reaching the pylons behind him. He dragged a wounded Marine to the pylon, waved at them to stop advancing, dashed for the far bank with a few others and took up a position firing carefully, defensively, to stretch out ammo. But there was no way to bring up more ammo or meds for the four wounded; before dawn they pulled back, bringing five dead Marines.

Back on the south bank near Le Loi Street he ran out into the street to grab an AK-47 from a dead NVA and worked his way back to C Company, just as they were inserted into the house-by-house, street-by-street slaughter in the old city, block by block of death, toward the Citadel.

TET WAS EVERYWHERE on TV. All the time. Newsmen, politicians and generals spoke of the offensive as if it were an inanimate event where you felt good because progress was being made. As if thousands of people weren't being torn apart and dying.

In the Duchess Suite at the Crown Royal Hotel in Vancouver, Tara knelt by the bed and tried to pray. Bring him home safe, Lord, and I'll do anything. What would be the hardest thing to do? I'll do it. Bring him home, Lord, and I'll quit smack.

The floor hurt her knees. So skinny these days. It didn't use to be like this.

Then it hit her like lightning that she was like this *because* of Troy. Because he was lost to her, and she still ached for him, and she bent down her head and told herself *Don't think about it.*

Just bring him back, Lord. Just bring him home.

. . .

EXPLOSIONS AND DEATH hung in the smoky streets. As the battle passed each block, most of the American dead were retrieved and piled on APCs for the rear, but weeping Vietnamese were still loading skinny underclad bodies on bicycles and two-wheeled wagons pulled by water buffaloes.

In the old city the Marines were fighting house to house, room to room, blowing holes through walls, throwing in grenades, spraying bullets and diving inside. Once in the corner of a room an old man in a white shirt and black trousers sat cross-legged beside an opium pipe, untouched by the grenades and bullets.

Amid the rumble of choppers came the random spat of M-16s and AKs as Marines and VC finished off enemy wounded. In a blasted garden a mother clutching a dead little girl watched them calmly. In an alley VC were trying to rescue a wounded comrade as Marines gunned them down one by one, and it seemed so strange they should keep on trying, dying. *They love each other*—it astonished him—*just like we do.* In a pink stucco house a crucifix hung sideways, in another a broken chalk Madonna, in an alley a jeep riddled with bullets, its tires flat, the driver slumped over the wheel.

Somewhere he'd lost his glasses, everything blurry. He shot at people and missed, but maybe that was because he was so sick of it, sick to death of death and killing.

After seven days' constant fighting they got an hour's rest. In a ruined hutch he found a bottle of Saigon brandy and downed it. There was a counter of broken dishes against the wall and a human leg behind it.

Beyond insane. The readiness of people to die was insane. All that mattered was love.

If Su Li was still in Bach Dang he'd get her out. Somehow. Or the VC might kill her. Because of him.

Dizzy from the brandy and hunger and filth and corpse stink he edged along the darkening street, choppers pulsing in the distance like a well-known heartbeat. Flies buzzed in blood glistening on the dirt. He moved north, downriver toward Su Li's home, between the VC and Marines through a maze of tiny streets with toppled houses and shattered godowns. Blood spattered the walls; bodies reeked under the rubble; NVA corpses swollen by the day's sun were belching and farting into the cool night.

The way ahead was blocked by NVA, dead Marines spread across the ground. He retreated to the house behind and eased through a broken window, waited, moved forward and waited again.

A man was breathing on the other side of the wall. Troy turned to back out but someone was coming that way. Sandals.

The man behind the wall sighed, a lonely quiet sound. There was a clink of crumbled concrete as he moved. He sniffed, an indrawn breath, softly swallowed.

"*An gai ninh,*" a voice behind Troy said—*Move forward*.

"*An gai ninh,*" repeated the man behind the wall. Uniforms rustled, ammo clips rattled. They were coming toward the wall; he was caught between them. He had a moment's hapless hope they'd take him prisoner, but here no one took prisoners. Trying to breathe silently he knelt to pick up a piece of broken concrete.

"*Quan di?*" another said—*What's that?*

Troy froze half-kneeling, chunk of concrete in his hand. A parachute flare blew overhead, the world suddenly black-yellow bright, shadows dancing across the doorway, the smashed wall and cratered floor as the flare hissed down. "*Lao danh!*" the man behind him said— *Don't move.*

Hopeless, he waited. An AK machine gun opened up to his right, beyond the wall. The first man stepped through the doorway, gun waist-high and Troy hit him in the face with the concrete and grabbed the gun, diving for the floor couldn't find the trigger then found it and sprayed the room fearing the clip would run out but it didn't and he leaped back out the door with the gun burning his hand and the man he'd hit came at him and he drove the barrel into the man's chest and fired again.

Another flare hissed down. Bullets whistled and smashed as he squirmed deeper into the rubble. Shadows leaped and dove. From beyond the wall a low whimper.

He had to go in there to get another clip. He waited. Machine guns snarled, mortars thumped into nearby houses; rifles crackled, bullets whacked into flesh; men cried and died. He bellied through smashed concrete into the room and waited for the next flare.

When it burst he scanned the room quickly: the shattered table with a body spread behind it, another in front of him on its back, a third in the far door. He took two clips from the closest gun and squirmed back out the door.

He couldn't make it through the NVA. Listening for the sound of M-16s he crab-ran over the shadowed rubble toward the Marine positions. Squads of NVA were running through the streets, in the darkness between the flares.

An M-60 opened up tearing the house apart over his head. Waiting to die he clung to the earth—if a flare fired now both sides would shoot him. The stench was awful. In the silence between the mortars he called out, "I'm a Marine, want to come in. Don't shoot me!"

Nothing. A bullet smashed a rock beside his head. "Goddamit you assholes," he yelled. "This is Lieutenant Troy Barden. I'm stranded out here and I'm coming in."

"Okay Lieutenant," a voice called. "Drop your rifle and make a dash for it. If you're not who you say you are we'll light you up like a Christmas tree."

A bullet tugged his shirt. "Don't shoot! I'm a Marine!" he screamed running eternally across open battered earth tripping on charred stumps and dove over the Marine wire onto ammo belts and mortar rounds.

He couldn't speak or stop shaking. The immensity of what had happened crashed in on him—that he'd made it. For a moment still alive. Hours, days, of expecting to die any second. He stared at the three Marines clustered round him. "What's the situation?"

"Static. We've taken some at this end and lost some at the other. Still no support."

"Those assholes!" Troy wrenched himself up. "Need to find my unit."

. . .

7

HE WAS GOING CRAZY. Too exhausted to sleep, he lay on a poncho atop rubble in the corner of a battered room, a rifle beside him, shaking with fear and fever, in a state of shock so vast it erased all else. The world spun insanely, nothing but a hammering of rounds and erratic mortar thuds and whine of incoming bullets and crackle of machine gun fire and rumble of choppers and the slow moan of a city condemning itself to death, the filthy floor shivering with explosions, the wailing of morphined wounded in the next room, the screeching of radios as men in terror tried to sound calm.

An overarching sorrow sickened him, despair so total there was nothing else, an icy hand crushing the heart, the exhausted realization that evil always wins. Finally he got up and went outside. A low misty dawn was breaking beyond the pillars of smoke, tinged with dew and blood and rotting flesh and cordite. Among the ragged wrecks of streets and buildings people were dying, many horribly, and there was nothing he could do about it. It was like World War One, you ran and ran at the walls of machine gun fire and there was no chance of surviving. He knelt down in the mud, crossed himself and prayed Su Li would make it.

"Here, Loot." A sergeant named Creasey handed him a cup of warm coffee.

"Oh Jesus," Troy said, "where'd you get this?"

"There's more. And get yourself some C-rats, Sir. We gotta move up."

Troy thought of Su Li. "Who says?"

"Captain Meader, Sir. He's the new CO since Quinn bought it."

Day after day the gray dismal sky and the mist and rain had made the ceiling too low for air support. And the order had come down on rules of engagement; the silly bastards in Washington didn't want the city destroyed. *Just kill everyone in it.*

With Captain Meader taking up the rear they trudged down a battered street of broken palm trees, overturned cars, shattered huts and fallen wires. The fronts of the houses had collapsed into the street that stank of half-buried flesh and smashed concrete. A squad of

Marines ran by, boots crunching damp rubble. Choppers were alighting in the flattened streets behind them.

The war seemed muffled, the mortars far away. They passed a clutch of NVA bodies slender and small as boys, almost feminine. They turned into a yard of broken trees and stooped one by one through a rocket hole into a house—two blackened rooms, a corridor rubbled with plaster and lath, a kitchen at the back with another hole blown out of it and slippery blood on the floor, Marines taking firing positions in the two rooms upstairs.

They ducked through the kitchen hole and ran one by one across a garden to the cover of two buttresses in the stone wall at the back. A bullet cracked off one, then a fifty cal opened up, chewing into the wall and knocking down rocks. Captain Meader came up. He was young with a narrow black moustache and seemed very frightened. "Other side of the wall," he yelled, "we think is garden and another house. We'll blow the wall, over there," he pointed, "where that big crack is. Then we toss in grenades, lay down fire and go for the house—"

It sounded like Lesson Seven from the Marine manual. Troy gripped his helmet as bullets hammered the wall. "What if there's no garden?"

"We'll know when we get there."

"Hey Four-Eyes!" Meader shoved a belt of C-4 at a chubby kid with thick grimy glasses that he kept pushing up his nose and sniffling. "We'll cover you," he yelled. "You pack it in good, halfway up that wall, where that long vertical crack is—"

Biting the side of his lip the kid made a waddling run along the wall to the crack. Bullets sang off the rock above him. The Marines fired back steadily at every window and wall. The kid packed the C-4 into the crack and ran back, caught halfway by machine gun bullets spinning him around as they ripped him apart. He tumbled to the ground; his helmet rolled a few times and sat face up. Blood began to well from beneath him.

Meader shot at the C-4 making a big thud of gyrating smoke and

9

dust and flying rocks. When the smoke and dust cleared the crack was a wide black hole, with a terraced garden beyond.

The kid quivered once. "Cover fire!" Sergeant Creasey sprinted for him, grabbed him and started back, stumbled, turned as if losing direction, dropped the kid and sank to his knees. His shirt puffed as another bullet ripped through him. He opened his arms like a crucifix and dropped face down, bullets knocking up stone and dirt around him.

"Volunteer!" Meader screamed. "I want a volunteer. We got two Marines down and we have to get them! Thomas!" he yelled at his radioman. "I want an Ontos now."

"Trying sir. Radio's down."

"Volunteer! Who's my volunteer?"

"They're both dead," Troy yelled.

"They're dead when I say so! Volunteer!"

Troy ran for the hole in the wall leaping over the dying Marines and tossed three grenades into the room beyond the hole. There was a silence then the huge outrushing *whack* of the grenades. He sprayed the room with bullets, reloaded and dashed inside to the right, another Marine left, to a door at the far end.

They halted panting on each side of the door trying not to breathe the smoke and dust. His rifle barrel was too hot to touch. Blood slid down his face. From beyond the door came Vietnamese voices, a radio.

Two more Marines bolted in, then Meader, who waved in the other Marines, leaving two to guard the hole.

Troy eased along the corridor toward the voices. They came from a room upstairs at the end of the corridor. On both sides of the corridor the doors were shut.

From the room above came more Vietnamese voices on a squawking radio, quick footsteps in and out. Maybe a command post. If his squad could sneak up the stairs they could get them all. A door squeaked open behind him and a man came out rubbing his neck sleepily. Troy hit him in the gut with his rifle and the man collapsed groaning and he clubbed him on the head. He checked the room: two rope-weave beds, a wooden table with a candle and a bowl of water.

With three Marines he advanced to the stairs. The voices upstairs were louder, a high singsong urgency. Sandals ran across the floor; a voice called down to what seemed to be a courtyard in the rear; a bicycle clattered away. Troy stationed one Marine at the bottom and with the two others behind him moved up the stairs. Their steps made no noise in the chaotic din of artillery, machine guns and small arms, the voices closer now. A throat clearing, something heavy slapping down on a table. At the top of the stairs was a door; he pulled the pins on two grenades, holding down the releases.

He kicked open the door, threw the grenades into the room and dove to the floor; the grenades blew in an awful roar; the other Marines waited two seconds then tossed in two more. Troy ducked through the door firing. A classroom. The desks shoved aside; maneuver diagrams on the blackboards, children's drawings pinned to walls.

An awful moan came from the back. He waited for light from a flare and stepped across the smashed bodies and desks. The moan hissed out. He upended a splintered desk and as the flare died he saw a crumpled body in VC black pajamas. A woman. He turned her over. The back of her skull was a shattered mass of blood but her face was untouched.

Su Li.

2

CANNON FODDER

HIS SKULL was horror and dust; he couldn't think or feel. For days he'd wandered heart-dead in a gray world of shrapnel, bullets, cordite, bodies and explosions. In the rare minutes he slept, Su Li came to him sweetly smiling, her slanted almond eyes and beckoning lips and the glory of her slim body in her *ao dai*. She's fine, she loves you, you're going home. She exploded in his grenade's blast, writhed in his bullets. Golden naked in the candlelight she reached up to him, sable hair and silken voice. "Let's go to America now. Tet all finish."

His heart stopped when he remembered. "You died for nothing."

She drew back. "So will you."

These constant conversations in his head were more real than the bullets and bombs, the ear-crushing explosions and constant rattle of automatic weapons, the screams of the dying, the stinking blood and sundered bodies. Every moment night and day he watched her die.

He was beyond crazy but didn't care. Everyone was crazy. Killing each other, officers showing how to kill better, weary despondent Marines running constantly toward certain death, sickened by the killing yet not knowing how to stop. And the ruthless fearless enemy —skinny little men like teenagers—fierce and determined because

12

you're destroying their country. The terrified civilians—how many dead children had he seen? The little girl clutching the baby duck was the worst, dead in an Ontos backblast, the gosling blown halfway into her chest, the girl maybe eight with long sable hair and a face in which you could already see the woman she would have become.

Why did people so love to hate? No explanation he could think of allowed for any God, not even Satan's weaker brother.

In the battle for the last streets he took risks no one else did. But it was the others who died. A kid whacked by a sniper ducking past a window where Troy had stood five minutes earlier begging for death. Three Marines cut down where he'd sauntered across without a shot.

Now the NVA were gone or dead under the ruins. The city reeked of cordite, phosphorous, blasted stone, bombs and rotten flesh. Civilians who had been lucky to flee were returning to stare sorrowfully at their ruined homes. Bach Dang was cleared; its streets rubbled. Troy found Su Li's mother outside her blasted home.

"I never knew," he said helplessly.

She looked at him. "She hated you."

He realized he was searching her face for a trace of Su Li. "I loved her."

"Love? Look what you do."

"I didn't want this war." He felt a heartbroken fool unable to express himself in Vietnamese. "Not when I understood..."

The old woman nodded. "Look what you wear."

He glanced down at his Marine utilities, dirty, torn, bloodied where he'd helped load bodies on a Huey. *It isn't me*, he wanted to say. *But it is*.

If he'd listened to Mick and never joined up he wouldn't have killed her.

If he hadn't re-upped.

If he hadn't found the weak place in the wall.

If he hadn't gone through that door and down the corridor and up the stairs. If he'd been killed first.

She might still be alive, might survive this crazy war. Someday an old woman smiling at her great-grandchildren.

MICK TRUDGED up the icy New Hampshire farm road, a girl named Heather beside him bundled in a long wool coat, their breath freezing in the sharp night. "I bet a yes," he said, crimping his lips against the cold.

"These isolated places worry me," she said. "You don't think they'll shoot us or set the dogs on us? Jeez, that last bunch..."

He took her arm, the two of them bumping together as they slogged through ankle-deep snow. "This place's like the farm where I grew up. That's a lovely cow barn, look at *all* that hay...has to be twenty percent alfalfa—"

The porch light snapped on; a white-haired bent man in blue coveralls let them into a warm wood-smoky kitchen, coffee on the woodstove. "Come in, come in out of the cold. What we can do for you?"

"We're volunteers for Gene McCarthy," Heather started.

He cut her off with a sharp wave of his hand. "I don't want to hear any of that!" He scowled at Mick. "You believe in it too?"

"Yes sir. Please listen a moment, to what we have to say—"

"Flora!" the old man called. "Come out here!"

A rustle of dragging slippers, a round gray-haired woman in a blue dress with white polka dots. The old man stared at Mick. "When I was your age I fought in the Battle of Villers-Cotterets. In France, the First World War. I didn't shirk my duty."

"That was a brave and right thing to do. But this is a different war." Mick watched the old man's face as he spoke, trying to reach him with the difference between necessary and unnecessary war, Heather telling them how the United States had split Vietnam apart, about the bombing, herbicides, and million civilian deaths. "Imagine," Mick said, "that you and I are Vietnamese, and our country is attacked...wouldn't *we* fight the invaders?"

Going back down the farm road, Heather took Mick's hand, the night colder, darker and more alien after the warm kitchen. "I give it a probable. She will for sure. She might talk him into it."

"When you described the bombings of the North her eyes glistened."

"How can they *not* vote for Gene! How can you vote to kill innocent people?"

Ahead of them his blue VW crouched snow-dusted on the shoulder. She held the door open to shine the dome light on a typed list. "The Jonsons are next. He's Republican, she's Independent. Forty-four Old Hardacre Road."

"Christ, we've hit forty-four voters already today and at least thirty're going to vote for Gene." He snuggled into the cold hard seat. "How many more on that list?"

"Maybe forty."

"In another week we can maybe do three hundred more..."

She kissed him. "Sometimes I get so tired of this I forget how important it is."

"Yeah, like getting so tied up in things you forget the beauty of life."

HUNDREDS OF MARINES HAD DIED in Hué. Thousands more wounded, many maimed for life. A thousand enemy and many thousands of civilians dead. One of the world's loveliest cities smashed. There was no way to explain it without accepting that humans were both insane and evil.

A sorrow so deep it numbed everyone. The Marines who had lived through it, exhausted by days of killing and expecting death, by seeing their friends die, deafened by the constant explosions and gunfire, seemed to know it had all been for no reason, an apocalypse.

By the end of February it was over. With deadly air support due to better flying weather and relaxed rules of engagement, the Americans were able to blast their way house by house to the Citadel, and then through its sixteen-foot walls and the acres of ancient buildings within. Countless NVA and civilian bodies still stank under the rubble or bloated in the canals. Asia's loveliest city was smashed, its people slaughtered, its magnificent architecture gone forever.

As Troy straddled a wall manning a machine gun over the battered Palace of Eternal Peace, he tried to imagine the millions of hours spent over so many centuries making this city so beautiful. What would those craftsmen think now? Was it worth building anything for humans?

From the desolate ruins of Hué he was transferred north to Fire-base Nimrod overlooking Route One. Captain Cross was there, thinner and angrier, on his third tour. "Charlie's been movin in," Cross said over the matchstick in the corner of his mouth. "We think he's traveling through; we're bombing the shit out of him but he keeps coming. Jesus, Khe Sanh's been gitting hit, what, a month now?"

Troy took every mission he could get, volunteered for every patrol, every night op or listening station. It was better he should die than someone who wanted to live, but the others kept dying while he lived on.

Captain Cross was hard and tight-faced as always, the muscles tense in his narrow jaw as he sent men out to die. Patrols for two to five days, strung out through the paddies and hills, at night up tight in foxholes under poncho halves, or out on perimeter watching for death. In the day they died from snipers and mines, at night from mortars and rockets, sometimes their own artillery, their own planes.

For days they worked the hills west of Khe Sanh hunting NVA stragglers from Hué. Burning the leeches from their legs, scraping the rotten skin from their feet, stomachs nauseous with dysentery, sleeping in rain and mud and mosquitoes and the din of mortars. Weeks in the same stinking torn muddy utilities, in the same stench of gun oil, shit, thatch, sweat, and blood. Attacked and attacking. Killing and dying with no purpose. Day and night the thunder of artillery and crash of bombs, the roar of napalm and hiss of phosphorous, the dead and wounded, the crushed jungle and seared paddies, turning the earth into Hell. The Hueys feeding on the dead, taking them away by the hundreds, then lowering themselves into the paddies to rinse the blood off their decks.

A stone raised against a brother, the Cro-Magnon's club crushing the last Neanderthal skull, Old Testament tribes slaughtering each other, Goths murdering Celts, Romans Etruscans, the Zulu the Bushmen, the Japanese the Americans and vice versa—who was fool enough to dream it could ever end? Except with that final weapon which takes all life, already in the hands of madmen...

We have to choose, he wanted to tell them, between war and love.

"BOBBY TOLD LYNDON he won't run against him if Lyndon pulls out of Vietnam," Al Lowenstein said. "But Lyndon told Bobby to get fucked. That's when Bobby announced."

"The Republicans will run Tricky Dicky again," Bella Abzug said.

"Bobby can clean his clock," her husband said. "But Gene can't."

Mick thought of the days he'd spent tirelessly canvassing for McCarthy with Heather in the bitter cold. "Hey look, Gene's the one who knocked Lyndon out of New Hampshire."

"Lyndon *won* New Hampshire—" Bella said.

"By three hundred votes?" Mick snapped. "A sitting president in wartime against some unknown from Minnesota? For you that's a *win?*"

"So Bobby's asking me to help," Lowenstein said.

"Against Gene?" Bella said.

"I told him I can't, it's my word."

"You helped talk Gene into it, so you can't switch to Bobby."

"Bobby's already ahead of Lyndon in the polls," Bella's husband said. "Did you hear that?"

"Walter Cronkite just said that the only rational way out of Vietnam is to negotiate. Did you hear *that?* He's suing for peace."

"He ain't the president."

TO DO EVIL was to do unnecessary harm. To hurt, damage another, except to protect yourself or survive. But Daisy couldn't find the cure for evil.

From all she'd learned, the desire to harm came from having *been* harmed. Most human viciousness linked to early experience in fear and sorrow.

Her father's alcoholism had been an attempt to drown early pain.

But by trying to solve her father's sorrows wasn't she derailing her own dreams?

Though, anyway, what were her dreams?

If you could learn what drove unnecessary pain? Not just for people, for all life? Wouldn't that be uniting her attempt to heal her father—and herself—with doing groundbreaking new research, that would give her power to go on...

What a crazy, stupid hope.

It's pain that teaches. Only pain.

No, that's not true. Joy teaches too.

She and Mick in high school, their naked thrusting under winter coats in the frigid back seat of his father's DeSoto. Yes, joy teaches too.

War and hate and violence, where were they rooted? Was it in the amygdala, fight or flight? The near-instantaneous unflinching response to danger, bypassing the frontal lobes. How do you take *that* back?

What brain nexuses influenced actions? Not just nineteenth century research on brain areas tied to behavior. Was the old argument about DNA vs. environment finally solved? No. But since long before the ancient Babylonians, Chinese and Greeks we've tried to fix the brain. Long before Luxor we were trepanning. Even when we lived in caves we were doing craniectomies. Why?

What did we have in mind?

She laughed, lulled by the music and the silky pillow against her cheek, the warm feeling of discovery, of self-affirmation. Deep in her bones feeling the truth of what she'd done.

Looking forward to what she could do.

About Mick, though, she had to admit she was a little empty. Seventeen hours a day of study and research. No time for life.

But wasn't she learning about life?

She should take a day off. She really should.

Probably every woman feels this sometimes. Unfulfilled.

TROY STARED at the hillside beyond the gully. Death there. Couldn't see it but it was there. He glanced at his fire team: Grinziak, Calloway, Quines, Ramirez. Two new guys he barely knew. Which would die? Because Centcom wanted a patrol up a hill they knew nothing about, even didn't remember the napalm scars half-way up the ridge, the shattered trees, the guys who'd died there before. *We might all die up there.*

He turned to Ramirez. "What d'you think?"

Ramirez scanned the ridge, chewed his chaw thoughtfully. "Shit place to die."

Troy inspected it again. "If we go right along our own ridge down the head of the valley and along that ridge on top?"

"They got us in their sights, man. No matter how we go."

"I'm not calling in Phantoms."

"To destroy a mile of jungle?" Ramirez squirted tobacco through his lower front teeth. "It's the Slopes' fucking country, man. We should leave it alone."

JOHNSON QUIT!" Tucker yelled as he came in the door. "It's on the radio!"

Mick ran to his stereo and snapped it on. "Took Congress totally by surprise," a Democratic congressman was saying. "We're going to circle the wagons and decide where to go next."

"It certainly puts the Democrats at a risk," the newsman was saying.

"The way Lyndon's popularity was dropping, he wasn't sure to win anyway."

Mick let out a war whoop and jumped so high his head cracked the ceiling. It wasn't possible! Al Lowenstein and the thousands of young people he'd inspired had done what he said they'd do just seven months ago: they'd brought down a sitting president.

McCarthy had come within three hundred votes of beating Johnson in the New Hampshire primary, close enough that Johnson knew he couldn't win the nomination now that Bobby was coming in. Mick's days of trudging through the snow to talk people into voting for Gene had then seemed pointless, doomed to failure. Now anything seemed possible.

The ogre was gone and the way was open for McCarthy or Bobby to win. With opposition growing against the war, a pro-war Republican like Nixon would never win. Romney was out of the race, Rockefeller couldn't buy a vote, and only an idiot would ever vote for a grade-B movie actor like Reagan.

Maybe democracy worked after all.

"If we all keep working," he told other anti-war groups, "we can do this."

Maybe peace would have a chance.

"CANNON FODDER. That's what we are," Lawyer Jones said. "There's a greater proportion of us blacks here at the front. More casualties. And we *know* Vietnam isn't about democracy or freedom. Because *we* don't have that, back home. So how can we pretend to be setting it up here?"

He chewed nonchalantly on a grass stalk and looked out over the pitted blasted hillside like a farmer over his crop. "I dig that word, *casualty.* Sounds kind of *casual,* doesn't it? And the plural: the *casual ties* that bind us—kinda pretty. But a casualty is somebody blown apart—happens all the time—and you have to go looking for his pieces. A head here, a foot over behind that bush...Or it's the kid lying there looking at his intestines...*Those* are casualties..."

"That Hanoi radio woman," Spike Jones said, "she says some good things. Like why are us blacks over here killing *them* and destroying *their* country, when back home our cities are burning and whitey treats us just like he does the people here? Why aren't we home, protecting our own rights, our own families?"

"When I get home—"

"You'll get home, brother."

"– I'm joinin the Panthers. Most of the Black Panthers are like you'n me, they been in the war. In the fighting." Lawyer turned to Troy. "You see, black brothers don't get to serve in the rear—you don' have no black rear echelon mother fuckers but you got plenty black frontline soldiers and Marines. What we gettin' exposed to in Vietnam make me realize we on the same wrong side back home—why were we helping whitey put the black man down? The colored peoples down?"

One thing I can tell you, the Beatles were singing on Spike's Sanyo, *is you got to be free.*

"Yeah," Spike said. "Maybe what we need, to be free, is a revolution at home? Instead of doing all the killing over here?"

THE MISERABLE MONSOON cleared by early April. Day and night Troy still thought of little but Su Li but he'd begun to notice the world again.

He would make amends though none were possible. As he lay awake in his poncho through the long cold rainy nights he began to decide if he survived he'd help to stop the war.

"Johnson won't run again," a Dutch photographer named Johann said. He had been lightly wounded in Hué and tomorrow was headed for the DMZ. "Said so last week."

Troy felt a burst of hope. That Johnson would quit the race seemed an impossible gift. "Why?"

"McCarthy almost beat him in New Hampshire and now Bobby Kennedy's come in. No way Lyndon could win the next state, apparently—what is it, Wisconsin?" He coughed mortar dust. "It's this bloody war's taken him down."

"Takes everybody down," Ramirez said. "Sooner, later."

"Nobody's for it anymore," Troy nodded at the Marines near them, the firebase. "Except lifers who aren't in the field. On my first tour most guys believed in it, cared..."

"Yeah," Ramirez said. "Got them killed."

A flare burst and Troy scanned the savage ruptured brush beyond the perimeter, all white-green in flarelight. "I believed in it then."

Johann coughed. "Why'd you change?"

Was it Captain Cross killing the beautiful teacher and the old man? The banana valley? The whole damn thing? "You're going up to the DMZ tomorrow, it's all Free Fire Zone, you'll see we've killed every person and waterboo, every pig and duck and chicken over thousands of miles..." Troy stopped to watch a patch of darkness in the dying flare.

"Evil's a nice thing," Johann reflected. "Allows us to compartmentalize, say it's not *us*, it's *evil*. Like Christians creating the Devil. To make God look good..."

"Back in the States, aren't people turning against the war?"

Johann shrugged. "If ever was a Pyrrhic victory, it was Hué."

"The most horrible thing happened..." Troy started.

"Yeah? What?"

"It's nothing. The whole thing was horrible...What we are."

"Anybody fought in Hué'll have nightmares for life." Johann picked at his teeth with a black fingernail. "Shoulda seen last June, the bloody Six-Day War. Christ when the fockin Mirages hit the Egyptian convoy we were doomed. I survived because this American guy wanted to climb the ridge for a look, so we were up there when the Mirages hit...The poor bloody bastards below..."

"My brother...my *adopted* brother, was in that war—"

A whistling hiss suddenly a scream whacked in as the first rocket of the night nailed the perimeter, mud and tree limbs thunking down. A loud glaring crack sending bolts of pain into your eardrums. "Bloody fockers," Johann grunted, "startin early."

"—He met a guy like you, he said," Troy waited as another rocket roared in, "told me in New York, before my second tour..." A third rocket blew up logs and earth that slowly clattered down. Automatic rifle fire was building from the northeast, green nasty tracers homing in.

"Corpsman up!" someone yelled. "Corpsman!"

Over the Prick Ten the shaky rapid voice of the F.O. giving coordinates to Firebase Nimrod, the first rounds slamming into the hills with great red-white bursts. "F-4s on the way," another voice said calmly, one Troy didn't recognize.

"I'm off to my hole," Johann grunted. "Nother blimy night in paradise."

"Hey Barden!" Captain Cross came walking up as if there were no mortars hitting, no danger. "Wanna lead a first patrol tomorrow?"

Troy listened for incoming. "Hadn't you better get down, Sir?"

"You want it?"

Troy shrugged. "Why not?"

LOVELY COOL DAWN, dry west wind, salmon-colored high cirrus, an undulant warm jungle of scintillating greens, reds and blues. The kind of day when your rifle feels light and the distance easy, in the simple joy of living

In midmorning he led the forward fire team down a long ridge of tall widely spaced trees. They spread out twenty yards apart, looking down both sides of the ridge. He signaled to Ramirez: *Come on up.*

Ramirez settled his helmet, slipped forward between the trees and crouched beside Troy. "What you think?" Troy said softly.

Ramirez chewed his chaw. Sweat ran down his dirty nose. "Fuckin sucks."

"That's my take. Something ain't right."

"If we send out three guys, a hundred yards ahead?"

"Somebody'll end up dead."

Ramirez raised his head to peer between the trunks. "I think so."

At the end of the ridge was a little oval paddy with three banana trees along the far edge, a tree line with scrub and bamboo behind. Ramirez watched the blue-green world around the paddy, the tree line and bamboo jungle beyond. "Can't see nothin," he said. He curled his upper lip, concentrating.

"I take half the team and circle right around the paddy on that high ground behind the bananas," Troy said. "You take the other and swing left, we meet on that hill there—"

A bullet hit Ramirez under the eye, his brains blew out behind him, bullets hailing branches and grass as Troy dove for cover but there was no cover, guys getting hit, screaming in the howl of bullets; expecting a whack through his helmet Troy rolled upright firing across the paddy, water spattering where bullets hit low. He ran to a rubber tree as bullets shattered its bark as he jammed in a new clip, turned and fired a burst into the banana trees, their fronds thrashing, waited five seconds and hit them again.

Wylie was down, the Prick Ten's antenna across his crumpled body. Troy scrambled for it, bullets sucking at his head, using Wylie's body for cover as he tried to call up choppers and support but there was no answer, just roaring silence as he pushed the button and waited and pushed it again, pleading with them to answer, blood dripping down his face from a round splattering Wylie's head, bullets hitting so hard even the earth seemed to groan and flinch.

"Pull back!" he screamed as he ran dragging Wylie and the Prick Ten through the wide trees. A burning steel beam tore through his gut knocking him down, pain so awful he couldn't breathe or think except beg it to end. He tried to get up so he could get hit again and killed but was too convulsed, couldn't find the Prick Ten; the pain took away his breath and blood came out his mouth.

Guns still firing, uphill somewhere, AKs and 16s. A few distant choppers like angels in another dimension. He lay trying to hold his stomach together. Soft rain fell through the bullet-blistered trees, cooling and cleaning the air. In his pain he thanked God for stopping the bullets, begged God to let a chopper find him, seeing the chopper hover down through the early mist, its interior like an ambulance full of soft white sheets and instruments, not the rattling metal floor where Marines bled to death.

The rain had gone. The sun was very hot and his throat burned with thirst.

There was water in the paddy. All he had to do was go down there.

He rolled to his side and saw no one on the hillside, just the bodies of Wylie, Keegan and Rowe downslope, Ramirez on his back at the edge of the forest.

He lurched to his knees. His trousers were heavy with blood; it had thickened on the leaves. He wondered if the VC would come back. Dragging his rifle he crawled to the paddy and drank but it burned in his gut and he pulled back moaning with pain.

Over his hoarse breathing he heard the childlike voices of VC coming downhill. He scrambled along the bamboo paddy edge, the raspy leaves hissing, his boots sloshing through muck. More VC voices came from ahead, a quick peremptory order.

He was trapped in a muddy bamboo-walled maze, VC ahead and behind, their tinny voices rising excitedly when they found his trail. Holding his belly he squeezed through the next bamboo wall into another flooded paddy, its green stalks bright emerald in reddish sun, the bare sidewall of a terrace ahead. He splashed bent-over and gasping along it, tugging his boots from the mud, rifle dragging in the muck, sweat stinging his eyes. He staggered uphill among the wide-spread trees, fell down; the pain made him get up and go on. He'd lost his rifle somewhere, should go back for it but there might be VC. He fell again and after a while got up.

Had to find his men, get them out. Then send a chopper back for Ramirez and the others.

He would tell them. Tell them all. No more war.

3

THE AWFUL GRACE OF GOD

"**H**E'S DEAD," the voice said in Vietnamese. Bare dirty feet, skinny legs, black shorts, torn tan undershirts. Hard steel poked Troy's eye: a muzzle.

Troy pulled away his head. "Let me be."

There was a moment's shocked silence that he'd spoken Vietnamese. One of them tugged at Troy's collar, spoke rapidly of which Troy understood *Officer, maybe, speaks Vietnamese. Intelligence.* Another kicked Troy in the stomach, the first VC restraining him. More VC came and stood around him silently.

"My Marines?" Troy said.

A brown moon face leered down. "We killed them all."

They dragged him onto a burlap sack, a man at each corner running, banging him over the ragged ground and into trees and branches as the F-4s he'd called for hours ago screamed down shaking the ground and whiplashing the trees, their huge bombs blasting the world, napalm and phosphorous firestorms sucking cyclones of molten air that even at a distance seared the clothes off men and set their ammo on fire. Each time a plane descended on them it was sure to kill them; twice the men dropped him to dive for cover but dashed back for him. *Like Marines,* he thought crazily, *they won't desert you.*

They slid him headfirst down a bumpy dirt tunnel of white roots and sharp rocks, into darkness, no air. A tiny light far below became a smoky yellow cavern under a hanging flashlight, stinking of burnt flesh and blood, bamboo racks of bandaged men along dirt walls. Men with shattered legs and sucking chest wounds and amputated arms in side tunnels on bamboo stretchers in the bloody mud.

He kept gasping but there was no air. So thirsty. Around him burnt men whimpering and begging, drip and spatter of blood. The earth far above them shuddering and groaning. More wounded sliding down, more bodies dragged up on ropes. The agony so bad he barely knew, clenched over his wounded gut, wrists tied to ankles so he could not lie straight. After a long time two men came and untied the torn shirt wrapping his wound, retied it and moved on. "What?" Troy gasped at them, "what are you doing to me?"

One man glanced back. "Wait your turn."

Much later they laid him on a bamboo table and tied a mask over his face. *Don't tell them anything*, he remembered. *But there's nothing to tell.*

An endless time later he grew conscious, not understanding, belly afire, aching with thirst. Slowly recognizing the smells of kerosene and sweat and disinfectant and blood. Doubling up to lessen the pain he realized his wrists were still tied to the sides of the stretcher. "Water," he gasped. "*Nuóc*! Please *nuóc*."

Chunks of dirt thunked down; the earth shivered like a beaten dog; between bouts of agony he wondered if these bombs were the thousand-pounders from B-52s. "Just one makes an underground parking lot," a pilot had once said in a Saigon bar. "A moving carpet of bombs going forty feet into the earth before they blow the world inside out."

Unending huge explosions far above, the earth shuddering, rocks and dirt falling on men who cried out, tunnels collapsing, men digging them out, ramming the earth aside. No air. It drove him crazy to have his wrists tied, couldn't escape the airless shivering deadly tunnel, claw his way to freedom.

"You not live one minute up there," someone said. He was being smothered under tons of earth; no matter how hard he tugged his wrists wouldn't loosen; each time he tried the stomach pain knocked him out.

Perhaps days later a gray-haired round-faced man bent over him checking the bandages around his stomach. *"Nuóc,"* Troy begged. "Please *nuóc.*"

"No water," the man said in English. "You have intestine and stomach surgery. No water." He nodded at the intravenous bag hanging on a bamboo pole. "That is water," and moved on.

Sometime later he was back. "I cut you open. I sew up every intestine, cut out sepsis. You very strong. You maybe live."

Chunks of earth were still falling. The doctor looked up. "The B-52s bombing everywhere west of Khe Sanh. When they stop we take you to Cambodia. Keep you there."

As if drunk Troy tried to gather his thoughts. "Why are you saving me?"

"They want you." The doctor nodded his head upward, up the hierarchy, up on the surface. "They tell me put you first, ahead our wounded."

The thought bothered Troy. "I don't want to go first."

"I don't want you to either." The doctor smiled, waited for a bomb strike to fade. "I want you to die."

Time passed slowly, second by long second dripping like the patter of blood turning the floor to mush, the steady throb of moans and weeping. He tried to think what he might have done to avoid the firefight, how he could have protected his men.

The ground kept rumbling, dirt chunks thudding down; they moved him to another tunnel; it collapsed and they dug him out and rigged a new intravenous bag and moved him again. "This not a bad bombing," the doctor said.

But it had gone on forever, the bombing, the horror of exploding death at any instant, the dread of tons of earth above crushing down, smothered or blown apart. "I don't know how you stand it."

"We stand it. No matter what you do we will win."

"I know."

"You were intelligence?"

"No. Second lieutenant, regular Marine."

"Then why speak good Vietnamese?"

There was no reason not to say. "I loved a girl in Hué. We were going to be married. She spoke English but I wanted to speak her language too."

"You *loved* her? Not now?"

"She died."

"Ah...so many civilians killed—"

"She wasn't civilian."

The doctor watched him warily. "ARVN, some officer's family?"

Troy hesitated but the hunger to speak of Su Li was too strong, to share her memory. The doctor listened carefully, fingers folded, head slightly cocked, a kindly sad face. "At first," Troy said, "she must have been ordered to spend time with me, find out what she could. Then she began to care," he waited for the shuddering earth to stop, "but couldn't turn her back on her country, her people..."

"How do you know she's dead? Many of us survived Hué."

In moments of quiet between bombs Troy told him. Cross-legged on the floor beside Troy's bamboo stretcher, head bowed, fingers linked, the doctor was silent. "It is unimaginable," he said finally. "That such a thing should happen."

"HE'S DEAD," Reverend Parrish called. "They just shot Martin Luther King." He came through the door of his Harlem community meeting room and slumped into a chair, hands over his face.

A woman screamed. More screams, weeping, yelling, begging questions, as people ran out the door looking for a television, some way to prove it wrong.

They returned in stunned and teary silence, others swearing, the young men hard and angry, some screaming epithets at the filthy whites, the anti-war people drained and hopeless. Reverend Parrish stood weeping uncontrollably as a silver-haired black woman tried to comfort him. Tucker tugged on his coat, turned to Mick. "I can't do this now. Can't do this fucking meeting."

Mick felt at desperation's end. "We *have* to come together. Us and the blacks."

"Not happening now, brother." Tucker stalked out, yelling, "This country's finished! It's *over!*"

Another hope turned to ashes, Mick thought as he halted at the door. This meeting to unite the anti-draft Resistance campaign with the Harlem community. To get their young men to Refuse. This meeting that now would never happen.

"The war in Vietnam is but a symptom of a far deeper malady within the American spirit," King had said. But who would listen now?

"We're gonna burn down every city in this nation," Clancy Martin was saying. "There gonna be fire and annihilation everywhere!"

"I feel like that too, Clancy," Mick sighed. "But it's not going to help."

"Vengeance!" Clancy glared at him. "*That's* what helps!"

"They wanted him dead," Leon Hamlin said, "to get us to rise up. So they can cut us down."

"You sayin you afraid?" Clancy answered. "You a coward?"

"I'm sayin wait a while, till things cool down. Then strike."

"Things ain't ever gonna cool down, brother. We got the people in the cities mad, they lose this great beautiful leader—"

"You didn't even like the King, man. You said he was a yellow nigger. You call him to his face, that day in Shreveport. A yellow nigger."

"Ain't no yellow nigger now, brother. He just begin the revolution."

THE WAR CAME HOME in riots in a hundred and thirty cities, forty-six Americans killed by the police and National Guard, 20,000 arrested. Now before the television coverage of the bombed cities of Vietnam came film of block after block, mile after mile, city after city from coast to coast America in smoky ruins.

In their hatred for whites, for the system that had killed Martin Luther King and thousands of others, black Americans were burning their own homes because the whites owned them. In response, Congress passed what it called the Rap Brown Amendment, making it a federal crime to cross state boundaries with intent to start a riot. "The catch," Reverend Coffin said, "is how you going to prove you *weren't* intending to start one?"

In his heartbroken speech in Indianapolis on the death of King, Bobby Kennedy spoke a few lines from Aeschylus, "He who learns must suffer. Even in our sleep the pain which cannot forget falls drop by drop upon the heart until, in our own despair, and against our will, comes wisdom by the awful grace of God."

America was falling apart. The killing it was doing was killing it. You have to accept it's going down, Mick told himself during the day, as he bolted girders and carried cable across empty spaces thirty-five stories high, and at night as he spoke at street meetings for the Resistance, wrote articles and letters to newspapers from *The Village Voice*, *LA Free Press* and *Berkeley Barb* to more traditional papers like *The Boston Globe* and *Portland Oregonian*, manned the phones, met with other peace leaders, with the Dems, once sat down with Bobby to talk about California.

"Growing up in Boston," Bobby said, "it's very hard to understand California." He shook his glass of ice cubes and bourbon and leaned forward. "I have to win there or it's over. So I need someone to organize the California peace groups, get them pulling for me. People respect you, Mick. You could do it."

"I can't run out on Gene."

"I know. And I honor your fidelity." Bobby sat back, started to rise. "It's a question with no answer."

Mick stood. "What is?"

"If it's better to be unfaithful and win. Or faithful and lose?"

"Like Al, I'm committed to a man who might not win. I'd much rather work for you but I can't betray Gene."

"All that matters is we stop this war." Bobby gave him a haunted look. "Or it's going to take our souls right down with it."

31

. . .

"IT'S JUST A MOVIE," Mick said.

"It's more than that," Peter Weisman said. "You're *there*, in space. Seeing the universe from a whole new direction. The myth of our future, the parable of who we are. Where we came from and how we got here and where we're going."

"Where we *can* go," Peter's girlfriend Lois corrected. "Given us lousy humans it's unlikely we'll get there."

"It sets our course," Peter said. "For the next thousand years."

"Who can imagine," Lois said, "what's going to happen in 2001? That's thirty-three years from now."

It was a movie that summarized human evolution and took it to the next level. The naked tribe in the desert that discovers a black monolith, and from it learns to use weapons to kill other humans, had evolved into space wanderers seeking the black monolith for the key to our next evolution. And our weapons now were not stones but supercomputers with brains smarter than our own.

Was the black monolith the watchful—or evil—eye of a civilization far more powerful than ours? And what did it have to do with humans murdering each other in Vietnam and so many other places? With the burning cities of America? What clues did *2001* give us on how to live? On the reason for our being?

True, there'd been an ominous rapidity to our evolution. No other animal had ever altered this fast: from ground-dwelling ape to master race able to extinguish all life. What black monolith *had* propelled us?

Could intelligence exist without evil? Didn't evil require choice? And wasn't the battle between humans and the black monolith really between us and amoral intelligence?

But what, really, was amoral? There were no answers. There were just questions. But unless you kept asking them you didn't realize what it meant to be alive.

"It makes you see," Lois said, "what we *can* be."

"On acid," Peter said, "is the best way to see it."

"Yeah, but for movies I liked *Morgan* better," Mick said finally.

"This guy goes to his ex-girlfriend's wedding dressed in a gorilla suit that catches fire—I almost died laughing."

"The best way to die," Lois said.

THE STUDENT TAKEOVER of Columbia University seemed at first amateurish and irrelevant. A lot of smart rich kids who weren't going to be drafted, a school Mick hadn't chosen because it seemed too numb and peaceful. But less than three weeks after King's death its students had raised up in arms. The Students for a Democratic Society and the Student Afro-American Society had occupied a construction site the university had taken over in a black area of Morningside Heights to build a new gym.

Rather than negotiate, the university called in the police who attacked and beat the students till they escaped to another building and took the dean hostage. The next day hundreds more students took over the president's office and other buildings.

When they invited Mick to speak he did so unwillingly. He could no longer fight against the soul-numbing awareness that it was all for nothing; nothing would stop the war; nothing could change the United States. But he woke that night thinking that if these young minds who would someday help to run the country could understand, see clear, in Timothy Leary's words, the country might evolve.

"You're here because of the war," he told the large group that had occupied Fayerweather Hall. "And because Columbia University does Pentagon research on how to kill people. Because Columbia is worse than a slumlord the way it runs its Harlem properties. Because the American culture of violence and coercion is what Columbia University is preparing you to take over and run..."

He cleared his throat, trying not to be emotional. "Vietnam's just a symbol of our nation gone wrong...A symbol of the repression of personal liberty, sending our young men to die for nothing and destroying a nation of strangers so the defense industry can make billions more..."

The megaphone's handle was slippery, the back of his neck sweaty.

Rows of faces peered attentively as if he had the answer to some global problem. *I don't have an answer*, he wanted to tell them. *I fear we cannot stop this war.* It made him feel an impostor, a charade. *We're just kids, playing at justice. Because for us it comes easy.*

After a week the police attacked the occupied buildings in force, injuring nearly two hundred more students and arresting seven hundred. And Columbia's mini-revolution was over.

LILY ON THE PHONE from Paris, three-twenty a.m., the girl beside Mick mumbling irritatedly. *"Oui,"* he said, *"tout va bien,"* trying to wake up, to understand Lily's high-speed French. "Like always," he answered, "I'm working against the war."

"And working still on the high buildings? Why you do this? It's crazy!"

"To make money. That stuff you have too much of."

"Will you shut up!" the girl beside him said, coming awake.

"I heard that!" Lily hissed, "there's a woman there!"

"It's your fault," he said in French, *"you* called me." He turned to the girl. "I'm almost done."

She rolled over. "Tell her get lost."

"André's going to Afghanistan for ten days," Lily said. "A diplomatic mission with Prime Minister Pompidou. The kids are on spring break with his parents in the Vercors. Could you come to Paris?"

4

NIGHT OF THE MATRAQUES

"LUNCH at Al-Ajami?" Lily tugged him along the Champs-Elysées. "Best Lebanese food in Paris."

Mick thought of the Six-Day War, he and Johann on the ridge as hundreds of soldiers died below. That he shouldn't have come to Paris, should've stayed in New York working to stop Vietnam...

"Hurry!" she laughed. "We just have a week..."

Al-Ajami smelled of mint, wild herbs and juicy meats, loud with voices in French and Arabic. Waiters brought plates of olives and raw vegetables and a bottle of rich Kerala from the hills above Beirut. "You tell me first," he said. "Everything since March last year, when I left Paris..."

"Your cheesy hotel on Raspail? That squeaky bed? *Mon Dieu* that was fun."

He grinned to hear her voice, see the lovely play of emotions across her cool classic face. "Let's go make love."

"Where, in that tiny apartment of your socialist friends?"

"My hotel. It's in the Seventh. Near you."

"Feed me first. I want time to see you, see your beautiful eyes, beautiful boy, see your lovely body move." She slid slim fingers down his ribs. "And remember why you excite me so much." She sipped her Kerala, smiled across the edge of her glass. "Before I let you excite me."

"You already excite me so much I'm dizzy." He took a breath. "So tell me—"

"I have a very placid life." Holding her glass against her cheek she watched people hurry along the sidewalk. "Mornings I write my wretched novels and in afternoons take Clément to soccer and Natalie to piano. Then shopping for dinner."

"I thought the maid did that."

"*I* do it. It's what keeps a family together, food. The kids make the salad and set the table and open the wine and cut bread and I do the meat and sauces and veggies, and then we three feast together like cavemen over a mammoth."

"Your husband?"

"André's always too busy at the Ministry. Sometimes he even sleeps there. Or like now, he's out of the country."

"Does he ever see the kids?"

"When he's here he sees them in the mornings before school. And Sundays." She snatched Mick's hand. "Don't glower like that! He loves them." She took a fat olive from the dish and gnawed it, gave him a reproving look. "How many girls you have slept with, since I see you?"

"Hardly any."

"You can't even remember how many. I hate it that other women sleep with you."

"They're not like you."

"You tell us all that. You're a criminal. A criminal of love...And what did you do, besides screw women, after you left Paris?"

He told her about Yugoslavia, Athens and Crete, the beach at Vai, his realization from *Under Fire*'s poor soldier that most people's basic problem was they were slaves of the state. Then the night playing music in the bar in Sitea, in the morning the CIA coup, the shattered guitar, the missing and the dead.

"It's easy to enslave people," she said. "If you tell them they're free."

The Sinai under the Israeli Mirages, the silly Egyptian bravado and pointless deaths. "DeGaulle's an idiot," she said. "To not give Israel the support we should." She nudged him. "When you came back to Paris from the Sinai you didn't call me."

"You told me not to."

Her eyes softened. "And since that time you are making a New York building? This steeplejack thing?"

"I was one of a hundred guys," he laughed. "*I* wasn't making it."

"And so high, you were not afraid?"

"Of course I was afraid."

"That's why women want you, you are so strong and not afraid."

"I *was* afraid."

"I hate that—"

"That I was afraid?"

"No, damn it, that other women want you."

He laughed. "You turned me down."

She bit her lip. "Don't *say* that."

He nodded at the fragrant luxurious restaurant. "Let's leave all this, go to Lebanon."

"Don't be mean." She squeezed his fingers. "You know I can't."

It pained him when he understood. "I'm sorry. I'm a bastard."

"You are a lovely man. Not ever a bastard."

"The best thing I ever did in my life was free that wolf."

"In Saloniki? I wonder where is he now? Alive still maybe? And you saved that musician's life in Athens. Maybe because of you that girl was not shot."

"What girl?"

"In the back of the Army truck. Who had been raped. And now you are doing all these protests, the Resistance, the Pentagon—how many lives you are saving?"

"I'm so tired of it. It's exhausting to organize a protest or a peace march. There's thousands of people to contact, to work with all these groups and get them to agree, to get their people involved. Then the radio and television and newspapers. Endless hours fighting a war we can't win and can't stop..."

"Like Gisèle Halimi's campaign, that you worked so hard on last year? Look what that got you."

He checked no one was looking, slid his hand up inside her thigh. "Still, Gisèle was the first woman to run for the Senate. I wanted her to win." He massaged gently between her thighs. "I like it better when women run things..."

The waiter brought plates of lamb and garlic-flavored white beans and many-colored vegetables, then baklava for dessert with Lebanese coffees and raki as they sat watching cars slide sleekly along the street, her hand in his. In the spring sunlight she looked even lovelier and he wanted her even more, inhaling her scent, seeing deep in her eyes, letting his open to her. His body ached for her, his voice quivered and his espresso trembled in his hand.

Her slender foot slipped up his calf. "I said I won't go to Lebanon. That's *all* I said I won't do."

HE UNBUTTONED HER BLOUSE, her breasts lovely and loose. She yanked her skirt over her head and shoved down her underpants and climbed on him, around him, urging him on with an intense frenzy then flushing bright and moaning joyfully, and as he came Mick wondered if their pretty little private orgasms had no purpose but to feed some great beast of the universe that milks us for this elixir of delight. She fell on his chest gasping and he had a lovely, tired, joined feeling, of each grateful to the other for what had just happened. He saw the gilded cornice round her bedroom's vast ceiling, the smooth plaster curving up into a pure white oval over the bed, the frilled silk curtains and the windows pale and translucent as TV screens, the windows, the Eiffel Tower pinned to the sky beyond them.

She leaned up dangling a curl of silky hair across his cheek. "*That* was not Tantra."

"I've been trying to decide why I'm crazy about you."

"Because you can't have me."

"That's not *it*..." True, a woman was more exciting if she was sleeping with other men too, but that wasn't *it* either. He shrugged. "It's just I love you."

"Shhh." She touched his lips. "We don't *ever* say that."

He kissed the lovely furrow between her eyes. "So what *is* Tantra..."

"Tantra is a way..." She stopped to think. "To enlarge life. To live much more deeply, not only in making love but bringing that lovely orgasmic eroticism into *all* of life. You learn to control your sex pleasure and make it last longer, to come again and again, and to expand that control and the wisdom of pleasure into the rest of your life."

He snuggled down into the warm pit of her belly kissing her fragrant cunt. She pulled up his head. "No, no time for that now."

He couldn't tell the time by the daylight in the window. "When's she due back, the maid?"

Lily squirmed round on the bed, breasts in the sheets, and found her watch. Mick thought of her husband lying in these sheets, of him fucking her.

"Your lover, does he come here?"

"Serge? Definitely not." She kissed him, slid away. "Now get out of here."

THE HOWLING PHONE shocked him out of a dream of saving Lily from the Wehrmacht in the forested mountains of the east. 'Why aren't you *here*?" Thierry said.

"Where?" Mick found the lamp button, pushed it, glanced round his dark-curtained barren hotel room. "It's four a.m.!"

"Where have you *been*? The CRS riot police attacked a protest at the Sorbonne tonight, beat up and arrested five hundred people, cops clubbing everyone, students, women with kids, old people, even tourists. We started fighting back, it turned into a huge battle, we fought the bastards all up and down St. Germain, St. Jacques, St. Michel, hand to hand with paving stones and their own *matraques*. We're going to the barricades."

"Oh shit," Mick said, coming awake. "Like the February Revolution—"

"How we brought down the king in 1848. *La France* is still that half-naked beauty atop a barricade, the flag of freedom in her hand..."

"So where are you?"

"Fifty-one rue des Fossés. Top floor. I'm living with Monique now..."

Mick had a moment's jealousy. Monique had been *his*, in the castle, the bedbugs, her skinny ardent body had been *his*.

"What about Romana?"

"She went to Nepal."

It made him grin, to think of it. What Nepal *was*, as opposed to what everyone thought it was.

When he got to Thierry and Monique's, people were sleeping all over the floor. "Don't you folks ever get up?" he said. "No wonder France is so screwed."

"We've been up all night, *idiot!*" Thierry exulted. "Printing leaflets and sticking up posters and taking over the streets." He waved a hand at the building, the power of Paris, of France. "These assholes don't know what's coming."

At dawn they went downstairs to a café for *café crèmes* and *pains au chocolate.* "We were just a few hundred students and teachers in the beginning," Thierry said excitedly, wiping crumbs, "and two weeks later it's nearly every student in France from grade school to PhD. We're going to take this from a minor fracas at Nanterre to the battle for France."

"People have the right to protest," Monique said, "without getting *matraqué.*"

"Of course they don't," Mick intervened.

"These protests are overdue," Thierry said. "The Sorbonne's curriculum's out of date, the profs distant and arbitrary. The whole school system has little meaning in the lives these kids live today..."

"Life's a magical, mysterious experience," Monique added. "Why should we spend our lives in dull schools and jobs, enslaved by a system we don't understand?"

"We *can* change that," Thierry said, "if we focus on higher goals, not money. The commercial and financial shouldn't be the final arbiter of value..."

"You have to pull in the middle class," Mick argued. "That's our problem with Vietnam. The government doesn't care if the students are pissed, as long as people pay taxes."

"In America the universities, they are exploding," Thierry said. "Like Columbia."

"It went nowhere..."

"Here the big question is unions. If they come in, we win France."

"If you win, who's losing?"

"We're such an old country. The medieval serf is now the little guy behind a desk. Instead, our slogan, *Jouissez sans entrâves—Live without limits.*"

"*Fuck without chains,*" Monique corrected. "Come without restraint."

"The losers are everyone who doesn't want that, the money, the laws, the military, the companies that will die in a new order, the real estate barons, the papers and TV."

"That's another great poster," Monique said: "*All the Press is Toxic.* Until you think about it you don't notice it's true."

Mick drained his *crème* and licked the pastry crumbs. Was it possible that an enraged and determined coalition of students and workers could initiate such sudden deep change? They were taking over Paris—could they take over France? What changes would they make? Could they truly banish the reverence for the industrial and financial gods, help people instead to live deeper and more rewarding lives?

Fuck without chains—it would take a revolution.

"THEY CAN'T WIN," Milton Greene said.

Mick grinned at Milton's stubborn pessimism. "They can make change..."

"There's going to be blood in the streets, lots of blood. Then things will go back how they were. And the young and stupid will learn it's not possible to change things, so the deal is to adapt to this world as best you can." Milton snickered. "That's called maturity."

They sat in the same café overlooking the Panthéon they had the year before, the same afternoon sun gleaming on its bright dome, but now the streets were smoky, sullen and empty, waiting for something to happen. "You still get lots of guys coming through?"

"AWOL guys? More than ever. Seventy thousand guys gone AWOL since sixty-five."

"If there's fighting in the streets here, will you join?"

Milton shook his head. "No way, brother. If I get arrested, I have to leave France, can't finish my degree. And Lamia's going to have a baby."

"When?"

"October. I told all my AWOL guys stay out of these protests. They don't have a dog in this fight."

HE MET LILY in a tacky bar in the Seventh jammed with workers arguing about the protests and students with petitions or announcing the next march. "Will the government give in?" he said.

"To these protests?" She giggled. "Of course not."

"There's a big one tonight. Every day they're bigger."

"They've been fools, the government, the police. It's easy to see why in the past we made such a mess of Algeria and Vietnam. We are the same now...Pompidou's in Iran, so André and a few others have raced home, are the government. De Gaulle's told them to bring in the Army if they have to."

"They'd shoot their own people?"

She smiled sweetly. "Doesn't yours?"

"So what's going to happen?"

"The protests are going to get very big and very ugly and then will be destroyed. People will die. Senseless."

"That's what your husband thinks?"

"He thinks it's all in bad taste."

Beyond the café window a Dalmatian with a pink collar was defecating on the sidewalk while the well-dressed silver-haired woman holding its chain pretended not to notice. In the narrow stone-paved street a white pigeon strutted and a dump truck idled smokily. Church bells were tolling three. "Let's go to your place."

She smiled. "With the maid to greet us?"

He slid his fingers up her wrist under the silk blouse. "So my room—"

"I don't have time..."

He collected his fifty centimes from the saucer, trying to remember how much money he had in his pocket. "Okay then, the Crillon. It's closer."

"It's the most expensive hotel in Paris and you have no money. And besides, I might meet someone I know." She lit a Gauloise, watching him through the smoke. "You *could* make a lot of money."

He laughed. "Then you'd go to the Crillon with me?"

"You're so animated and smart and brave. And you *love* money."

"I don't love money, I love life."

"To enjoy one you need the other...You love food and wine, beautiful women, books, sex, fast cars."

"Sex is free."

"Sex is *never* free, darling boy. There's dinners to be bought and clothes and perfume and movies and silk underwear and hotel rooms. Then there's babies to pay for and growing up kids. You know how much it costs to grow up a kid? Millions of francs."

"So come sleep with me. *I'm* free."

She squeezed his hand quickly. "You must go back to the States. Now. Our government is getting very nervous...They're very large and stupid. And ruthless. They don't like Americans..."

As she slid from her chair her gray skirt slipped up her gray nylon-sheathed thigh and the delicious memory of her flesh came back to him and he knew it was true what she'd said, that for fun you need money. Outside the café she kissed him on both cheeks but he took her hard little cheekbones in his hands and kissed her lips and she drove an avid tongue down his throat then broke away. "Don't call for a while..."

"*Merde*," he muttered as he stepped on the turd the Dalmatian had left. It was yellow and soft and came up the side of his shoe. In the street the strutting white pigeon was now a reddened lump of fluff. He wiped his shoe on the curb and went down the steel stairs of La Tour-Maubourg metro and took it to the Austerlitz station line then to Cluny-La Sorbonne and the flat where Thierry, Monique and their friends were planning the revolution.

ARM IN ARM they marched down Boulevard Saint Michel, thirty people wide and half a mile long, singing "La Marseillaise" and "Je Ne Regrette Rien" and handing joints and wine back and forth, guys and girls kissing as they walked, fondling each other. An overpowering glow of community, sharing, caring, of fun. When the government saw how many and peaceful they were, how could it not listen?

At Rue Gay-Lussac blue CRS buses blocked the boulevard, the CRS in their black uniforms and masks massed in front of them, slapping their black clubs, *matraques*, in their palms. The marchers came closer, those in front trying to slow but the enormous crowd behind them pushed them on.

Teargas launchers flashed; silver flying cylinders rained down in blinding choking fire, everyone trying to shove back against the others still advancing behind them. A whistle blew; the CRS ran forward in close ranks, hammering everyone down.

The teargas congealed his lungs, he couldn't breathe, couldn't run, eyes blinded and burning, face and throat afire, arms raised against the bone-crushing *matraques*. Slowly they retreated down a street of burning cars, fighting the CRS with fists and sticks and trying not to fall under the whistling smashing clubs. He stumbled over a fallen girl, snatched her up and carried her.

Four girls and two guys with wooden pickets blocked the way yelling *"Stop! We fight them here!"* The black CRS phalanx coming fast, flames reflecting on their steel helmets, shields and *matraques*.

A flowerpot smashed onto the street; the CRS halted to load teargas canisters and fired point-blank; one hit Mick in the shin knocking him down in awful chemical choke and eye-searing blindness; someone yanked him up and they threw pickets like javelins at the CRS and retreated again. Choking, gasping and rubber-legged he sprinted up a side street but CRS were coming twenty yards away and he dashed back into Rue Saint-Jacques but more CRS had arrived, one swung his *matraque* two-handed into Mick's forehead; he fell smashing a car fender, the *matraques* thudding his back as he scrambled through an open door up dark stairs, two CRS clattering up behind him.

His searing eyes saw only a kaleidoscope of flashes. He stumbled fast up six stories onto the slippery steep roof, Paris in teargas clouds and Molotov flames far below. The two CRS thundered onto the roof behind him.

He backed to the edge of the roof. One mistake on the cold greasy tiles and he'd fall six stories to the street. The terror from the Shawangunks cliffs came back, the Himals, melting his muscles, the terror of being far too high and steep on vertical rock with no rope and aching to jump just to end the terror and a *matraque* cracked the tiles as the first CRS swung and missed and Mick edged back, the CRS coming for him. Mick reached the slippery roof ridge and inched along it. Surely the CRS would stop now, wouldn't risk dying just to kill him. He backed further along the edge. The CRS scampered up toward him like a malignant black beetle, the second CRS behind him, both tied to black cables tethered to a rooftop chimney so *they* couldn't fall.

The roof ended in horrible black space with far beneath it the tiny street of burning cars and crumpled bodies. He turned toward the CRS and almost slipped off, grabbed the gutter as the CRS swung his *matraque*.

If he slid any further he'd go off the edge. On his squeaky rubber soles the second CRS was coming down the roof. "I give up," Mick called.

"Asshole!" the CRS panted. "I'm going to kill you."

Mick tried to find the roof edge below the gutter. By holding tight to this concrete lip he could keep from slipping. The CRS crept nearer. Mick slid lower till his legs hung over the edge.

He was shaking so hard he almost fell. Like a spider on a thread the CRS dropped toward Mick, *matraque* ready, soles squeaking.

Voices yelled far below—how Mick hungered to be with them, they whose lives wouldn't end in this awful smash into the street. Keening sirens, police whistles, loudspeakers, the rat-a-tat explosions of Molotovs and the whooping wails of ambulances. Hiss through the air as the *matraque* smashed the tiles by his fingers.

Broken tiles slid past over the edge. *Whack,* the *matraque* hit again and he grabbed the hole where it had hit and more tiles dropped over the edge as Mick snatched a tip of rafter, splinters and nails, legs swinging, and the *matraque* smacked into his left hand knocking him off the roof falling in horror then crashing onto a balcony of aluminum chairs two floors below. Someone yanked him inside; he ran across their apartment whacking his knee on a glass coffee table that shattered, and ran hobbling down the stairs but CRS were in the street and he had to limp back up again, banging on doors as the two CRS from the roof came running down.

An old man snatched him in, shut the door and slammed the bolt. He had skinny urchin elbows, a long bald head on a bowed neck. "You want water?" He used *tu* as though Mick were family or a close friend.

"My eyes!" Mick fell to his knees with the pain. The old man made him lean backwards over the sink and ran cold water into his eyes but that made them burn more. The CRS were banging *matraques* on the door. The old man yanked him across the kitchen to the bedroom opening a tall oak armoire with a woman's long slippery dresses hanging down, a cry of fright from a girl huddled behind them.

"I've brought a friend!" The old man shoved him in beside her making her cry out.

"Sorry," she whispered. "You banged my head."

"Sorry."

"How bad are you?"

"My hand's broken. My head hurts. *Matraques.*"

"Me too," she sniffled. "God it hurts."

"Your head?"

She put his right hand on the long swollen gash across the top of her head. Blood was pulsing through her hair onto her clothes. The *matraque* had driven a barrette deep into her skull. She moaned with pain when he touched it.

From the distance came voices, a door slam. His broken finger bones grated against each other.

"Your eyes are burning?" She made him lean across her and with her tongue began to lick round his eyes. "Yuck," she spat. "They got you good." Bending over his upturned face she pooled his eyes in her saliva, the soft tip of her little tongue flicking over his eyeballs into the corners and under the lids, then she sucked them clean and spit it away. "You're bleeding bad."

"That's your blood. You're dripping on my face."

"I give you my blood." She wiped more blood onto Mick's face. "So you'll look bad, maybe we can pass police lines. Saying we're going to the hospital."

Her blood tasted salty. "If they find you they'll just hit you more."

"Oh God, it hurts so bad...We were just marching. It doesn't make sense."

Every time they bumped it hurt her; they could barely breathe in the darkness, with no air in the armoire and their lungs and throats and sinuses afire with teargas. His fingers howled with pain. Keep going another minute, he told himself, and then one more.

After a time it grew quieter. The armoire door screeched open and orange glossy flamelight rushed in from the street. "They've gone," the old man said.

They stood bleeding on his Oriental rug and glossy herringbone floor till she noticed and tugged Mick into the kitchen. Their blood spattered on the white octagonal tiles like a modern painting. The old man took them down two flights to a chunky woman in a flowered dress who bandaged their heads with torn pillow cases. She led them along the street around debris and shattered burnt cars to a bulldozed barricade and an ambulance, its orange light chasing shadows round the walls.

People were jammed in the ambulance, most with head injuries, mouths agape in pain, fingers clenched, blood running down their faces and clothes, a girl cradling a broken arm like a dead baby, a boy by the door moaning desolately, less for the pain it seemed than for a shattered world. Mick shoved her in and squirmed in beside her, fighting the pain each time the ambulance lurched and bumped.

"Shit!" the driver said. Ahead a bus lay on its side shooting up oily flames, a line of CRS surrounding it. The ambulance driver reversed, tires squealing, the injured screaming. He banged through another street smoky with teargas and burnt tires to an avenue with a tall chestnut tree toppled in the middle, shifting crowds and the sea roar of voices, the grind of steel and clash of glass, Molotovs blazing.

Rue Le Goff was blocked by a smoky barricade jammed with people. Fifty yards beyond it CRS were climbing out of a bus and running toward it. Mick tucked his broken hand inside his shirt and jumped from the ambulance, climbed the barricade over a battered car and piled paving stones, sewer grates, steel fencing, parking signs, traffic sawhorses and broken-down trees, and at the top a velvet armchair on its side with a white doily pinned to its back. "Have they attacked yet?" he asked a tall kid in a baseball cap.

"Twice. Both times we beat them back. This time there's more."

"They're tightening the noose."

"If we hold the center the city will turn."

He was right, Paris felt edgy, ready to swing. "People in the apartments, all throwing stuff down on the CRS—they're on our side," a girl said.

"The workers, Renault, and someplace down south, taking the factories over, setting up workers' councils."

"Sud-Aviation, at Nantes, they've come in," the girl said. "Four thousand workers."

The CRS moved closer.

"We have a million marching, the radio said..."

"De Gaulle's left the country...If we can hold out three more days all France will come in."

A woman from a *boulangerie* was handing out sandwiches. A girl with a water bucket moved among the people soaking their scarves. Oily teargas coated its water. More people climbed the barricade, behind them the street a solid mass.

"We'll get caught here," the kid said. "Spread out down there!" he called through a bullhorn. "Be ready when we need you."

Holding his broken hand against his chest Mick went down the barricade toward the CRS. Their line tightened. A kettle sailed down and clattered into them. The street was slippery with water thrown down from the apartments to disperse the gas, and littered with bricks and timber and paving stones and empty teargas canisters, a broken lamp, a dead black cat, shattered bottles, a flower still upright in its broken pot. Battered, burnt cars crouched along a curb like chastened dogs.

He felt wild elation. The pain pounded in his left hand like a drug. "Eve of Destruction" flashed through his mind. There was no danger. Every step toward that black CRS mob fired him with life, a dizzying adrenaline tight-muscled rush.

He saw everyone's eyes on him, from the barricade and balconies above, the excitement of being the one who first attacks the enemy, escapes and does it again. A Cheyenne counting coups, defending the tribe.

The CRS now thirty yards away. Ten yards ahead five bricks lay where someone had dropped them.

5

FUCK WITHOUT CHAINS

H E THREW A BRICK that clattered off a CRS shield. The CRS fired a teargas canister that for an instant seemed faraway then spun past him and clanged into the barricade. One CRS broke from the group and ran at him, another, then five more.

He slung the bricks like fastballs knocking down the first CRS then the second and one turned back but Mick hit him and he went down on one knee and Mick ran up to grab his *matraque* but it was leashed to his wrist so he snatched his gas mask and dashed for the barricade as stones whizzed overhead from the barricade into the CRS and they broke ranks and fell back.

He tugged on the gas mask slippery with the CRS man's cigarette sweat and ran forward with the others, hurling granite cobblestones into the CRS, teargas bursting round his ankles. In the gas mask he couldn't breathe or see so he tossed it aside, the kid in the baseball cap beside him hurling stones with a long-limbed steady rhythm and Mick felt a great affection for him, the teargas now so thick they retreated to the barricade coughing and choking and the CRS came running through their own gas and the stones whirred at them again, the grunt and whack of granite on heads and shoulders and several fell, the others leaping over them till they too were hit and, seeing themselves alone pulled back, dragging their injured with them.

"Three days." The kid wiped at teargas. "We have to last three more days."

"Like guests and fish," a girl coughed.

"We've taken part of Paris," a round-faced boy with cracked glasses said. "They can't take that away from us."

A guy holding a transistor radio to his ear ran up. "We've lost Saint-Michel, hundreds injured!" he yelled, holding a hand over the other ear. "More CRS coming!"

Through the smoke, explosions, moans, cries, and yells of anger came the rumble of engines in the streets to the left. The CRS at the end of the street fired more canisters that fell short and the wind blew the gas back at them. When it dispersed they came closer and fired again and a table came whistling down and smashed into pieces before them, one leg bounding end over end and as they fell back Mick charged them grabbing up teargas and hurling it at them as the crowd poured over the barricade behind him with a great war cry, the tear gas falling among them as the CRS backed past the corner, chairs and pots and pans sailing down on them from above. "This way!" someone was yelling and there was a side street he ran down through clean air toward more CRS attacking the barricades there.

They caught the CRS on the flank, two busloads in their black beetle uniforms and shiny helmets, raining rocks and sticks down on them, and rode over them like a wave, kicking and punching and grabbing *matraques* as the cops fled for the buses, one bus pulled away nearly running people down but they caught the other and tipped it over against parked cars, steel shrieking and windows popping, CRS scrambling out the shattered windshield like wasps from a hive.

Attacking and withdrawing, they ran effortlessly through the streets, and everything seemed easy, beyond excitation, the freedom of annihilating the oppressive certainties of a life he did not want to live, breaking out of the maze he had so long taken for the world. Never had he felt so free, so alive, with such fierce power to break the world and remake it as it should be, just break the world, unconstrained, take things back to the start.

BARRICADE BY BARRICADE, street by street, the CRS were closing in. They had driven them out of the main avenue and intersections of Boulevard Saint-Michel and the traffic circles on the edge of Luxembourg Gardens. They held a triangle of the Rue Gay-Lussac and the smaller streets paralleling Saint-Michel that were hard to defend and easy to teargas, and where the barricades were small.

An old man came with a bucket of water to soak their kerchiefs, his hands shaking. Mick dropped to the street and fell instantly asleep, waking when someone yanked his shoulder. There was a thunder of running boots and roar of voices, crash of lamps and pots and bricks and bottles, acrid burning cars and teargas and the damp earth uncovered by the paving stones, and the sweat and fear and anger of a hundred thousand people.

They were too jammed up, it was hard to throw without hitting someone's head in front and those standing on the slippery wet jumbled stones, bodies moving wraithlike through clouds of teargas and the flash and stink of Molotovs and the CRS kept coming swinging *matraques* into the front line who were falling or scrambling up the barricade and for a moment they were looking straight down into the masks of space creatures, alien and deadly, the gas so thick they had to withdraw, running and stumbling and dragging their injured back to the next barricade further up Gay-Lussac.

In the blazing cars and teargas, the thunder of voices and Molotovs, the sirens and screams, the grunts and whacks of truncheons and sticks they were losing ground. War face to face, medieval, the CRS armor, helmets, steel-toed boots and *matraques* against the students' sticks and rocks, the CRS gas masks against the students' sodden toxic kerchiefs, CRS shields against the students' trash can lids.

Anyone who fell was instantly swallowed up by CRS and horribly beaten. Mixed with the terror of the fighting, the whirring thudding *matraques*, the boots, the choking eye-searing gas, was the fear of falling down, the absolute knowledge of crushing pain if you fell, a shattered head and maybe death.

BLEEDING COUGHING PEOPLE crowded Thierry's apartment. Mick fell asleep on the floor, awakening with a short-haired girl beside him, her hand across his chest, a rusty bloodstain down her cheek. People were sleeping everywhere on the floor, under blankets, rugs, coats, a white lace tablecloth. Bloody handprints ran along the hallway and into the WC; puddles of blood had dried on the kitchen floor. He found a cup of cold espresso on the sideboard and drank it. A woman came in and ran cold water on a towel and went out holding it to her head.

Thierry shuffled in, one eye battered shut, a rip down his cheek. "This'll bring the bastards down." He washed his face and wiped it on his shirt. "It's all over the radio, two thousand injured last night alone, over a thousand seriously. The good *bourgeois* of France don't like to see their kids beaten. The government's coming down."

"I have to get my hand fixed."

"I'll go with you. They can sew up my face."

"You look better that way."

"Do I?" Thierry paused. "Like a dueling scar? Chicks would go for that..."

Three people from Cohn-Bendit's group came in. One of the girls had her head half-shaved and a huge compress on it, streaks of hardened blood down her neck. "We won last night," the other girl said, a short blonde. "Even if we lost the battle we won the war."

"Bullshit," Thierry said.

"We've come to get you," she said. "A meeting, decide what to do next. There's going to be a general strike."

Mick went to the hospital alone, traveling roundabout by way of the Place d'Italie to avoid cops. Twice he saw them catch people and beat them down and throw them in vans and drive off. His hand was hurting terribly now, the middle finger big and black, and with every step, no matter how softly he tried to walk, it roared with pain.

"Three fingers are smashed," the nurse said, angrily shaking his X-ray at him. "We'll put them in a cast for now, but soon you must have them set."

"Set?"

"Operate to pin the bones together. They're shattered. Fragments."

"Afterwards, can I use them?"

"The fingers? They'll never bend. You're very lucky that's all you have." She looked at his skull. "*And* a bad concussion."

He bought a bottle of Chartreuse to go with the morphine the nurse had given him, and walked back to Thierry's through the dregs of teargas and gasoline smoke and the rotten soil of the uptorn streets.

The guitar was finished. No more songs, no more nights making the love of music, the enchanting melodies of truth. "Fool," he swore silently, "you did this to yourself. This wasn't your fight." He was being punished for losing focus. His job was to fight the Vietnam War, not riot in Paris. And now he'd lost the guitar playing he loved far more than any revolution in France.

"You can be a singer," Thierry said.

"Fuck you."

"We're remaking France. Fuck your hand."

He called Lily twice during the street battles. "You've got to tell me," he said. "What's going on?"

"André doesn't say."

"Get him to talk! What are they going to *do*?"

Down the phone line there were circuits ringing far away, lovers wheedling and dealers doing deals all over the world, the universal whine. Pompidou being briefed, grocers ordering lettuce, parents trying to reach their children. "I don't know any more," she said.

"Try to find out—"

"Nothing I can do to André is as bad as what he can do to me..."

"THE RICH AND POWERFUL," Mick said, "have us fighting against each other. "The cops I hit with bricks, they're just normal guys defending their way of life, their families, their country. Just like us, they love and work hard and hope for the best. We have to stop fighting each other, us and them. If we going to change the world."

Days and nights were a haze. Stunned by head injuries and weeks without sleep, by fear and tension and total confusion, by the sour aftertaste of adrenaline, they tried to negotiate with the government while it cheated and lied. They had lost the battle of the streets, but thought the government had lost the war for the hearts and minds of France. They didn't realize that the hearts and minds of the people didn't matter.

They were young and full of ideas and dreams and didn't realize that people with families only cared about getting by. About things not getting worse. People didn't believe, not for a second, in the brotherhood of man. They didn't see any hope of equality, nor of true freedom. Silently, invisibly, the State controlled them.

What the students and workers had wanted, Mick realized, was the right to influence how they worked and what they were forced to learn, a chance to open each life to all its marvelous possibilities. But how could a commercial, industrial world survive this?

"The trick," an accountant named Didier said, "is don't provoke it."

"It still can put you in the Army, get you killed," a red-haired girl called Suzanne said. "The State even owns your house—if you don't pay taxes they take it back."

The talk made Mick's head hurt. From his pocket he took a chunk of hash and fumbled it one-handedly into a pipe and lit it.

"See that?" Didier mocked. "You can't smoke that, the State says. Even though it does no harm. But it's okay, the State says, to smoke tobacco, which will kill you."

"They get taxes from tobacco," Suzanne said, tucking her long hair down one shoulder.

"Hash makes you see clearly," said a boy named Etienne with a bandaged head. "But the State doesn't want you to see clearly. It wants you to keep your head down and keep slogging and pay taxes and do what you're told."

"That night when I got arrested in Place Rostand?" Didier said, "we were standing there with our hands clasped behind our heads like prisoners of war...Here was this guy ahead of me in a camelhair coat and Saint Laurent scarf, some businessman who'd joined the protest or been caught up accidentally."

Didier shoved his glasses further up his nose; it seemed a truculent act, as if warning them not to disbelieve him. "In an instant I saw that's *who* we were: prisoners of war. The State's. What is the State? A vast power composed of us yet controlling us, can even order our deaths. A power that wants us to think we're free—we millions of cells that make up its body—but if we become inconvenient it snips us off like a hangnail."

"Or a nasal polyp," Etienne said. "In medical school that's what we were studying, when this all started."

"*Felicitations*," Didier grinned. "So it came to me in a flash, seeing the man in the camelhair coat, hands behind his head, that he was very lucky: he'd blundered into reality. As I had. We hadn't been smart enough to know we'd always been prisoners and always would be. On work release, to be sure, as long as we behave. But the moment we get out of hand, interfere with the normal operations of money and power—even worse, show others that *none* of us is free, but that it's possible to confront this power we barely knew existed..."

"This is how we lose," Suzanne said. "Pissing our time away with talk. You *know* what we have to do."

"Individual insurrection is the only way to win," Didier said.

"That's a copout," she snapped. "We're *never* free if others aren't."

"Then none of us will ever be free."

"True, but it's only in constantly battling we can remain half-free."

"Real freedom is inside us," Mick said. "Not kicking the CRS. Though that was fun too."

"Simone de Beauvoir," Suzanne said, "criticizes revolutionaries for being too single-minded. It's fine to have a revolution to improve the world, but revolutionaries use it only to give meaning to their lives, they forget the human context."

"What imprisons us," Didier said, "is a structure of thought. A false way of seeing the world. Schools and then work till you're too old to get it up, and..."

"When my grandfather was ninety," Suzanne said, "he could still get it up."

"When you attack a building," Etienne said, "you attack the whole reasoning, the accepted beliefs, the trap."

"What trap?" Suzanne said near-derisively.

"That it has value, that this huge mass of concrete is good for us. That we need it. This gross structure that's really a cage, the newspapers whose purpose is to misinform us, the teachers training us to be perfect workers in the industrial world...they're images we must learn to see objectively. That we may not want. Not need."

"The true symbol of the State," Mick said, "is the *matraque*. The State is the *matraque*; the *matraque* is the State."

"I like that," Suzanne repeated. "*La matraque, c'est l'état.*"

The *matraque* like the State was heavy and hard, moved fast and inflicted great pain. It could be used to warn, to threaten, to hurt, to kill. Unlike teargas and bullets it caused little collateral damage. It carried far less political risk than guns, because a country that turns its guns on its own people can no longer pretend to be free.

But if the *matraques* had not worked, the State would have used its guns. De Gaulle's heavily armed paratroopers would have attacked if the street battles had spread. Whatever it took, the State would win. And if by some madcap destiny *we'd* won, he thought, *we'd* become the State, and defend our grip on it just as fiercely as did the ones who owned it now. Look what happened in Russia.

"What you're saying," Didier declared, "is that wisdom has no influence on evil."

Mick stood and rolled his head from side to side to loosen his neck and soften the ache in his skull. Triple codeines plus lots of hash and Chartreuse and espressos had put him on a high mellow plane, a jet at fifty thousand feet. The broken fingers pulsed pleasantly like an old injury that reminds you how much you loved the game. He held his good hand out to Suzanne, nodded toward the bedroom. "Come tell me about your grandfather."

"**WE ALMOST WON,**" he told Lily. The words sounded empty, a boy's boast.

"No, dear," she said. "France, you must remember, is a fashionable woman. She likes a fling now and again, something that gets her blood hot for a few weeks. But then she'll tire of it, worry what it's risking, think about her assets, her properties, her clothes and jewels. And," she held his good hand against her lips, her warm breath through his fingers, "she'll send the boy away."

"We could have pulled it off."

"You never had a chance. The world doesn't want students in charge. All that idealism is far too dangerous. And Moscow? A student takeover in France would lead to one in Italy and then Holland and then how can they keep down the students in Prague?"

A row of little girls in blue smocks walked by the café window single file holding hands, a teacher at back and front, past the charred corpse of a car and a blackened wall. A little blonde peered through the window at them, giggled and faced forward.

"When I was in tenth grade in Fontainebleau," Lily said, "my school was across the street from the forest. For the two-hour lunchtime my boyfriend and I left school separately and met in the forest, it's hilly and rocky with caves and boulders among these huge ancient trees. We had a place surrounded by brambles and inside a little grassy mattress and we would make love, eat the lunches our mothers had made us, smoke a cigarette, check our homework and then crawl back through the nettles, shake off the grass and sticks, and go separately back to school." She wrinkled her nose, making Mick think of the joyous grin of the little girl who had just passed. "My grades sure improved."

"*Fuck without chains,* that's what the revolution taught us." Suddenly he felt free. "Fuck the revolution."

Lily chuckled. "I'm sure you've tried."

He reached across the table and ran his good fingers through her silky hair. "I can be so free with you. Because I can't have you."

"Don't worry, someday you'll have a wonderful marriage."

"Like you?"

She leaned forward, mock serious. "No, darling boy. Much better. Find a girl like you—open and loving and not too bright—"

"I've learned that fighting in the streets won't win the revolution. Not here. Not in the States."

"Did I ever tell you about the student who killed Batista's police chief, at the start of the Cuban Revolution?"

He shook his head, wondering if she'd slept with the guy.

"I knew him. The police chief of Havana had raped his girlfriend, and so one night he snuck into the restaurant where the police chief was eating, a private club, got past the bodyguards and shot him. After the revolution he married the girl and became Castro's police chief, till Castro had him killed because *he* wanted to fuck his wife."

"Anyway," he said, "I'm going back to work for Bobby."

She sat back, fingers folded, thinking in her silent, face-turned way, looking out the café window at the night. "He could stop Vietnam."

"It haunts him."

"Our intelligence guys say he'll get killed too."

Mick shook his head. "Because of Jack's murder there's better protection now. The Secret Service wouldn't let anyone near Bobby."

She watched him in silence. "How many men are killed by their bodyguards? Or betrayed by them? What about King?"

"He wasn't guarded. And there were half a million loonies after him." Mick had a sour thought of how quickly he'd accepted King's death. "I've been fighting in the streets for weeks. King was killed April 4 and I was fighting the National Guard in Chicago three days later and then Cleveland then the Federal Marshals came after me and I left for France to see you then Thierry calls and the next thing I know I'm ducking *matraques* and it's all shit, it all comes to nothing."

"That's not true, sweet boy."

"And now I'm losing you."

She squeezed his good hand, hers small and cool. "You mustn't fall for women you can't have. That's just avoiding love."

"And you? How do *you* avoid love?"

"Practice." She looked him in the eye. "What will you do, for Bobby?"

"Organize peace groups."

"I thought they were for McCarthy?"

"Bobby can win. McCarthy can't. That's my message. The alternative is probably Nixon."

"André says Nixon is one of the four truly evil men he's ever met."

The thought made him laugh. "The others?"

"Batista, of course. Stroessner. Franco."

"Interesting, all three Spanish speaking."

"It's what the Church does to them."

He caressed the sharp bone of her cheek. "Don't let it die, ecstasy—"

"You lose it, like your sense of smell."

"I'll come back to Paris. Or you, come to New York..."

"I can imagine your hippie apartment." She rubbed her lips across his bandaged hand. "You're headed to some prison, Mick."

"Maybe not."

"And I'm going to raise my children well." Outside the café she smiled and kissed him, licked the tip of his nose. "Now go, pretty boy. And don't come back."

He turned away sadly thinking they had walked out of each other's lives forever.

THE EARTH LURCHED and shuddered as a new round of bombs hit. "Thousand pounders," the doctor said. "That's bad."

"It doesn't drive you crazy?" Troy whispered.

"Of course. The B52s have bombed every fifteen minutes for twenty-three days now. It's because we are so close to Tay Ninh. But we're lucky—the bombing is worse there."

"Humans are such bastards..."

"Soon America must run out of bombs."

"You don't understand my country."

"I am sorry your beloved died. Mine have too."

"Here?"

"No. A little village near Hanoi. Navy planes. My wife. Three daughters."

Troy wanted to reach out but his wrists were bound. "I'm so sorry."

"So," the doctor sat back, "you are not with intelligence."

"Does that mean you'll shoot me now?"

"Not me. But you would be wise to pretend. To not say."

"Why do *you* help me?"

The doctor spread his hands, explanation or benediction. "For your beloved? Because you are a good man? Because it's my job? When I was sixteen I fought at Dien Bien Phu. For two months I was terrified every instant. I still am. Of those French shells raining down. So many of us blown to bits. Pieces of your friends all over you."

"And here you are."

"When the French war was over I decided to heal people rather than kill them. And we had won the war. I thought there would be peace."

"My brother in America is fighting for peace. Started a whole movement, speaks all over the country..."

A clod of dirt hit Troy's face; the doctor wiped it off. "I don't think peace will ever be possible. Think of Lao Tzu: is it better to seek peace on your own, or improve the human condition?"

"If you were one of my men and lying wounded out there," Troy said, "I'd run out to get you, no matter how much danger. You'd do the same for me."

"That is the problem."

The thousand pounders came back, hammering the earth. As tunnels collapsed the soldiers dragged out the dirt-covered stretchers, piling the wounded men together. The light died. In airless darkness Troy thrashed at his tied wrists, other bodies crushing him down, no air.

"Untie me!" he screamed; no one could hear over the thudding bombs. His lungs heaved, begged for air but there was nothing. Blood writhed in his arteries and screamed for air. He wanted the others to die so he'd have their air. He sucked in the vacuum, distending his lungs, head back, jaws wide, trying not to squirm because that made him need more air.

He ripped the right wrist free and tore loose the other, crawled from under gasping bodies bumping into someone. "There you are," the doctor said in English, snatched at Troy's face. "Peace be with you."

"Have to get out!"

"The tunnel's blocked. There is no way out. We will die here."

Troy shook his head, remembered the doctor couldn't see him. Bombs kept shuddering the earth. The tunnel had collapsed on them. He lay under the wet cold dirt and began counting to a hundred between each breath. He would be here forever. And never be found.

DAISY TOOK TIME off from Stanford to work for Bobby Kennedy because she couldn't imagine what else to do. The war was getting more and more evil and even in her Stanford ivory tower she could not ignore it.

It was like when Pa was hitting Mom. You had to try to stop it. You had to help the good. Like helping the people in Mississippi. It was all the same.

Bobby's people sent her canvassing Daly City neighborhoods, asking how do you feel about Bobby? *Please tell me you're for him* because I've thought long and hard about this, and he's the only one who can stop this insane war.

Most said yes. We like Bobby. We hope he can change things. Men with missing front teeth leaning out of aluminum doorways of trailer homes; women slowing their Mercedes at their front gates to answer a few questions.

Bobby was going to change things. Things that most people wanted changed.

The campaign was endless, breathless. She ate poorly and got a bladder infection from being so busy she forgot to pee.

Be funny if Mick O'Brien showed up. Someone said he was running part of the campaign, out of LA. Funny to meet up.

Thinking of him left her weak.

Maybe I'm not truly happy. Maybe I'm not happy at all. Anhedonic, that's what it's called.

How do you know if you're happy? When I was doing pure research I was happy. Sort of.

Be fun if Mick showed up.

THE HORROR of the bombs moved on. *Let them hit someone else,* Troy begged.

Clods of the dirt jamming the tunnel tumbled into his face. Cool air rushed in, strong arms carried him toward the surface as he sucked in the sweet beautiful air of tunnel muck, cordite, phosphorous and guts.

The earth's surface seethed like a volcano, huge craters of rubbled rock and hissing coals, snakes of burning phosphorous, pools of bubbling napalm, here and there a blistered trunk glowing red. Clusters of soldiers were digging frantically where tunnels had collapsed.

Soldiers ran up with five other wounded, three on litters. "You," one soldier said to Troy, "you can walk."

It was impossible. He rose to his feet, tried a step, another, gritted his teeth at the soldier. "I can walk."

"You must," the doctor whispered. "Or they will shoot you."

"Where are we going?"

"Over the border. Cambodia."

6

BOBBY

A DIRTY ENVELOPE was waiting in his mailbox when Mick got home from France. It had no return address, but there was Troy's handwriting, clear as day.

I've given this letter to a war correspondent going home because it won't get past the censor.

One's mindset changes so much in war. You and I grew up taking care of people: family, neighbors, even the people who bought our milk, we made sure it was clean and fresh. We looked out for them.

But here we set out mines to blow each other up, we shoot each other, we even (not I) torture each other and desecrate each other's bodies, we burn each other alive with phosphorous and jellied gasoline. Yet the people we kill and torture are like our neighbors back home—they love their families and take care of each other just like we do.

When I saw you in New York after my first tour I didn't tell you I'd met a girl in Hué, a teacher. But she wouldn't leave and marry me. So I re-upped mostly for her, and for the guys I wanted to protect, not leave behind. I couldn't stay home knowing they were in danger.

When I first met her she entranced me. Not by how she looked, though she was beautiful, but by her inner calm and kindness. It sounds crazy but she was solace for the world. But as I came to know her she changed. She seemed divided, torn, loved me but didn't want to. Now I know why.

She was VC, a section commander. At first she tolerated me to get information. Then we fell in love and it drove her crazy, and finally she said she'd marry me if I'd leave Hué, next year.

In the Tet offensive I led an attack on a VC command post. I killed her not knowing who she was. After I saw her body all torn with bullets—my bullets— held her dying with her blood all over me, I was crazy for days, weeks. I couldn't grieve because the other Marines would know. I couldn't let them know.

Do you know what it's like to be crazy with sorrow but not able to show it? I wanted to kill the person who killed my beloved, but of course that person was me. Me, and my country and my Marines.

I'm choking with sorrow. Now, weeks later. I don't want to bring you down with my sorrow but to tell you that you were right and I was wrong: this war is evil, and we who fight it are evil.

I say this not because of Su Li, but because I knew all along the war was wrong but my pride wouldn't let me tell you. I wasn't here a week when my C.O. shot a young woman and an old man for nothing, then burned their village and killed everyone in it. I've seen village after village destroyed with phosphorous, napalm, artillery, hundreds of civilians murdered to increase body counts. Nearly all the prisoners we take we kill.

I've seen horrors even Dante never dreamed of. And for what? Because we don't have the courage to speak the truth: that this is an evil war and we're doomed to lose.

When I think of how some people glorify the military, how a professional officer is given automatic respect, honoring the killers, it makes me sick. The men who created this war are evil. If I make it through this tour I'll try to make amends. I'll go to medical school or become a teacher like Su Li, try to give back to the world.

I'm sorry for everything I said to you about courage—it takes more courage to stand up against what's wrong, to fight against this war, than take the easy way and join up. The easy way lets you feel good about yourself, patriotic, brave, all that shit. The courageous thing is to fight what you know is wrong, but the sad thing is that it doesn't matter—the generals have their firepower and they're blowing up this beautiful world and there's nothing you or I or anyone can do to stop them.

This war has taught me that morality is up to the individual, not the nation. The individual alone must decide wrong and right, because the nation is immoral.

Thank you for being who you are, and for all you've given me. I hope if I make it through and see you again you'll forgive me.

Your loving friend and brother,

Troy

P.S.: I met an old Williams classmate of yours, Link Doolittle. He's a First Loot up near Khe Sanh, his second tour. Says you were smart and a great jock but why he liked you best is you cared about people. Not bad praise, huh?

Tears burned Mick's eyes; he felt a stab of love for Troy, for the courage it had taken to write this, the horrible pain that had provoked it. He sat on his ancient couch and reread it, could not imagine the horror Troy was living, the unfairness of it. If he could go to Vietnam, find him, get him to leave...But Troy wouldn't do that.

To have loved that girl and killed her.

Strange to think what Link Doolittle had said. The big lunkhead from Nebraska, Mick's freshman roommate. Who later destroyed Mick's shoulder. How could he say that?

Was Link not what he'd thought he was?

When Troy got home they'd be brothers again. Like that first day when he'd shoved Troy out of the locomotive's way, when they fought to save each other after riding the freight train to Washington, on the baseball field at Nyack High: *We'll always take care of each other.*

Now Troy was in pain and danger and he couldn't help him. The only person who could help him now was Bobby Kennedy, because only Bobby could stop the war.

The California Primary was two weeks away. Hubert Humphrey, the pro-War vice president, didn't dare run in the primaries but had locked up a lot of delegates through the old-boy network. Gene

McCarthy had won in five states, but only in Oregon against Bobby. Gene couldn't beat Nixon. If Bobby could win California he'd be America's next president.

The best way to take care of Troy was to help Bobby get elected.

ON THE TWA 707 to LA, full of gin and tonics, he smiled affectionately down on the farms, fields, rivers, cities and forests below. America so huge and beautiful, varied and plentiful. Like Bobby said, full of good-hearted hard-working honest people.

He winced as the cast on his fingers bumped the tray table. CRS guy had wanted to knock him off that roof. When he was hanging from the slippery slates and gutter, the people and lights so tiny below. At night this horror woke him; he'd sit up, look around to make sure he wasn't on the roof, tell himself he was safe. But an operation to fix his smashed fingers was three hundred bucks. Where did anybody find money like that?

He'd give his guitar to Tara. The first thing Evil did was kill music. The Athens cops smashing his guitar, beating Nikos for singing. Because music connected people, made them happy, made them dance, love each other, want to fuck, not want to work or fight.

So of course the first thing you had to do was kill music.

Looking back at the battle of Paris he saw it had been about the chance to live deeper, explore life, deal with each other through freedom, goodness, faith, trust, and caring. To focus on higher human goals, not money.

Fuck without chains was to enjoy sex without the shame that drives humans to build cities and make money and slaughter each other. Orgasm without restraint, give yourself fully, live who you are...

We deserve our shame, the Bible tells us.

Bullshit.

If we lose our shame, can we stop killing?

WITH TWELVE DAYS to the June 5 California primary Bobby was still behind McCarthy in the polls. His LA headquarters was a volcano of cataclysmic mayhem pulsing out and sucking in energy and information, an infinite soup of orderly chaos and chaotic order, a blur of passion, fear, excitement, and exhaustion.

His first day Mick was sent with seven others to Watts in a pale blue Falcon whose seat springs had cut through the blue plaid vinyl cover, and which would not stay in second unless the driver held the stick.

Down a prim street of two-story houses he went door to door with a divinity student named Ian Holzer, tall and skinny in a white shirt and drooping black slacks, a bony nose and glasses. Midmorning sun seared the fog. The damp air smelt of garbage, sewers, chemicals and exhaust, loud with Motown, singing, arguments and radios and televisions.

"Why should we care," said a skinny short-haired kid playing hoops, "what some whitey wants to do about some other whitey?"

"How old are you?" Holzer smiled at him benevolently.

"Sixteen."

"You'll turn eighteen while the next president's in office. You get the wrong one, he'll send your sorry ass to war."

The kid smiled, at the ingenuousness of adults, specifically white ones. "War be over, man. Long 'fore then."

"It's already the longest war in our history," Mick said. "And it's barely started."

"How come you don't have no Negro people workin with you?" A narrow-faced kid with buck teeth, in a sleeveless khaki t-shirt, made a show of peering behind them as if to discover someone. "I don't see no black faces."

"So come with us," Holzer said. "Let's talk to everyone we meet."

"They say he rich, Bobby Kennedy," called out a muscled kid in dreads. "How come he don' give you a better car?"

More kids gathered, bouncing basketballs, laughing and putting each other down. Mick wondered why they weren't in school, remembered how he'd hated it, but wondered now what they thought the world was going to offer them without an education. Why had they given up?

Had they never, really, had a choice?

"Talk to your families," Holzer said, "anybody who can vote. How important to vote for Bobby. That he *will* stop the war, bring better schools and jobs to Watts."

"You can easy get a job," said Dreads. "White boy, pretty blue eyes, nice college. All the money already on your side of the fence."

"To get into college," Holzer called, "all you got to do is study in high school."

"If Bobby Kennedy get voted in," said the first, "they just shoot *him* too."

"How many of you," Mick said, "know somebody who died in Vietnam?"

There was an embarrassed pause as if he'd said something almost shameful. "Timmie Roberts he just got kill." A tall kid in a torn yellow jersey pointed at a blue-shuttered house across the street. "He live there."

"Don't all of you," Mick said, "know somebody who's died in this war? Who'll die next? How many? Why? For some white politician who can't even get them guns that work or tell them why they're there?"

"What about you?" The bucked-tooth kid said, "You got a college education and all. A de*ferment*?"

Mick shook his head. "I turned in my draft card. I can get arrested just for being here."

"You crazy, man." The boy turned away and Mick feared he'd lost him, that in the boy's eyes self-impalement was never wise, nor was any principle worth dying for.

Dreads pointed at his cast. "What happen to your hand?"

"Cop clubbed me. Broke three fingers."

"Yeah," Dreads said. "We know about that."

THAT NIGHT HE STARTED calling anti-war groups for Bobby. Most supported Gene McCarthy because he'd challenged Johnson first. "But Gene can't win," Mick kept saying. "Bobby will. You want Nixon and four more years of war?"

Al Lowenstein had been an early McCarthy supporter and refused to change. "I've told you, Mick, I have to keep my word." He was running for Congress and had a primary election soon, and Bobby had just called him to wish him good luck. "That's Bobby," Al said. "Even if you're not with him he cares about you. Hardest damn decision I've ever made."

Chet Dickinson, a Vietnam veterans' organizer, was sympathetic. "All that counts, Mick," he drawled, "is we *win*."

"That's my point, Chet. We have to be rational. The Republicans will run their usual smear campaign, they'll eat McCarthy alive. But Bobby can destroy them."

"It's true, everyone wants another Kennedy. After what happened to Jack."

"Can you talk to the other top guys in Vietnam Vets? Try to pull them in?"

"Everybody says wait till after California. If Bobby wins that, he's golden. Everybody'll come in."

A WARRIOR PRINCE reclaiming his murdered brother's throne, Bobby was electric, a powerful fiery being who could be soft as cashmere or sharp as steel, a mind so fierce and bright it encompassed almost everything, understood almost everything instantly, yet aware of all humanity's weaknesses, all of his own.

Just being near him, Mick realized, galvanized him. He loved him, would do nearly anything for him. Yet Bobby didn't ask for this, didn't want it. What he wanted was to use the gifts God had given him to better the world, or at least reduce some of its sorrow and evil. And because he was up against such overwhelming odds it made you want to help him.

He wasn't that big, five-ten maybe, wiry and intense, a razor mind and quick tongue, a fighter's stance and cocky Irish grin. He would walk through a room talking to three people at once about three different things yet smile at everyone and if he'd met you before he'd nod and his bright eyes would say *I know you.*

His brother's murder lay on him like an open wound. You saw it in his kindness, his scarred smile, the times he faced the darkness and you knew he was seeing Jack, wishing him back, missing him terribly and only asking to measure up.

So you loved him. You had no choice. To not love him would be like not loving God. Not loving kindness and fair play and determination surmounted by endless pain.

One night Mick was grabbed to drive Bobby and his aides while Bobby planned the next meetings and threw questions at people, "Did you call Gunther? What'd he say? That's bullshit. Make him do it. Then call Callaway, Martinez, make *sure* of them. Did you get Lanslow?", as they raced from corner speech to corner speech all over San Diego, Bobby reaching out, holding hands, listening, sad or smiling, his caring for each person so immediate and intense that whole crowds were moved by it.

Standing on a car roof or a porch leaning his lithe young body toward them he spoke urgently of halting Vietnam, establishing racial justice, protecting all that made America great—its people, history, freedom and land. There was no hypocrisy: he cared totally about these issues and had the will and means to change them. He was a giant killer. He alone could stop the war.

Gene McCarthy was campaigning hard on California campuses, Bobby in the ghettos, the black and Hispanic communities. Bobby seemed driven, not out of ambition but something else, a haunting need. "He *has* to stop the war," Tim Hanson told Mick. "That's what drives him hardest."

Tall and athletic, Tim was one of Bobby's closest aides, a conservative Catholic from Philadelphia who had worked for JFK. It was after two a.m., they sat exhausted in the campaign suite at the Ambassador.

"And he wants to reveal who killed his brother," Tim said.

"Who was it?"

"The CIA's Cuban exiles. Everybody inside DC knows this. It was Mafia guys pissed at Castro for shutting down their casinos and whorehouses. The Agency paid them to knock Castro over, that plan cooked up by Dulles and Eisenhower—"

"The Bay of Pigs."

"Jack thought it was crazy. The Agency and Joint Chiefs told him the exiles could win on their own, but that was a lie. The intent was to send those guys ashore, then force Jack to bring in US troops. He refused. The attack fell apart, and Emilio and his friends decided to kill him for it."

"But why Oswald?"

"He was the dunce. Some stupid fuck with scrambled brains, full of fury and hungry for glory...They just got him all wound up and sent him in the right direction, somebody to blame afterwards."

"So why kill him?"

"They planned to kill Oswald even if he hadn't been caught. And Jack Ruby was dying anyway. Chance to prove himself to his leader, and a lot of money to family in blind accounts. Like some Wehrmacht corporal charging Russian machine guns for the Führer."

"The other shooters?"

"Cuban CIA guys. Up on that knoll. And one in a car."

"Bobby knows all this?"

"Lots of people in the Agency, they loved his brother."

"Why doesn't he *say*?"

"All this is buried deep. One of the shooters is already dead and no doubt they'll kill the others. It's Bobby's word against the Agency's, against Lyndon Johnson and the Pentagon. And the question is, going forward, do you tell the country its beloved president was murdered by an in-house team for the benefit of the guys running the show? Or do you let them keep thinking the country's wonderful, nothing like that could ever happen, it was an accident, really, one evil man, not *us*? Particularly since we're in a very unpopular war?"

"A war that wouldn't have happened if Jack had lived." It was unutterably wearying and hopeless. "So many needless deaths."

"But Mick, it's no big secret, the Bay of Pigs guys. That they killed Jack. What Bobby wants to uncover is for whom and why. The real reason they hit Jack."

"Because Jack fired Dulles, all the rest of those CIA thugs?"

"That too. But the real reason was the Nass."

"NSAMs?"

"National Security Action Memorandas. Jack wrote three, numbers 55 through 57, right after the Bay of Pigs. I was there when he signed them. They substantially reduced the Agency's powers and took it out of the clandestine operations business." Tim took off his glasses and rubbed his face, a weary, rough sound. "Then, nearly two years later and a month before Jack was shot, he signed number 263. It began the pullout of Vietnam. Which Johnson reversed the day after he became president."

Mick stared at a strange metal fish hung on the far wall, a pattern of thousands of little holes in a brass sheet.

"Better you know." Hanson rubbed his eyes and put back on his glasses. "Maybe someday you can use it."

"What would I use it for?"

"You're a good man. People rely on you, believe in what you say." Hanson took a slow breath. "A natural leader."

"If Bobby wins..."

"He's going to open it wide. A real inquest, reform the Agency, throw out the scumbags and Mafia hit men. Track down every evil bastard tied to his brother's death."

"They *know* this?"

"Of course," Tim shrugged. "Bobby has a whole investigation going, *sub rosa*, inside the Agency."

"They wouldn't dare do it again?"

"Kill Bobby? Never. This time everybody'd know. It'd put an end to them."

BOBBY BEAT MCCARTHY forty-six to forty-two percent. The Ambassador Hotel ballroom blazed with laughter, joy and song, thunderous with clapping hands and people chanting, "We want Kennedy! We want Kennedy!" Mick felt an exultance he'd never known, a rush of knowledge that *yes*, when things turn evil you *can* change them.

In the happy din and pandemonium he hugged people he'd never met, laughed and nodded to words he couldn't hear, raised his broken fingers in a victory sign. Ethel Kennedy entered the ballroom, Bobby behind her, Ethel the prim, shy conservative Catholic girl with so much wisdom and brains behind her affectionate smile.

Through the roar of happy voices Bobby spoke softly, waiting for them to calm. "I send my high regard to Don Drysdale," he began, and people cheered more. "Who pitched his sixth great shutout tonight..."

It was quintessential Bobby. He'd won an astounding victory, could go on now to win the presidency and change the world, and his first words were congratulations for someone else's victory. In his flat Boston accent Bobby went on to thank everyone, slowly, sincerely. Then he turned to the nation.

"We have certain obligations to our fellow citizens...What's been going on in the United States over the period of the last three years—the divisions, the violence, the disenchantment with our society, the divisions whether it's between blacks and whites, between the poor and the more affluent, or between age groups or about the War in Vietnam, we can start to work together...We are a great country, an unselfish country, and a compassionate country, and I intend to make that the basis for my running—"

He was so overwhelmed by cheers you couldn't hear him. "The country wants to move in a different direction," he was saying. "We want to deal with our own problems within our own country. And we want *peace in Vietnam.*"

Again he was drowned out by cheers. Tears rushed to Mick's eyes. *Yes you can change things...*"All of us are involved in this great effort,"

Bobby said, "...on behalf of the United States, on behalf of our own people, on behalf of mankind..."

Again impossible to hear. Mick kissed the woman beside him. "And whether we're going to continue the policies," Bobby said, "that have been so unsuccessful in Vietnam, of American troops and American Marines carrying the major burden of that conflict. I do not want this, and I think we can move in a different direction."

Once again, a Kennedy was asking us to be the best in ourselves, do our best for the world. Once more a rich powerful man was reaching out to the poor and powerless, the sufferers, the victims of war, and promising to help them.

Mick laughed to think how Troy would appreciate Bobby's citing the Marines.

"WHO'S GONNA BE THE NEXT PRESIDENT!" a voice yelled into the microphone.

"RFK!"

"RFK!" Everyone chanting, laughing, singing, clapping hands, the women in wild flat party hats. "They can't stop us now," a girl screamed as Bobby waving and smiling cut through the kitchen, the shiny pots hanging on racks, bumping round the stainless steel counters, the sense of joyous momentum, of hope and good, Mick thinking he'd write Troy and tell him the end is near, Bobby'll win and we're going to stop the war.

In the happy roar and pandemonium he saw someone he almost remembered, a pale, hard-faced man watching Bobby from a distance, hair so blond it was almost transparent, a tan suede jacket despite the heat, brown slacks. The man Mick had seen in Bali after the killings began, the man with the murdering soldiers, the man Erica had told him about. With a snarl Mick started for him as over the yelling and happy voices came a bang, a scream, yelling, more screams, the gun going *bang bang bang* as people fought for it, flailing arms, a man shot down, a woman, Bobby on his back in an aureole of grace and blood, a white-coated youth kneeling to put a rosary in his hands.

In the sudden chaos roars of sorrow and rage rose from the crowd. "They shot him!" people were crying, and it was too late, it was all gone; in a broken-hearted instant Mick understood America's last hope was gone; the war would go on. Millions more would die, and many more millions suffer, for the men of steel had won again.

"Would a doctor please come," someone was begging into the microphone that moments before had radiated the joy of victory. "Please somebody help us!"

Shoving people aside, Mick hunted everywhere for the blond man in the tan suede jacket, but he had vanished the instant the shot was fired.

He sat alone in his room. A splash of Bobby's blood on his trousers was holy but the young god had died. He called Tara; her phone rang in the Berkeley night. No one to talk to. Nothing to say. Nothing could explain this away.

The blond man in the tan suede jacket had never existed. No way to find him now.

If Bobby had lost California, the killers would have waited. If he'd been defeated there would have been no need to risk killing him. But if he won California it would be the start of a momentous surge to the presidency, which meant stopping the war, opening a real inquest on his brother's death, going after the CIA. So if Bobby won California he had to die.

How easy to enlist a drone like Sirhan Sirhan: a few drugs, hypnotic suggestions channeled into his lurid little brain, then lead him to a gun and point him at the target that you've convinced him he hates. He will even think he did it of his own free will.

Like they'd done with Lee Harvey Oswald.

On the 707 back to New York Mick stared hopelessly through the perspex at this vast land that had lost its soul. And the greatest proof it had lost it was that it did not know.

WITH THREE BROKEN fingers he couldn't steeplejack but found a job at Chemical Bank from eight at night to four in the morning matching stock buy/sell confirmations with the day's list of trades. The sheer immensity of the money silently changing hands each instant of each day was unfathomable, billions of dollars buying and selling pieces of paper that decided the fates of companies and people all over the world, the ownership of lives.

It seemed arcane that the stock market had power of life and death over the economy. In a normal economy, companies created and sold things or provided services to individuals and to other companies from whom they also acquired goods and services. It was a resilient market, a natural functioning interplay of supply and demand. But once these companies could be bought and sold on a market, once there was speculation to drive markets up and down artificially, then this once-natural economic network, this web, becomes prey to recession, depression, bankruptcies and purloined hopes.

Bobby now seemed unreal, his death a place Mick couldn't go. The country was sinking into a cauldron of hatred and murder. Since there was no chance to improve things, it made sense to get out of the way.

With his Chemical Bank wages he rented a beautiful three-room, rent-controlled apartment on the top floor of a six-floor walkup on Christopher Street at ninety-six dollars a month. Every other apartment was an Italian family; the building was clean, quiet, and filled with marvelous cooking smells.

At four-thirty a.m. he got home from the bank, rolled a joint and sat with a bottle of Lancers on the soft couch he'd bought second-hand, and waited for the sun to rise beyond the rooftops. He stretched, loosening the neck muscles cramped by hours of leaning over ledgers, rubbed his eyes grainy with numbers.

Everything life needed was here: a coffee table to put his feet on, a red-leafed coleus in its little pot beneath the window, a bookcase of cinder blocks and planks, a vibrant Madras rug on the red-painted plank floor, a corner bedroom with a big bed and two bright windows looking out to the Hudson River, a kitchen with a wooden table and four chairs, plenty of sink and cooking space and no roaches. He was sorry the country had gone to hell, but there was nothing more he could do to stop it.

The United States had abandoned Khe Sanh after losing a thousand dead Marines and five thousand wounded trying to hold it. After firing more than a hundred and fifty thousand artillery rounds and nearly a hundred thousand tons of bombs and rockets and billions of bullets at this relentless, resourceful, fearless foe. No, General Westmoreland insisted, it wasn't a second Dien Bien Phu.

Like Troy used to say, Marines were bullet magnets. You sent them where you wanted them to die. And they didn't have the right to say no.

SETH CALHOUN banged on his door one morning about six, almost furtive, near-embarrassed, hair plastered down with morning drizzle. "Miranda and I are splitting...I've been walking all night, man. Don't know what to do."

Mick made coffee while Seth paced. "I'm quitting my job. So she wants out."

"You're the eternal grad student. You don't *have* a job."

Seth shook his head dismissively. "You know what my job's been since the day I finished Williams. You know our family, our tradition of the Navy then the Agency. The PhD at Columbia was to give me a believable persona, the mild-mannered fun-loving American professor helping out in foreign lands. It's why I didn't have to go to Nam even though I did ROTC..."

"I wondered about that."

"At first you think you're doing the right thing. Protecting our country. A nice feeling. Never occurs to you that you might not be protecting it at all. When you start seeing how things really are, you don't want to believe it. You make excuses for it. You don't want to lose that nice feeling of giving yourself to your country."

"So what does Miranda care about your job?"

"Her family..." Seth shrugged. "If I quit, she's disgraced. Won't have it."

The memory of Miranda pulling up her dress on the porch in Williamstown came back, of her frantic orgasms in his sweaty bed, the rip of her nails down his back. Her goddamn ocelot. "Maybe you're better off."

Arms folded, Seth stood looking out the window. "Nice sunrise."

"Where's Cynthia in all this?"

"Hah! Miranda's beloved sister?"

"Is *she* taking sides?"

"She's in her third year of law at Columbia. Of course she's taking sides."

"May I be so rash as to inquire..."

"You got to understand, our clan is an absolute mafia. Omerta, loyalty, duty—all that."

Mick laughed at the idiocy of it. "But why are you quitting the fucking Agency?"

"Because of Bobby. They killed him because he was going to reopen the files on Jack's death."

"They know you know?"

"Who knows what the fuck anybody knows. Any more."

"Why the sudden conversion?" Mick felt a hateful distance. "Why do you care that they killed him?"

"I loved the guy." Seth looked out the window. "Despite myself. He was real."

"Would they kill you?"

Seth made a *moue*, a downward cut of his mouth. "They don't bother with little turds like me."

AS SOON AS HIS BROKEN HAND was usable he got a job with Dunlap & Sons, moving people's furniture from apartment to apartment all over New York. After a few weeks he bought a beat-up '56 Ford van, put an ad in *The Village Voice* for "The Village Mover—*Expe-*

rience, Care & Efficiency, $6.95/hour door-to-door," fifty-five cents cheaper than the competition. Next morning the phone began to ring.

Despite the July heat and traffic it was ecstatic to push himself to the limits carrying furniture up and down endless flights of stairs, fitting it tightly into his van, tying more on the roof then weaving through Manhattan's dismal congestion and smog to the next apartment, often no bigger or better than the last. The intense exercise was fabulous, not even playing football had felt like this.

"It's made me hate intellectuals," he told Peter and Lois. "They all have five thousand books and a piano and live at the top of a six-floor walkup."

Many of his clients were working girls; often after an exhausting day he helped them unpack, bought a bottle of wine to celebrate their new home, sometimes made love with them for hours but was up at seven to start the new day. He didn't need sleep, lived on raw fruit, yogurt, red meat and sex, worked twelve hours a day seven days a week, and by the end of August had saved a thousand dollars. One weekend working seven a.m. to midnight both nights he made four hundred bucks, a new high.

Russian tanks had rolled into Prague; the students fought them first with flowers and then Molotovs. "See that," he told Sparky, one of the men he'd hired part-time. "Communism's as bad as capitalism."

It made no sense to go to Chicago to protest the Democratic Convention. It made no difference. It was just like Prague, stand up to the tanks and get killed. If a country's run by Nazis, be invisible.

Hubert Humphrey watched passively from his suite high above the bloodied streets while the police attacked the demonstrators, some Democratic senators decried the "Gestapo tactics" of Mayor Daley's cops, and televisions worldwide once more covered bloody street battles in America.

When it was over Humphrey was nominated over Senators McCarthy and McGovern, though he had received just two percent of the popular vote.

Bobby's murder by a fanatic Palestinian had changed America, the world, and human history. His greatest goals were to end the war and to end poverty; he would have achieved the first and possibly the second. He was young, animated, caring, brilliant and energetic. And he was a fighter; he would have fought for the country he loved. And he would have won.

Mick thought again, as he had so many times, of the CIA agent in the corner of the room, the one who'd organized part of the Indonesian coup, a hard-faced man in a tan suede jacket, who disappeared the instant Bobby was shot. Could he be tracked down?

With Bobby dead, Nixon won the Presidency and would enforce an even harsher war on Vietnam. Millions more would die, trillions more dollars wasted, a nation's honor tarnished, all because of one man with a gun in the kitchen of the Ambassador Hotel.

A SELECTIVE SERVICE letter came ordering him to report to Whitehall the following Tuesday at 7:30 a.m. for immediate induction. He called Lou Graziano. "You're a high-profile guy," Lou said. "This Resistance stuff? Of course they want to take you down."

"I won't kill people who've done me no harm."

"They don't want to *draft* you for Chrissake. They want you to refuse so they can send you to jail for ten years."

"Can we get a postponement?"

"They want you too much. You've become too big an anti-war figure. It's a vendetta."

"So what do I do?"

"Don't say I said this, but disappear. Canada maybe? Or do ten years in Leavenworth, your choice. The downside of disappearing is if they catch you, they jail you even longer." Graziano chuckled. "Funny how they jail the guys who don't want to kill, not the ones who do."

As soon as Mick put the phone down it rang again. Tara's hoarse voice, "Troy's dead. He had me down as next of kin, is why they called me. He was killed in action, but his body wasn't found."

7

THE CRAZIES

EVERYTHING HAD DIED at once. He'd lost his brother to the horrors of Vietnam, and it didn't matter that he, Mick, had been right and his brother wrong. It didn't matter anymore that the Vietnam War was evil. It didn't matter that the one man who could stop it, Bobby Kennedy, had just been murdered by those who intended to expand the war.

It didn't matter, but nothing else mattered except it. Or nothing mattered, and he'd been a fool to believe anything did.

He wandered aimlessly from room to room like a madman, sat and wept and walked around and sat again. He made and drank coffee without knowing, looked out windows without seeing, had to remember to breathe. He wanted to call Tara back but didn't. None of this matters, he thought. All that matters is Troy's gone.

When after two days he went outside the world seemed glaring and jagged, people like puppets, the air toxic. He walked as if undersea, bought things, cooked meals, paid his rent, and remembered none of it.

He did not go to his induction at Whitehall. Any day now they'd come for him. That didn't really matter either.

"Get a grip," Peter said. "You being in prison for ten years won't help Troy. It won't help you. It wouldn't be payback."

"Payback for what?"

"For Troy's death. You couldn't protect him from what happened before he met you. From the way he was."

"That's what Tara said. Whatever the Boys' Home did to him, he could never escape it."

"He was always seeking structure, the family he'd never had. Then he had you guys, but the need remained. Like the way people who were hungry as kids never lose their fear of starvation. You can't fill an infinite hole."

HE TRADED THE '56 FORD VAN for a Triumph 350 bike, tied a backpack with a sleeping bag and a few clothes on the back, and drove west, on the road again, and as long as he went fast enough he couldn't think about anything else.

He could tell himself that now he was free. Free of everything. This was how the world really was—everyone you loved died and the evil in humans outweighed the good. The sooner you understood this the freer you were.

Farmers were haying their fields in the Pennsylvania hills, the dust of the reapers gilding the air. The Ohio farmlands rolled away, thick with heavy-eared corn; fat Holsteins and Guernseys studded the pastures and white barns and homes gleamed in the September sun. It all seemed so innocent, so honest and hard-working. There was no way to understand. You just had to learn not to care.

Hard-working farmers were often perceived as virtuous, but what was virtuous about a life of endless repetitive physical toil?

To Escape
From Hairy Apes
Women Jump
From Fire Escapes
Buy Burma Shave

The first night he camped by Lake Erie on a beach with an oil slick. The second night after midnight at a muddy Minnesota lake, the third in the Badlands, still hot in September, the fourth in Montana.

Bozeman was a bright cool town under the vast sky, rimmed by hills of tawny grass and sea-green lodgepole pines, the air thin and sharp. In a cowboy café on Main Street, the radio playing

How does it feel,
To be on your own, with no direction home
A complete unknown, like a rolling stone...

He glanced through *The Bozeman Chronicle* for construction jobs. There were none, but it was fall roundup and ranches were looking for hands. It took five dimes to find one who was still looking. "Can you work cattle?" the man said.

"I grew up on a farm."

"From Big Timber go north toward Two Dot then take the Crazy Peak road northeast twenty-one miles. Where the dirt road crosses a stream you'll see the Circle B gate on your left. We're nine miles back that road. Can't promise anything."

It was a quick ride east thirty-seven miles along the Yellowstone River to Big Timber. A cool wind was drifting down from the mountains and afternoon sunlight gleamed on the meadows and torched the cottonwoods along the broad river. It was easy to imagine how this had looked to Lewis and Clark, the seas of buffalo and antelope, the wolves loping patiently behind the herds, the sky dark with geese and ducks, passenger pigeons and a hundred other birds.

The Crazy Peak gravel road ascended overgrazed eroded prairie into tall timbered hills. Above them steeper conifered slopes were studded with granite cliffs and spires, the black peaks ridged with fall's first snows.

He opened the Circle B gate, re-chained it behind him and drove up the dirt road along a flashing stream through stands of fir and pine, a cold breeze flowing down from the peaks, the road steepening through jagged hills then easing into a vast meadow with a white

84

house and large red barn at the far end, dark forest and white peaks above it.

Two German shepherds came barking then wagged their tails when he knelt to greet them. A white-haired man in a green shirt limped onto the porch and whistled at the dogs. "As you can see, they won't kill you." He was about six feet, thin and hard-faced with long wispy white hair and aqueous eyes. "That motorcycle's damn noisy. We heard you all the way from the county road."

"Sorry. I need to get it fixed."

"You ever broke cattle?"

"No but I grew up on a dairy farm. And like I said, I can ride."

The man glanced at the sun notched between the western peaks. "Too late to do much today. Come have dinner and we'll bunk you for the night and try you out tomorrow."

The kitchen was lit by two gas lanterns, warmed by a pine fire crackling in the black woodstove. The pine cupboards had formica tops and red-checkered glue paper. There was a white sink with a wooden drain board, a black rotary telephone on a pine table, a red and white doily beneath it. The woman sitting at the pine table put down her knitting and smiled at him. She was solid-set, in her sixties, gray rolled hair, a roundish face and glasses. "This's my wife Fern," the man said. "I'm Clyde Gottson. What you say your name is?"

"Dave," Mick said. "Dave Willson."

Clyde turned to Fern. "Dave's from Massachusetts. Grew up on a dairy farm."

Dinner was thick roast beef and mashed potatoes and string beans, dark bread and butter. "Those are the last of my fresh snap beans," Fern said. "Frost got the rest."

She brought out cheddar cheese and half an apple pie. "We don't have much milk. Didn't keep a cow this year."

"They're all up in the hills with calves," Clyde said.

After dinner Fern picked up her knitting, a small blanket of blue and maroon wool. Clyde opened the woodburner and put in another split of pine. "We've got three mares you can choose from. A barn-sour spooky Appy named Belle, a big quarter-Appy mix with a mean streak named Ho'ota, a flashy young mare who likes to kick named Taffy. We also keep an old barrel paint, kids grew up on her. But she won't go up that mountain."

The bunkhouse was behind the barn. The German shepherds trotted silently beside them. "Pick any bunk you want," Clyde said. "We'll ring the bell at five."

Six steel beds with bare mattresses, a low pot-bellied stove against the slab pine wall. He lay by an open window, warm in his down bag. The stars were diamond-sharp; coyote calls echoed through the valleys and elk bugled in the hills.

When the bell clanged he climbed quickly out of the bag, feet stinging on the cold floor, dressed and crossed the dark yard into the warm woodsmoky kitchen. Fern had made bacon and eggs and mashed potatoes and raisin bread, with cherry pie and coffee.

Through the sweet smell of dawn-wet grass they walked to the barn. Clyde called over the horses. Mick picked out Ho'ota the big, dark quarter-Appy, and saddled her and they rode up through the glistening meadow into the cold conifers and up the ridge, the horses huffing with the climb, into a vast cirque with black walls to south and west.

The eastern sky was red. Clyde leaned forward on the saddle, the horses blowing and shaking their heads. "There's a hundred eleven cow-calf pairs in this valley to drive down to that pasture by the road you took coming in." He glanced at Mick. "How long you think it'll take?"

Mick looked at the far jagged rimrock, the vast sea of pine and spruce and fir tops touched by first light. "A week?"

Clyde smiled, whistled up the dogs. "You head west with Cassie, straight toward that rimrock. Any cattle you find, drive them ahead of you. There's a little lake up there, under that cliff, it's about six miles from here. Let's meet there at one o'clock, and push them together and down."

Mick rode in golden early light up through the tall timber over the needled slopes, in and out of light and shadow in the resiny breeze, lop-eared Cassie bounding ahead and trotting back and racing ahead again. Ho'ota climbed steadily, ponderosa branches and spider webs tickling his face. This is what it was like to be a Cheyenne, he thought. A Sioux. Free in the undegraded infinite beauty of the world.

Ahead Cassie barked, a calf bawled, and his horse swung obediently toward it, pushing the calf and its grunting mother ahead, then three others, then four more. One cow kept straying, her calf squealing behind her, but each time Cassie flanked them and drove them back. More cattle joined in, trampling the forest floor. Their reeking, fly-buzzing feces splashed and spattered the flattened grass, drowning the scents of pine and sage and dark earth.

The cattle herded up before a creek, not wanting to scramble down its banks and up the other side. Cassie darted at them barking sharply and nipping at their hocks and drove them through the dogwoods and willows, muddying the water as they crossed. Ho'ota stood ankle-deep, sucking water and shivering her sides and snapping her tail to keep off flies. He short-roped her to a tree and walked upstream above where the cattle had crossed, knelt in the stream and drank.

By noon he had more than fifty cattle milling ahead, bawling and squealing. The black rimrock glistened overhead in the hot sun. Ho'ota perked her ears, smelling Clyde's horse.

Clyde sat by the shore of the little lake. "Still think it'll take a week?" he called.

Mick unsaddled Ho'ota and let her drink, washed her down with a few hatfuls of water. They ate the BLT sandwiches Fern had made. The lake shore was jumbled with boulders fallen from the cliffs. Trout dimpled its surface. Mick stripped and dove in. It was so cold his lungs felt crushed; he scrambled out and dried off with his shirt.

"Up this high," Clyde said, "that water never gets warm."

Mick glanced at the peaks. "Why they called the Crazies?"

Clyde crumbled a bit of cookie and tossed it to the fingerlings along the shore that grabbed at it and whirled away, darting back for more. "One story is an old Blackfoot woman lived up here alone. Her people'd all been killed—it was after John Bozeman opened his trail and all the whites came through looking for gold and killing Indians.

She wandered these hills that had been her tribe's, crazy with grief and loneliness...

"Other story is that one of the first white families lived up here, the Blackfeet slaughtered them all except one woman who went crazy, lived up here alone...Take your pick."

They saddled up and pushed the cattle all afternoon down through the dark timber, the earth stained with their brown manure and gouged by their hooves. After sunset they drove them out into the wide valley south of the house where the cattle all milled bawling inside the jack fences. "Good grass here," Clyde said. "Keep 'em till we truck out the calves tomorrow."

That night they had steaks and coffee and pan-fried potatoes and apple pie. In his sleep Mick still felt Ho'ota moving beneath him with her undulant grace; calves bleated and cows grunted, the cold air sharp with cow dung and the resin from broken branches.

Outside the window Orion rose into the late sky, twinkling and cold. A frigid breeze whispered under the floor. He went outside and down the meadow under the stars. Across the valley four Indians crested the ridge through the lodgepoles, moving fast, bows in their hands.

He went with them, feeling limber and powerful in the infinity of prairie, sky, and peaks, like them slender and muscled, the same dark-tanned sharp cheeks, dark eyes and white teeth. Through every sense and pore he felt the cool piney air, the grass at his shins, the stony needled forest floor through his moccasins.

In the dream he woke feeling an old woman's coarse hand on his cheek, saw her black eyes out of the darkness. "I love you, Grand-mother," he said. "I've missed you."

He dreamed again: a road diagonal across the ridge, the pines dry and stunted, the grass cropped, the streambed dry. Cattle gnawed brittle grass splashed with their own excreta, from which flies swarmed to bite their flanks.

. . .

"THESE PROTESTS in Mexico City," Clyde said as they sat by the woodstove one night, "it's a terrible thing."

"I didn't know..." Mick said.

"You should read the paper. The Mexican government killed a hundred twenty students just for gathering in a public place to protest how their lives are run? Like what just happened in Prague, the Russians killing all those students. It's just not free there."

"Think of what *we* just put up with," Fern said. "That Democratic convention!"

"I don't think protests work," Mick said.

"Sadly I don't either," Clyde said. "Though there sure is plenty to protest about."

"I'm just happy to be up here," Mick said, "in the clean air."

"And the forest," Fern said. "I never tire of seeing it."

Clyde scanned him. "You haven't been drafted yet?"

"Till recently I had a school deferment. No doubt I'll have to join soon."

Clyde gave an offhand shrug. "Don't know what I'd do in your shoes."

"I expect I just have to defend my country..."

"I had a brother, Jimmy. Dead now, God bless him. The meanest son of a gun—"

"On God's green earth," Fern said.

"Now Jimmy would get in fights then expect me to back him. But he was attacking good people, my friends, other nice folks. One night he slapped this woman, and I told him you may be my brother, my closest flesh and blood, but you try to do that again I'm taking you down."

"What he do?"

"He tried, so I knocked him out."

"He was better after that," Fern said. "A changed man."

Clyde opened a whisky bottle and poured Mick and himself a full glass. "Now that we've moved down all the cattle and cut out and shipped the calves, I could use a hired hand for hunting season. We've got three dudes coming from Texas next week, oil company bigshots.

Jerry Montano's coming over from the Circle J to cook and guide them, but he could use a second man. I've got a fine old Remington .270 I'll lend you."

Mick held the whiskey in his mouth, letting it burn. "What would I do?"

"See to the horses, help pitch camp and cook, wash dishes. And Jerry'll want to put you out on stand with these guys too, in case they miss a shot."

TAN DUST ROSE from the horses' hooves as they ascended through sagebrush along a flashing creek up into the shade of the lodgepoles, Jerry Montano leading on his brown paint, the three dudes, then Mick on Ho'ota leading three pack mules.

After a few miles they climbed from the trail up into aspen forest of wind-dancing yellow leaves to a stream dammed by beavers, white aspen trunks reflected in its riffling gold-green depths. They pitched camp above the last beaver dam, "where the little fuckers don't shit in the water," Jerry explained. He was a solid-looking man in his forties, round-faced and black-haired with a scar down one weathered cheek, a worn white beaver skin cowboy hat, worn jeans and cowboy boots run down at the heels.

They cut fir saplings and nailed them between trees to make a corral, pitched three tents, built a fire pit and latrine, fed oats to the horses and cooked a dinner of steaks and pan-fried potatoes. After dinner Mick washed the pans and dishes while Jerry got out the blackberry brandy and whiskey for the three dudes. They were all from Dallas; Brett Drucker was the president, he said, of an oil rig company, "and these two cowboys," he nodded at Rush and Gordon, "are unlucky enough to work for me." A little over six feet, an ex-college lineman years out of shape, balding with a frizz of gray hair above his ears, round-shouldered, burly and pugnacious, Drucker gave the impression of being less smart than persistent.

Hands stinging from the icy water Mick stacked the clean dishes by the fire. He checked the horses, hung the saddles and bridles on the top rail of the corral so the porcupines couldn't chew them, put Ho'o-ta's saddle blankets on a flat area near the fire with his sleeping bag on them.

"What, you aren't going to sleep in the tent with Jerry?" Drucker guffawed. "What's he do, grab your ass?" He grinned across the fire at Jerry. "Jus' jokin."

"I like to see the stars," Mick said.

"How long you been wrangling, kid?" Rush asked.

"Just started. But I grew up on a—"

"Just started?" Drucker snorted. "So Clyde Gottson sent me out with a greentail?"

Gordon chuckled. "That's a good one, Brett...A *green*tail..."

"Mick's done plenty huntin' and ridin'," Jerry said.

"Hell, Mexican, how would you know? I never seen a Mexican could shoot straight."

"As I remember," Mick said, "they shot the hell out of the Alamo."

"You makin fun a me kid?"

"No. You are."

"You're a real long-hair," Drucker muttered. "How come you're not in Vietnam? What are you, one a them protesters?" He turned to Rush. "Every kid should go in the Marines. That's what I say. Serve his country in time of war."

"You were in the Marines?" Mick said companionably.

"I grew up between wars. My country weren't at risk then, and I had better things to do. But if I was young now like you are and my country's fighting a war, I'd be the first to join up."

"You probably still could...My brother just died in Vietnam; he used to say need lots of people, quartermasters, fuel dump managers...you're in the oil business, right?"

"I'm a CEO, kid. I don't do fuel dumps." Drucker poured himself more blackberry brandy. "But it bothers me seeing a longhaired pinko who should be serving his country."

"Tell you what," Mick laughed, "I'll join up when you do."

Jerry grinned. "Tomorrow after breakfast we're going to set you guys out on three stands with good shots downhill where elk trails cross. The elk should be moving pretty good, some should come by at least one a them stands."

The night was bitter and clear, the stars stainless steel in the black pit of space. Toward dawn it snowed, a light cape over the ground and branches. At five Mick lit the lantern, built up the fire and broke through the ice on the stream for coffee water. "Shit," Jerry Montano said, rubbing the back of his neck as he came out of his tent. "Cold up here."

They ate over-easy eggs with bacon and pan-fried toast, the three dudes filling their cups with blackberry brandy and adding coffee. "Colder'n hell up here," Rush said, swinging his arms.

"Twenty-seven below," Mick said. "What the thermometer shows."

For three days the dudes sat out on their stands in the bitter cold. On the fourth Jerry told Mick to sit with Drucker. "I'll take care of Rush and Gordon. I got a feeling maybe today elk come by you two guys. Better two guns than one."

They sat on insulated pads on the snow, Drucker shivering and sipping blackberry brandy from a flask, Mick listening for elk among the soft thud of snow clumps falling from the fir boughs, the chittering of chickadees and the far complaining of crows.

"You see, kid, the oil business's like the outdoors." Drucker burped. "Survival of the fittest."

"Hush," Mick whispered, "I hear something."

"So it's all very fine to treat your neighbor like yourself but don' forget he's takin the bread from your mouth." He burped again. "That's what I say..."

"Elk!" Mick hissed. "At least two. They're going to cross that clearing down there. It's about thirty yards, if there's a bull he'll probably be second, following the cow."

The footfalls neared, hooves on rocks and soft snow and downed boughs then an elk cow trotted across the clearing, and twenty yards behind her a young bull, two points to a side, golden umber chest. With a huge blast Drucker's Weatherby Magnum went off. The cow stumbled, caught herself and scrambled for the dark timber, the young bull darting downslope into cover.

"Jesus Christ!" Mick yelled. "You shot the cow!"

Drucker kept blasting away at the patch of low fir boughs where the cow had vanished. He shot his magazine and looked at Mick with fierce exasperation. "That wasn't no fuckin cow!"

Mick checked the picture in his memory of the sleek-bellied cow outlined against the dark timber. "Yes it was, Brett. She didn't have antlers."

"Fuck you, kid!" Drucker scowled and turned away. "You don't know shit."

Mick took Clyde's .270 and started downhill. "Let's see if she's hit."

His back felt naked as he descended the slope with Drucker scrunching and puffing down behind him, ravens calling, clumps of leaf-thick earth dislodging underfoot. At the open spot where the elk had crossed there were the sudden deep hoof marks where the cow had sprinted, then on the left a crimson spurt along the leaves, another ten feet further then a smear waist-high along the fir boughs. "She's gut-shot," Mick said angrily.

"Don't call my goddamn bull a she!" Drucker coughed up phlegm and spat. "C'mon, get tracking."

The cow had run through uphill through the fir forest into a steep canyon of huge black boulders. Her bleeding had slowed, just a spot every twenty feet or so, but still easy to follow on the snow in the canyon bottom and where her hooves dug into the earth. Panting from the climb Drucker fell behind then stopped. "Hey kid," he called. "You go ahead. He'll be right up ahead. I'll go back to camp and have them bring the mules."

"We don't need the mules."

"To pack out the meat." Drucker's nasal drawl was almost plaintive.

"I doubt we'll find her."

"You find my goddamn bull, kid." Drucker turned and started back down the canyon. "Or stay out there."

The canyon steepened to a wide half-timbered grassy slope, the air at eleven thousand feet cold and thin, the elk's tracks easy to see where they had bent down the dry grass. To the north, a thousand feet below, the conifered hills rolled away like the sea, granite on their crests, huge forests almost black in their shadowed valleys, snowy peaks blazing above them in afternoon sun.

The elk's tracks climbed this grassy slope for half a mile into thick firs and spruce. Mick moved silently, smelling elk and the steely odor of blood, kneeling often to scan between the trunks for the motion of a leg, to listen for footfalls or broken twigs or a nervous huff. Then through a slot between the dark trunks he saw her.

She stared at him, her head low to see under the branches, ears tilted forward, her flanks heaving. She licked her lips, tilted her head to see better, licked her lips again. Slowly she limped out of sight. Mick snapped on the safety of the .270 and turned downhill. The wind had turned icy, the valleys near-black, the sun sinking like a tiny ingot among the white peaks.

When he got to camp they had finished eating, Drucker, Rush, and Gordon round the fire with blackberry brandy, Jerry washing dishes and pans in the stream. "There you are," he called. "I was ready go find you."

Mick squatted beside him. "I was two valleys away, couple hours."

"Drucker was sure beat when he got here. Where's his bull?"

"He winged a cow. I tracked her five miles maybe, blood trail died out, the sun was setting, she was moving good, so I came home."

"Drucker's gonna be pissed you didn't get his animal."

"He shot up the whole forest, couldn't hit a thing."

"Your dinner's in the Dutch oven."

Mick took a pan from Jerry's hands. "Washing dishes is my job. Get your ass out of here."

"We do it together." Jerry rubbed his hands together to warm them. "Fuckin water's freezin."

When the dishes were done Mick crouched by the fire heating his hands. "Well here's the tracker," Drucker called, "who can't even find a bleeding animal." He punched Rush's shoulder. "You shoulda seen him...Couldn't even tell it was a bull!" He mock-squinted across the fire at Mick. "You need glasses, boy."

Mick took his steak and potatoes out of the Dutch oven. The plate was warm, the steak hot and juicy, seared enough to magnify the taste, the potatoes steaming and thick, sopping up the blood. He sat by the stream eating with his hands and tipping his tin cup into the icy water, thinking about what wine to have, decided on a Margaux.

"My bull ain't gonna be worth a damn," Drucker called. "Not after he's laid there all afternoon and night with coyotes chewin on him. Even if you *could* find him."

Mick dragged his mind from the memory of Lily riding naked atop him, a crystal glass of Margaux in her hand. "I'm sorry, what?"

"You heard me. You're a bad guide and a bad tracker. And I'm going to tell my good friend Clyde Gottson about it. Your days're numbered, kid."

Mick licked blood off his fingers. "It was a cow. No rack."

Drucker kicked at the fire, a few coals bouncing past Mick's feet. "You don't hear so good, do you?" He stepped round the fire, towering over Mick. "Why'd you *lie* about my bull?"

"You better tell him, kid," Rush said. "No more lies."

"Hey guys," Jerry stood. "Back off it."

"Shut up, Mexican," Drucker said. "I'm dealing with this." He stepped down hard on Mick's foot. "Ain't I, kid?"

Mick stood and moved back from Drucker. "Go sleep it off."

Drucker swung, his fat red fist in its thick-sleeved jacket coming round like a slow swing of the bat; Mick shifted his head and the punch grazed his temple nicking his ear. He stepped forward and swung over Drucker's upraised forearm smashing into his cheekbone and jaw and Drucker went over like a logged tree flat on his back.

"Jesus!" Rush said. "You didn't have to do that."

Drucker moaned, rolled on his side. Mick took his sleeping bag and saddle blankets and climbed the hill behind camp into the firs till he found a little open of soft grass under the white stars and black night, the air clear and cold as a knife.

In the morning Drucker's face was blue and swollen. "I got a broken jaw. You sucker-punched me. We're going down to press charges against you. You'll be in jail tonight."

It was early afternoon when they reached the ranch. "I'm sorry you

95

didn't get your elk," Clyde told Drucker, "but you had no right to hit my man."

"He sucker-punched me first. Ask Rush and Gordon. We're going to the Livingston police." Drucker scowled across at Mick. "See you behind bars, sucker."

Mick watched their van trail its tail of dust across the meadow. "I'm truly sorry, sir. He came at me for no reason. And it was a cow."

"Jerry told me all that. I'll back you, when the sheriff shows up."

Mick shook his head. "I hate to leave. But I have to."

Clyde looked at him searchingly. For the first time Mick appreciated the fineness of his features, the sculpted nose and cheeks, the wispy white hair and reddish skin. "Okay, Dave," Clyde said. "We'll pay you in cash through this coming Friday."

"You don't have to do that."

"And if the police ask me what you're driving, we'll tell them you hitched in. And today I took you down to the Crazy Peak road but I don't know where you went."

"THE FBI," Lou Graziano said, "got you on their top ten."

The pay phone slippery in his hand, Mick glanced around the busy Bozeman street as if someone might hear. "Since when?"

"Since a couple weeks. September twenty-sixth, to be precise. Already they had you for conspiracy to counsel, aid and abet draft resistance, that's a minimum five years. Now they added a big second charge: crossing state boundaries to foment a riot. You could get ten for that. Where the hell you been?"

"Traveling."

"So your warrant's all over the system, any state or local cop can see it...Maybe you should change how you look?"

"Can I get across the border?"

"First place they'll look."

Mick waited for people on the sidewalk to pass. "Is it still safe to call you?"

There was a moment's silence. "Probably not."

8

SMILE ON YOUR BROTHER

THE ACNE-FACED COP in the white Chevy pulled into the spot next to Mick's, got out, slammed the door and stared at him. "I clocked you at a hundred thirty. Before I lost you. You out of your mind?"

Mick had a stab of fear that the cop had seen him on the wanted list, was playing with him. "Sorry. I never opened the bike up before, wanted to see how fast it'd go...I heard there's no daytime speed limit here in Montana."

Lundgren said the brass nametag on the cop's chest. "Let's go sit on that bench." He handed Mick back his license. "Why you trying to kill yourself?"

"I wasn't." Mick stared at the whitewall tires of a passing car, at a rattling pickup, at the yellow cottonwood leaves carpeting the grass. Now he was going to go to jail forever. "I was just letting the bike out..."

"No normal young man with a reasonable head on his shoulders tries to kill himself. So is it some girl?" The cop shrugged. "Let it pass. Six months later you'll have somebody new and won't even remember this one."

Something about him seemed good. "My brother died last month," Mick said. "No, he didn't die last month but that's when I found out."

"Jesus I'm sorry. How?"

"Vietnam."

For a while the cop said nothing, staring down at the grass between his black shoes, tapping his cap against his knee. "I wish we all could do something for you—"

"Stop this war."

"Yeah, but that won't bring him back. Listen, kid, you got to walk this road alone." He looked into Mick's eyes. "Don't waste his death or your time being unhappy. That's just weakness. Instead make the world a better place. In his honor."

"That's crap."

"I should crucify you but I'm letting you go. On a couple conditions."

Mick let his breath out slowly. "God bless you. Anything."

"Promise me you won't speed or in any way risk your life —"

Mick nodded, swallowed to hide his emotion.

"And promise me whatever search you're on you don't give up."

Mick bit his lip. "I promise." He shook the cop's hand and walked to the Triumph, turned to the cop, eyes glazed with tears. "God bless you, I promise."

THE HITCHING POST in Great Falls was a cowboy bar full of good-natured rough men in big hats and blue jean jackets jostling and joshing each other over horses, football, and dice. They made him want to grin with their friendliness and happy machismo, their love of horses and machines and beer and trucks and women and this wide western land.

He bought a Schlitz and leaned with his back to the bar. He could live here, change his name, sign on with some ranch. How could the FBI find him? This country was very big and porous and if you changed names often, kept your head down and left no paper trail, how *could* they find you?

A slim girl in denim shorts, red leather boots and a see-through blouse with a lacy bra underneath came out on a low plywood stage rocking her hips to *Suzie Q*, twirling her ass and kicking high, spreading her legs at the men pressed against the stage. She had a comely face with sparkly brown eyes and light brown hair down both sides. After a few verses she slid off the see-through blouse, her breasts round and tight in the pink lacy bra.

The song slowed to the sensual throb of "Within You and Without You" with the twanging uncertainty of the sitar behind it and she belly danced sinuously, a Kama Sutra lesson, then slipped down the denim shorts and stood rocking her crotch at the ring of men, her hairs dark under her panties.

And the people
Who hide themselves behind a wall
Of illusion

She knelt thighs wide, hands out behind, twisting and swinging her pelvis making him wonder how can she not be fatigued. Dizzy with desire he slid a dollar into the hem of her panties.

She grinned and sprung to her feet like a sapling freed of snow, an effortless single motion. *Let's spend the night together*, jabbing her hips to the drive of the bass she pushed her breasts out at him, *now I need you, more than ever*, she untied the bra letting it slide from the high strong beauty of her breasts and his legs were trembling and his stomach weak.

He tried to slide five dollars up the thigh of her panties but she ducked away and when she swung her hips forward again he shoved it in the waistband frayed and skinny as a string. She flashed him a beautiful smile and sprung up with that sudden vertical leap, danced right up to his face grinding the pink see-through panties in his face and he could smell her rich cunt smell, seeing her long-fingered hands and her clean unvarnished nails and her cunt hair gleaming in the red floor lights.

Later when the music had died and the lights went out and he was in the parking lot kicking the bike alive she came up to him. "Thanks for the five."

He knocked snow from his boot. "You're so beautiful and your eyes are so goddamn kind."

She shivered tugging the false fur collar of her skinny coat up round her neck. "Can you give me a ride? My truck is broke. I don't want to fuck or anything, just a ride home."

His chest tingled as if he'd been offered a great quest. "If I can get it started."

They rode slowly along the frozen Great Falls streets over snow like down, her skinny arms round his waist and her sharp little chin in his shoulder.

It was a trailer court between the feedlots and grain elevators on the far side of the tracks. A little muddy street, the bike skittering through the icy ruts, the trailers on both sides silent as coffins.

"Here!" An Airstream with a tan Ford 150 on cinder blocks beside it. "Your hands're *so* cold." She took them in her skinny hot fists. "Christ you got no gloves." She hugged his fingers against her, off-balancing him on the bike. "You have to be quiet. If you want to come in."

He locked the bike and followed her through an open gate of broken pickets. The aluminum door squeaked, the kitchen linoleum gave under their weight. In the night-lit living room she tugged off her coat and boots. "Right back."

She tiptoed down the hall and creaked open a door, went to a second one then came back to him soft-footed over the carpet and they reached for each other, her lips electric and hot as she twisted and writhed against him. "Jesus," she whispered, smothering his mouth. "I never fuck the clients. Jesus!"

Half-dressed they tumbled on the couch gasping and swearing, fucking in the wild joy of it, then he lay panting with his cheek between her breasts in the dizzy elation of after. He kissed down her belly into her delicious odors of sex and her own intoxicating smell.

"Enough!" she gasped. "Get up here."

He stretched out along her. "Thank you, thank you."

"Other guys don't look at me like you do. They look at my cunt. You, you were looking in my eyes."

He raised up on one elbow. "I still am."

She kissed him, a quick peck. "I gotta sleep."

Nestled against her he slid his leg between her thighs. "This helps you sleep."

She giggled, pushed him off. "I get up at six. The kids get up at six-fifteen, have to be on the school bus at six-forty. I gotta be at work at eight."

"Work? What kind of work?"

"Secretary at Malmstrom."

"Malmstrom?"

"The Air Force base."

The propane heater huffed on and roared steadily for a few minutes then subsided. Next to her on the narrow couch he listened to the ticking heater, the snow hissing at the door, the far-off howl of a coyote starving in the night.

Make the world a better place. In Troy's honor.

At six-thirty her five-year-old daughter and seven-year-old son inspected him with quiet gravity as he made peanut butter and jelly sandwiches and washed apples for their lunch boxes. "Sam likes chocolate milk," Crystal called from the shower, "but Liz wants white."

When Crystal left for work at the Air Force base he walked into town for a coffee and doughnut and a *Great Falls Tribune*. It was Wednesday, October 23; an American spacecraft named Apollo 7 had returned to earth. John Lennon and Yoko Ono had been fined a hundred fifty pounds for marijuana possession, Jackie Kennedy married Aristotle Onassis and the Pentagon ordered another twenty thousand soldiers back to Nam for involuntary second tours, bringing the total of US troops in Vietnam to 530,000. Already 30,000 young Americans had died there; every month 1,000 more died and another 10,000 were maimed for life.

And on the back page of section three, "PFC Randall Oliver of Townsend, son of Ralph and Denise Oliver, was killed in action in Pleiku Province...Warrant Officer Charles "Buckie" Archembault, only son of Wayne and Maureen Archembault..." and it was impossible to imagine, the loved ones in their holocaust of grief.

"C'mon people now," the radio chanted,
Smile on your brother,
Everybody get together,
Try to love one another right now

He walked back to the trailer court with the paper under his arm in the lovely Indian summer morning, the hills aflame with aspen, a cold sting in the air. Maybe everybody could get together and love one another. And if we focused on getting into space maybe there'd be no more need for war.

A police car's brake lights flashed as it stopped at Crystal's trailer. Two cops climbed out and looked at Mick's bike. One went back to the car and sat talking on the radio, the cruiser's door open, his left foot on the ground. The other knocked on the trailer door, waited, banged again.

Mick watched from behind a cottonwood tree. With a crowbar one cop popped Crystal's door. They glanced around and went inside. Mick walked fast back into town. Now he'd lost the bike and couldn't get away, couldn't take a bus or hitch. He'd lost his clothes, tent and sleeping bag. They'd know he was on foot, be looking block by block. Either he had to sneak out of town with no winter clothes, or find a vehicle fast.

Five blocks later a blue Ford van leaned against the curb with a FOR SALE sign.

Mick went up to the house and knocked till a man with snakes tattooed up both forearms opened it. "That your van?" Mick said.

"Yeah." The man burped, rubbing his forearms, trying to wake up.

Mick tried to not seem rushed, nervous. "Can I drive it?"

"So early?"

"Just blew a valve on mine, need to find something this morning. To get to work."

"It's got just the front seat and a bed in back. Me'n the old lady go camping in't. Drives real good, man." He coughed, spit on the grass. "Needs a little body work is all."

It had a cracked rear window and one working taillight and said *Enamorado Plumbing* in faded yellow letters on its sides. It had a shimmy and kept veering left into oncoming traffic. "You need to take it down to Motor Vehicles," the man said. "Put your name on it."

"I'll do that now. Where are they?"

"I should go down with you, sign it there."

"Don't bother, just sign it now. I'm going to stop for breakfast on the way."

He gave him seven hundred even and took a back road southwest to Missoula and over the Bitterroots into Idaho. The van was in the man's name, D.T. Jones, so as long as he didn't get stopped he might be okay. For a while.

At a rain-whipped Gulf station in the Bitterroots he called Crystal. "Hey how are you, Honey?" she said. "There's cops all over looking for you."

"What you tell them?"

"That I don't even know your name."

"I can't come back. Not for a while. Probably a long while."

"Yeah." She cleared her throat quietly. "I figured that."

"You keep that bike. Tell them I gave it to you."

"They took it already, Honey."

The pay phone bonged that time was up. He fished for more coins, didn't have them. "Tell the kids hi!" he called as the phone bonged again and died.

IT TOOK SIX MONTHS for Daisy to bury Bobby. In her heart. She pushed through her required courses and left Stanford in January for San Francisco with a thesis still to do on the roots of human evil, the relation between neurosis and the modern way of life. And how LSD and peyote could help.

She was still, she'd realized one night alone with a bottle of pinot grigio empty on the table in front of her, chasing the same connections between cognitive neuroscience and anthropology, now with philosophy thrown in too.

Human evil: no one wants to talk about that.

She'd found a studio apartment for $129 a month on Genoa Place, a narrow street under Coit Tower, worked days on her thesis and nights at Vesuvio's on Columbus Avenue, across the alley from City Lights Bookstore, first as a waitress. Two weeks later, when the second bartender broke a leg in a motorcycle wreck, she told the boss, "I can do that," and got the job right away based on her energy, her smile, her nearly-uncovered breasts, and her rapid assimilation of the many drinks bartenders must know how to make. "It's easy," she told the boss, "you separate them into family, genus, and species. The family is the basic liquor, like gin, the genus is any additions— like vermouth—and the species is the martini, the final drink. Effortless."

There were happy days walking to work when she felt light as air, effortlessly independent, extravagantly free. She had love, freedom, and happiness. Her love was the thesis, which entranced her for hours of intense awareness. Freedom came from bartending at Vesuvio's, more money than she'd ever had before. And happiness was this warm little studio in North Beach, with two windows looking over the East Bay to Alcatraz and Berkeley beyond, morning mists over the steely water with the sun rising above them, a cup of coffee warming her hands and the joyous awareness of a day of research to come.

If only, she sometimes wondered, her mother had had this same independence, this same chance to become herself, what could *she* have done, become? It had been her mother who had given her this freedom, by dint of her own hard work, overriding the misery induced by an alcoholic husband...But what if...

What if every person had the possibility to become what they could be, reach at least some part of their potential? Could LSD help make that happen? Clinically there were plenty of indications, but the politics were becoming dreadful. What if?

On work nights at Vesuvio's Daisy never got home till two a.m., sometimes with a guy, which meant she got no work done on her thesis till late morning. The guys were so much fun, but that wasn't *it*, really. So what was *it*?

Such thinking was circular, led nowhere. She would do her dissertation on the causes of human evil, the relation between neurosis and crowding, the write-up of her studies on LSD. Stay right here in North Beach and make money.

But no, these late nights were killing her. Her brain wasn't focusing. She was losing ground.

She'd saved enough money to move out of San Francisco to somewhere rural and cheap, to spend six intense months finishing the thesis.

Then more research.

Then the truth.

SPLASHING THROUGH the mean little main street of Weiser, Idaho in the rainy dusk Mick saw two figures huddled under a poncho, a suitcase between them. He didn't want to stop but it was raining hard and he wouldn't have wanted to be out in it.

They tumbled in, a woman maybe thirty-five, chunky with chopped blonde hair and a red face, sitting in the front, a girl maybe seventeen, chunky too in a pale open way, in the back.

The woman smelled of wet clothes and cigarettes. She kept wiping water from her brow as it ran down from her hair, and looking back at the girl.

"Where you headed?" he said.

"Bend." She glanced back, not at the girl this time but out the back window, turned to Mick holding out a damp cold hand. "What's your name? I'm Trudy."

"Dave," he started to say.

"Dave?"

"No, Steve. I said Steve. Steve McKinnon."

She leaned forward scanning the road. "Where *you* headed?"

"Oregon, the coast. My girl's there." He leaned over the steering staring through rippling windshield at the blurry approaching lights of trucks. Damn—he'd picked them up because it was raining and he felt sorry for them and now he had them half way across Oregon. He glanced back at the girl sitting lock-kneed on the bed, buck teeth pinning her lower lip.

"Don't worry," Trudy said. "We can sleep in the woods."

The rain grew harder, colder, sleet building up in the corners of the windshield. "I'll sleep up front here," he said. "You two take the bed."

"Spunky's small, she can sleep up here. You and I can stay back there." She coughed her smoker's laugh. "I won't attack you."

He chuckled, embarrassed. "It's not that."

A jackrabbit darted into the road, he braked hard, it crouched yellow eyes ablaze and whumped under the van. "Shit!" he said. "God-damn it!"

"Don't swear in fronta Spunky!"

"Fuck Spunky." He drove along feeling sad for hitting the rabbit and guilty for what he'd said.

"Bugs Bunny never dies," Spunky said.

"This one did," Trudy answered.

"How come?"

"He got in the way," her mother said. "What's the lesson?"

"Never get in the way?"

"Now go to sleep." Trudy eased herself back in the seat.

After midnight he took a BLM dirt road about three miles into low hills. She woke the girl and they went in different directions to piss. The rain had stopped; the night smelled damp and resiny from the piñon and juniper trees, and tart with sage. Strips of black starry sky rushed through the clouds.

Squatting on a rocky outcrop he smoked the last of a joint Crystal had given him, thinking of her, her warm little place, the two kids. If he'd slept a while longer...

It was impossible to imagine what ten years in Leavenworth would be.

He'd been stupid to register the bike in New York in his real name. He could afford no more mistakes, would have to be flawless.

Impeccable. He laughed at the thought of it: impeccable meant *without sin.*

Had to become someone else. A real person so if some cop stopped him his license would be good and he had a social security number and could get work. A whole different person. So no one could connect him to him.

Impossible to imagine what ten years in Leavenworth would be.

When he came back the girl was curled up under her coat in front and the woman under her coat on the far side of the foam mattress. Inside the van smelled of wet stale cigarette smoke. He lay down awkwardly beside her.

She sniffed. "Hey you don't have to go outside to smoke dope."

He felt guilty for not offering to share. "Do you want—"

"No way. I got so many visions going through my head already it's like a Greyhound bus station. I don't mind if other people do. Just don't give none to Spunky."

"What kind of visions?"

"Like that movie *She Freak?* Whoo that was scary. That's what it's like inside my head. Or *Wait Until Dark?* Whoo that's a good one to stay away from..."

In the morning the sun was bright and the wind cut like a knife. He built a sagebrush fire against some red rocks and they had coffee and Cheerios with powdered milk. "You live well," Trudy said, and a minute later, "we're lucky to have found you." She patted his shoulder. "You're our lucky star."

"I just saw you in the rain, that's all."

"Most people wouldn't of stopped. Back in Mountain Home even people you know won't pick you up. Pretend they don't see you."

She lit a Virginia Slim, keeping it in the middle of her mouth, lips parted over it. "I married a man that owned the Buick garage in Mountain Home. So we had some prominence. But he hated Spunky, cause of how she is. We got divorced and most people wouldn't speak to me. After a while I lived with Leonard. He was a real drip, that one. Said he was getting a heritage but all he got was his mom's dancing shoes, the ones where you go on your toes. Too small for me. I'm a hefty girl. So I married Ollie. He thought he was God's gift to women, the dumb drunk. He's the one who did it."

"What?"

"What he did to Spunky. That's why I moved in with Babs. My sister. But Ollie come after us. He whacked me around real good, see?" She pointed to a missing upper front tooth. "Then he spanked Spunky and was gonna take her in her room and do it to her again and I hit him with his championship baseball bat, the one he bought from the fifty-four World Series when Dusty Rhodes hit that homer off Bob Lemon, remember?"

"Then what happened?"

"He fell down. What's bad is it broke the bat. I grabbed Spunky and a few things quick, and here we are."

"What's in Bend?"

"My mom's sister Edna. She don't want us but we got nowhere else. Do we, Spunky? She runs a café, her husband was in a log mill but broke his back. They give him seventy-five dollars and found him a job in a gas station. But he can't walk so *they* fired him and he went on the county but they closed him off so Edna runs the café by herself."

TARA'D SCREWED A HUNDRED GUYS or more, why should one death matter? Troy and she were never fated anyway. They'd murdered their own child then pretended they could still love each other.

She sat on the back porch of her rambling Berkeley house with the black cat in her lap, staring down but not seeing the canyon of redwoods and rhododendrons below, hearing but not hearing the distant cacophony of traffic, the breeze flowing through the eucalyptus leaves.

She should have felt cool after shooting up with some White Angel.

But nothing would ease this pain.

What a prick Troy was to go to Vietnam. When he didn't *need* to.

Then to go back a second time. *Wanted* to die. Didn't want her, he wanted death. So why was she crying? Why every night did she ache to hold him? What was human touch anyway?

What were humans?

Like Janis sang so well,

Freedom's just another word for nothin left to lose

The White Angel a warm solace in her bones. Sybil always trying to get her off smack, didn't understand how she *needed* this lovely onrushing feeling. And it wasn't true what Sybil said, that she was losing it, forgetting her songs, getting off beat. No, the more smack she did the closer she got to Buddha's truth: *All attachment is toxic.*

Was it because they'd murdered their own child?

She'd start rehearsing with the band again. That'd shut Sybil up.

Thank God for smack. Where would she be without its sweet caress to ease pain and confusion, and to mellow every day? Someday she'd quit it too. Damn right she would.

Not yet.

JUST PUT ONE FOOT in front of the other, Troy told himself. Then pick up the other foot and swing it forward and put it in front of the first. Easy if you just think about that one foot, not how far you have to go. Don't admit you can't go any farther. Because then they shoot you.

They had walked for days through bomb craters and blistered forests and the remains of villages stinking of corpses. The doctor said they were in Cambodia now but that couldn't be because the bombing was even worse than Nam, the bombing and the stink of defoliant that burned your throat and made you so sick you had to force down your food, and the VC were throwing up and pissing blood just like he was.

Sometimes there were pieces of forest still standing but the leaves were gone, the huge trunks sepulchral and bare like columns in some gigantic temple of death, towering corpses frozen in rigor mortis, so sickening and sad and empty that he refused to see it any more,

109

refused to think but couldn't stop, wondered sometimes if this weren't really happening and he should shake himself out of it, come back to life.

Maybe it was Hell and he couldn't get out of it.

But the pain in his gut was so horrible it had to be real. Sepsis, the doctor said. It had come back and now there were no antibiotics and even if there were they'd go to the VC wounded, guys with sucking chest wounds and third degree burns and truncated arms, one older man, a gray-haired teacher from Hanoi the doctor said, who walked on a bleeding stump tied to a stick and never whimpered, never said a word.

In his constant agony Troy sometimes asked how much longer, promising himself he could go another hundred steps, then another fifty, but the doctor said he didn't know, soon would come a base hospital and all Troy had to do was keep going a little more, climbing in and out of craters and over shattered scattered trunks, his feet soaked in the muddy water stinking of Agent Orange and burnt exploded steel.

In his delirium he sometimes wondered where in his own vast fruitful country all this murderous steel had come from, this high explosive, where had it been assembled, who had trucked it to the trains that took it to San Diego and put it on a ship to Guam to be loaded into the belly of a B-52 and flown across the globe to be dropped here, thousand-pound bombs falling thick as autumn leaves?

It made no sense that humans could be so evil, that any person could do this.

To trick himself into walking further he'd think about what he'd do when he got back to America, pretending that some day he could, that he'd go to med school and return here to help heal this poor ravaged tortured place, these silent anguished people. At night lying in pain in a brush shelter hearing the bombs and rockets hitting nearby he talked with Su Li and told her his plans, that everything he did from now on would be for her. *I love you*, he said time and time again, inhaling her lovely scents of skin and hair, glorying in the beauty of her soul. *I love you too*, she'd answer, *Oh how I love you*, and her words eased his nights and kept him going in the days.

"Few more kilometers," a voice said, the doctor. Troy reached out and held his shoulder, less for support than to give thanks to this quiet man who had lost his whole family to American bombs yet took care of Troy just like the other wounded, seemed to live Hippocrates' ancient teaching: *Do no harm.*

That night they reached it, a cluster of camo tents and netting beneath tall spreading trees, the wounded lying on cots, wrapped in clean bandages, nurses and doctors rushing about, the lovely smell of rice and fish cooking on low smoky fires, and tears poured down his face and he wanted to fall down on his knees at the joy of it but kept walking, stronger now, into the hospital, head spinning, throat choked, and they led him to a cot and cut away his soiled bandages and a small woman in black pajamas knelt beside him with warm water washing his wound speaking softly in Vietnamese, words he understood, "Better now, all pain goes," and he wondered where in this godless universe such an angel had been found.

She fed him mashed rice spoon by spoon, hitched his drip to a tall stick driven in the ground, returning to see how he was doing. "Antibiotic," she said in English, then in Vietnamese, "soon all better now."

The doctor came, beyond weary, felt Troy's forehead. "You maybe make it."

"Then what?"

"We trade you, maybe?"

Troy held his arm. "You didn't keep me alive, all this time, just to trade me. It's because you're a good man..."

Somewhere it was raining, thunder. The doctor looked nervous, stood watching the east. The thunder loudened, wasn't thunder.

Bombs. B-52s.

The earth began to shake, the camo nets shivering. The stick with his drip bag toppled. People were running, yelling, grabbing the cots one by one but the thunder was upon them, the dead trees lashing to and fro like wind-driven grass, and through the dusk a wall of fire raged toward them, a vast red-black-white hurricane a hundred feet high and half a mile wide, his cot tumbling, men screaming, mountains of earth and trees spouting into the sky and falling upon them, the roar of bombs crushing his ears, crushing his body, vast explosions rending earth and splitting apart the air, and he wondered just before it hit how badly will it hurt to be blown apart, obliterated to the end of time?

9

EARTHSOUL

BEND WAS DANGEROUS with nowhere to hide from the blue city police cars, black Oregon State Police cruisers, brown Deschutes County Sheriff Fords and the unmarked cars he didn't even see. Everyone seemed to notice his Montana plates.

Edna's Restaurant was a railroad diner on Main Street. He dropped Trudy and Spunky at the corner, bought a cheap sleeping bag and tarp at Western Surplus, filled the tank at Cities Service north of town, bought an Oregon map and asked the man how to get to Portland. He then cut through back streets to continue south on logging roads into the National Forest in the Cascades. Logging trucks bellowed past dragging trailers piled high with Douglas firs, and the snarl of chainsaws echoed over the hills where clearcuts spread in all directions like the saturation bombing in Vietnam.

He felt shaky, uncoordinated. His gut burned and his arms trembled. The constant fear and watching were wearing him down, his eyes gritty and sore, his muscles aching, his thoughts weary. He had to hide, stop moving around, but nowhere was safe. Much as he wanted to call Tara in Berkeley that would be the end.

The clock on the van's dashboard said three twenty-two a.m., but it was twenty-four minutes slow compared to a bank clock in Bend, so it was really about quarter to four. He parked at the end of a deserted logging road and took his sleeping bag and tarp into the hills where he could hear and see anything coming up the road.

YOUR CARES WILL LESSEN *if they are faced cheerfully*, said his fortune cookie next noon at The Magic Dragon in Grants Pass.

"What'd you get?" said a girl down the counter.

He told her. She opened her cookie, dropped its wrapper in the remains of her ham and eggs, laughed. "Your cares will lessen..."

"Maybe they save money by buying just one fortune."

"Or," her eyebrows raised mock-seriously, "*our* fates are linked..."

"Which way you going?"

"I'm hitching to a place near Gasquet."

She had mahogany braids plaited down her breasts and tied with scraps of purple ribbon. She was tall with slightly Mongol eyes, high cheekbones and a pert nose. Her name was Shawnee and she sat forward intently on the van's passenger seat, knees in her hands, peering through the Coast Range mist at the narrow sinuous highway.

"Where's Gasquet?"

"Just over the California border. But I take off before that, a dirt road."

"Where to?"

"Earthsoul. A commune."

She had a joint they smoked driving through a light rain, tires hissing on the asphalt, drops from overhead boughs splattering the windshield, water crashing down a roadside ditch, the van gasping on the uphills.

The weed was powerful and made his body tingle. "What's it like, Earthsoul?"

"We live on what we grow and share everything. We don't take anything from the Sham World."

"Sham World?"

She waved her hand at everything around them. "Cities, towns, other people. Who think and do what they're told and never realize they aren't happy...Tom's our mentor. He started it three years ago and now there's almost a hundred of us."

"What do you grow?"

"We have chickens for eggs and goats for milk and cheese and plenty of greens, and pigs for meat too..."

"You must get bugged by the police."

"We're fourteen miles up a dirt road. Their shocks can't take it. Last one was a year ago; he popped an oil plug and they had to tow him out."

"Doesn't it make you feel isolated?"

"Earthsoul? No, everyone's cool, we're all friends."

"I've often wondered what it was like, a commune."

"Why don't you hang out a few days, see if you like it?"

Before Gasquet she directed him up a logging road into the eroded bulldozed hills of scrub oak, madrone and raspberry thickets, poison oak and stinging nettles where a vast redwood forest had recently stood. A few redwood saplings stuck out at weird angles from the landslided hills or tilted up from bulldozed streambeds of muddy boulders and huge upended stumps with outflung roots.

Runnels had cut the road, jouncing the van as it bumped across them. It took an hour to reach a long cedar-shaked hut on the crest of a ridge, a shiny Ford pickup and Pontiac wagon beside it, about thirty slab huts and tents on platforms crawling up the slope below it, a few old vans and jalopies parked by them.

"Here's my place." It was a hut of redwood boughs to which overlapping planks had been nailed horizontally, a low roof of hand-hewn shingles with a blue tarp atop them. "I made it all from logging slash."

Inside was a double bed against the back wall, a white-enameled cookstove with a round thermometer in its door, a plank table and benches, a pole in the corner with a few clothes hanging, a bright Oriental rug on the umber earth.

She introduced him to a guy named Jeremiah, his sharp brown eyes on Mick's. "Sure," Jeremiah said. "You can stay a few days. "Shawnee's *Us*—you're her guest."

Something about Jeremiah was out of context: maybe the tangled russet beard and moustache, the ragged ponytail, the strength beneath the nondescript brown shirt, the disinterested hostility in the flat brown eyes. Sitting on Shawnee's dirt floor drinking her tea Mick felt disconnected from everything, so lonely it ached his gut and enervated his bones. He could not decide if he was safer here or more endangered.

But *where* would be safe? If he kept wandering like this they'd surely get him. He had to find somewhere they wouldn't look. Wouldn't *think* to look.

Earthsoul might be it. Maybe fifty couples, some with little kids, all young and long-haired. All dope-smoking casual love leftist anarchist political free spirits, the men in jeans, work shirts and occasionally a hand-made deerskin vest, the women in cotton skirts, jeans and Indian blouses. Friendly yet distant, as if he was allowed for a short time in their community but not part of it.

The rules were simple: everyone worked in the community gardens, milked the goats, made cheese, gathered and cut firewood, repaired the buildings and tended the spring and latrines. Beside the stream at the foot of the ridge stood a wood-fueled hot tub where people hung out in the evening and often made love. Everyone shared food and shelter as necessary and partners when asked. "We don't have monogamy here," Jeremiah said with a sideways smile at Shawnee.

"You can't *own* anyone," she added.

That night in the common hut they ate chicken stew from a huge aluminum pot set in the coals, throwing chicken bones to the skinny anxious dogs, drinking spring water and herb tea. Everyone quieted after the meal and waited for Tom to speak.

He stood, a tall rangy man with gray-white hair and a truculent chin. "Tonight reminds me when I visited a commune in Australia," he said softly so everyone strained forward. "Called Southern Cross, for the constellation...They were all into free love and sharing produce of their work but some of them worked harder than others, and," he slapped a fist on the table, "some were jealous, and others were free!"

He explained that no one was free if they constrained the freedom of another, tried to possess another. That wasn't love. Love was letting go, letting the loved one be and do everything they wanted, dreamed of, feared.

Palms on hips he scanned the room. "That's the message for tonight, sisters and brothers: *WHAT* are we doing, each in our own way, *TO PREVENT OURSELVES, AND EACH OTHER, FROM BEING FREE!!!?*" He raised his hands for quiet, scanned the room briefly and backed toward the door. He nodded to a longhaired blonde girl who sat in the first row, and gestured to another, dark-haired, in a back row. They rose and followed him from the room. "Where they going?" Mick said.

"The Long House."

"What's that?" he was whispering, as if in church.

"Tom's place. Every night he picks a girl or two, or three. It's his due."

"His due for what?"

"For starting Earthsoul. For turning the earth around."

They washed the dishes in another huge vat, then spread out to go home, picking mates, being kind and choosy and going with the flow. "Tonight," Shawnee gripped his arm tightly, "I get to keep you."

"This Tom guy, what's he do?"

"Puts it all in perspective. Reminds us of the joy of *Now*."

"So you have to screw him, too, if he asks."

"All us girls do. With anyone who asks. And they have to screw us too, if *we* ask." Nestling her hand in the crook of his arm she led him down to her hut with its bed of squeaky coils that made him wonder when they made love if the whole commune could hear.

After breakfast a stuttering guy named Prescott showed Mick a pile of live oak logs to cut and split. The wood was hard and tight-grained. "You don't have a chainsaw?" Mick said.

"No internal combustion engines here."

Mick nodded at the Ford pickup and Pontiac wagon by the Long House. "What about them?"

"They're how we transit to the Sham World. To take what we need from it."

Anyone with a specific skill, Mick learned, could provide that skill to avoid garden time or firewood gathering or other basic community tasks. Thus a tough greasy guy named Dusty was the commune mechanic, and Prescott the head carpenter. Others at the top like Jeremiah did no community tasks except for show; their role was to run the commune. Tom of course had duties that preempted any work.

IT TOOK A FEW DAYS to learn where the money to keep the commune going came from. He was following a path through brush and slash past a blowout where logging roads had collapsed an entire hillside into a stream canyon. Beyond it was a narrow green valley of second growth redwoods, and between them tall shapely marijuana plants stretching to the end of the valley. Rows of plastic pipe fed by gravity from a sandy stream had a feeder at each plant. The scent of the weed was rich and heady; its iridescence barely different from the young redwoods glorying in the sun.

"Of course," Shawnee said. "That's what we bring the Sham World. To help it."

"Who keeps the money?"

"Earthsoul."

"Who takes it to the bank?"

"Tom, of course."

If the commune was growing weed in these amounts they were selling it in big quantities too. And such large transactions sooner or later attracted cops. Worried, he drove the next day out to Gasquet and called Lou Graziano. "You crazy?" Lou yelled. "They got tracers on this phone! Can come grab you, wherever the hell you are!"

"I'll talk quick. Lou, is there any way I can turn myself in, like for a reduced sentence?"

"You *nuts*? You'd never get out of Leavenworth."

He stood numbly by the phone in the rumble of loaded logging trucks, a few uncut boughs dragging their green needles along the road. He wanted terribly to call Tara in Berkeley, Crystal in Great Falls, even Clyde Gottson in the Crazies. Lily in Paris. Or Daisy—Oh

God if he could only talk to her just once. *No*, a voice said, *you will always be alone.*

He was in limbo with nowhere safe to go, not even here. Not daring to flee, he worked at the tasks assigned him in day, ate the wholesome, uninteresting food, made love with Shawnee on her creaky bed. There was nowhere apart, nowhere to be alone unless he went out in the clearcuts and then all he saw was the horror of logging, the slash piles, the huge disconnected stumps, the red earth like wounds, the ravines of erosion. There was no peace from it, nowhere to get away, no nature. He felt disconcerted, invaded, hungered to go somewhere else, but anywhere he went could be fatal.

One hot afternoon Dusty came into Shawnee's hut. She looked up at him, elbow on the table, finger at her lip. "Hi," Dusty said, looking at her, then Mick. He nodded at her, the bed. "Want to?"

Her wide dimpled smile and big white teeth, a sparkle in her eyes. "Why not?"

"I don't want to talk," he added, hand on her shoulder following her to the bed. "I just want to fuck you."

Mick got up to leave, a little discomfited. It was strange you could be talking with someone and the next thing you knew she was fucking someone. Dusty's hairy ass was twitching up and down as he drove grunting into Shawnee, her distraught cries and gasps of pleasure seemed bizarre and funny. Mick went down the dirt street, a strange emptiness in his chest, a skinny puppy running up to greet him, naked kids barefoot in the mud, sniffly noses and bright red cheeks.

Rena lived in the last house on the right. She and Hart, a soft-voiced quiet man with a dark curly beard, had two kids, but he wasn't there. She was a solid woman in her late thirties with a bland face and tired eyes. "It's what you're supposed to do when your lover's making it with somebody: *Love someone else.* I'm glad you came to me."

When he got back to Shawnee's hut Dusty was gone and she was making cocoa on the woodstove. "Where were you?" she said.

"Down to Rena's."

"You fuck her?"

"Of course."

She stood unbuttoning her shirt from the bottom up. "Want to do me?"

"You've just been fucking Dusty—"

"Yeah." She slipped off the shirt, slid down her jeans. "Nothing makes me hornier than fucking."

That night Tom gave a long talk. Pacing, facing down and speaking softly as if ruminating, then raising his eyes to sweep the group, voice thundering. "And *if* you listen, *really* listen, to Nostradamus, you'll see we're near the end of time—wars, environmental sacrilege, worship of money, worship of evil, even by the churches...*Most of all,*" he roared, "by the *churches!*"

Back and forth he trod, exhorting, whispering, a few times nearly weeping, while the throng sat immobile before him with adoring eyes. "If you're not *emotional* about this, *deeply* emotional," he raised his arms in an embracing gesture, "I don't want you with *Us.*"

The lecture was over. Motioning to Shawnee and another woman Tom led them back to the Long House. Feeling adrift and solitary, Mick went down to Shawnee's hut. On the way a girl with a pixie face took his hand. "Shawnee's taken for tonight, but I'm not." He considered making love with her, imagined her slim little body writhing beneath him. "Sorry, Annie, I'm just not into it tonight."

"You've got to get over other guys doing it with her."

"That's not it."

She went on as if he'd said nothing. "The thing about lovers is they make your major relationship even closer." She squeezed his fingers. "No one's naturally monogamous; we all have wants and desires we don't express, our culture's so repressed and church-ridden, but to get past that is such an aching freedom."

Her earnestness disarmed him. They went into Shawnee's hut and made love for a long time, slowly the way Lily had taught him in Paris, and each time she came he felt nearer to her, more deeply linked, her ecstasy far more important than his, this elfin stranger he'd hardly ever talked to.

"Jealousy," Annie said, stretching her small lean body along him, "it's a fear trip, that our lover won't love us as much as whoever else they're fucking. It's a loss of control...But when we love them for their complete selves it's a far closer union, a deeper happiness. Like you and me, what we just had. It was wonderful...How could anybody criticize that?" She tucked on her underpants, jeans and shirt. "Woody loves it when I make it with somebody else...He's going to want to ball me all night."

In the days that followed, Mick realized that though Tom scorned the outside world he could not live without it. It bought his weed and supplied him with recruits, groceries, fuel, telephone and other services. Most importantly, it gave him something to rail against, his validation: *if the world was wrong, he must be right.*

In love with himself, he used his religion to secure others' love, a half-saint for whom only the most passionate devotion was acceptable. His "helpers," acolytes like Jeremiah, attacked any criticism or doubt, completely brainwashed and defensively empty of all reflection, ready to punish anyone not like them.

Tom derided the Sham World as a fabrication, Land of the Living Dead, where humans lived without awareness. Beyond this Sham World was a wider one, Land of the Spirit, the deep awareness all humans should have and know. Then a third world where only a Medicine Man like Tom could go: World of the Eternal Spirit.

Yet he taught valuable tactics like using wide-angle vision to meditate, walking barefoot to stay in touch with the earth, how to survive in the wilderness, build a debris shelter that would save you in winter, make a bow drill and start a fire, find good plants to eat, snare rabbits, *survive.* "Like Buddha says," he intoned, *"Your salvation rests on your shoulders!"*

Reduced to basics, Tom demanded that they:

Become self-reliant. Don't depend on the Sham World.
Love the earth thy Mother.
Love each other. No boundaries.
Don't trust anyone but Us.
Spread my teachings to everyone you can.

A great liar obsessed with himself, Tom neither respected or had interest in anyone else unless he thought he could get something from them, in which case he became instantly charming and convivial. But Earthsoul, Mick had come to realize, was a cult. Like religion, patriotism or nationhood—the most dangerous. In any cult was the unspoken understanding that one's deepest allegiance, even more important than a loved one or oneself—was to the cult. And to disagree was treason.

Often in his harangues Tom would say if he had twenty minutes he'd show them all how to reach soul truth, but then meandered on with a half hour of sentimental trivia about himself, that he had his own swami, the prophet essential for all cults, and the Maharishi himself had taught him to speak in tongues, and if one listened with the heart they'd understand.

When a new couple was officially inducted into the commune, he led a sacred pipe ceremony where everyone smoked from a long pipe while Mick watched from a distance, disgusted by their credulity.

One noon Tom claimed to know every word of Scriptures and could recite long passages of the Koran. Mick thought of the old man Ben Younès in the Sahara. "Please recite something from the Koran," he called out. There was a shocked hush; everyone stared at Mick but Tom only smiled and shook his head, "I don't have time for that. I don't have time to prove myself to unbelievers."

"One sura," Mick persisted. "Just give me one sura."

"Jeremiah," Tom called. "We've got an asshole here."

Jeremiah appeared, large in the doorway. "I thought as much."

"Get rid of him. He's a virus, could contaminate us all."

Mick stood. "You're a fraud, Tom. And Jeremiah or whatever the hell your name really is, get out of my way or I'll break every bone in your face."

"I can call it down on you any time," Jeremiah smiled.

Mick walked out of the Long House downhill to Shawnee knitting something out of raw wool. "I'm heading south to San Francisco. Want to come?"

She gazed at him, an animal who'd never free itself from its trap.

"Someday you're going to look back on all Tom's taught you, and wish you'd stayed."

He checked his tires for nails. "You're right, he's taught me a lot. Taught me to trust myself and no one else." In his rear-view mirror as he drove off her head was tilted over her knitting as if he'd never been there at all.

10

MODOC

A T THE JUNCTION of the Gasquet road he stopped, not knowing which way to go. He'd told Shawnee he was heading south to San Francisco, but with the intention of going back to Oregon or east to Nevada. Oregon was only five miles up the road but it felt risky and less forgiving. Nevada was just deserts and gambling. They might be less likely to look for him there.

The driver of an empty logging truck gearing down for the climb toward Oregon glanced at him. *Anti-war activist caught in rural California mountains.* Kind of place you'd expect someone to get caught.

He turned toward Nevada. He was living on a nervous edge, not thinking straight. So afraid that everything seemed dangerous: a little girl in a yellow raincoat in Happy Camp smiling at him, a grocery clerk clucking sharply when Mick dropped a tuna can in the checkout line, his hand shaking as he paid. The gas station attendant in Weed glancing at his license plate. "Where from in Montana?"

"Oh, uh, the Crazies."

"Huh? You've got a Great Falls plate number."

"Yeah, just moved. Haven't changed registrations…"

He tried to be relaxed and not afraid, reminded himself that no one at Earthsoul had known who he was, not even Shawnee. How could the Feds track him anyway? Unless by now they knew about the van.

After dark he switched plates with another Ford van in a diner lot in McCloud and took Highway 299 toward Nevada. This northeast corner of California was empty, barren plateaus and low pine forests, and on the map a small back road that cut east through the Modoc Indian Reservation over the Warner Mountains into Nevada.

The rain turned to sleet then snow almost horizontal across the windshield, the wipers dragging, the truck slithering on the turns, tires spinning on the climbs. "Damn this!" he yelled, angry and so alone he feared his heart would stop. He was going to get stuck out here in the snowstorm, a gift for the cops.

His headlights danced across a white abandoned Victorian house that sat back from the road, its windows dark and empty. He turned up the drive, skidding sideways in the ruts, parked behind the barn and walked out to the road to rub a pine branch across his tire tracks.

The back door was open; the hallway boards sank under his feet. In the parlor, snow had blown across the floor and piled up under the empty windows. He went to the barn and broke some wood from a stall, went back inside, knelt by the fireplace and yanked back his hand when he felt its warmth.

"So," a deep calm voice said, "you comfortable here?"

Mick turned toward the voice. "This your place?"

"I been here first. Now you come in."

Mick backed into a corner, trying to locate the voice. "Look, kid," it said, "I been watching since you came. I wanted to kill you, you'd already be dead."

"I'm moving on tomorrow. I'll leave tonight you want."

"Nobody ain't moving on tomorrow. Not in this storm. Got any food?"

"Three cans of beans, a can of Dinty Moore stew, some peanut butter and bread."

"I've some meat hanging in the barn. And I'd enjoy some conversation." He stepped into the firelight, a huge old man with a face like polished stone and a nose like the blade of a maul. "Where you headed, middle of the night like this?"

"Idaho, see my girlfriend."

"You're going the wrong way."

"I've got time, seeing the country."

"This girlfriend must be something, you don't care to see her." For a while the Indian watched the snow dance through the pane-less windows. "Where you come from?"

Mick rebuilt the fire. "San Francisco."

"I been through there twice." He chuckled. "Once Soledad, once San Quentin."

Mick watched him, thinking it through. "What for?"

"Armed robbery, assault. But I'm done now. Not going back no more."

"It must be awful, prison."

"Day by day it kills you. Hour by day by week by year it kills you." The Indian knelt before the fire warming his hands. "You make a good fire, kid. Teepee style." He glanced up at him. "I'll share you some venison you share me some beans."

He came in from the barn with a slab of deer meat sliced off the carcass. "Been there two weeks but it can't age, it's too damn cold." He drew a huge knife from a sheath on the outside of his calf, split a plank and made two skewers. "Don't cook it too much. Makes it tough."

The meat was tough and gamy but full of taste. Mick opened a can of beans and gave the Indian his spoon. "You eat half then give it to me."

The Indian gave him an appreciative look, handed back the can a little over half full, went to a window and wiped off the spoon in the snow and gave it to Mick. He held out a hand. "You call me Jack."

"Jack? I'm Stu. Stuart Elliott."

"Captain Jack. Named for my grandfather. He killed lot of white men."

After a while the fire settled down. "Where you sleepin?" Jack said.

"This's your house. You tell me where the guest room is."

"I sleep here, close to the fire. All I got is my coat. You can sleep here you want. There's plenty room. I'll break some more banisters, bring them down."

Mick thought of the big knife on the Indian's leg. "I got a bed in my truck."

"Gonna freeze your ass."

"Yeah. Probably true." Mick moved to the door. "I've got coffee, for the morning. You got a pot we can cook water in?"

"There's a pail somewhere."

"Stay warm."

Jack gave him a conspiratorial grin. "You sleep easy."

Inside the van was frigid; his breath froze on the windows. He locked the doors and crawled fully clothed inside his sleeping bag. After a while he got no warmer, could not stop shivering. He thought of the Indian's knife. The Indian could've killed him long ago. But maybe he was stringing him on, wanted him to fear before he died.

Finally he waded through deepening snow across the barnyard and into the parlor. Jack lay huddled under a bearskin coat in front of the fire. Mick quietly put more banisters on the fire and lay down in his sleeping bag to one side. "Lucky you not freeze to death," Jack said.

"Did I wake you?"

"I'm always awake. Even when I'm sleeping. Life's better that way."

"Me too. But I don't want to be."

"Shit," the Indian chuckled. "For that you got to go back and change your life."

ALL DAY the snow came down. It rose above the open windows and piled into the room. They burned all the stalls in the barn and part of the siding and all the banisters and rails but couldn't get warm. "I'm the only guy you ever meet," Jack said, "jumped across the Volga River."

Mick didn't understand. "The one in Russia?"

"I was twenty-one. Was the year nineteen twenty-one. I'd got into the last of the fight in Europe in eighteen then got sent with a lot of other Army guys to help the white Russians fight the communists. We were up in the hills north of Moscow, the source of that huge river, where it's so small, couple yards, you can jump across."

"What was it like, fighting the communists."

"We lost. That should tell you everything."

"What about Vietnam?"

"It's a white man war." Jack leaned to look out the window. "Tonight," he said.

"Snow's too deep."

"There's tractor chains in the barn. We make them small, to fit your wheels. I ride with you to Bidwell."

"What's there?"

"A few of my people. I want to see them, before I move on."

"Why?"

"You stupid? So I don't go back Soledad."

"What if somebody like me was on the run, from the FBI?"

"Yeah?" The Indian eyed him speculatively. "What of it?"

"If you were me, how would you do it?"

"Think of Captain Jack."

"Captain Jack?"

"My grandfather. His real name was Kintpuash. He was our leader, the Modoc people. Modoc just means The People. We were a small tribe but very strong and free. Our land was from the middle of what you call Oregon far into northern California and Nevada. We could live in the lava desert and the pine mountains and prairies and marshes and everything in between. The other tribes, Klamath, Paiutes and Shasta, all feared us. But we lived in peace with everyone till the whites came."

"When was that?"

"What you call the eighteen-forties. Even before then we'd had white trappers come in, screw our women and trade us guns and liquor for pelts. But after your Gold Rush the white man came into this land in thousands and thousands, settlers, miners, militias, soldiers, criminals, freebooters, maniacs and murderers, wagon trains half a mile wide and three miles long one after another across our lands, miners blowing up our rivers, people cutting down our forests...We asked the government, the army, to stop them but nobody stopped them. The only way to stop them was kill them..." Jack sat back, spread his hands wide. "See, nobody knows all this. It's vanished."

"There *was* no solution."

"We killed hundreds of them but more and more keep coming. My grandfather said we have to stop the killing, we have to solve this with the white man. We're only fifty warriors and a hundred women and children—how can we keep fighting ten thousand soldiers?

"We agreed to many peace talks and each time our little piece of land got smaller. Finally we were squeezed in with the Klamaths who hated us, and we couldn't trust them so we left their reservation and went to our old homelands on Lost River, and when the Army attacked us we killed more than a hundred and never lost a man.

"They cut off our water but we escaped through a pass in the lava beds, and we beat them at Sand Butte and then Dry Lake and other places, killing almost a hundred more.

"They asked for more peace talks. When my grandfather and our other leaders came to the peace talks the soldiers took them prisoner and hung them. They sent the rest of us to Oklahoma. Only twenty-five ever made it back...

"Imagine," he said softly, "this powerful tribe of strong, brave and free people just vanished. In the blink of an eye.

"It was always the same. The Sioux, the Nez Perce, every tribe in America...Couldn't keep our land. Our way of life. Whites hemming us in more and more each year, and you know that all the other tribes have been killed off or gotten nothing, how do you protect your land, your way of life? At least a little piece of it?

"The answer is you don't. Your tribe, your way of life, are dead. Just like somebody put a bullet in them." Jack glanced round the room as if seeing it for the first time. "And the beautiful natural world is dead. Before you white men came, all this land was deep grass. Your cattle made it a desert. You cut down the trees and make roads everywhere. Your cities stink, your air kills people. All the animals hate you." He chuckled. "I don't mean you personal, kid."

"Yeah, but it's true."

"You whites won't stop till you've killed everything."

"I've wondered if that's our role, a geologic one. Changing the nature of life."

"With you, life don't have no nature."

"So your grandfather didn't escape."

"Nobody does."

"And I was asking, if I were on the run from the FBI..."

"First change your looks. Change your ID—your driver's license, Social Security and draft card—you got a draft card?"

"Of course."

"Change all your habits, places you go, things you do. Go where they never think you'd go. Never go where they think. Don't attract attention. Never hitchhike, never have a busted car, never speed, always obey the law, never hang around anywhere, stay out of bars, never case a place, be careful how you get laid and what you tell her, be friendly but distant with folks..."

"And?"

"...And get used to your own company. Because you're the only friend you're ever gonna have. The only one you can trust."

"Doesn't sound like fun."

"As your tracks get cold their hope fades, their motivation. Time's on your side. But if they really want you, they never give up."

WITH A COLD CHISEL and a ten-pound hammer from the tool shed Jack cut a tractor chain in half then split it lengthwise, breaking the thick steel links like twigs, chunks of hot metal flying. "Why *are* you on the run?" Mick said.

"Broke parole. That gets me five more years. I already done twenty-two. All I did was go to Susanville. Man there owed me money. I had to buy a car to get work, like I was supposed to with parole. But when I got to Susanville they grabbed me and I had to use all that car money to make bail."

They laid the chains down in front of the back wheels and Mick drove onto them, then Jack tightened them with a steel cable on the inside and outside of each tire, twisting the cable by hand till the chains were snug. "Try it slow," he said.

The chained wheels dug into the packed snow and the van lurched ahead. Mick drove it twenty yards down the drive then backed up. "Tonight we go," Jack said. "Before they plow this road."

"Won't they be waiting for you in Bidwell?"

"I know when they're there. Bidwell is a small place."

They finished all of Mick's food and all the deer except the bones, which Jack boiled in a pail and they drank the broth. By ten the sky was clear and a half-moon shone brightly on the snow. Mick drove the van carefully to the Bidwell road and turned east, the chains clanking against the rear wheel wells, the van floundering forward.

Three times they had to crawl alongside the rear wheels to tighten the cables. They came over a pass and the desert spread out before them, in its midst a fistfull of lights twinkling in the glacial night. "This Fandango Pass," Jack said. "We ambush wagon trains here when they come to the top of the slope, kill many people." He huffed unbelievingly. "And still they keep coming."

"I'm sorry you lost," Mick said, had the feeling of speaking to Jack's grandfather, *the* Captain Jack. "I'm sorry you didn't get to keep your land. Your way of life."

"Whatever you do," Jack poked Mick's shoulder hard, "don't move too much. Like deer hunting, it's the flash of movement that gives the buck away. The smart old guys, Kid, they just lie still and let the hunter go past."

"Takes guts."

Jack pushed him. "Everything good takes guts, kid."

Fort Bidwell had a short main street lined with bare cottonwoods, one store and the boarded broken windows of another, a few small clapboard cabins and trailers on tiny plots, at the end of town a yellow cement building that was either a school or prison. "Go south to

Cedarville," Jack said. "You won't need the chains. Then across the alkali desert into Nevada. Maybe nobody bother you."

Mick glanced at the wind-cut frozen town. "You shouldn't stay here either. Remember how they got Captain Jack."

"Do like I say. Stop being you. Start a new life."

HOW STRANGE to stop in front of the post office in Virginia City, Nevada, seeing a photo of himself clean-shaven, and beside it an artist's drawing of him with a dark beard. He did have a beard now but had dyed it and his hair blond, yet in the mirror over the stamp display the man looking back at him was the same.

Athletic build, 5'11"
Blue eyes and chestnut hair but may have changed his appearance.
May or may not be with a young woman.
May be driving a blue Ford van with Montana license # 1-5662.
If you see this man immediately call your State Police or local sheriff.
ARMED AND DANGEROUS. DO NOT ATTEMPT TO
APPREHEND.

How crazy to call him that. Only person he was dangerous to was himself. Then he realized the reason they were saying that was to portray him as too dangerous to be captured, giving a reason for him to be killed.

He walked the sidewalk trying to be invisible. When he glanced back, people were staring at his photo. He had to leave right now, couldn't even risk collecting the forty-two bucks they owed him for painting the storage sheds behind the Rock Shop.

Like Captain Jack said, *Depend only on you.*

"Of course you're dangerous," Lou Graziano had said when Mick had called him two weeks ago from Gasquet. "They want your problem solved—know what I mean? So be real careful. If you turn yourself in, do it in a public place. With lotsa media. Otherwise maybe they just take you out."

HE SOLD THE VAN for nine-twenty in Reno and six blocks away bought a BMW bike for six ninety-five. On the registration the former owner's name was Dennis Kurtz of Carson City; Mick found the motor vehicle department in Reno and told them he was Dennis Kurtz and had lost his license, and got a temporary one. He had a month to register the bike; by then he'd have sold it and disappeared again, and let the bastards try to find him.

He drove up the Sierras toward San Francisco. Near Donner Pass a hand-painted sign on a trailer park lawn,

1 Cross
2 Trees
3 Nails
4-Given

It made him laugh then feel sorry for anyone who believed they were responsible for the death of Christ, for the fall of man. That Christ died for their sins. A malicious horrible guilt to impose on anyone. But so many bought it. And loved it.

The kind of people who were hunting him down.

Even more evil was the concept of Hell, where you eternally suffer infinite pain. Only a fascist psychopath could imagine such a thing, let alone propagate it. Was it just jealousy and revenge, the dank mutterings of the transgressed and unappreciated? *I may suffer in this life while you prosper, but I will have eternal joy and you will suffer infinite agonies forever.* Not a bad exchange, if you were nutty enough to believe it.

Nixon had beaten Humphrey and was going to expand the war. Another insane exchange people seemed so good at.

That Bobby would have stopped the war seemed almost forgotten. And that that was why he was killed.

Mick tried not to think of it because the thinking brought him nothing he didn't already know.

A KNOCK ON TARA'S BACK DOOR, hesitant then louder, a woman with a strong squarish face, large bright eyes and reddish curly hair a little gray in the roots. She gave Tara a wide grateful smile, stuck out her hand. "Are you the Tara O'Brien? Did your family take in a boy named Troy many years ago?"

Tara stepped back. "Why do you ask?"

"I'm Ginnie Barden. Troy's mom."

Tara slumped against the door, hands to her face. "Oh my God...We thought you were...How do you know?"

"I just found out. Every year on my week's vacation I go looking for him. Except his name was Daniel, our name for him, my husband Cal's and mine...Last week I got the name of an old priest from the Boys' Home...a lovely old man...Told me how to find you..."

"Oh my God." Tara stumbled into the kitchen, found a chair and sat. Seeing this strange woman with her bobbed hair and pugnacious nose and bright, wide-set eyes, and seeing only Troy.

"Can I come in?" the woman said.

"Oh Christ please." Tara wiped her eyes. "Look, can I make you coffee? Tea?"

The woman glanced round the vast kitchen, the humming refrigerators and shiny sinks, the wide polished floors, and sat at the kitchen table with her handbag on her lap. "After Daniel was born—Troy, I mean—I got a job at the Cleveland Bomber Plant making B-29 parts for the war. One day they told me that Daniel's Dad was dead. A place called Corregidor."

Again she scanned the kitchen from one end to the other, taking it in. Looked at Tara. "I fell apart, came down with brain fever. They thought I'd die. Three months in a hospital, didn't know where I was. When I woke up Daniel was gone. No one knew how or where...Please," she bit her lip, "please, how is he? When can I see him?"

11

I WANT YOU

"HE CAN'T BE DEAD." Ginnie Barden sat on the front edge of one of Tara's wide white leather living room couches twisting her hands in her lap. She stared at the vast bay of stained glass windows where it was raining outside like the tears down her cheeks. She kept snuffling at a tissue Tara had given her and stuffing it up her sleeve. "They're just saying he *might* be dead."

Tara nodded, wanting to give hope when she had none. "They think he is."

"So now I know he's *there*, I could go over there, try to find him. Maybe he's just in some hospital somewhere, they mixed up his name." Ginnie laughed sharply, burst out crying. "Maybe if I gave them his real name..."

"You can't go over there. It's a war."

Ginnie sat straight. "To hell with their wars. They killed my husband. Now after all these years they've killed my son—"

"You never had...another family?"

"Never ever kissed another man after Cal. You knew him you wouldn'a wanted to either."

Tara felt the air corrode in her lungs. She had to think of something to say. "How did you meet him?"

"One night in a pool hall in Cleveland. He was playing against everyone and beating them. He made over fifty dollars...noticed me watching and came up and said, 'C'mon, let's buy a quart of whiskey and rent a room together...'" She wiped her eyes. "Isn't that funny, when you think back on it? Those days we were much more uptight, as you'd call it now. I'd never even been with a man...I was eighteen...These days you young people jump into bed with everybody..."

She turned from the stained glass skylights back to Tara, her head tilted, her eyes shining. "So what was he like, this Daniel of mine?"

How could Tara explain? This person she'd hated and loved? "When he first came, I didn't like him. He'd escaped from the Boys' Home and he and my brother rode the rails together. They were only twelve."

"Sounds like something he'd do. My husband Cal, I mean."

Tara shivered. This was real bad and she needed a hit. She wanted to scream with sorrow, said, "I'll be back!" She went into her bedroom and shot up; it seemed hours passed; she came back and smiled at Ginnie Barden.

"You doing okay, girl?" Ginnie said.

The onrush of good feelings from the hit was oceanic. Tara suddenly loved this woman, with her squarish shoulders and bobbed, graying hair. Loved her for Troy, for the Troy neither of them had had. *Makes you see clearly sometimes*, she realized, *White Angel*.

"The longer Troy lived with us," Tara said softly, "the more I cared for him. He tried very hard to pay us back for taking him in, did well in school, always ready to do chores and help Ma and Dad." It got easier the more she said; after a while she made coffee and then bourbon on the rocks for her and a bourbon and Coke for Ginnie.

"For twenty-five years I've hoped to find Daniel. And now I find out maybe he's dead." Ginnie was trying not to weep. "And that maybe we'll never know."

I loved him too, Tara said silently. *Your son. I've lost him too. And our child.* How could she tell her that she and Troy had been lovers? Had murdered her grandchild?

Ginnie nodded as if agreeing with something Tara hadn't said, craned her neck to stare up at the broad redwood beams of the towering ceiling, the stained glass skylights with their rainbow of colors down the tall cream-colored walls onto the vast slate floors. "Lovely place you have here, dear. I'm sure you enjoy it." She turned, hands on knees. "I've listened to your music."

Her mind on Troy, Tara came back. "Oh..."

"It's magnificent. Simply magnificent. You make a human heart glad."

Tara burst into tears. "Oh Jesus don't say that."

"On my wages I can't go to the opera, but I listen to it on Cleveland Public Radio. You sound like that wonderful woman, in the opera—"

"Oh stop now—"

"You know the one, the Greek one. You got a voice like her. Maria Callas."

Tara shook her head, faced down with fingers clenched, tears pouring into her lap. *Please God bring him back.*

Ginnie took a deep breath and looked out the broad window at afternoon sun on the wet grass. "So where's your brother now, dear? Would'n he be Daniel's brother too?"

Tara looked up, wiped at her face. "He's gone away. No one knows where."

NORTH OF THE GOLDEN GATE, Highway One became a narrow twisty road around seaside ravines and precipices, often cut to one lane by landslides. It came down to the sea at a narrow town called Stinson Beach, then swung north around Bolinas Lagoon, a sparkling estuary rimmed by steep hills of towering firs and redwoods.

The road was one-lane and dusty; Mick ate dust behind a black '56 Mercury with glass packs, waiting for a chance to pass. But on the short straights the Mercury pulled to the middle and Mick couldn't pass, so he finally rode up on its rear blaring the BMW's horn and giving the guy the finger.

The guy yanked the wheel to the side and stopped. Mick pulled up, knowing he should keep going but too angry. "You asshole!" the guy yelled. Taller than Mick, a military haircut and olive t-shirt.

"Why didn't you let me pass you fuckin jerk?"

The guy kicked at Mick's face but he ducked aside grabbing the guy's cowboy boot and twisted him down falling on top of him and they both started laughing at the idiocy of it. "I don't give a shit," the guy laughed, wiping gravel from his cheek. "Hey, buddy, I'm sorry."

"Me too," Mick laughed. "I'm sorry too."

"How silly to get all pissed off."

"Over nothing."

They sat beside each other sharing a joint in the warm sea breeze in the calls of sea birds and squawk of scrub jays, the lagoon shimmering in morning sun. "I'm a fucking Marine," the guy said. "Taught to fight. Can't learn when to stop."

"You were drunk anyway. Can't fight like that."

The Marine went to the Mercury and came back with a quart of Black Label. "My brother was a Marine," Mick said.

"Holy Shit! Where?"

"He's dead."

"Oh fuck."

"That's why I'm so pissed. So nasty. Sorry I turned on you."

"Hey brother," the Marine put his arm around Mick's shoulders.

"I tried to make him stop. He did a second tour. That's when he died."

"Hey, brother." The Marine shook Mick's shoulder. "Hey brother."

"He wrote me this letter, I got it after he died. Saying how it was all a waste, he shouldn't have gone, how he fell in love with a teacher in Hué ..."

"Fuck Hué, man. What a nightmare."

"He killed her. She was VC." To Mick it seemed the distant hills were dancing. "And then he got shot and disappeared..."

"That's atrocious." They watched the dip of curlews over the cumulus patterns reflected in the water. "All the friends I lost, man," the Marine said. "So many killed by our own planes and artillery. What right do they have to kill us like that?"

"Me and my sister, we couldn't stop him. She loved him too."

"It's all right, brother. It's all right." The Marine said nothing more, then, "No, that's a lie. It's *not* all right, it'll *never* be all right. Not forever."

IT LOOKED SAFE, a narrow road cutting left around the lagoon's north shore, seals sleeping on sandbars in the sun, blue herons and white egrets roosting in the trees. The road passed a few unpainted houses and a white church and graveyard and ended at Bolinas, an unkempt Victorian village between lagoon and sea, with two streets, a post office, hardware store, gas station, a bar named Smiley's, a two-aisle grocery store called Pepper's, and a great crescent beach under Dover-like cliffs.

Above Bolinas town was the Mesa, fields and pastures, dirt roads where children played barefoot, chickens wandered, and dogs slept in the sun, scattered ramshackle houses in groves of coyote brush, pine, eucalyptus and manzanita. Dented cars and pickups with peace signs and anti-war stickers rusted in front of houses where the Stones and Hendrix drifted through open windows. Beyond the Mesa a dirt road wandered past RCA Beach, where a few people lived in driftwood houses; beyond that the rocky fir-clad headlands and stony beaches of the Point Reyes peninsula faded northward into mist.

For three nights he camped in the hills and watched Bolinas by day. It was a laid-back place, mostly long-haired, bearded guys and barefoot, long-haired girls. Never a cop car. Lost at the end of the road, it wasn't part of the world, and no one cared who Mick was or where he came from. *I'm Dennis Kurtz*, he told anyone who asked, but a first name was all that mattered.

On RCA Beach the massive gray waves rolled out of the fog and crashed into surf and hissed up the sand in fast white fingers. Gulls and terns cried darting over the crests; strings of brown pelicans rose and fell between water and sky; the cold wind smelled of kelp, seaweed and wet sand. Twelve driftwood huts stood under the cliff that rose two hundred feet to jagged headlands of tan grass and juniper scrub.

It was a place Troy would have loved but it made no sense to think that. Mick walked the slushy sand, slinging rocks into the surf remembering Troy throwing rocks at barracks windows but there was no sense in thinking that either.

The residents of RCA Beach were young couples or loners who had built their driftwood huts themselves and had a relaxed attitude about household amenities. If they had cars they parked them on the bluff and hiked down a narrow stream canyon to the beach. They fished and hunted for food, drank the water from the stream and washed their dishes and bathed in the sea, used its fast-moving south-ward current for a toilet, grew grass and a few vegetables on the bluffs and paid no attention to the outside world.

It took six days to build his own hut at the south end of the beach. Eight wave-worn wooden pallets with driftwood planks nailed atop them made the floor and a small front deck facing the sea. The walls were thin logs or driftwood four-bys sunk in the sand and sided with overlapping horizontal driftwood planks and translucent mylar to roll up and down for windows. It had log rafters and hand-split redwood shakes, and a chimney that exited one wall via a rusty pipe that had once been a culvert. On the driftwood plank floor lay a small Mexican rug with an orange sun half-risen from azure waves that he had found by the side of the road, a foam mat for his sleeping bag, a small potbelly stove, a table with a bowl of yellow apples and red tomatoes and a jug of Sonoma red.

Twice a week he drove the dirt track back across the Mesa to Bolinas to buy provisions at the two-aisle store. At night he cooked dinner on driftwood fires and lay in his sleeping bag on the sand hearing the hiss and rumble of the surf and clatter of wind-scattered pebbles down the cliff, watching the stars and galaxies and wondering if the FBI could find him.

WHO EVEN *WAS* THE FBI? Could be anybody, you couldn't tell. Was it the chick with the long curly reddish hair and the peace sign on a silver chain between her lovely tits? Or the bearded carpenter who spent a week in town then vanished, but who seemed to have talked to everyone? Could be anybody to nail you, and then you're on a bus to Leavenworth, wrists and ankles chained, ten years waiting.

You tried to not be afraid. To act normal, so people wouldn't sense the fear, but you feared it didn't work. Could never relax for fear of letting go. Like the World War Two slogan, *Loose lips sink ships*: any indiscretion would send you to Leavenworth.

Yet Bolinas felt peaceful; no cops ever invaded this tiny southern outpost of Point Reyes peninsula. So you had to relax, stop showing fear, being uptight. Because that was the thing that would give you away.

And it was easy to slip into the life of Bolinas. Everyone worked as little as they could or not at all. Most were young, a fellowship of everyone against the war. Grass was everywhere and smoked by everyone. It was normal in meeting a stranger that one or both would pull out a joint to be shared. In a new place one could ask anyone, providing they were long-haired and hip, where to find grass. It was the young against the government, against the older people who had made the war, made the country what it was.

But for the risk of the FBI he felt free. He still had nearly forty bucks from Clyde Gottson's ranch. Every morning when he awoke he was free to do what he wanted. He could lie in his sleeping bag drinking coffee, smoking grass and reading, or get up early to enjoy the gorgeous dawn, or wander through a field of horses down to town to sit with friends on the beach smoking grass and enjoying the inward roll of the waves and swooping gulls, or with luck going with a girl into the long grass along the cliffs, the fragrance of her sex and the strident smell of the sea, the crushed wild leaves.

Some days he ran north up the coast in sun and sapphire sea-light through the manzanita and eucalyptus, in the lighthearted pace of everything new all around him, the land untouched by road for seventy miles along the steep-cliffed coast around Drake's Bay down the other side of Tomales Bay to the ranch town of Point Reyes. Or south from Bolinas atop the Coast Range to Mount Tam then down along the wild seaside cliffs to the Golden Gate, miles and miles of freedom. Funny that when you didn't have to be anywhere you had time to see where you were going.

Or he could risk riding the bike over Mount Tam to San Mateo or Mill Valley, sit in a café and read, wander and look in stores, have an ice cream. Or across the big damp bridge into San Francisco's traffic, crowds, cooking smells and filthy sidewalks, wander down to the Haight and see the imitation hippies, or the stoned teenage girls who'd had more sex in a month than most women in years, or the jagged-out pretenders trapped in what they'd sought but never understood.

It was amusing how Bolinas in some senses had reverted to an almost medieval or tribal male hierarchy: how much of a stud you were. How cool. How together. It mattered a lot to be *together* in your head. People whom Bolinas rejected were the squares, the unhip, the straight dope-haters and war-lovers, people crazed by money.

The women's hierarchy had earth-mother overtones. To have a good man, a strong tough man. That was paramount. If you didn't have a man then to be open to life, to men. If you did and had children, to share them with the community, share the chores of mothering. To be into music and gardening and nurturing. And to like fucking. To like fucking a lot and not be shy about it.

HE TRADED WORK on a redwood fence for a Bear 55-pound hunting bow, eight arrows, and a bow quiver. The arrows had both razor heads and blunt points; he wandered the sunny seabreeze hills shooting blunts at tree trunks and dirt outcrops till he could knock the top off a dandelion at thirty yards. The hard pull of the bow felt good, and the unerring sense it gave of trueness was like a drug. When you want to hit something you look at it. Raise the bow, steady the arrow under your chin, but *see* the target. Don't aim the arrow. Don't look down it. Focus completely on the target and when it is time you let go...

And he sensed that by shooting arrows, by seeing the target and letting his body, his subconscious, do the rest, he was learning to be free.

After he built the first fence the neighbor wanted one. He didn't mind the work, it was simple. Every eight feet you dig a two-foot hole with a post-hole digger. You paint the bottom two feet of eight-foot rough-sawn redwood four-by-fours with creosote. You stick them in the holes and in every other hole you pour two bags of concrete and mix it with a garden hose. You check every post with a level to make sure it's vertical and come back the next day after the concrete dries.

You run rough-sawn two-by-fours horizontally between the posts, one six inches off the ground, the other across the top of the post. Then you nail on your vertical redwood laths or one-by-fours or one-by-sixes. If you're using planks, you can cut a pattern in the top, even a half-trapezoid, that will make it look even better. You use only hot-dipped galvanized nails that don't rust or pull out of the wood.

With the money from this fence he bought a Gibson Sunburst acoustic and sat in the sun on the deck of his hut playing for hours, kneading the broken fingers till they worked together again, till the songs inside him were reborn.

One day when he'd just finished playing a long blues progression that had come right out of his soul, he leaned back against the sun-warm rough planks of his hut watching the sea and understood that in this moment all in his life was perfect.

On the Mesa there were parties nearly every night, pools of pure happiness, crazy states of elation, music, fellowship, drunkenness, guitars and lust. Everyone yelling over the music through the marijuana air,

I want you,
I want you
So bad...

143

ALYSSA came out of the grass haze of a bedroom in a red gingham dress through which her body showed. She was tall and slender and had a green Chartreuse bottle in her left hand. She had black hair down her back and a high-boned, longish, almost Semitic face, a nose too big for the beauty of her eyes. She glared at a burly blond guy coming out of the bedroom behind her. He gave her a hostile apologetic glance; she shook her head, pushed through a clump of people and brushed by Mick into the kitchen.

Mick filled his cup from a Gallo Hearty Burgundy jug on the wine-sticky table, singing with the record,

Pretty woman, stop awhile,
Pretty woman talk awhile.

Laughing at the stoned elated glee of it all went through the kitchen out onto the back deck where she stood staring into the night.

"It's too dark." His body tingled like a radio tower. "You can't see anything."

"I don't want to."

"Then why're you looking?"

"I could kill him."

He drained his wine. "He's a jerk."

"Goddamn bastard I loved him."

"You were stupid."

She shook her head, yanked back a strand of hair over her shoulder. "I'm not sleeping with him anymore."

"Sleep with me instead."

She laughed under her breath and made that quick shake of her head again, as if trying to clear it more than denying something. "Fuck all you men."

The stereo was playing *Why don't you come with me little girl, on a magic carpet ride,* and he thought about what it meant. "He keeps coming back," she said.

"Want me to beat him up?"

She snickered. "Peace and love—and where the fuck are we?"

"Move in with me on RCA Beach for a while. That'll chase him off."

Through the darkness he could see the shoulder straps of her dress rising when she shrugged. Electric lust shot up his spine. The Chartreuse bottle tasted of her mouth. He could feel the tendons in her hand. Toward the sea an owl called—*killing in the darkness. Beauty is death.*

She opened a heart locket at her neck and put a tab on his tongue. "It's Owsley." ·

Hand in hand they walked barefoot down the dirt road under the myriad stars, cool grass and cold mud between their toes. The night smelled of manzanita, ocean and sage. From a distant house came *"Cowgirl in the Sand"*,

When so many love you, is it the same?

Sitting on the cliff edge over Agate Beach they drank her Chartreuse and kissed and watched the silvery surf unravel on the sand far below.

He kissed down her belly into her sweet silky cunt. "Twenty years ago," she leaned back sighing, spreading her legs, "if a woman fucked she could get pregnant. Now with the pill we have this marvelous gift of sex—And it's free."

His head on her thigh, infused with her cunt's marvelous fragrance, inhaling it, tasting it, he understood and knew he understood in one magical moment of clarity that a cunt was truly, as he had so often believed, divine. This and nowhere else was the door to heaven, this magical place where life is made.

And that despite all the fussings about God being three folks in one or a dude on a flying horse or whatever, yes there is a God and God is sex. Sex and nothing more. The only God that creates life.

Love, he realized with a laugh, love doesn't create life. Nor does faith. Nor silly things like discipline and honor. Only one thing creates life: fucking. Pure unadulterated fucking sex.

God is sex. Sex is God. *How come it took me this long to figure it out?* He slid her dress higher. "You taste *so* good—"

She tugged it down. "Let's not do it till we're high..."

Her head on his shoulder, her hair tickling his cheek, he watched the darkness between the stars, felt the blood thudding through every cell, every synapse, felt her warm skin and fragrant hair, her gingham dress, her Chartreuse lips, the crushed grass and redolent soil.

Then he could see them both from above lying on the grass, her head on his arm, her hand on his thigh, his hand on her hip under the tucked-up dress. Rising higher he could see the wide silvery fields and manzanita. *Music is your only friend*, the faraway music was singing,

Until the end...

There was a path in these words you could follow. *Was* beauty your only friend, the path inside, deep as you could go? And when the end came, music and love were all you'd had? Or was there something else? Or was there nothing?

Nothin ain't worth nothin but it's free...

He went higher and could see wider below, the shadowy manzanita and scrub oak and darker blotches of pines, the gray roof of the house where Jim Morrison was challenging and beseeching death, the gleaming cliffs of RCA Beach and the white roll of the sea. He rose higher, the Mesa like a map then California with the Modoc reservation in its upper corner, then the earth spun away, the sun too, stars slid away, the Milky Way twirled into a point and vanished; he could go anywhere, there was no time, just being, an endless universe to see and be in.

"Hey," she jostled him. "You high yet?"

1 2

THE TRIBE

LIVING WITH ALYSSA wasn't easy. She took all the space, her rumpled sleeping bag, many shoes, calico dresses and see-through underpants scattered over the tiny floor, her Fender Bassman amp hogging the corner, her guitar in front of his between the drift-wood studs. "I don't stay with any guy very long," she announced. "I like hardball."

He laughed. "What's the connection?"

"A single's one guy, a double two—I've had lots of singles, a couple of doubles, one triple—*that* was fun. But never had a home run."

"We can solve that."

She liked to sing in bars and coffee houses in San Francisco, but it took gas money to get there in her Dodge Power Wagon, a four-wheel-drive monster that looked like a World War Two Soviet Army truck. "Let's take my bike," he offered, but there was no way with her guitar and her huge amp she always dragged to sing-outs.

Sometimes they came home together and other times he ended up in North Beach or Noe Valley or the Fillmore with someone else. "How was it?" he'd say to Alyssa next morning as they drove in her Power Wagon back to Bolinas, and she'd tell him how it felt to ride a strange man, how many times she'd come, was he long and skinny or long and thick. "It's not true," she said, "that all black guys have big dicks."

She was a much better guitarist than he, had a mellow voice that reached down and cauterized the root of your spine. She sang "Suzanne" like Judy Collins but sweeter, with a tremolo like Buffy Sainte-Marie, her voice soft with sorrow,

There are heroes in the seaweed,
There are children in the morning,
They are leaning out for love
And they will lean that way forever...

and it was true, he realized, you could fall in love with beauty and mistake it for a person.

One afternoon she was sitting on the driftwood floor singing and playing guitar so softly he didn't hear till he climbed the stairs,

I have torn everyone
Who reached out for me.

"You're cold!" She put down her guitar to hold his hands.

"Been hunting. Didn't see anything."

She warmed his hands against her belly. "I counted our money."

He took a drink from her wine glass. It had been a jelly jar and had a cartoon of a little man with a red beard, plaid shirt, and six-shooters. "I didn't know it was *ours*."

"We have six dollars and eighty-nine cents," she said, "and your half dollar."

"That's for good luck. I can't spend it."

"Dennis, it costs *two dollars* for gas just to *go* into the city!"

"In your damn truck? So we take my bike."

"Not with the guitar'n stuff."

She began to play again, low and silky,

She just can't be changed
To a life where nothing's gained
And nothing's lost
At such a cost—

He broke a stem of grass from a clump drying on the wall, the resin so strong and sticky he couldn't rub it off his fingers. He rolled the joint and she smoked singing in her soft husky voice, *"Ain't no use in turnin on your light, babe."* He lay beside her drinking her wine and caressing her cunt lazily while she played, *"I'm on the dark side of the road..."*

"I'll get a deer," he said. "And there's plenty of fish. Who needs the city?"

"One of us has to earn *some* money. Or we can't buy anything."

He took a toke, lay back. Reflected sunset on the ceiling planks was beautiful. "I can't imagine wanting to buy anything," he grinned, teasing her.

She leaned over him moving her hair from side to side to tickle his face. "Seriously, let's make some money. I'll waitress, you work construction..."

"You're going back to San Francisco State."

"Not till fall. And only if I want to."

His arm had gone to sleep; he moved it from under her head. "Yesterday in Point Reyes I saw a Bentley. Young guy, hip, open sunroof with the warm breeze coming in. Made me think of Lennon. Of what it's like to have money. So that you never have to do anything you don't want."

"Donna went to the city today and came back with lots of magic mushrooms. They cost twenty-four bucks..." She stretched, arching her back. "So *that's* a reason people need money."

Through the window he watched the sunset darken on the waves. On the beach, people were gathering by the fire. He went with her to the water's edge to piss then they walked hand in hand to the fire with two joints, a half-gallon of wine and two guitars,

To dance across the diamond sky
With one hand waving free,
Silhouetted by the sea—

Donna and Tom were passing the mushrooms around. He chewed down four, ignoring their bitter taste, and put four in his pocket for later, pushed a chunk of rockfish onto a willow skewer and held it to the fire. A girl named Sherrill was laying potatoes on the coals. Some people seemed high already. When the fish cooled he chewed it off the skewer, tough and pungent, charred outside and bloody inside. It tasted wonderful and ran down his chin,

Take me on a trip upon your magic swirlin ship...

Jugs of Gallo Hearty Burgundy stood in a row along the cliff like fat little soldiers. He opened one and drank deeply, took a hit and smiled at his surroundings. How peaceful this little village on the sand, the stilted huts and stone paths, their brave little fire. How alive and bright against the stars, the looming cliffs, the waves. As if humans could live forever.

It would be just like the FBI to find him now.

THE BUCK climbed the ridge through manzanita and jack pines and glanced back. Young, not used to being hunted. With kin nearby, more nervous than afraid.

Mick eased closer, silently on moss, roots and rocks. Raising the bow he drew the arrow till the nock was under his chin, his eyes focused on the buck till all he could see was the soft golden place behind the left shoulder where the heart was. The buck licked his lip, batted an ear at a fly. The bow sprung and the arrow hissed toward the buck and as he was turning away it plunged deep into his chest, and he stumbled and trotted off through the manzanita.

Mick waited five minutes then climbed the ridge. The buck lay in sea daisies and columbine. His eye did not blink when Mick touched it. The arrow had gone through him halfway out his ribs and the tip had broken off when he fell. Mick dragged the buck's head downhill, cut his throat and sat watching the blood drain over the pebbles.

Beyond the world's edge the sun had set and the distant orange clouds were paling. *Don't feel bad*, he told himself, told the buck he was sorry, thanked him but couldn't think of anything to give him in return. *Because of you we'll live better* he told the buck, but the buck didn't care if humans lived. Preferred they didn't.

Dusk brought a cool wind down the ridge toward the sea. *I will become your flesh*, Mick told the buck, *your spirit*. A golden stairway where each step is greater awareness, a brighter love of life. But the buck didn't care. He'd wanted to live.

When the blood stopped Mick gutted him, saved the heart and liver and left the head and guts in the scrub. He tugged the body over his shoulders, forelegs down one side of his chest and rear legs down the other, picked up his bow and his backpack with the heart and liver and descended the darkening ridge toward RCA Beach.

Seeing candles in the windows and the fire smoke twisting away in the wind made him think of the thousands of years of hunters coming home to a fire, to other humans and safety, and he felt a moment of peace and contentment.

He skinned the buck by the fire, cut apart the quarters and hung them under his hut. Sherrill came over. "You got one!"

"On the ridge behind Lava Lake. A young one, he'll taste great."

"You're all covered in blood." Her eyes sparkled. "We'll have meat for days."

Donna's dog Clover came sniffing at the skin, waited till Mick's back was turned and rolled on it. "Stupid girl," he yelled. Wagging her tail she rubbed against his thigh, looked up at him appreciatively as if to say *I smell so good like this*.

He ducked in the frigid surf to wash off the buck's blood and dried by the fire. A woman named Kate brought a salad of miner's lettuce from the stream and radishes and little onions from her winter garden. Mick thin-sliced the buck's heart and liver and fried them in an iron pan with butter, garlic and onions while a girl named Audrey opened three jugs of Sonoma red. "It's truly blessed," someone said. "This life we lead."

"We thank this deer," Mick said self-consciously. "For giving his life so we may live." It sounded hollow, and he resolved never to kill for other people again.

WHEN ALYSSA WENT BACK to San Francisco State and a storm wrecked his hut he rented a small barn behind a house on the Mesa for twenty dollars a month from a girl named Teresa. It had no running water so he fixed a hose from the house, found an old iron stove for five dollars in Olema, built a bed of two-by-fours and plywood, set a door on two-by-fours for a desk, and bought a six-foot-long two-handled logging saw to cut firewood in the hills.

Teresa was blonde with a cheery laugh, uneven front teeth and a wanton grin as if you and she shared a lustful secret, a fire you could feed any time you chose. As if everything reduced to sex.

She also had a blond five-year-old named Cody and a white kitten named Tom. Cody adopted Mick as an ally against his mother's strictures, for he hated school as much as Mick had, and soon after Teresa left for work in the morning he'd show up barefoot and grinning at Mick's door and say school had been canceled. "Cool," Mick would say. "We'll hike up into the forest and I'll show you how to live off the land."

The twenty dollars he paid Teresa for the first month's rent killed his savings; he needed a job. But for that he needed a Social Security card with Dennis Kurtz's number, and for that he'd first need a new driver's license with his own photo on it. But the cops and FBI inspected new driver's license photos all the time.

He'd put it off as long as he could.

"THE WORLD'S UGLIEST DOG," Brian Newman said as they sat smoking weed and drinking beer on the front steps of Smiley's

Saloon. He nodded across the street at a speckled splay-legged hound with basset ears and kinky fur.

The dog had his nose buried in a female's rear. "But he gets laid more than any other dog in town," Mick noted.

Brian cackled, downed his beer. "Has to be a lesson there."

Dogs wandered everywhere like people, in and out of Smiley's and Pepper's, sitting on the sunny wharf watching the lagoon empty into the sea, going about their business in packs or alone, scratching fleas in the middle of the street, trotting purposefully toward the beach perhaps to look for friends or chase halfheartedly at terns and gulls. Most came up to people good-naturedly, wagging tails, friendly recognition in their eyes, and after a quick pat and lick on the hand loped off to their friends playing in the surf.

"Ugly as I am," Brian said, "You'd think I get laid all the time."

Before coming to Bolinas he'd been a social worker in the slums of Los Angeles, till he realized he'd been "part of the problem, not the solution...The people we were handing this pittance to, they're never going to grow out of it, not when that money keeps coming in."

He shook his head at the memory of it. "One day this eighteen-year-old girl asks me how she can find a job. After I leave the apartment I'm standing on the landing checking who I had to see next and through the door I hear her mother yell at her, 'Don't you dare talk that job talk, girl. You make a baby and get your lazy black ass down to the welfare office'n sign up. That's the only kind of job you need.' I had to quit, man. I had to quit."

THINK OF BOLINAS AS A TRIBE," Head said, wiggling toes in the sand as they sat waiting for the surf to rise. "A tribe of maybe two hundred families? Everybody knows everybody, right? Not interfering with each other, but when something attacks us from outside we come together."

"The Neolithic village," Mick said.

"What we fight for," Brian exhaled, "is to be left alone...As long as nothing attacks us, we're free..."

"Bolinas is a mirror where you can see yourself change." Head tugged his long blond hair back from his face and took a hit. "Once you change, you can step through it...And see the world without your reflection in it." Squat and muscular with hair to his shoulders, he was a former Notre Dame linebacker who'd lost a foot from stepping into a punji trap in Vietnam. Now he surfed with his peg leg stuck in a hole in his board.

"We have morals," Brian took the joint. "We have ethics."

"We live by our own rules, not interfering with how others live. That's the basic law: everyone lives how they want. But there's a community ethic about what's moral and what's not, right? Like it's immoral to steal or damage people's stuff, to screw up the environment, to hurt a woman or child or old person, that kind of stuff."

"And contrary to our government," Brian said, "in Bolinas to kill people is considered immoral but to bang somebody's woman is cool."

"That's because nobody's somebody's woman," Head said. "They're all free."

"Yeah," Brian mused. "Thank God for that."

13

HELL'S ANGELS

THE CALIFORNIA DEPARTMENT of Motor Vehicles filled a low concrete building in San Rafael. A cop stood at the door lazily thumping his nightstick into his palm. The lines were crowded; Mick tried to fit in, feeling an outsider, glancing occasionally toward the cop who seemed not to notice him.

"I need a California license," he told the woman at the counter, showing her Dennis Kurtz's Nevada one.

"Four dollars. Go over there." She pointed him to a camera where a bored man was taking photos. "Where you want I send your new license?"

He put four dollars on the counter. "I'm moving—"

"You got to give an address."

"Can I pick it up?"

"Try two weeks, maybe it'll be here."

WITH HIS NEW LICENSE he got a new Social Security card and answered an ad for a jackhammer operator in Tiburon. The contractor, a freckled sandy-haired man about forty named Vern Jacobs, was building a house on a hill overlooking San Francisco Bay. A five-hundred-foot driveway had to be cut out of the rock to get there.

Vern had a compressor hitched to the back of his pickup. "It's an eighty-pound hammer so be careful. Just follow the stakes and cut down eight feet in the middle section and taper to grade at both ends. Let me know you need something."

Mick lugged the huge jackhammer and coils of red hose from the back of Vern's truck. "I haven't done this in a while. Why don't you remind me what goes where."

Vern hitched the hose to the compressor and the hammer, fired up the compressor, squeezed the handle of the hammer and it spat and jumped like a demented dragon. Nonchalantly Mick took over, stood it on the rock ledge beside a stake, gripped it carefully and slowly squeezed the handles. Off it went like a bronco with a burr in its saddle, roaring and clattering against the rock. He managed to keep it vertical and in no time it was eating into the rock like ice cream, knocking out huge chunks that he kicked aside as he worked, the hardened steel point smashing banging and bouncing and jamming his shoulders, the compressor snarling, the hose writhing and hissing like a sea snake.

In an hour he'd learned how to lean into it, let the jackhammer do the work so it didn't jar his body to jello, how to keep his feet clear so they weren't smashed. It was fun, this war against solid bedrock. On breaks he shut off the compressor and staggered around numb and deafened while Vern pushed the rubble aside with his Cat.

Each day he cut more driveway down through hard green stone. The work was fun and tough, making the sweat pour off his tanned torso in the hot Marin sun. The strength it took to hold that jumping vibrating eighty-pound hammer sideways against the stony hill was enormous, but his muscles kept getting leaner and stronger, and when he put away the hammer at five o'clock and stood looking over the Tiburon hills to the Bay and gleaming San Francisco, sweat drying on him in the cooling breeze, he felt full and complete and happy with himself. *Il faut imaginer*, he smiled, *Sisyphe heureux*.

You have to imagine Sisyphus happy. Because he was.

· · ·

EVEN BETTER were the mornings with rain pattering on his barn roof and pinging into the buckets. Naked under a poncho he barefooted across the muddy yard to Teresa's house and called Vern.

"How bad is it there?" he'd ask nonchalantly.

"Sorry, Dennis, we can't work. Too damn wet."

"It'll clear up by tomorrow, Vern. See you then."

Back to bed, rubbing mud from between his toes, the girl drowsy and pleased he was back. Later there were rain drips hissing on the stove, the warm room tinged with oak smoke and the smell of new cornbread, cups of strong black coffee in which the rafters reflected like doors into a secret room. The elation of a day all his own, to do what and when he wanted, the miraculous joy of life.

And the wonder of the nights, elation tingling up his back as astride a creaky wooden stool he slid the black Mustang he'd bought with his first pay from Vern out of its pink velvet case, uncoiled the jack and plugged it into a big black Marshall amp. The warm snap of the Marshall's tubes firing up, the rhapsody of fingers over the strings —sure, the left hand was still slow, he'd never be a guitar god, but the broken fingers had learned a new language, a more difficult one, and the song they made was different.

Easy to get into, one-on-one with the music, sharing songs against the night,

Lacy lilting lady
Losing love lamenting

They went on forever, these nights, till he was hoarse with singing, laughing, cheap whiskey and wine and lovely grass, the laugh and tear lines down the corners of his cheeks, and sometimes the girl he'd been playing to all night would take his right hand, the Mustang in its pink-velvet case in his left, and he'd follow her home to the Sausalito Hills or Muir Beach or North Beach or wherever she lived, and wake up the next morning in a sparkling epiphany of sunlight, drained and at

157

peace, with fresh-ground coffee and fresh oranges in bed, the peels between their thighs, or to jump on the BMW for the Café Trieste's hot sweet cappuccino and Italian pastries, their flaky thick sugar molten in their mouths, and Saturday mornings the café's owners Gianfranco and his father sang arias while the Gaggia espresso machine hissed and traffic rumbled by on Grant and Columbus, distant as the moon.

Working for Vern he needed a truck, so for a hundred seventy bucks at the Point Reyes Garage he bought a '49 Chevy with three on the floor and a top speed near fifty. It was so beautiful it stunned him: the three back windows, the perfect angled headlights on the sweeping fenders, its lovely lines from the side. "A work of art," he told Brian.

"Like poetry," Brian said. "It's when you're old that people see how good you are."

"EIGHTY THOUSAND of us marching," Lefty said. "Just for People's Park. Just for a bit of green grass and to rid Berkeley of teargas, guns and official murders. We jammed the streets for two miles, people waving from windows, little old ladies running out with flowers, not a hostile face in miles, just smiling people, old and young..." He shook his head at the wonder of it, passed the jug.

"Can you imagine," he added, "walking arm in arm past rolls of barbed wire across streets backed up by soldiers holding M1 rifles on you? In America?" He reached for the jug. "Like it was in fascist Spain or something. Communist fucking Russia..."

"Lucky they didn't shoot your ass off," Head commented.

"And all the time there's cops in blue jump suits on the roofs with high-powered rifles and shotguns, helicopters circling like vultures over the trees." Lefty raised the bottle in a mock-toast, "A police state in the offing. They have so much desire to kill. Cataclysm coming. See it *first* in California."

"Nah," said Mick, thinking of Paris a year ago. "Won't happen."

Lefty rarely came to Bolinas; his turf was Richmond, where he had joined the Black Panthers after his brother had been shot in Oakland. "What's different about the Panthers," he said, "is we scare the police. We are armed, well-trained, and dangerous. You fuck with us we fuck real bad with you."

"I'd avoid that," Mick said. "Just on principal."

"It's not like the old days, brother, when every black man's scared of the police, cause they beat you and jail you and sometimes shoot you whether you criminal or not."

Mick took his arm. "Remember, brother, nothing's worth spending your life in jail for. Nothing's worth getting killed."

"Oh yeah? Well you just ain't a black man, Brother."

That was of course true, Mick realized. But he'd run out of empathy. Empathy for the whole fucking situation. The whole universe.

And what he cared most about the Berkeley People's Park thing was that Tara wasn't there, was doing a concert in Austria, then someplace else—Madrid, maybe?—and safe from all this.

You never knew where she was now. Concerts pulling in a hundred thousand people, hours of this raging magical blues and soul that simply tore down your eardrums then the rest of you. He had to admit he'd been wrong: Tara was becoming a stunning success. And the band too. But her voice was the driver, her voice gave it soul, passion. This was someone who'd gone down past the gates of hell and come back up to make a better world.

Holy shit.

As for People's Park, Mick realized, that having grown up in forest and farm country, he had scant interest in efforts trying to save little false green patches in big filthy cities. *Don't live in a city* seemed obvious, *if you want to see green...*

AT A HELL'S ANGELS party he sold the BMW bike for five hundred twenty to Claire, the girlfriend of a Hell's Angel named Scotty. The party was in the Mill Valley hills in a rented ranch-style house at the end of a dirt drive under tall eucalyptus, at least fifty bikes on the ragged lawn, most of the Angels drunk and high on speed, some shooting up, a few black-jacketed girls looking bored and stoned. Some of the Angels had knocked out the living room picture window so they could throw out chairs and sit in the sun.

Claire was slim and muscular, with a crew cut. They shared a joint and a bottle of Jack, sitting with their backs against the living room wall listening to the Beatles and watching Scotty and four others smash the picture window frame from the wall and kick out the sheetrock, insulation and siding. "Scotty's such an asshole," she said. "Thinks this makes him look brave."

"So why you with him?"

"I like girls not guys, and Scotty doesn't try to fuck me. I'm queen of the pack, all the drugs and girls I want..."

"Front door," Scotty panted. "Now we got us a real front door."

A tall black-bearded Angel slapped away a stud hanging to the left of where the window had been. "Motherfucker's still too small." He beat the wall with his fists till it gave way; splinters and sheetrock clattered into the yard, flecks of fiberglass floating like pollen in the sun.

Scotty ran at the stud to the right of the hole and smashed through it almost falling into the yard. He rubbed his shoulder and kicked at the bent-out wall. "This house needs repair," someone guffawed. "That wall shouldn't even *be* there. Should be a patio, something. Fuck, shoot the architect."

They smashed away the wall with bare hands and broken studs and as they got to the corner the ceiling creaked down. "Termites!" someone yelled. "Place got termites!"

He and Claire moved to the shade of the garage sharing another joint and a bottle of red. He felt very mellow from the grass and Jack Daniels, liking her upturned sunburned nose, thin eyebrows and tall smooth brow, her tough assertive chin, thin lips in a wide mouth. "I can eat pussy," he said, "better than any dyke on this planet."

"Yeah, right," she snickered.

"Let's go down in the bushes. I'll show you."

"They're poison ivy."

Behind them a house wall crashed down, glass tinkling. "They're going to ruin the whole fucking place," she laughed drawing on a cigarette and shaking her head as she tamped ashes on the grass. "Last week we rode up the coast, stopped in some bar, Fort Bragg I think, ten of these guys and me. They're all drunk and pissed off cause it's raining. This logger comes in takes a stool and Scotty's giving him shit, you know, about the place and the shithole rain, and the guys are talking shit to the gal behind the bar."

"Scotty should've known better—"

"So the logger leaves. The guys are laughing about what a jerk when he comes back yanking on this monster fucking chainsaw and the goddamn noise is deafanin and he's swinging this chainsaw at the guys—Christ it *had* to be *five* feet long—herding them into the bathroom then cuttin down the door and the guys all squirming out the window. Some a them've got pretty big bellies..." She laughed. "What a *hoot.*"

The magical mystery tour, the Beatles were singing, *is dying to take you away.* The song vanished in a great scream of wood and metal as another wall came down. "Most of them can't even get it up," she said. "That's why they try so hard. They're actually fearful little boys. Why they always ride together."

"Where will these guys stand, if there's a revolution?"

"They'll hide in the bushes and come out afterwards to beat people up."

"Pan Am's taking reservations for the first passenger flight to the moon. Maybe we should send them there."

"Yeah, maybe."

"So why are you here?"

She looked at him curiously. "Life just unfolds. I go where it sends me."

Riding on the back of the bike as she took him home to Bolinas he wondered was it true that life just unfolds, you can't ever get what you want? Or do you get what you need, in the Stones' ironic phrase: whatever destiny or God has cooked up for you is what you need.

She downshifted expertly for a steep section of the narrow twisting coast highway, skirting an empty place where half the pavement had dropped off the cliff. *Just a flick of her wrist and we'd be down there.* She accelerated; leaning forward he slid his hand up her lovely tits under her leather jacket and she laughed and let go the throttle to slap him.

The sun was setting over the ocean with an explosion of fire and light, the horizon so wide he could see the upcurve of the round earth in its center.

How horrible to lose this lovely life. Ever.

14

MAYBE TONIGHT

THE MOON silvered the lissome hills and sparkled on the quiet sea. The sky was clear, immaculate. Like Diana the huntress, Mick thought, the moon was beautiful, cold and inviolable. He shivered in the July night and stepped back into the crowded noisy living room.

The moon's image filled the TV screen, tufted mountains and ringed craters and a gently curving gray horizon. Dispassionate disembodied voices issued commands and reports.

It was what Jack Kennedy had promised and now it was happening but JFK wasn't here. Bobby wasn't here. All that was gone.

"If it succeeds," Lawrence Ferlinghetti said, "it will be a considerable achievement for an animal that five thousand years ago was living in caves."

"That was the Italians," Mick said. "The Irish were already living in wood houses back then."

"Of course," Ferlinghetti's eyes twinkled. "And writing poetry too."

The moon's gray granular curve filled the screen. "Lunatic," Mick said.

"Crazed by the moon? Maybe we all are." Ferlinghetti had an impressive stature and kindly watchful face. "It's two-sided, this landing, isn't it? Makes us reevaluate human genius, *what we can be*...But it's rape, somehow, too, isn't it?"

"What do you suppose we'll do if we can't get off the earth?"

"You're not imagining we'd learn to live together?"

"If we began to explore the universe could that unite us? End war?"

Ferlinghetti chuckled, held his glass up to the light. "This wine's dreadful. Can't believe I paid four dollars a bottle for it." He took the bottle to the kitchen and came back with three bottles of Barolo.

"That's beautiful stuff," Mick said, "you should save it for yourselves."

Ferlinghetti pulled out the first cork. "No matter how hard they try, Californians can't make wine that tastes Italian."

"Or French."

"You know, Kubrick's right. Clarke, those guys."

"That we'll be traveling beyond the solar system by 2001?"

"But not if we keep spending all our money on war."

"No nation that fights frequent wars will long survive."

"Sun Tzu?"

"The same." Mick scanned the room, a mix of Bolinas longhairs, carpenters and shipbuilders and famous poets and beautiful women. Minor poets of all sorts strutted, pecked, drank wine and chatted venomously. Richard Brautigan leaned against a redwood-paneled wall; it had a lovely chair rail, Mick noticed, half way up. Brautigan twirled a moustache and winked; Mick gave him the finger. Brautigan made a *Who, me?* gesture, arms wide.

"So how come," Mick said, "with all this magnificent pussy here you're not getting any?"

Brautigan rubbed his belly. "I get all I can stand."

"That's my point."

"This acid," Brautigan grinned. "You had some?"

"Yeah, about twenty minutes ago. Hasn't hit."

"The blessed Owsley was here, doled it out. Mag-*fucking*-nificent!"

"Yes, God bless him. He does the Dead's sound systems—did you know that?"

"Thought he was a chemist." Brautigan burped. "I'm high but clean, you know? Can see forever."

"It's Clear Light, this acid." *The thousand-yard stare*, Mick thought. *I love you Troy.*

Brautigan snorted a laugh. "God I love it here."

"Ferlinghetti's house?"

"Shit no. I love it *here*. On earth. This life."

"I love it too, man. I love it too."

"Creeley's here." Brautigan drained his glass. "Poor fucker."

Mick laughed. "Would you stop it!"

"That woman. They drive each other nuts."

"Like Pogo: *Cherchez la femme?* Too easy, man."

"No I don't mean that. Nobody's more ready to acquiesce in the superiority of women than I." He raised his glass. "To womanhood, well may it please us."

Mick leaned against the wall wondering if Brautigan was a good poet. He was ragged as hell but sometimes came across with a hit. A feeling you couldn't deny. And he could drink most folks under the table. But how silly most of these apprentice poets with their little feuds and jealousies, their terrible verse, in most cases lacking the insight and beauty of good poetry, their incredibly fucked up lives, and their astonishing supposition that their ineffective, usually self-published "works" added any value to the world.

Just as modern art had been a response to photography, when it became too hard to draw reality like the camera did, had modern "classical" music with its atonal cacophonies resulted from the intrusion of fabulous rock music suddenly on radio and phonograph? Was poetry similarly a victim, of the cinema perhaps, which places you *in* your feelings? Or was writing a real poem, with rhymes and all that other tough stuff, just too much work?

He drank a lot more wine. The acid began to hit, insidious. Lovely. *Jesus I could live like this forever.* Every woman in the room made his prick hard. Every whiff of wine and weed and sagey Mesa mist made his heart soar. *I could live like this forever.*

Angelica Bailey leaned against the far wall in a low-cut blouse open-latticed down to her lacy short skirt, her husband the locally famous poet slouching haughtily beside her. Mick wondered did he even *know* how many guys in this room she'd banged while he was away somewhere doing readings?

He caught her eye from across the room, mouthed silently, *Want to fuck?*

She raised her eyebrows, smiled and nodded toward the back door, raised five fingers.

After two minutes he stepped onto the back deck. Three people were arguing about how long it would take to walk to the moon. The screen door clacked. Angelica's arm brushed his. "We have to be quick."

They went out into the grass. "How different," she said, "the world suddenly is."

"In some ways I'm sad. And in some ways almost proud to be human."

"Not easy, these days."

He could see her dusky nipples through the latticed blouse. "Adventuring together into the universe while we kill a thousand people a day?"

"Adventurers are always killers." She raised the short lacy dress above her hips, pushing her cunt against him. "You should know that."

"Amazing to look up there and think other humans are walking there."

"I worry about those guys, can they get back..." She tucked aside the crotch of her underpants. "Yes, *yes*. Come inside me like this. Standing here. Oh God *yes*."

She went back to the house first. When he came in the television was saying, "Tranquility Base here. The Eagle has landed."

The gray grainy surface of the moon was like a bulldozed dump. After a while blocky white feet descended a white ladder and plumped down on crusty soil. "One small step for a man," a scratchy long-distance voice intoned, "one giant leap for mankind."

"Such bullshit," Brautigan cackled. "Some PR hack..."

But wasn't it here that human paths diverged? One path hewed to the earth, honored the moon as a goddess, and eventually went extinct. The other, the clan of this man crunching the moon's crust and broadcasting across two hundred forty thousand miles, was the future human who would travel to far galaxies and create new worlds to take up arms in our relentless war between bright life and endless universal night.

He headed back to Ferlinghetti's kitchen for another glass of red.

"MICK! IS THAT *YOU?*"

He spun round spilling his wine, the woman's voice behind him so lovely, achingly familiar. "Mick!" she cried, "it *is* you!"

He reached for her. "Don't say my name!" Held her close, breathless, stunned, inhaling her, feeling her body against him like a man who reaches shore after swimming for days at sea.

"Why?" she laughed, hugging and kissing him. "And what's with the blond hair? Are you some secret agent? Mick O'Brien, Agent 008, *We Only Live Twice?*"

"Daisy, stop!" He touched her lips. "*Shush.* Oh God how lovely to see you." He pulled her closer. "I thought we were extinct, you and me." He didn't want to kiss her, for that meant taking his eyes off her, kissed her as if the world had ended and begun anew. "Daisy all these years I've missed you—"

"Then why didn't you *write*, silly?" She wiped away tears. "I wrote *you!*"

"I *did* write you dammit. You never wrote back."

"Mick, I did! Every day!"

"Stop saying my name!" He led her through the crowded chattering people past Angelica watching curiously, Creedence Clearwater singing,

Some folks are born, made to wave the flag
Ooo, they're red, white and blue
And when the band plays Hail to the Chief
Ooo, they point the cannon at you, Lord.

They passed the glaring TV of the affronted moon, down slippery back steps into the field where moonlight glistened on the dew. "Magnificent desolation," an astronaut's voice was saying.

"Daisy, I'm not me."

She looked at him grinning, not understanding. "What *are* you then?"

"The FBI's hunting me because I helped start the Resistance."

"I know you did. I saw you on TV."

"Why didn't you find me?"

"I assumed you were...with someone..."

"Now they say I've crossed state borders to start a riot, other stuff. All lies. But if they find me I do ten years."

"Oh my God!" She stumbled against him, straightened. "Oh my God."

"Everybody knows me here as Dennis Kurtz."

She near-laughed. "Oh Jesus."

"It's awful, Daisy. I'm scared all the time..." He pulled back. "You look so wonderful!"

She reached for him. "I thought I'd never see you. Never again."

"I can't believe it's you!" He kissed her deeply, tasting her lovely lips, forgetting everything else. "I've lived here for months. When'd you—"

"Last month from SF. I've rented a place here, a fishing shack really, to finish my thesis. I used to work nights at City Lights, that's how I know Ferlinghetti. Mick, we were *crazy* not to stay in touch." She kissed him deeper, her body hard against him.

"I missed you so. *I've missed you so!* At first it was just awful, then I got used to it, then I made it go away. Are you with somebody now?"

"No. Are you?"

"Yeah," he nodded, felt her recoil. "With you."

She pulled him tight. "This's our third time. Tappan, then Nyack, now Bolinas."

"When are we going to stop getting torn apart?"

"Maybe tonight?"

The moon rippled in a puddle he stepped across to put her bicycle in the truck. She sat against him on the old leather seat as if they'd simply transferred from Dad's DeSoto to this moment. "I like it," she said. "Your truck."

He kissed her, pulled her close. "I can't wait to make love," she whispered through the kiss. "I want you inside me."

As they drove in the night, fragrant with eucalyptus and sage down through the sleeping town to her shack on the lagoon he told her about Troy. "It's a year now. A year and two months. And seven days."

"I can't think," she said finally. "Can't believe he's dead...Stupid to say that, people always say that...It's just that someone so *alive*. How can they die?"

"A bullet kills them."

"That our government, our nation, *we*, could do this. Kill this magnificent young man...No explanation. Nothing that makes sense."

"He always wanted to be an astronaut. Get us out of this silly backward solar system, he used to say."

"Remember his room, all those planes hanging from the ceiling—"

"Each one painted perfectly. He knew everything about every plane."

"I was in his geometry class sophomore year—"

"His favorite subject. That and physics and astronomy. He loved astronomy...I should've never invited him home, started the whole thing."

"No. He was lucky to meet you."

"He'd be alive today if he hadn't."

"You mustn't think that."

He snickered. "Why? It's true."

She faced him. "All we can do in life is try to help others and take care of ourselves and do as little harm as possible. You didn't kill Troy."

"The US government killed Troy. For no reason I can understand."

"The same US government that just landed on the moon."

SOMETHING LONG missing from her life had just been returned. The world was full again.

What to make of Mick's sudden reappearance? Fate? Pure accident? The mathematics was impossible.

Mick so solid and beautiful, unchanged but different. Just to be next to him made her hot and wet. Couldn't call him Mick, had to remember *Dennis*. Instead of that slender, lean boy so unsure of himself, now he was larger, muscular, aware of the world and himself. With power in his hands, his body, in his soul. Have I changed too?

In all the times she'd heard about him, seen him on TV, his speech at the Pentagon, his articles, she'd never thought she'd be here with him, not ever again.

In her imagination she'd surveyed her shack on the drive home from Ferlinghetti's—she'd made the bed and the table was cleared and no underpants were on the floor or dirty dishes in the sink. Her body vibrated with the truck's errant shudder, its erratic engine and yowling gears. When Mick pulled up in her drive she reached for him and they kissed and kissed, his hand between her widened thighs till finally she gasped *Let's go inside*, the hot ache for him surging inside her.

The tossed pillows, magic bed, every instant felt and loved and they were kids again in the back seat of the DeSoto, his whole body steel-hard, gently breaking her down till all the walls inside her fell and she was free, and they flew away together.

"I'VE NEVER COME SO MUCH." She lay alongside him, sweaty and hot. "This lovely warm feeling pouring through you and you're floating on a river of pure sensation wider and wider till your whole body convulses in the ecstasy of it, the most delicious agony, you want it to never end, just to keep on pouring and soaring through you... fluid and warm and complete and aching and beautiful..."

"The little death."

"It's easy to see that sex is God, because sex creates life. But sex is God also because of the little death, each time we make love we're reborn..."

"When you come you realize how silly and unimportant most other things are."

"...And doing it on acid? Impossible to describe how beautiful, how perfect and lasting, how loving...Anyone who's had this, who's known how deeply we can live, how can they not be a better person the rest of their lives?"

And in the end, the Beatles were singing,

The love you take
Is equal to the love you make.

Hours later he woke from a dream of being in a large place like a supermarket full of people wandering. He met a young man with long dark hair who looked like him. "Why are we here?" he asked him.

"To find out what it is."

"What *what* is?"

"Life."

He woke understanding that this was the task he had been given in life. That in good years and bad, joys and sorrows, his unerring goal would be to understand life, to seek the meaning of this vast mystery encompassing us. To find out what life is and spread the word, like a scout returning to the tribe from distant and dangerous lands.

Through wide-open windows came the rustle of the sea on pilings, the gentle slap of waves on rock, the scents of eucalyptus and wild-flowers, seaweed and salt, the sleepy complaint of gulls and crows.

Daisy lay sleeping beside him as if she'd always been there, her hair splayed across her pillow like Leonard Cohen's *sleepy golden storm*. Her face was perfect, sculpted by a god. Her skin glowed in early light, her breathing like a light breeze in the trees. *Now I know*, he thought, *what it is to love.*

What it is to live.

The last wintry night in Tappan in the DeSoto's frigid back seat, the sorrow of her departure, and the ache of her absence were all tolerable again because she was here. In all those years how strange that nothing had changed. She was the same Daisy he'd fallen in love with in the third grade.

But a woman now, brilliant and determined, lover of many men, hungry for truth. Like he'd said last night, *I'd marry you right now if we could. But it would doom you.*

He didn't want to doom her. He didn't want to do anything that could harm her. She, so long missing, had always been, he understood, most important in his life. As if every act in his life had tended toward this.

All the other women, in this moment he loved them too. *Every love act is unique*, the words came. *You can't compare them.* Each a universe to itself. Each brings the gift of greater knowledge and erotic joy.

And each moment with Daisy reminded him of how fast life was progressing, how little already they had left.

Even if he didn't get arrested.

HER FISHING SHACK was one long room with a kitchen at the front end, a red rug, a couch, armchair, and a pine table and three wicker chairs in the middle and a dresser and a mattress on the floor at the far end. Tacked to the back was a privy that hung out over the lagoon; for water you went up the trail to Smiley's bar and filled a bucket and brought it back to heat on the propane stove. The front windows opened out onto a deck that looked over the sea swirling in and out of the lagoon and beyond its silver expanse to the eastern hills of oak scrub, eucalyptus, and pine and the luxurious greenness of Kent Island. The tall redwood and fir slopes of the Coast Range rose behind them.

Red Guatemalan blankets hung across the burnished redwood walls; a black potbelly stove squatted in a corner. The worn fir floor gleamed in the sun and felt warm against his soles. There was a constant roar and lash of the sea, the scratching of manzanita twigs on glass, the cries of gulls and terns, the rattle of the stovepipe and wind whistling over the shingles.

Every night two raccoons clambered in through a window to sleep on each side of her head and nipped him if he moved too close. "That's Curly," she said, "and that's Kate."

"They look the same."

"Kate's a girl, silly. Curly's a boy."

They were almost human with their long fingers, warm inquiring eyes, their love of play and affection. To lie in the candlelight rubbing a raccoon's belly while it grinned and sighed with pleasure brought back the night of hunting coons with Clem and Carl so long ago. How could anyone want to kill these sly, smart, loving creatures?

What was wrong with humans?

HER PHD IN NEUROLOGY was nearly done and she had retreated to Bolinas to finish her thesis. "I'm broke and it's cheap to live here. I've got all my clinical data and case histories, so now it's six months of writing them up, doing the synthesis and deciding what it all means."

"Me too, I'm trying to decide what it all means."

"Stop being philosophical. I'm trying to understand something."

"What's that?"

"The clinical result of administering mind-altering chemicals to patients suffering from certain mental illnesses like alcoholism."

"Like your father?"

"*His* father was a drinker too, knocked *him* around a lot. It's almost genetic, this kind of behavioral tragedy, how it repeats down the generations. We need to find better ways to treat it."

"Acid brings you face to face with things. Maybe why it cures alcoholism. But the government says it's dangerous, can kill people—"

"I've studied one thousand two hundred and fifty-seven research papers on LSD and nearly fifty thousand individual case studies of people using it, and I found *not one death*! And almost *no* long-term negative reactions!"

"I've never met a person who's had a bad trip. But the media says it happens all the time."

"LSD has a higher cure rate for alcoholism than Alcoholics Anonymous. Hundreds of FDA-approved studies for the National Institute of Mental Health found it's beneficial for autism, alcoholism, sexual problems, compulsive disorders, fear of death in cancer patients, so many other research findings."

He nuzzled her. "I've got some sexual problems I wanted to talk about."

She pushed him away. "We've all spent years studying this, and now it's a federal offense to possess it! Due to the fussing and moaning by these right-wingers and ministers and other fruitcakes!"

"It's how they win elections. By making people fearful."

"It was the CIA. *They* developed it."

"That's what Leary said, that time I met him at Millbrook."

"You met him? Some of my professors and other researchers blame him for killing LSD."

"By pushing so hard? He and Alpert should've won the Nobel Prize."

"Not just *them*. So many fine researchers have been working on it. All their time and work's down the drain now. I did three years of analysis and it's all useless."

"Mushrooms, LSD and peyote take down the walls separating us from the world, and we see how beautiful and intricate and essential life is, how valuable every moment is. They make us happier. So of course the government is against them."

"Leary's just a focal point for hate and outrage. The government dredging up these silly marijuana charges..."

"Daisy I don't give a damn. Let's make love."

"...usually from very structured male-dominated or authority-figure homes. That's the link between conservatism and religion—the father figure, the need for security, for answers...Thus they fear anything that might give people new ways of seeing things. They don't understand *they're* the cause of the very problems they rant against."

"And you? Aren't you still trying to cure your father?"

She nodded. "The father inside me maybe."

He slid off her underpants. "Acid's dangerous."

"Used wisely it's therapeutic."

"What I mean is it's dangerous to the status quo, to the powers that run this country, this world, who try to force us all to do their bidding. Bellicose patriotism, religion and money—acid frees you from all three."

"Maybe that's what they fear. That we'll all get free."

"You and me, honey, we're already free..."

But he couldn't imagine this coincidence of finding her again. No, it wasn't coincidence, was it? That if it hadn't been for the FBI hunting him in New York he would have stayed with his moving business in his nice apartment with all the exciting things there, wouldn't have driven the motorcycle across the country, ended up in Montana, chased from there, wandering till finally finding Bolinas, where by an equally inexplicable twist of fate so had Daisy, so that he and she were again reunited, as they had been at Nyack High so long ago, while they had hungered for each other all this time...Was there some divine hand that had brought them back together? No way coincidence could explain it.

And strange too that they'd both worked with Al Lowenstein, she in Mississippi in '64, he in New York anti-war groups from '66 to '68 —yet she and he had never made the connection. Nor the time they'd both worked for Bobby. Like many other things we can now connect, he thought.

Al was running for Congress now, Daisy'd said, from Long Island. It looked like he had a good chance. It bothered Mick that he hadn't been able to contact Al since he'd gone underground, that he couldn't go back and work for him.

"Al wants to get into Congress," she'd added, "because of the Bobby thing."

"What Bobby thing?"

"Al says that ballistic and forensic evidence shows that Sirhan Sirhan alone didn't shoot Bobby, that they totally invalidate the official accounts. And he wants Los Angeles and federal authorities to reopen the investigation into the assassination. He thinks if he gets into Congress, he can force them to."

Mick remembered the tall blond man he'd seen who'd helped direct the massacres in Indonesia. Who'd been thirty feet from Bobby at the Ambassador Hotel when he was shot.

"This is dangerous," Mick said. "They'll shoot Al too."

"He knows that. It won't stop him."

15

KEY TO YOUR HEART

TARA HATED CHOPPERS even more than doing concerts, and the band wasn't even getting paid for this one. "I'm driving," she told Blade.

"You won't get within *miles*," an organizer named Gabriel said. "The roads are clogged shut since three days ago. Nobody had any idea how big this would *be*..." He had long curly hair knotted in a ponytail with a blue kerchief. "*Every*body's choppered in, Melanie and Joan, Gracie and her guys, David, Stephen and Graham—they're doing a set with Neil did you know?—and Creedence, even Jimi and he *hates* flying..."

And now the rain. Slanting sheets of silver rain. A half million kids getting drenched, getting high, getting laid. *O brave new world.*

She took the window by the chopper door. The seat belt crossed your shoulders pinning you in, like they knew you were going to crash. The door shut and you were sealed inside a time capsule, a crypt. The engines screamed, the tail lifted tipping them forward, the ground accelerated past as the copter lurched up into the slanting rain.

Getting dark, the roads below jammed with parked cars, vans, and school buses, thousands and thousands of them spilling out into ditches and fields like the detritus of a vast battle. Trails of headlights going back for miles...How many cars were there, anyway, in the world?

An anthill of endless people in glistening slickers and plastic sheets, bonfires, flitting, flashlights, more and more and more people, *Give me your huddled masses.* The crowd went on and on and did not end. "Jesus," Sybil yelled. "How many are there?"

"Six hundred thousand," the pilot yelled back. "What the cops say. So maybe a million."

"One out of every two hundred people in America," Gabriel said. "Right here in Woodstock."

"This, children," Blade intoned, "the biggest mother concert we *ever* gonna do."

"Arlo Guthrie says the New York Thruway's closed," the pilot said.

"He's so fuckin stone all the time," Luis laughed, "how he know?"

"Cops turned away another half million, radio said."

Fifty feet above the immense speaker towers the pilot circled the stage where tiny figures strutted. "Who's that?" she called.

"Country Joe," he called back. *"And it's one, two, three,"* he sang off-key, *"what are we fighting for?"*

"Don't ask me, I don't give a damn," Tara sang back.

"Next stop is Vietnam," Blade sang, and they all came in together.

Come on generals, let's move fast
Your big chance is here at last,
Gotta go out and get those reds—
The only good commie is one that's dead.

the song that most honestly summed the insanity of the war,

Come on mothers throughout the land,
Pack your boys off to Vietnam...
Be the first one on your block
To have your boy come home in a box

"If people," Sybil said, "would only listen."

"Latest poll," the pilot called back, "seventy percent of Americans have an IQ of ten. They agree with Nixon on Vietnam..." He swung the chopper down in a wide flare spraying clouds of rain.

"You been there?" Blade called.

"Marines. Two tours. Medevac. Lost every good friend I had." Rain slid in sheets down the windows. "Last night Joan Baez was speaking of David Harris—"

"Her husband—"

"He just got ten years in Federal Prison for draft refusal. What every man should be doing." He shoved the door open and handed her a huge joint. "Fine Burmese, courtesy of Mile High Airways." He kissed her forehead. "Rock 'em tonight, darlin."

She kissed him hard. "Where you going to be later?"

He smiled through his handlebar mustache. "Flying around."

Yanking on her scarlet raincoat she splashed after Blade and Sybil across the field up a long ramp, rain hammering the boards, up slippery steps onto backstage. The crowd before her spread beyond the horizon, more than half a million people dancing and clapping in the pelting rain to the orgiastic thunder of the speakers.

Too many people. She shouldn't have come. *Damn Blade.*

"Listen, people!" Country Joe yelled to the vast crowd, "How you ever expect to stop the war if you can't sing any better'n *that?*"

Someone bumped her elbow. "When you on?"

"Oh hi, True." She backed away looking up at him, trying to remember a weekend somewhere, maybe Chicago, of booze and coke and weed, guitars and wonderful sex. "Some time the middle of tonight? After Johnny Winter I think." She shook rain from her hair. "Crazy, nobody'll be awake."

"Sure they will. Got nowhere to sleep."

"They don't have tents?"

"Most of em don't. Should have been here last night. Amazing connection we had. Canned Heat was fantastic—then us, then the Dead, then Creedence and Janis."

"How'd she do?"

"She was *on*."

"Great." Tara felt sharp fear. *Damn Blade. Never should've agreed to this.*

"Everybody was *on*. It's like we're all playing to a higher power, a new vision of life. A million kids and there's no fighting, everybody sharing and living together in these atrocious conditions..."

"For music. The great God Music."

"Yeah. The love of what we do..." He nodded at the crowd. "We're part of a real change, Tara. Showing that people can live better. Without war."

"Fuck I don't care. I get so scared before we go on..."

"Yeah, you told me, remember? That weekend in Milwaukee..."

"Wow. Now I remember."

"Still shooting up?"

"Just a little."

"No such thing as a little."

"Hey," she shoved him. "I'm in control."

He handed her a tab and a bottle of Jack. "Give up horse, do acid. Just a tab a day, three weeks. You'll kick horse. Promise." He gripped her biceps in hard guitarist's fingers. "I did."

She knocked back the acid. The whiskey warmed her all the way down. She took out the joint. "Pilot gave me this. Burmese."

A raw savage guitar ripped through the speakers, fast and wicked. "Jesus!" she said. "Who the hell is *that?*"

"Don't know." True glanced around. "Should ask Alice."

"*Go ask Alice,*" someone sang walking by, "*I think she'll know...*"

"Yeah," True said, "Man, did they fly last night."

"Who?"

"Airplane..."

"Gracie Slick," Gabriel said, "has this unbelievable vibrato..."

"Some chick named Alice," True said, "has the latest schedule." He tugged a soggy mimeo from his pocket. "Oh yeah, some Brits called Ten Years After."

"Never heard of them."

"Guy named Alvin Lee, vocals *and* guitar."

"Jesus!" Luis said. *"Listen to that!"* The guitar climbed, faster and faster, up the neck and down like lightning, the guitarist singing, screaming, exultant, ecstatic, for five minutes, more, more and more entrancing, on and on like an orgasm that keeps building and never ends. Then slowed to a coaxing whisper, *"I'm coming home...see my baby,"* the joy of love, the happiness, the magnificence of something far beyond explanation, building slowly now, faster, guitar cutting hard, sharp and nasty, minute after minute of impossibly difficult fast fingering, the guitarist singing at the same time

Gonna love you, baby,
Love you all night long

With a grateful beatific grin Alvin Lee staggered to a halt, bent-kneed with exhaustion as the crowd's joyous screams and thunder rattled the stage. Right fist raised in triumph, the red Gibson hollow-body on which he had just done what could not be done by any human being clutched in his left, he turned from the chanting cheering crowd and stumbled toward her, fist still raised. When he saw her his long narrow face widened in a weary grin. "How's things, Love?" he whispered hoarsely.

"You know me?"

Rivulets of sweat were pouring down his face and chest. *"Every*body knows *you."*

"What you just did—" She wiped at tears. "I've never heard anything like it."

He shrugged. "We did it for *them*. All those good people out there."

"Everybody talks about Jimi but *you* are the *true* guitar god."

Seeming stunned by the majesty of what he'd done, Lee wandered backstage as the crowd roared on.

The rain abated; wrapped in her scarlet raincoat, her face half-covered, she wandered the crowd while The Band poured their golden Biblical stories into the sodden night. Never had she seen so many people, everyone passing wine bottles and joints and pipes around. More people than lived in some whole states.

People screwing everywhere, on wet grass under plastic sheets or jammed into tents, dancing naked, smoking hash, stoned on mush- rooms, acid and peyote, smoking weed, standing in long lines for the toilets, for first aid, for plates of food handed out by the Hog Farm. Signs advertised weed for fifteen bucks a bag, acid, mushrooms and peyote four bucks a tab.

She shared the Burmese with a girl with rain down her face, a guy cross-legged in a poncho, a tall black man with a goatee who squeezed her hand and whispered *"Thank you Tara."*

"Don't take the brown acid," a woman called working her way through the crowd. "Tell everyone, the brown tabs are bad. Bad acid, full of speed. Don't take it."

She tried to remember if the tab True had given her was brown. "Oh well," she said, "what the fuck."

"I will!" said a tall skinny blond guy in a waterlogged blue bandana.

"Later, love." She laughed at herself for considering it. What band was it whose singer always got a blowjob before going on? If it worked for him maybe she should try an orgasm just before going on, maybe calm her down...The Burmese was making her happy, the acid really hitting, The Band finishing up. Jesus, was she on next? No, Blood, Sweat and Tears—

She pressed her way through the crowd back to the stage. Just enough time to needle a quickie and slide into the acid and with Benny she'd be *on.*

"Where you been, girl?" Sybil snapped.

"Out in America."

"You'll catch your death."

She stripped off her wet clothes. Naked under her scarlet raincoat she grabbed Benny and marched barefoot onstage, wind yanking the coat wide. "I'm Going Home" kept snatching her mind, she couldn't kill it. She chugged more Benny, grinned at Blade hunched over the keys, Tiny standing watchful, the bass guitar hanging off his huge frame, Sybil with her sticks raised. She swung her hips and stuck her tongue at Luis sultry-eyed and serene, his axe slung loose over one shoulder. She swung round and faced the crowd which spread to the ends of the earth, suddenly not afraid, almost savoring it, let it slide awhile, yanked the mike off the stand.

"We *love* you!" she screamed, fist in the air. "*You* are the start of something *new*! *You*! A million of you celebrating the *good* of people, the *love* of *music* and *beauty* and *peace* and *nature* and *each other*! WE LOVE YOU!"

The crowd roared and cheered and whistled. Sybil opened with a steady tick-tick and Luis slid in behind her with a soft backbeat till Tara slipped into their faithful opener, their door into the magic world of beauty and song,

If I mistreat you, honey, I sure don't mean no harm,
I'm a motherless child and I don't know right from wrong.

With every song they got more down into it, raw and hard till every note rang true and every word hit like a hammer and the world shrank to pure awareness, nowhere but *this*, no past or future, just the music crashing in on you with the perfect consonance of meaning and sound,

Here I am can I reach you? We are all in this together...

Something bit her leg, a fucking bulldog, and she screamed in the middle of a verse yanking her leg aside but there was no bulldog just the sting in her calf and skipping a line she caught up with the song, from the corner of her eye seeing Blade watching her.

She cried out in pain and surprise as it bit again but she stayed with Luis' solo soaring over the crowd where girls were dancing bare tits bobbing, the song reaching out, haunting, her voice and Luis' guitar two souls seeking each other but she missed a note, got behind, getting fucked up dropped out a few beats and came back in too late again—*how could that be?*—tried to pick it up foot tapping but that was the bulldog leg and she feared he'd bite and couldn't get the beat thinking *This is a smack hallucination, I've got to stop doing smack, no more smack starting tonight.*

It's not me fucking you up, Smack said huffily. *Just look at your friends.*

Yes it is you, asshole. The enormous humanity beyond the glare took her beyond fearing and she slid into the melody, eased into the next line then the next like water downhill, down through rocks of time as if the universe could last forever and she fell behind again, chasing the beat trying to catch up.

Smack was right. She couldn't finish the tour without him. But once it was done no more smack. She tore happily into the song, catching up, ripped it alive up and down the middle sighing like the wind in the trees, the people standing and screaming and Jesus it felt good to finally be so *on*. Wind blew the raincoat as she rocked her body to the beat, naked and free.

They were done, drained, shriven. Fist high, she turned from the mike, ran back to it, screamed, *"WE LOVE YOU!"* Backstage the roadies, everyone, cheering and clapping, yelling, "You were fantastic! You were beautiful!" She collapsed on a chair, pulled the raincoat tight, elbows on the table.

"The worst and best," Blade said to her. "You ever been."

"What the fuck," Sybil said, "happened to you out there?"

"I'm quitting smack." She looked at Luis. "I am."

He smiled. "Fine to me, baby."

"You have to choose," Sybil said. "Between life and smack."

Tara scowled at Luis. "Look at him. He does it."

"I watch my limits, baby," Luis said. "Why can't you?"

Because my need is bigger. Tara wondered what that meant, glanced down at her calf. Fucking bulldog hadn't left a trace.

"We are all one family!" someone onstage was screaming. "One tribe! People, good people! Let's all stay here! Start a new nation!"

Gabriel shook her shoulder. "Somebody wants to come backstage,"

"No way."

"Says she's your sister. But she's um," Gabriel looked at Blade, "she's a Negro."

Tara laughed. Goddamn her throat hurt.

"Says her name's Joan of Arc. But that was some French chick, right?"

Tara jumped up. *"Where is she?"*

Joan seemed taller, more slender, more radiant than before. "I *just* found out last night," hugging Tara and swinging her round, "'bout you being *here*, girl! So I told my man Montrose I'm going to see that Tara girl of mine. See how she doing. We left last night, driving all the way from *De*troit, girl, just to see you—"

Tara laughed happily. "You rescuing people still?"

"Four nights a week emergency room, honey, that's enough rescuing for me—"

"Come meet the band. This's Joan, we met in the Detroit riot, after Motown..."

She smiled at Joan shaking hands and hugging people. This was so unexpected it made the rest of her life seem flat, monotone, no happiness. "Where's your boyfriend?"

"Montrose? He's out there by that little pond."

"Let's go somewhere, eat."

Joan giggled. "Honey it's almost one-thirty in the morning? This the middle of *no*where."

"So what!" Tara laughed. "Let's go find someplace."

Joan hugged her. "You haven't changed a bit now have you?"

"I'm so happy to see you." Tara took her hand crossing the field. "I'm going to quit horse."

Joan said something Tara couldn't hear over the rain. "What?"

"I said you never should have got into that, honey. Didn't make you a better singer. You were better before."

Montrose was a large very black man with a high forehead and pugnacious face that softened instantly to a grin. "You're even prettier than your picture."

She tugged Joan's arm. "I can't believe you came. Makes doing this concert worthwhile...Don't know why I'm crying...Tired out I guess, I hate concerts."

"I'd die of fear up there front of everyone!" Montrose hugged her to his huge hard frame. "I heard so many good things about you."

CSN was singing as she and Joan and Montrose walked the muddy, crowded road of dancing, singing people,

Fear is the lock,
And laughter the key to your heart.

HOW STRANGE TO BE ALIVE: what did it mean? Mick watched the candle waver in the sea breeze and tried to understand. But could he understand the process *by which* he understood? If so, did he understand the process of *that* understanding? As in physics, there were no significances, only relationships. As with Alice, the mirrors were infinite,

One pill makes you larger
And one pill makes you small

They called it navel-gazing because that's what it was. You looked back down the tunnel of life to your birth and before. Tried to explore it. To understand creation.

The quest for understanding was life's deepest joy and task. There was no shame in thinking deeply, in trying to understand life and how best to live it, in exploring the mysteries of being. On the other hand, to ignore the myriad unknowns of being, to fear mystery, to live without inquiry or exploration in hated jobs, dully completing one task and going on to the next, in endless commutes, deadlines and bored relationships, in the vampire trance of TV, media, entertainment and pastimes, in numb despair of never knowing freedom or even that it existed—that seemed the greatest shame of all.

Dawn tinted the redwood hills; the clear blue sky was a symphony of silence, a crow's call a mile away sharp as a stiletto. Every ridge stone and conifer crown shone with unique light. Each pebble and leaf, each bird and shard of light and bead of water had immanence, being and remaining within itself, present throughout the universe, the Great Spirit often foolishly called God.

The night he'd found Daisy he'd had a dream of wandering through a supermarket kind of place, asking anyone and everyone *why are we here?* The kid like him had said *to find out what life is.*

Impossible, but you had to try. You could learn. You could get part way.

Life is a clue to the mystery of the universe: it fit perfectly with his dream. Only when we found out what life was could we go on to the next clue, the next mystery.

And if we didn't solve this one we didn't get to go on: as in non-evolution, we'd be stuck here till we vanished.

Everything could be a dream, imaginary. But this candle, the muted music, the rustle of wind down the tin chimney, the polished grain of the pine table—all had impenetrable significance.

Every life, human, animal, insect, and plant had infinite significance. Even the wind was alive. We humans, who did not even know our own reality, how could we know others'? Did it matter? Even to matter was a concept of inconsequential dimensions.

"Listen to this," Daisy said. "*Sun breaks over the eucalyptus grove below the wet pasture* Gary Snyder, talking about Marin — *distant dogs bark, a pair of cawing crows; the twang of a pygmy nuthatch high in a pine...*

a soft continuous roar
comes out of the far valley,
of the six-lane highway — thousands
and thousands of cars
driving men to work."

"Anthropologists say Stone Age people didn't work near as hard as folks today."

"If you had your way, you'd never work at all."

"I'd work on what I want to. Like a Cheyenne, hunting buffalo, wandering the sacred earth, killing my enemies..."

She held up Ferlinghetti. "Here's another one:

On freeways fifty lanes wide
on a concrete continent
spaced with bland billboards
illustrating imbecile illusions of happiness

...and they have strange license plates
and engines
that devour America..."

She closed the book. "Strange they call it a *free*way. When it costs us the earth."

"Tara used to say humans work for cars, not the other way around."

"Must be terrible for her, not knowing where you are."

"I wrote her last month. Brian was driving to Toronto, he mailed it from there."

"What if I go see her somewhere she's not being followed? Agree on a time when you can call a pay phone near her?"

"After all these years it'd blow her mind to see you."

"Let alone talk to *you*."

FIVE DAYS A WEEK after breakfast Daisy put her Olympia portable typewriter on the pine table and spread out file folders and reports, black coffee at her elbow. Mick carried his tools to the truck and drove over Mount Tam to work for Vern on a new house in Sausalito, digging ditches for the foundation forms then building the forms and setting the first joists into the joist holders on the concrete walls.

Weekends were free to lie naked in the sun drinking coffee and vodka with orange juice, smoking grass that made lazy gray haloes over their heads, in the warm rhapsody of his guitar, a happy strangeness to the world, doors into the future, everything woven in a web of understanding by the sun,

Our house is a very, very, very fine house
With two cats in the yard, life used to be so hard
Now everything is easy, 'cause of you

"Nothing's better than sitting with you in the sun, coffee and a joint beside me, playing guitar."

"You should be in a band. You really should."

"My left hand's too slow, the broken fingers." He thought of Alyssa. "There's a million people out there better than me."

She ran her fingers down his broken hand. "If it's what you love most..."

"What I love most is to be free."

She grinned. "You're not?"

"No one who has to work five days a week should imagine they're free. And once you *have* to have that job, you're no longer an employee. You're a slave."

"I'm happy doing my thesis. That's work, ten hours a day, six days a week..."

"Yeah, but that's different. You love it."

"What if your work was playing guitar, five days a week?"

He thought. "I don't want to *have* to do anything. Except what I want, right then."

She laughed. "Good luck."

"It sounds selfish but it's not. Why are we trained to think we *can't* be free? That we have to work and pay taxes and be ready to die if someone says to? When did we agree to give up all this freedom?"

"It's the old war between individual and tribe...Like these causes we've fought for, against the draft, for civil rights, stopping the Vietnam War—"

"Those causes killed my freedom. Organizing a meeting took hours, days. To help organize a march of fifty thousand people you give up freedom for weeks at a time."

"So," she tilted her head, "it's senseless trying to create a better world?"

He shrugged. "Sometimes I think so."

"When I worked in Mississippi during Freedom Summer, in '64, six percent of blacks were registered to vote. Now, just five years later, it's almost seventy percent, one of the highest in the country. Isn't that creating a better world?"

"But for all those black people who died, most whose names we'll

189

never know, or for whites like Schwerner and Goodman, was it worth it?"

She stared at him as if shocked, making him realize again her depths he'd not yet imagined. "If there were even one death," she said, "that would be a good question for God."

"The real question is, how much do we owe the tribe? And when they do wrong how long do we stand by them? And if innocent people are being murdered, shouldn't we as fellow humans help *them*? Particularly if we're part of the cause?"

"As a member of the tribe you're guilty of its sins? But if two hundred and fifty thousand Americans hadn't died in World War Two, we wouldn't be free today."

"That war would never have happened if in the nineteen-twenties Woodrow Wilson and Clemenceau hadn't been determined to ruin Germany's economy forever. What caused Hitler and Fascism was the resulting starvation and misery."

"If your country makes you choose between fighting a war you think is evil or going to jail, how can you be free?"

"No one facing death is free." He picked up the guitar,

It's gonna come
So don't be dumb
And think you've got
Forever.

IN THE INFECTIOUS JOY OF PEYOTE he moved effortlessly through the room of golden auras. Everything had meaning, a perfect existence—Daisy's Roman terracotta oil lamp on the pine table, the wrinkled floorboards, the yellow lapping flames behind the wood stove's mica door, two glasses of red wine on the table, the woven Guatemalan placemats, an overturned fork, a few glistening crumbs.

The microcosm *was* the macrocosm. You were *here* but could be *anywhere*: an igloo's cold steaming ice walls, a white bear rug on frozen snow, one candle and a seal skull of frozen meat. A spacecraft to another world, humans weightless inside, new galaxies drifting past. In the Roman Senate with early sun on the marble steps and the Tiber gleaming beyond the palaces below.

The superior person curbs evil and furthers good, the *I Ching* said, when he opened it randomly.

And thereby obeys the benevolent will of heaven,
which desires only good and not evil.

To do good was to lessen suffering. To do evil was to maintain or increase it. But that got complicated. Like when God told Abraham to sacrifice the lamb instead of his son, what was good for the son was evil for the lamb. There was no absolute good.

So we had to do the best we could to not kill or harm unless we needed to in order to protect or sustain ourselves. And to make sure the good we sought didn't entail greater evil down the line.

And you did good by following the path with heart. Like Castañeda said, *Does this path have a heart? If it does, the path is good...*

His cheeks ached with smiling. The twisted wick of the Roman lamp threw out a holy golden light, the warm air full of ecstasy; he could taste it and feel it on his skin, scented with salty mist and oleanders and the velvety rumble and hiss of the sea. Daisy's smile halted time, her sculpted face, the tendons in her neck and the cascade of her auburn hair, in the depths of her eyes the awareness of her own death, and his.

Everything was sacred, lamplight on the wall, Judy Collins singing *In my life, I've loved you more*, sea wind and perfumes of a thousand flowers, chatter of swallows in the eaves, gulls on the wind and jays in the scrub. In peace and perfect understanding.

I didn't know we could ever live like this.

16

MY LAI

"**Y**OUR CHICKEN SHIT has to be old and dry," Head said. "The fresh stuff will burn your plants. You dig a half-bucket of old chicken shit into the hole for each plant, mix it with good soil and a bit of compost."

Almost everyone in Bolinas grew great grass, but nobody's was like Head's. Two whole football teams, he used to say, could get high off one joint. "I call it parapet weed," he'd said. "Like in San Francisco, there's these buildings with stone parapets sticking out the tops? They're trying to pass a law these parapets have to be removed, right? 'Cause if there's another earthquake, man, they're gonna drop ten, twenty stories and hit the heads of the folks down below. That's my weed, man. Parapet weed."

Mick took another hit. "In the Himals they mix weed with opium —you're stoned but mellow, can go on forever."

Head grinned. "Yeah, we used to smoke that in Nam before going out on patrol. Made it easier, Man, what you had to do."

"What was that?" Mick said.

Head took a long toke. "It's important, real important, space your plants five feet apart. That way they get sun down their sides, but are still close enough to grow tall instead of out. And be sure to cull all the males. That's *sinsemilla*—'no seeds'—that way the females keep on producing more and more resin, more and more THC. Trying to attract some pollen..."

"They just get hornier and hornier," Brian Newman said.

"And not too much water, right? Let 'em get thirsty now and then. Like people, it's good for 'em."

Watching the long steady roll of the sea, Mick thought of the Sahara. Nobody even *knew* what thirst was. Nobody could imagine. "It eats you up inside, thirst does. Till you're weightless. Can blow away like a bird. A leaf."

"The day I don't have weed," Head said, "I'm gonna blow my*self* away."

THAT US TROOPS HAD MURDERED 504 women, children and old men in the village of My Lai on March 16, 1968 surprised few who had fought in the war. Covered up by the Army until November 1969, it however ended the last pretense that America's Vietnam had any justification or morality.

To get maximum benefit from the opportunity, the GIs had raped many of the women and girls before killing them, with their combat knives cutting "C Company" into their chests—some while still alive. Tragically, one GI was wounded in the foot, while reloading his pistol to finish killing a little girl.

General William Westmoreland, Commander of US forces in Vietnam, congratulated Charlie Company on doing an "outstanding job." *Stars and Stripes* announced that "US infantrymen had killed 128 Communists in a bloody day-long battle."

When a courageous soldier named Ron Ridenhour reported the massacre to his superiors, the Army did nothing. Finally, under some pressure, it instituted a token investigation by Colonel Oran Henderson and Major General Samuel Koster, both who had ordered the killings then watched the slaughter from their helicopters overhead. Then a major named Colin Powell, from the same unit as Charlie Company, was ordered to have a look at the soldier's report and whitewashed it completely. "In direct refutation of this portrayal [of atrocities]," he said, "is the fact that relations between American soldiers and the Vietnamese people are excellent."

Finally an investigative reporter, Seymour Hersh, published the truth, backed by interviews with the soldiers involved, in the *St. Louis Post Dispatch*. At the Pentagon one can imagine the horror—not at what had happened—*but that it had been revealed*. But after all, with so many incidents to hide—how could they keep them all under wraps?

In the weeks that followed it became clear that My Lai was one of many villages similarly destroyed by American troops, in which thousands of people, usually women and children, were murdered, and the murders covered up.

It made Mick so sick at heart he could not think or eat, could not sleep. He felt lost in a cloud of evil and lies, could not talk to anyone who still supported the war. "I've always hated the Nazis for what they did," Daisy said. "But I thought that the Nuremberg war crimes trials made this kind of horror impossible now. Look how wrong I was."

In reality, Mick said, My Lai was just a metaphor for the whole American war in Vietnam. "You invade another country and kill millions of people, most of them civilians—isn't that just thousands of My Lais, one after the other?"

She thought a moment. "It works out to three My Lais a day."

As more and more evidence was revealed, the Army was forced against its will to find someone to prosecute. Captain Medina, who personally may have killed more than 30 people, and Second Lieutenant William Calley, who personally killed up to 50, and thirty other GIs were charged. Colonel Henderson, he who ordered the killings then watched from his helicopter, was too high-ranking to charge.

More than 70 other GIs who either participated or did nothing to stop the killings were not charged. Medina, defended by F. Lee Bailey, was acquitted and then given a job by Bailey in a helicopter company he owned. Calley was pardoned by his fellow war criminal, Richard

Nixon, whose approval rating by the American people reached a new high that month of 67%.

"I will not be affected," Nixon said, "by opposition to the war."

For most people it seemed impossible that Americans had done this, unless you had been in Vietnam and saw it happen all the time: how many VC prisoners shot on the spot? How many thousands of villages burned and people shot down in the fields for the crime of not doing what America wanted?

Napalm and black clouds emerging in newsprint, said Allen Ginsberg in *Wichita Vortex Sutra*,

Flesh soft as a Kansas girl's
Ripped open by metal explosion—
...on the other side of the planet
caught in barbed wire, fire ball
bullet shock, bayonet electricity
bomb blast terrific in skull & belly, shrapnelled throbbing meat
While this American nation argues war...

"MY LAI'S NOTHING NEW." Tim Cardin shrugged. "Massacres like this, we're doing them all over Vietnam. The basic idea is to kill every Vietnamese—then we've won the war, right? I was just a grunt in the Ninth Infantry down in the Mekong Delta when we did this thing the Pentagon called Operation Speedy Express..."

A friend of Head's, Cardin had built a hut on RCA Beach when Mick had lived there with Alyssa. Tall, stringy and dark-bearded, he was a good surfer and sometimes worked fishing boats to make money. "For months we bombed the shit out of the whole province, even though there were no fucking VC. Day and night we hit them with B52s, gunships, napalm, white phosphorous, F4s, any tool we had to kill. Our sniper teams were whacking old people riding water-boos, kids with rice baskets on their heads."

Cardin swallowed, looked out to sea. "There was this General

Julian Ewell, and his deputy commander, Colonel Ira Hunt, they used to fly over us in Ewell's command chopper, screaming at us to kill everyone, farmers in their fields, villages full of civilians, waste them, man, waste them. Then we had to count the bodies, even the water-boos, and report them as enemy combatants..."

"That's how the officers get promoted, by their body count," Head said. "Westmoreland, he was the king of civilian body count. Sending out choppers on night missions, just wasting villages...Next day the Ninth goes in there and adds up the dead, adds them to the body count."

"Only way guys can deal with this constant murder of civilians," Cardin said, "is pretend they aren't people, just *gooks*, they don't feel pain, don't care when their kids are set on fire or their families get blown apart."

"Yeah," Head said. "Like the Japs in World War Two, they thought *we* weren't human."

Cardin snickered. "Maybe they were right."

"Interesting thing about all this," Head added, "is that *we*, America, invented the international laws used to judge war crimes: the Nuremberg Principles, which we developed just twenty years ago to judge the Nazis. And one of the things the Nuremberg Principles say, is that it's a crime to do something just because your government or superior officer tells you to, if there is a moral option."

"In war," Cardin said, "there never is a moral option. Every war is criminal and immoral."

"In Troy's last letter," Mick later told Daisy, "he talked about stuff like that. Said it happened all the time."

"This isn't the country I used to love."

"It's the country we've become."

"And once you do this kind of evil, how can you ever be good again?"

"A REVOLUTION?" Brian pushed back his Cleveland Indians cap. "Because of My fucking Lai? Compare us to France in 1789, Russia in

1917, you see it couldn't happen. We don't have the hunger, the implosion of the existing societal structure, the power vacuum in the center..." He scratched his head with the cap brim. "But like Russia we have an unpopular foreign war, the loss of respect for the central government—"

"We've had riots in hundreds of cities," Mick said. "Major civil disobedience, escalating violence, and we're the best educated and freest people in history."

Brian snickered. "Tell that to some kid in the paddies ducking bullets. Some guy in Sing Sing for refusing the draft."

Mick watched him. "What do you mean?"

Brian's eyes widened. "What the fuck you think I mean? How many guys all over this country're doing time for refusing to fight in this evil, illegal and immoral war?"

Mick shrugged. "I wouldn't know."

Brian slapped him on the knee. "You should get more involved, Dennis. About what this country's doing."

Mick stood his surfboard to brush off sand, wanting to tell Brian the truth but couldn't. "Right now I'm involved in what those waves're doing."

Brian stood and lifted his board. "It's when people're uncommitted like you, man, that's when dictatorships happen."

FROM A PAY PHONE in San Andreas, Mick called the Berkeley pay phone Tara and Daisy had agreed on. It rang and rang and he felt sorrowed and empty; then she picked it up with her familiar, coarse "Hey!" and he was back with his little sister again, before Troy, the train tracks south, Ma and Dad dying, the war, before everything.

"So how you been?" Stupid questions, how do you sum up the year of sorrow, fear and joy since he'd gone into hiding? The phone beeped: twenty-five more cents.

"The band's doing great—we hit twenty-one on last week's Billboard, did you see?"

"I didn't know—"

"You should go back to France. It's safer there. Amazing you found Daisy—you were at a party, saw each other?"

It all poured out. He felt shriven, healed. His little sister. His own flesh and blood. "I can't get over Troy."

"Don't talk about it, Mick."

"Nobody calls me Mick. So strange not to have your own name."

"What about Mexico? Down in the Yucatan? Would you be safe there?"

"I don't know, Tara..." He changed the subject: "So what's new with you? How's your love life?"

"Me and Luis, we're still going. Someday I'm going to stop being a motherless child." She was silent, then, "You won't believe who found me."

"Yeah? Who?" he asked, half-caring.

"Troy's mom."

"His *what?*"

When he hung up he felt worse than before. The strangeness of Troy's mom brought Troy's death near again; he wanted to meet her but didn't, wished again he and Troy had never met. Had it been his own selfishness, his wanting a brother, that doomed Troy?

Or even if he and Troy had never met in that deserted barrack that afternoon so long ago, even if Troy had grown up in the orphanage, wouldn't he still have ended up in Vietnam? Unloved, maybe unskilled, no connections. The first to be drafted?

But maybe he would've gone to Vietnam and come home again. Alive.

DAISY WENT TO IOWA to see her mom, and the night before she was due back, Mick traded an hour's plumbing work on a Sausalito houseboat for four tabs of Clear Light, and on the way home stopped at the store on the corner of Route 1 and Sausalito Boulevard for a jug of red. It was nearly dark; it had rained and the pavement gleamed. As he came out of the store a cop car cruised by; instinctively he ducked behind a sign.

That he'd been stupid enough to hide made his gut congeal. *"Never act scared,"* hadn't Modoc Jack told him? *"Never* act guilty." Tomorrow instead of being home with Daisy he could be on his way to Leavenworth.

As he slid into the driver's seat a voice behind him said, "Why were you hiding?"

It was a cop in a tan uniform, hand on his pistol. Another cop by the passenger door. "I didn't try to hide anything. I was going to go back in, that's all."

"Back in?"

"To get my girlfriend some Boone's Farm."

"Why didn't you?"

"Short of money."

"Got a license?"

"Sure." Trying not to tremble he pulled Dennis Kurtz's license from his wallet.

It should be okay. The photo on the license was of him with long blond hair and a beard. Should be no problem. *Be cool, man.* He took a slow, long breath. *Be cool.*

The cop dropped the license into his own pocket and walked to the cruiser. "Ain't no biggie," the other cop said. "Just checking that you're you."

He could probably outrun them out the back of the store but that was all marsh and there were buildings and cyclone fences on both sides. And they might shoot. His back tightened, imagining the bullet.

The first cop came back. "Sorry, Dennis, but there's an outstanding warrant for your arrest."

"What? I haven't done anything!"

"A parking ticket, kiddo. Two years ago in Truckee. You should've paid it."

They cuffed his wrists behind him and locked him in the back of the cruiser. *Be calm.* Fucking Dennis should've paid his parking tickets. *I* should've paid them. *I'm* Dennis. I'm not this guy facing ten years.

Oh shit: the four tabs of acid in his pocket. First thing they'd do in Marin County Jail was check his clothes.

He was never going to be with Daisy again.

"So it's third and one." The first cop was driving. "What's the asshole do? He throws the ball. I coulda throwed *up*."

"Didn't nail it?"

"Short. Almost fucking intercepted."

If Mick pulled down real hard he could slide his cuffed wrists all the way to his hips. But it would tear his shoulder loose to push lower. Pictures flashed through his mind—Link Doolittle the linebacker ripping it loose, Daisy waiting by the pine table for him to come home, a corridor down a long line of clanging steel cells...

"After you're booked you can make a call," the other cop called back. "You got somebody, make your bail?"

Mick halted, crouched over his cuffed wrists, transfixed by pain. "Sure. Maybe."

"Too late tonight but they can get you out tomorrow."

He twisted the cuffs past one hip. Now the other. He gasped, sat back.

"You okay back there?"

"Sure." He slid the cuffs under his feet and up to his lap and twisted his humerus back into the socket. "Fine."

He reached into his pocket for the plastic bag of LSD but the shoulder hurt so bad he dropped the bag and now there were four tabs for the cops to see.

"I hope this whole passing fad," the first cop said, "is just a passing fad."

Highway 101, not far to go, streetlights brightening the cruiser's interior. He fumbled on one side of the seat, then the other.

Found one.

"That's what fads are, aren't they?" the other cop said. "Shit that's just passing?"

There was no crack between the seat and back to shove the tab into. He could try to push it under the front seats but standard procedure might be to search the car after they bring somebody in. With joined hands he raised the tab to his lips.

Three to go.

One under his foot. Easy.

Two to go.

The cruiser decelerated onto the courthouse off-ramp. Tipping sideways he felt one under his thigh. Three down.

One to go.

He swallowed the plastic bag as the cruiser pulled into the jail lot. The other cop opened his door. The fourth tab lay in Mick's lap, bright in the jail's yellow lights. He snatched it as he got out. "This way," the cop said, behind him.

He popped it in his mouth.

"Hey," the cop yelled. "How'd you get round those cuffs?"

TARA WISHED SHE'D TAKEN THE CHOPPER. The roads to the Kansas State stadium were jammed; there was no way she could reach the performers' entry. She sat in the idling XKE furious at herself, she'd be late, no time to change, get her head into it, they'd have to keep the opening act, a Motown band called Rare Earth, on too long.

Funny how Motown's founder, Berry Gordy, hadn't wanted to sign them because Blade and Tiny were the only blacks, that she and Sybil were white and Luis a PR, and now Berry was signing all-white bands like Rare Earth...

The traffic inched forward. The VW bus with the Grateful Dead stickers in front of her shuddered, spit a cloud of oily smoke and died. She slapped her ebony steering wheel in frustration, swore at them. She'd have to start warming up now, walk on stage like she was, in torn Levis and a tan blouse.

Rain beat at the windshield, the wipers slapping it back and forth. She snapped the radio on, off, began running her voice up and down the notes, catches of song. Jesus she sounded awful. She reached behind the passenger seat for the bottle of Benny.

A chopper fluttered over, rotors silvery in the rain, lights flashing, and she felt fury at herself again for not taking it, for being late. It hovered and dropped toward the stadium, between the light towers, hidden by the bleachers.

In front of her the VW bus's starter went *yuk-yuk-yuk* but didn't catch. Cars were inching past on both sides but she was blocked behind it. A concert sign went cartwheeling past in the wind, paper cups and soda cans chasing after it.

Over the howl of wind and hammering rain and the motors thrumming and throbbing came a great *Boom* then a crackling roar as an oily cloud burst into the orange sky. She leaped from the car and sprinted up the road between the moving cars and dodged across the parking lot telling herself the chopper didn't crash that was just landing lights, it wasn't their chopper it was a TV news one, a medevac for someone collapsed in the crowd. Maybe it was just stage effects, could be anything...

Gasping and soaked she dashed up the stadium stairs, people screaming and running out knocking her down, others crowding toward the arena where flames leapt like a pyre. *"What was it?"* Tara screamed. *"What was it?"*

"The band!" a boy yelled as he shoved past toward the flames, camera held high. "The helicopter crashed! With the band!"

17

CELL 131

VERY HIGH ON ACID in Marin County Jail, he was headed for Leavenworth.

If he could keep remembering he was on four tabs of acid, that this wasn't the normal world, maybe he wouldn't go crazy.

His forehead ached from smashing into the steel door but that was okay because it shook some sense into his brain. Blood had crusted above his eyes and down the sides of his face. His hands throbbed from hitting the concrete—he'd *almost* punched through it, kept sucking the blood from his knuckles so *They* wouldn't see it. Made the floor sticky too.

Had to stay in control.

Control of what? *Ha ha.*

Rattle of steel bars as other prisoners in their gray-blue jumpsuits screamed curses at each other. A huge black man with drooping mustaches blew a kiss across the aisle at Mick. "Hey, sweetie, I'm gonna be the first to have your baby-white ass!"

Sliding molten walls of orange ice, the ceiling stars, the roof gone and you could fly away. He went out into the universe and it was home. Falling stars were cigarette lighters, chuckling mushrooms, a house amid a flooded river tumbling slowly, gray stones, pale toes, sunset over silver oceans—he could be anywhere, just choose it.

Look inside your mind," she said, a lazy southern voice on the edge of desire. *If I could have you*, Mick said but she just kept saying, *Look inside your mind.*

He could follow it like a staircase that went down in circles into the earth. Pink walls, gray floor. You stopped believing your self-created picture of yourself.

Who *are* you?

Is there a *who* there?

Are you just myth? Imagination?

Go down another level: you are a self-replicating, self-protecting chemical structure. Your soul evolved as a survival tool.

So did evil.

Before they transferred him to Leavenworth he had to escape. He scanned the steel ceiling looking for cracks. Make yourself tiny and go between them?

Had to be a way.

Go down another level: we are the seed of life.

Love is also an evolutionary tool. Why it exists.

There is only one Life, and we are all its cells.

CELL 131 had pink concrete walls, a rusting green-painted steel door, a steel toilet bowl in the corner and a concrete slab for a bed. The cell was about six feet square but the bed took up half; he could pace two steps, turn, and pace two steps back.

It seemed improbably evil that Frank Lloyd Wright had designed this. From the outside, with its thick pink concrete walls and aqua tile roof it looked like a Mexican insane asylum. And now he was inside it, and getting more stoned every minute.

In another cell a radio was playing,

I shot a man in Reno
Just to watch him die—

It seemed improbable too they would let that song play *here*—wasn't this the place they weighed your soul before they sent you on to hell?

Cell meant two things. And you were locked in both at the same time.

EASY TO WATCH HIS BRAIN, red seas of capillaries patiently pulsing, billions of cells, axons and neurons throbbing with messages, queries, taunts, fears. Infinite rooms of infinite voices calling. You could shunt aside a signal, shut down a net, pull the truth back out of a synapse and replace it with a lie. Truth and lies were chemical impulses, nothing more.

What to do became so easy to understand. Every question its own answer. The body knows, the mind wants.

Before they shipped him to Leavenworth he had to escape.

Explosions of glorious color. He punched the door, surprised at the pain. If he'd been able to almost punch through the wall, the door might be easier.

If he got ten years, they might let him out in seven. Daisy'd be gone. *You won't survive prison,* Lou Graziano'd said. *They'll make sure of that.*

Every question carried its answer inside it like a pregnant woman's belly.

A harassed railroad clerk wearing a green eyeshade was selling tickets, counting money, answering questions, typing a telegram and talking on the phone at the same time. He had a crew cut waxed up in front and arm bands on his sleeves like a casino croupier.

"No wonder you're crazy," he said. "I'm your mind."

"Close the ticket window," Mick said.

"Can't. These people need tickets."

"Shut it. Leave the phone off the hook."

"I'd be derelict—"

"And take off that silly eyeshade, lock up the office, walk down to the pond and go swimming."

"I don't have a suit."

"Go naked."

Spider on the ceiling laughing. Mick craned his neck to peer closer. Eight hairy legs, sinister torso, huge gleeful eyes, wide salivating jaw—he saw them from a bug's viewpoint before it was torn apart and swallowed down that red vortex. It was big as a fucking house this spider and he was stuck in its web under its red drooling jaws.

"Lesson Number One," the spider said in a soft raspy voice, spraying him with spit. "*Watch your step.* You got caught in my web because you didn't." Its sharp jaws jabbed down ripping him apart, blood spraying, *I'm dead,* his last thought as the blood emptied from his brain.

Silent ships on a silver sea, skeleton masts, the water viscous and still. A blackened egret dead on a tarry shore. "Lesson Two," the spider said. "*Some dangers can't be foreseen.*"

Sperm bumbling at an egg like drunken pollywogs. *Drive deep* into the vagina, down the red-hot throat of life—the future goes to the strongest, the first in, *the lust to fuck divine.* "Lesson Three, the spider said. "*Sex is God.*"

The boats again, *wooden ships on the water very free* ringing from the radio, all those harmonies with every other melody in time, rivers of song rushing to the sea,

Go, take your sister then by the hand,
Lead her away from this foreign land,
Far away, where we might laugh again...

He was going to be fine on four tabs of Clear Light in Marin County Jail. He laughed aloud, hugged himself, sat on the concrete bunk and watched his mind tumble through infinities.

"Lesson Four," the spider said gravely. "*The warrior goes to war hungry to harm his enemies. Not fearing harm himself.*"

He stretched out grinning on the concrete bed, hands clasped under his head, and floated nightlong in a million worlds, had sex with a million women, loving every single one, sang a million songs, each his own, swam tropical beaches and climbed peaks in a million other dimensions and times.

"*I* am the first mind," his gut said. "I'm never wrong."

"I keep you alive," his leg muscles said.

"I been here before all of you," his prick said. "So just do what I say—"

"*The men don't know,*" Alyssa sang cross-legged naked on his prison cell's cold concrete floor, her concert Martin atop her open thighs, her beautiful cunt so lovingly visible, "*what the little girls understand—*"

He reached down to her magical tits. *Oh this perfect world.*

"Fifth and final lesson," the spider said. "If it feels good do it *is* the path with heart."

FOR HIS ONE PHONE CALL in the morning, he tried Smiley's and got Jack Royce, a carpenter rebuilding the bar's front stairs. "Can somebody go see if Daisy's back—

"And if she isn't?" Jack said. "You gonna sit in jail till she gets home?"

The longer he stayed in jail, Mick realized, the more likely they'd figure who he really was. "She's supposed to get back today—"

"I ain't seen her...Anyway, I'll make your bail."

"I can wait for her—"

"You don't want to stay where you are."

"I don't know how much it is—"

"I got three hundred bucks. One parking ticket can't be that fucking much."

Mick suddenly wanted to weep, felt the soaring joy of one who might be saved. "Man," he sighed, "have I seen some shit..."

"Be there in an hour."

"I'm still so stoned," Mick said as they rode in Jack's battered blue Econoline out of San Rafael toward Sausalito so Mick could pick up his truck. "I felt so alone...In the entire universe I was the only living thing."

Jack gave him a broken-toothed grin. "Four tabs? Amazing."

Jack had lived many years in Japan and was well-known as an artist in the *ukiyo-e* style, the seventeenth century *pictures of the floating world*, so Mick held him in the respect one has for those wiser and more aware. "Never," Mick said, "did I have a moment of fear. But I kept forgetting I'd taken acid, and that what I was going through wasn't normal."

Jack laughed as if to say maybe it was. Mick leaned back into the sun-warmed seat, liking the rattle and clatter of the van and the kaleidoscope of passing green hills and blue-white sky, hungry to see Daisy.

When he got home the house was empty. He opened the jug of red, thinking how different his life had been yesterday when he'd bought it. He rolled a joint and sat on the deck watching the lagoon flow into the sea, thinking this is what it'll be like when I come back from Leavenworth and there'll be no one.

With a hollow rumble her white Karmann Ghia pulled up behind the house. He wanted to weep with joy, run to her, but smiled and kissed her as if nothing had happened. She was weary from the flight and from being with her mother. "She's fifty-nine. She's all alone now that my Pa's disappeared, but she won't admit she's lonely. How's she ever going to meet someone working in a library in a small town in Iowa?"

Mick's memory of Iowa was of rolling forested hills, white barns and miles and miles of corn. "I'd think that'd be a good place—"

"She still talks about my Pa. That if only he hadn't been a drunk..." Daisy shrugged, a helpless gesture that made Mick sad because it was so unlike her. "I think she'd still take him back, if he *came* back."

Mick thought of fighting Percy Moran years ago in Tappan, being hit in the head by his heavy lunchbox. He wondered where Percy'd disappeared to. It made him sorrow for Daisy, for her pain that could never be healed. Nor, he realized, could the pain of losing his own Ma and Dad.

The four tabs of acid had made everything seem clear, all difficulties easy. *That's why they call it Clear Light...*"I've decided to stop going over the Hill for work, it's too dangerous. Jack Royce and I, we're going to work together in Bolinas, lots of construction and rehab jobs right here."

"Does Jack *know*?"

"Who I really am? Hell no. Only you do. You and Tara."

"Why were you talking to Jack?"

He told her what had happened.

"*Why?*" she was almost weeping. "Why did you hide when the cops passed?"

"Instinctive. I'm always at risk."

"Now you're even more at risk. And now one of those cops who let you go is going to see the Most Wanted list and say *Hey isn't that the guy we took in last week?*"

BEFORE DAWN they paddled the old Grumman aluminum canoe far into the lagoon and floated silently watching the stars die in its silvery expanse. Thousands of birds were calling, splashing, clattering the water with wingtips as they took flight. Slowly the sawtoothed ridge of firs and redwoods above the lagoon caught flame; first sunlight hit them with intense instant warmth, turning the waves red-gold.

Egrets and herons roosting in the redwoods dropped in long lazy circles toward the Lagoon. Multicolored fingerlings flashed in schools through the green-gold water. Seals barked and rolled on the sandbars, turning sandy flanks to the sun.

Drops from his paddle tip *tick-ticked* across the water. Sea grass rustled softly under the hull. Coots called, scattering before them. A vast flock of ducks whirred over. The sun flashed on the high waves beyond the channel. "Look!" she called, "an arctic tern. He flies all the way from Alaska to Antarctica, every year." She turned to face him. "Like you, wandering all over the world and now you've come back to me."

"I'm going to have to leave you soon. They're bound to catch up."

She turned round in the bow. "You know I missed you every single day since Tappan?"

He laughed. "I missed you more than you missed me."

"So let's get married."

"No way. As it is, your failure to turn me in could be a felony...Like we've said, you don't know why I've changed my name, I won't tell you, you don't know I'm being hunted—"

"We'll go somewhere, New Zealand maybe."

"I won't be chased out of my own country by a mob of fascists."

KPSF WAS PLAYING TARA's band's songs one after the other—strange, when sometimes you could go for days and not hear one. Mick put down his Skilsaw to listen; it was the one he loved best, Tara's wistful pure voice rising and falling in perfect melody against Luis' searing guitar, soaring contralto against the guitar's fiery staccato, its notes hitting so fast it brought tears to his eyes that any human being could do such a difficult, perfect thing.

For the station to play so many in a row, the band must really be getting famous. When he'd talked to her she hadn't mentioned a new album. He felt happy and proud for her, for the band, wished as he so often did that he could see her.

"As the band's only survivor," the disk jockey said, "what will Tara O'Brien do now? For the moment no one even knows where she is, or what her plans might be..."

He dropped the saw, jumped in the truck and drove over Mount Tam across the Golden Gate and took the Bay Bridge to Berkeley. From a pay phone on Shattuck he called the home number she had given Daisy but it didn't answer, didn't answer all day. Finally he drove home through a fog so thick in the headlights he couldn't even see one stripe ahead on the highway.

One sorrow after another. When was enough?

JACK LIVED IN THE WOODS beyond the Mesa with his wife, a self-described poet named Gillian, in a house he was building by hand from the eucalyptus he'd cut to clear the land, with a chainsaw dropping the huge trees and ripping the steel-hard logs lengthwise into posts, beams, joists and planks.

"Why you building that huge place for her?" Mick said. "She isn't gonna treat you any better." He couldn't understand Jack's stubborn refusal to admit pain, whether it was a saw-cut finger or Gillian's latest romance with another supposed poet of exquisite sensitivity and enough money from his daddy or some university grant to prance about in literary guise and smile down his nose at those with more significant goals. "Like when you cut your finger last week, you can't make yourself immune to pain."

Jack wiggled a toothpick under his yellow moustache. "If you love someone you let her do what she wants. She wants to fuck young guys, we can work through it."

"This whole thing about preserving relationships—making it *work*? Such bullshit! Like the Beatles, *we can work it out*? They're joking, man...If a relationship is *work*, ditch it."

Jack spit a tobacco fleck. "Since when are you such a fucking expert?"

"This whole Bolinas fake poetry scene pisses me off, the pecking orders, jealousies and one-upmanships of a bunch of so-called poets full of self-centered drivel with no rhyme, meter, form, idea or any skill at all! The kind of meaningless shit found in university presses funded by unsuspecting taxpayers, that has helped to bury real poetry under six feet of sewage—"

Jack grinned. "Since when has the human race not been stupid?"

They had demolished the kitchen of a Victorian vacation home off Bolinas beach, baring the old rough-sawn Douglas fir rafters to create a cathedral ceiling, and were installing a stained-glass skylight of a red poppy in a field of golden grass. Plaster dust coated their hair and sweaty faces; fiberglass insulation itched their arms and necks.

"If it isn't fun to be with her, if you're fighting and hating and making each other miserable, it's better to be alone. Or have fun with someone else."

Jack's right eye squinted when he smiled. "You and Daisy, you don't fight?"

"Hardly ever. But then we—" He'd been going to say *but we were together years ago*, but couldn't, not even to Jack. Though it hurt to not be honest. "Last week we got in an argument about where we'd put the canoe paddles—stupid shit like that."

Jack stubbed out his home-roll and stuck it behind his ear. With his engaging ironic smile, broken-toothed grin, ragged golden beard and tangled hair, he seemed a cherubic satyr. And with his middleweight's shoulders and fighter's stance, scarred knuckles and busted nose he was easily the toughest man in town, with no harm in his heart for anyone.

Living seven years in Japan had influenced his painting style, his brush use, forms and colors, so his work seemed both a synthesis and clash of east and west. In New York he'd made a good living selling his work, but had tired of the New York literary and artistic scene, "the self-advertising fakes and frauds who steal the spotlight and give nothing back, the Andy Assholes of the world," meaning those like Andy Warhol who made up for lack of talent with publicity and illusion.

Mick climbed down from the scaffold to brew more coffee and roll another joint. They sat on the back deck smoking and drinking coffee and looking at the patio Mick had made from granite paving stones that had been cut in the mountains of New Hampshire, shipped round Cape Horn as ballast in clipper ships, and used to pave the streets of San Francisco, then torn up and replaced with asphalt, and trucked up the coast by Jack to become a patio in Bolinas.

"MacAdam in Scottish means the son of man," Jack chewed on an edge of mustache, "and that's who's covering the world with tar."

"And why we live here. Hardly any paved roads. Fucking world leaves us alone."

"Yeah?" The broken-toothed grin. "Till when?"

18

KENT STATE

ALL DEAD. Sybil and Luis and Blade and Tiny—all dead. Tara floated in a numb maze, every second with them but they weren't there, just a chemical memory in her brain.

Had she known it would crash? Why hadn't she warned them, insisted they all drive? Why had she been spared?

Her whole life had led to this. The farm, Troy, piano, smack, men: all illusion.

She stayed inside her house in Berkeley not answering the howling phone or the door because of the journalists. When she glanced out her front bay windows, they took pictures; she sat in the back garden with the cat on her knee, ducking inside every time a copter came too close.

When the door knocker clacked one afternoon she ignored it. It stopped, started again, loudened. "Tara!" a woman called. "Tara!"

It stopped. Tara moved to a window and saw Troy's mom. Tara stood chewing on a knuckle as Troy's mom walked away on the concrete sidewalk through the dappled shadows of the trees. Then Troy's mom stopped, fiddled in her handbag, came back with a pen and paper and stood on the front porch writing a note she slipped through the mail slot.

The slot clattered shut. Tara stood behind the door clenching her fists and biting her lip.

Dearest Tara,
I am so sorry. Please let me see you. I came by Greyhound.
Staying at the Copper Penny motel (629-4509, room 12).

Tara yanked the door open. "Ginnie!"

"IF WE'RE GONNA HAVE A REVOLUTION," Brian said, "it'll be the Weathermen who lead it. They have the will; they understand what needs to be done."

"What needs to be done?" Mick said innocently.

"Think about it, Dennis. If we're destroying another country, if we've killed three million people, most of them civilians, then to do nothing, isn't *that* violence? Aren't *you and I* responsible too? Not just Nixon and those who vote for him?"

"I didn't vote for him."

Greg shook his head. "You're an American? With a nice job, you make good money, you benefit from living in this country? But you're not trying to stop it from committing genocide? Then you're participating in the genocide too."

Mick had had too many of these conversations with Brian and they cut to the bone. As if Brian was trying to learn what he'd really done in the past. Even how Brian said "Dennis" was nearly sarcastic, as though he got the lie and was making fun of it. *I fought this war for years*, Mick ached to say, *and now they're going to jail me for it.* But he couldn't say it, had to seem mild-mannered and disinterested, one of Nixon's silent majority.

"Ever since the Weathermen split off from SDS," he said casually, "they've seemed more and more radical. Aren't they the ones who blew up that townhouse in New York last week?"

"Three of them died making bombs to blow up an Army base. So?"

Mick shrugged. "Too far out to me. Those soldiers are American too."

"Dennis," Brian looked at him entreatingly, "what do you think those *soldiers* will do when they get to Vietnam? They're going to kill people, murder civilians like in My Lai."

"C'mon, Brian, that may have been an aberration."

Brian stood disgustedly wiping sand from his hands. "I can't *believe* you. How many other civilian massacres do you need? You're smart and you care about people, but you just don't get it: we need a revolution *here*, because it's the only way to stop this war."

Mick looked at him. "And you think the Weathermen are going to do it."

"Maybe. Maybe not. But I'm ready to join up. We've tried non-violent protests for years. We've marched and petitioned and voted and begged. I got hit on the head at Berkeley and beaten by federal marshals in Washington. The guys in power are happy to have us protest because they know that doesn't stop a thing. What stops things is violence against *them*. They're cowards—good at dealing death to others but afraid of it themselves. What do you think Nixon, Reagan and Johnson did in World War Two? They sat it out, while hundreds of thousands of guys died on Pacific beaches and in Europe..."

Mick thought of Troy's dad, of his own father in the carnage of Tarawa.

Brian spat angrily. "I've tried to work for peace," he said almost tearfully. "But I can't take it anymore. Either you're part of the solution, or you're part of the problem." As Brian walked away Mick sensed he'd lost another friend because he couldn't explain who he was. He started to run after him, to tell him the truth. But wasn't that just putting another burden on Brian? And increasing his own risk too?

I hate this war. But I can't kill other Americans to stop it.

How could he tell Brian he'd known Diana Oughton, the girl

haunted by napalm, one of the three Weathermen who'd just been blown up in the Greenwich Village townhouse?

A LOVELY GIRL with a warm soul who included everyone in her kindness and cheerful smile. He'd met her at that conference in Chicago where a black activist had blamed the Jews for black problems, and where Mick had finally given up hope of uniting black and anti-war groups.

After the Greenwich Village explosion, the police had found the tip of a little finger and identified it as hers. Her sweet smile, silken hair, lovely body and magnificent mind, her caring for others, had been vaporized.

"As if she'd been hit by napalm," Daisy said.

"I'VE BEEN TALKING TO THE FBI," Lou Graziano said. "They say you come in, maybe they cut your time. To seven years maybe, instead of ten."

Mick tried to imagine it. When he got out he'd be thirty-three. "I'd go crazy."

"Lotsa guys do seven years and come out fine. It's character-building."

IT WAS A SUNNY MONDAY AFTERNOON. Mick had taken a three-day weekend and was lying in bed with Daisy while she read Ovid aloud, translating as she went, *"Thrill, woman, to your depths with passion, that both may take more pleasure in the act."*

"He's saying when a woman's really turned on, that turns the guy on even more?"

She sat up, curling her toes. "I always wanted to write a book on pleasure."

He loved to watch her cunt, soft, golden and hairy, when she sat like this, arms loosely across her knees. "A book?"

"On what it does for us. Where it comes from, what it is."

"Isn't it the same as *if it feels good do it?* Pleasure's how you know what you want."

"And if something feels bad, *don't* do it."

"But if you run into a burning building to save a child, getting burned feels bad."

"But letting the child die feels even worse." She traced the scars across his shoulders and ribs, her breast against his arm. The way he risked his life with such casual abandon terrified her sometimes. *I've been too much of a scientist. Expecting causal encounters. Newtonian. Foolish.* She fingertipped a bit of fuzz out of his navel. *How beautiful he is, but he doesn't care. Doesn't even notice.*

A trace of sperm had dried across his belly, sticky. *How funny,* she thought, *this is us. This and the mysterious eggs inside me. Seed of the universe. It's this we should pray to, not some damn cross.*

Someone was banging on the door. "Don't answer," Mick said.

She slipped into her kimono, glanced out the window. "It's Jack."

Mick felt an instant's relief, realized he'd feared it might be the FBI.

Jack had his usual home-roll hanging from his lips. His face was grim; Mick feared he'd had another fight with Gillian.

"National Guard just shot four students in a peace demonstration, Kent State University. Wounded a lot more."

Daisy stared at him. "Kent State?"

"That's where she went," Mick said. "Undergrad."

"Oh Jesus." Jack took her hand. "I'm sorry."

She stood. "How can they? How *can* they?"

"They were demonstrating against Nixon's invasion of Cambodia," Jack said.

"It's time." Mick stood. "The revolution." He felt fury, sorrow, fear and fierce determination. No way to know how it would develop, but this would start the Revolution. He might die, people he cared about would die, but now it had to come.

"They were just standing there," Jack said. "When the Guard opened fire. Some of them were just walking to class."

They went with Daisy to the pay phone outside Smiley's so she could call her former college adviser. How strange to stand there in the sunlight, the beautiful lagoon in front of them and the magnificent hills beyond, Daisy with tears down her face, saying into the telephone, "But why? No reason, just did it?"

They walked back to the house. Gulls were rising and falling over the waves, the sun was bright, the air full of flowers. "He says all the kids were good students. One of the boys killed was in ROTC. One of the girls killed, Alison Krause, was photographed yesterday putting a flower in a soldier's gun barrel. That's the kind of protest it was."

"Nixon says the kids were bums," Jack said. "That was his word."

Jack came in and they talked for a few minutes, the next steps. Mick had a sense of the revolution starting: there would be payback for this, but how?

That night he lay for hours beside Daisy, his mind spinning with fears and solutions. Where to start? The government was so big, so powerful and omnipresent, what acts against it could make a difference?

Somewhere tonight the families and friends of those Kent State students were mourning; elsewhere those of soldiers dead in Vietnam, and elsewhere the endless Vietnamese families mourning their dead. How was more killing going to make it better? Sure, the ones behind the war deserved to die, the Johnsons, Nixons, Rusks, Westmorelands and all the other war criminals, but how to kill them without bringing down apocalypse on everyone else?

But as the days passed it became clear nothing would change. A government that was happily killing thousands of its young men across the sea had, apparently, no qualms about killing a few more kids at home. There were of course the furious editorials and congressional fussings, but after all, hadn't the students provoked the Guardsmen and couldn't you say it had been an accident?

The leviathan of middle-class America barely took notice. The Gallup Poll reported that 58 per cent of Americans blamed the students, and only 11 per cent the National Guard. And in the colonnades of power there were no doubt many hearty chuckles: *young bastards got what they deserved.*

Across the United States over nine hundred college campuses were shut by strikes and demonstrations, and on May 9 over a hundred thousand people demonstrated in Washington against the massacre. President Nixon escaped to Camp David while the 82nd Airborne was called out to confront the demonstrators.

A few days later police killed two students and wounded twelve more at a peace demonstration at Jackson State College in Mississippi, but these were blacks so the fuss was minor. And the war rolled on; the United States Air Force expanded the carpet bombing of Cambodia, and to Mick it was clear that the country did not see itself as evil, nor its actions wrong.

In sum, there was no hope of stopping the war.

NOT THAT SOME SENATORS didn't try. In the summer of 1970 Oregon Republican Mark Hatfield and South Dakota Democrat George McGovern co-authored an amendment requiring the US to cease all military actions in Vietnam by the end of 1970 and withdraw all its forces by June 1971.

One bright afternoon in early September as Jack and Mick were framing an addition to a house on the Mesa, Jack turned up the radio, calling, "Listen to this." Mick unbuckled his tool belt and sat on a sawhorse. "It's a Senate debate," Jack added. "McGovern, talking about Vietnam."

"Every Senator in this chamber," McGovern told his fellow Senators, *"is partly responsible for sending fifty thousand young Americans to an early grave. This chamber reeks of blood.*

"Every Senator here is partly responsible for the human wreckage at Walter Reed and Bethesda Naval and all across our land: young men without legs, or arms, or genitals, or faces or hopes.

"There are not very many of these blasted and broken boys who think this war is a glorious adventure. Do not talk to them about bugging out, or national honor, or courage. It does not take any courage at all for a

Congressman or Senator or President to wrap himself in the flag and say we are staying in Vietnam, because it is not our blood that is being shed."

"Holy shit," Jack said. "The man speaks the truth."

"Despite Senator McGovern's powerful critique of the war," the announcer went on, "under pressure from the Nixon Administration the Senate today easily defeated the measure."

Jack looked at Mick bleakly. "I'll be dead before this war ends."

It didn't matter, Mick realized, whether the State was wrong or right, when it was threatened it would defend itself. As in the failed Paris revolution of '68, if protest against the State becomes serious, the State will turn violent. The State's greatest and most entrenched interest is always and only to defend and perpetuate itself.

The State is not the sum of the citizens. It is just the State. If the citizens get in its way it will crush them.

When *Life* published the photos of beaten and emaciated Vietnamese prisoners chained in tiny cages at the US prison on Con Son Island, the State didn't flinch: "Those prisoners are war criminals," insisted a Nixon spokesman. But to the rest of the world America had descended to just one step above the Gestapo.

"LIFE CAN BE SO PAINFUL," Ginnie said. "Sometimes more than we can stand. But we go forward."

It would be easier, Tara thought, with smack. What they made morphine for: to reduce pain. But since the band had died, she hadn't done any. Joan of Arc would be proud of her. Maybe she could call Joan. That was part of life going forward, like Ginnie said.

"Okay," Ginnie swished her ice cubes in the remnants of her Benedictine, "here's what you have to do—"

Tara *was* going forward, even if she didn't want to. How awful to admit that the band had ceased to be people, had become the dead. As if they had always been only part of her imagination. Tara looked at Ginnie. "What's that?"

Ginnie went to Tara's kitchen and came back with the Benedictine bottle. "As of right this minute," she patted Tara's hand, filled their glasses. "As of right now, darling, you start planning your solo career—"

"Ginnie, they're hardly in the ground."

"It's been six weeks, sweetheart. You locked in this house."

"I don't care about singing. I don't care about music. Anything."

"Of course not. I didn't say that. I said it's time to start living again."

She had been thinking that, Tara realized. "I can't sing on my own."

"They have them, these, what, studio musicians? You make your own band. But from now on you're Tara O'Brien. All by yourself."

Tara saw Sybil; Sybil nodded, turned away. "I don't know...I can't do it."

"And people will love you even more. Because you survived this. And kept on giving them the gift of music."

"AL LOWENSTEIN'S JUST REVEALED IT!" Daisy said, held open a page of *The San Francisco Examiner*. "The pathologist who did the report on President Kennedy's body after he was shot? Said he got hit by three bullets. Two from the back, but another from the front."

"So there *was* another shooter," Mick nodded. "Beside Oswald."

"Lowenstein thinks it was ordered by Allen Dulles, the CIA head."

"Because Kennedy'd fired him, opposed the Bay of Pigs?"

"The same Allen Dulles they put on the Warren Commission, that was set up to investigate the whole thing? It's absolutely evil."

"If you want to hide a crime, what better way to do it?" The whole idea made Mick's insides melt. Was the truth going to be buried? Forever?

"Al wants to reopen the investigation. Tie it in with Bobby's assassination, which he thinks, based on evidence, was CIA too." To think of Bobby gave Daisy a stab of heartache. "Mick!" she grabbed his arm. "We have to tell Al he shouldn't!"

Mick thought of the CIA killer, the tall blond man, who'd been in the background when Bobby got shot. "What, try to uncover it? He should."

She turned away, shook her head. "It will just get him killed too."

"Al's a member of Congress. No one's going to shoot him."

She looked at him in disbelief. "Wait and see."

THE SENATE TRIED TO STOP THE WAR AGAIN. An amendment introduced by Republican Senator John Cooper of Kentucky and Democrat Frank Church of Idaho, both World War Two combat veterans, would halt US air attacks against Cambodia, end funding for US troops in Laos and Cambodia, and restrain US backing for South Vietnamese troops outside South Vietnam.

Astonishingly it passed the Senate but was defeated in the House after Nixon lobbied intensively against it. Determined to keep the war alive, Nixon fought even the amendment's watered-down versions. Though it finally passed both houses in December, at this point it contained only minor restrictions on the war. The US carpet bombing of Cambodia, christened Operation Freedom Deal, continued unabated.

"All year long," Mick said to Daisy, "these politicians have been debating this bill. In the meantime how many thousands of young Americans have been killed? How many ruined for life? How many hundreds of thousands of Vietnamese, Cambodians and Laotians? And look what we've got after a year of speeches and negotiations: a minimal reduction of air operations. That's not going to stop this war."

The truth was that the government was controlled by evil men who intentionally did great harm. What some of our generals and politicians were doing in Southeast Asia would've gotten them hung at Nuremberg. There was no way to stop or diminish it; the best one could do was become invisible so it didn't catch you too. Learn to live with it.

But if you didn't defend your liberty yourself, how could you expect someone else to do it? The kid who didn't want to go to Vietnam but let himself be drafted and then killed or crippled never realized he'd had the freedom to refuse, or didn't dare to use it, preferred to risk death rather than stand up for himself.

The question really came down to freedom. If you were willing to fight, and perhaps die, for America, it was to defend it. What did you want to defend? Freedom. And what did you lose when you went to war? Freedom. And maybe your life—the ultimate loss of freedom.

WAS FREEDOM really, Tara wondered, what Kris Kristofferson said,

> *just another word for nothin left to lose,*
> *Nothin' ain't worth nothin' but it's free.*
> *Feelin good was easy, Lord, when Bobby sang the blues*
> *And buddy, that was good enough for me...*

In four lines he'd brilliantly distilled a great philosophical truth. The first two described the human condition; the second two answered: Yes, we live in a world where the only meaning is nothing, but love and beauty are good enough for me.

Four of the finest lines in poetry, for their resolution of a timeless question, and for the power of love, loss and spirit that flowed from them.

She had long ago given up the hope of being like Janis, like Gracie. Or in a different way like Baez or Buffy Sainte-Marie. They were more touched by the gods; hard as she tried, she couldn't get there.

What *was* she, anyway? *I'm someone who loves music, that's all. Who wants to offer it to you so it can touch you as deeply as it does me.*

Just sing the truth.

19

STANDARD OIL

A GREASY STENCH woke Mick. His eyes and throat stung. He slid from bed trying not to wake Daisy and went outside. Beyond the deck the lagoon gleamed dully in the cold January dawn; on the long far curve of Stinson Beach the golden sands were black as a parking lot.

Jack's blue Econoline came clattering up to the boathouse. "You see this shit!" he yelled.

Mick stared stunned and hopeless at the ocean laced with oily rollers, patched by cloud shadows and speckled with white dots of birds that could not fly. "It'll kill everything. Ruin the lagoon, wreck the Pacific flyway...the birds...the seals..."

"Two Standard Oil tankers collided, under the Golden Gate." Jack tugged hair from his face. "A million gallons. Clint wants to build a boom, try to keep it out of the lagoon."

Mick imagined the lagoon black, dead. "It'll never work. The tide through the channel's insane, the waves."

"He's got his derrick truck and lots of logs. Grab your tools, meet us at the end of the Channel—"

Mick thought of the press, the police. "Have to wake Daisy."

"Tell her we need her." Jack jumped into the Ford; the starter scratched and caught; the differential clunked as he dropped it into reverse, bald tires slithering. *How evil,* Mick thought, *that stupid contraption's killing the world.*

Inside the house dawn light gilded Daisy's gold-auburn hair and naked shoulder, her lovely face in profile, simple and discreet, long lashes shut. How different the world had been just minutes ago. "Hey you," he nudged her. "Hey you, wake up."

The lagoon grew golden with sunrise. Even a mile away he could see the white flecks of great egrets and snowy egrets, the gray specks of blue herons and smaller darker shapes of night herons and green-backed herons, the clouds of ducks, scaups, sandpipers, curlews, coots, pelicans, dunlins, stilts, bitterns, plovers, terns, teal, grebes, loons and so many others the oil would soon trap, once the tide changed and the oil poured into the lagoon.

Far out to sea the tall rollers gleamed darkly; to the south the buildings of San Francisco shimmered like white marble. The beach stank, black and strewn with oily seaweed. In a tar pool a loon called mournfully, frantically evading a waist-deep woman trying to bring it ashore. Flocks of ducks, grebes, pelicans, gulls, terns and cormorants struggled on the slick waves, crying high painful screams and uselessly flapping oil-thick wings.

The sand once white as salt where children played in day and people made love at night now stuck to their shoes, acrid and tarry, covered with dead fish, crabs, and birds. Up and down the beach people were carrying oil-soaked birds into town.

"We always get what we pay for, don't we," Daisy said.

"It's the birds who are paying—"

"The way they always do. That everything pays for what we do."

He felt numb, worse than anger. "I hate the human race."

"Cops'll be here," she said in the way she had like Troy of echoing his thoughts. "TV cameras. Somebody could recognize you."

He could go to Leavenworth for trying to save the lagoon. But it was already too late to save it.

AT THE LAGOON MOUTH the fog had rolled in. Clint's truck, loaded with logs, had backed down on the sand. Jack, his woven cap atop his tousled hair and another home-roll between his lips, was drawing diagrams in the sand with Clint and Head. "If we put the boom here," Clint said, "tie off the cables, use nets of straw to soak up oil...maybe we can block most of it..."

"Have to pick the least turbulent place in the channel," Head said, "to bury our deadmen to secure the cables..."

"Only place to bury deadmen," Mick said, "is where a Cat can get in."

"The rest of the pits we dig by hand," Head said. "You saw town? Jammed with people from all over Marin, come to help. Hundreds more every hour."

"Journalists too," Jack said. "From SF, LA, back east, Europe, everywhere—"

"Why weren't they covering this *before?*" Head yanked at his long hair and shoved it down his collar. "Doing stories about how dangerous tankers are and how we need to improve their navigation equipment? Who needs these journalist assholes now!"

Ted Lacey, round-faced and friendly in a blue down vest and white hardhat, had come from Standard Oil. "We'll get the oil out of the lagoon, boys, best as we can."

"We don't want the oil to get *in*," Clint said.

"Be an act of God to stop it—"

"If your God allowed this," Clint said quietly, "He should be shot." Black-bearded with long pony-tailed hair, and dressed in a torn gray sweatshirt, tar-stained jeans and leather work boots, he stood a half-foot smaller than Ted. "To stop your oil from destroying the lagoon what we'll need is not God but thirty-two telephone poles and five thousand feet of one-inch braided steel cable and two truckloads of two-by-twelves and two-by-sixes and three crates of spikes and nails and four truckloads of baled straw. Or hay if you can't find straw—"

"And where do you suppose—"

"—And two Cats to dig pits to anchor deadmen. And an amphibious duck—I know where you can get one in Stinson—to ferry supplies back and forth, and lots of tall lights with generators. So we can work all night—"

Ted shook his head. "It won't work, son."

"It won't work if you don't get the stuff."

"I'm an engineer. And I tell you we just *can't* get it."

"Tide's out for seven more hours. We'll need the boom in place by three hours after it changes. That's when it'll start to flow into the lagoon. With all your oil."

"We can't pull it all together that fast, son. I'll make some calls but..."

They watched Ted walk toward the line of people waiting at the phone booth outside Smiley's. "Asshole," Head commented.

"Call Curt at Point Reyes Lumber," Clint said. "Tell him Standard Oil wants five thousand board feet of Doug fir Grade Two construction, all the dimensions we wrote out."

"He won't take my word."

"He has questions let him talk to Ted Lacey. That'll be me. And ask him who has telephone poles, does he have any cable—"

"Have to get that from Eagle Metal Supply in San Marin," Jack said.

"Can you do that? Tell them Standard Oil needs it right away. A hundred bucks extra if they get it here by three-thirty."

KLIEG LIGHTS turned the sea black and faces to bone, sucked color from the truckloads of lumber stacked along the beach and the tawny bluffs above. The roaring generators and snarling Cats drowned the rumble of surf and yelling voices. Across the flattened sand, weary men, all young and long-haired, were dragging telephone poles down to the shore, carrying lumber, unrolling six-foot wooden spools of braided steel cable, driving spikes into the lumber framework built on the poles, unfurling nets and filling them with hay and roping them to the amphibious duck to tow into the channel.

There was a constant singsong rattle of hammers and the deep ring of the sledges driving home the bigger spikes. From time to time came the sharp *braack* of chainsaw as someone notched a pole, the sputter of a motorboat, or the whine of a pickup truck gunning its engine up the sandy ramp to town.

As each new boom section was towed into the channel Jack and Mick rode out in the duck and climbed over the side to connect it with the previous one, riding the two logs up and down in frigid thundering waves, the two logs swinging apart and crashing together and banging into the duck. Mick's legs grew numb and he feared losing grasp of the log, of a cable, of being washed off by the surf, smashed between two logs and sinking in his drenched clothes.

"Wind's shifted to northwest," Clint said. "That'll bring the storm." His eyes were shadowed with exhaustion, his face, burned by cold and wind, was drained of all expression. There was a cut under one eye that had bled long and hard and had dried to the color of black paint. Mick reached a numb hand into the water. It was slick, greasy.

Daisy came from the Bird Rescue Center on Wharf Road. "We're saving so few of them. What must it be like, floating for hours unable to fly, dying of oil poison, freezing because oil ruins their insulation, then drowning on the beach, snatched up by enemy beings, boxed inside in this hell of light and voices, that agony in the gut? You can see it in their eyes."

Before midnight it was done, a huge net stretched from pylons set in the sand in a long arc across the channel to Stinson Beach. A frigid breeze came down from the mountains. Mick and the others crouched exhausted round fires of two-by ends and driftwood, steam rising from their clothes, their chapped hands held out to the flames.

"We did it," someone said. "When the man said it couldn't be done."

"A cop wanted to arrest me," another said. "For endangering myself with oil."

"The world should be arrested for endangering itself with oil."

"Tell all these fucking journalists—"

A girl in a black pea jacket brought hot coffee and sandwiches from Smiley's that they ate dunking in the coffee. Kiley Farrell, a UC physicist building a sailboat on the Mesa, laboriously undid his laces with swollen hands, tugged off his squishy boots and extended soaked feet toward the fire. "Feels as good as fucking sex, this does."

"Is there any other kind of sex?" somebody said. "Oh yeah, there's oral, and—"

"*Life* is sex," Kiley said. "Every time I see a woman, that's sex."

"No wonder it's taking you so long to build that boat."

Kiley had a square, open, friendly face, a short brown mustache over a wide mouth, soft blue eyes, a thin nose and high forehead. "I've spent a lot of my life on the sea...it's been like the final frontier, the one place humans couldn't wreck. Now I see I was wrong— we're going to destroy the ocean too." He shook his head. "It's taken three years to build this sailboat, wanted to sail around the world...Why?"

"Why what?" Head said.

"Why do we do this to the world?"

"You're burned out, brother." Head squeezed Kiley's shoulder. "We all are."

"I've worked so hard, we all work so hard, to try to protect the earth..." Kiley's voice trailed off in weariness and the incipient negativism that weariness fed, the feeling of can anything, anything at all be worth this, this effort?

Mick turned his back to the fire letting its heat soak into his sodden coat, looked at the boom and smiled. What we can do if we try.

If we can't make a better world maybe we can at least save some of this one.

THE STORM STARTED after midnight. Gray mountainous waves came rolling all the way across the Pacific, and here was the first place they hit. He could hear them booming far out to sea, wind gnashing their tops, the nearing roar of rain. The sky grew low and black; wind flattened the fire and hailed them with oily sand.

The boom cables howled in the rising wind, strung round a pylon driven deep into the beach and linked to a deadman. The boom logs shuddered and banged as the sea surged, their straw nets whipping to and fro, the boom a huge sea snake writhing on the waves.

Wind slammed into Mick and the others nearly knocking them down and chasing burning branches down the beaches, a cliff of black water raced up the channel, the boom stretching like a slingshot, cables wailing and logs grinding. The next wave hit it and the next. The cable grew taut, hummed like a bowstring.

IT SNAPPED three hours later when ten-foot rollers crashed up the channel, and the boom floated up both sides of the channel in long bedraggled lines of oily straw.

Sleepless, soaked and frozen, they watched the oil slick race into the lagoon. "We need stronger cable," Clint told Ted Lacey. "Need to build a double boom of poles with a matrix between of two-by-fours and hog wire filled with straw."

Racing back and forth in the amphibious duck they rigged the old boom together, a night and day of searing labor in bitter wind and icy water, shivering constantly, clothes always soaked, hands unable to feel. When the new cable and timbers came, they rebuilt the boom and pulled it across. That night it broke in a different place and they tied it up again, a vast pool of tarry water rising behind it.

Standing exhausted on the sticky beach Mick watched the repaired boom ride the shuddering waves. He could not see the stars nor hear the sea or voices. Could not remember when he'd last slept. When he'd last been warm or dry. But always on the watch for cops, ducking the TV and newspaper cameras, keeping his face down.

He wondered where Daisy was then remembered she'd gone home for two hours' sleep after two straight days and nights at the bird rescue center.

"We're trying every cleanser on these birds," she'd said, "but they've already swallowed so much oil trying to clean themselves that almost none are going to make it."

The Cat driver slept over his controls, head on crossed forearms. Others huddled in the Navy duck drawn up on the sand. The klieg

Lights stared down with disembodied mantis eyes. Mick took a ten-inch spike from his pocket, placed it carefully in the middle of a two-by-twelve over a creosoted log and with a five-pound hammer drove it home.

"FANCY SEEING YOU HERE!" Johann the Dutch photographer, out of the past with his imperturbable grin. "First Athens, then the Sinai, now here!"

"Shut up!" Walking him down the beach Mick told him.

"Crazy, man, crazy!" Johann said. "You should get out."

"Yeah? Where to?"

"Anywhere in Europe, the Europeans hate the war. To them you're a hero."

"Fuck that."

"Remember those articles you did on the Six-Day War? They were good, man. Why not go to France, be a journalist?"

"I don't want to *be* anything, Johann."

"What's your new name, again?"

"Dennis Kurtz."

Johann laughed. "Doesn't fit you. Doesn't fit you at all."

"When you take pictures make sure I'm not in them."

"Hilarious they'd jail you ten years for opposing a war everybody knows is evil...It's like jailing somebody for trying to stop the crucifixion." Johann stared at the oily sea. "I was there, Vietnam, up north with the Marines. Some of the finest kids you'd ever meet. They all thought the war was wrong. Hated it. Were trapped and knew it."

"My brother was a Marine. He died near the DMZ."

"God, man I'm sorry. When?"

"Last summer."

"Christ I was there then. Maybe we—"

"Johann!" a woman's voice. "I need some pix!"

"Christ, that's Jennifer," Johann said. "Reporter from UPI Chicago. Perfect bitch."

Mick moved away. "Let's talk later. But remember, no pix of me."

"You don't exist." Johann waved, turned toward Jennifer. "You don't exist at all."

THE OIL in the sea lessened each day as more washed up on beaches and rocks. They strengthened the boom and added two more; some oil had reached the lagoon but not enough to destroy it, and was soaked up by boats patrolling with nets of straw. Thousands of people from all over northern California were cleaning the beaches, still finding newly oiled birds, scrubbing the rocks with straw that they gathered in burlap sacks and barrels, raking oil off the beaches, digging up the tarry sand.

"I was holding this arctic tern in my hand," Daisy said. "This little bird who flies all the way from Alaska to Antarctica and back every year, this little bird, and he was dying and looked at me—I can't explain what I saw in his eyes..."

"There's like sixty species dying, somebody told me."

"We've counted five species of grebes, five of terns, three of loons, six species of gulls, seven species of ducks, three species of cormorants, storm petrels, murres...The murres and scoters are getting it the worst, sanderlings, auklets, thousands of birds dying the most horrible deaths...We can't save them, no matter what we do they die..."

When the oil hit a week earlier everyone had been stunned, with no time to feel, only to fight back, days of exhausting work that left everyone numb. Now that they could pretend the worst was over, they were facing what they'd lost. The shock had worn off and they could feel the pain.

"We have to find a way to live without oil," Mick said to Clint.

Clint glanced at Mick's truck. "And what'd you come here in?"

"Same thing you burn in your fishing boat. That makes your nets."

"And what're we going to do when it runs out?"

Mick grinned. "Live the way we used to?"

Clint let out a hiss of exasperation. "Yeah. Sure."

ON THE WILD side of the San Andreas Fault, facing the sea, they had turned their backs on America, seeking to build their own vision of the individual and tribe. But America had hunted them down. As the weeks passed, they realized that it wasn't enough to live the right way and ignore the world, for the world would come and get you. You weren't safe, even here.

"We thought we could leave the world," Daisy said, elbows akimbo, hands in the pockets of her slim jeans, looking down the still-darkened beach. "But it won't leave us. At some point we have to make a stand."

"Then we lose our freedom. A cause is just another slavery to tie ourselves to."

"The lagoon almost got developed as a marina a few years ago but a few determined environmentalists saved it." She kicked a stone. "If we love places like this, we have to go to war with Standard Oil. With the American Way."

It was like Dave Mason's song,

Shouldn't have taken more than you gave
Then we wouldn't be in this mess today

"In the long run we can't win. You know that."

Her look bore in on him. "So, we give up? Run to the next place and stay there till *it* gets attacked?"

He turned from the stained, empty beach. "Nirvana's always getting wrecked."

"So? Life's in an endless war with death. Hunted by death's henchmen—the generals, politicians, oil men, developers, murderers and priests—by death's pathological hatred of life. Someday death'll win and there'll *be* no more day, no more life, just eternal night...So what? So as long as we're alive we have to fight for life."

233

"That's easy for you to say. Everything's a social experiment. Trying out life."

"And you?"

"I *know* what I want."

"And *I* don't?"

"That's bullshit what I just said. You're not *trying out life*. I love you because you *are* so deeply alive—no, that's not why I love you, I just love you." He was angry at himself for almost crying. "You make me so goddamn happy..."

She wrapped him in warm arms. "It's been so awful. Since the spill..."

"The smell will go away, the beach will get better, I'll keep working with Jack till summer and you've finished your thesis—"

"Then we'll go to Mexico, live on the beach at Playa del Carmen, it's so lovely, nothing but a few fishing huts..."

"I don't care where I am if I'm with you." He kissed the fragrant top of her head where the lovely auburn strands parted, tensed at hearing Jack's Econoline. It choked and died; Jack shouldered the truck's door open and eased out avoiding the loose springs in the seat, tugged his wool cap tighter on his dangling curls, shook ashes from the home-roll hanging over his beard, hitched up his jeans and sauntered over.

"Not another damn spill?" Mick said.

Jack pulled a tobacco packet from his shirt pocket and rolled a cigarette to replace the stub he'd just tossed. He licked it shut and stuck it between his lips, squinting at Mick as he lit it. "Was a guy around town today showing photos of you. Wanted to know has anybody seen you."

20

STAIRWAY TO HEAVEN

"**THEY'LL BE WATCHING** for your truck," Jack said. "I'll give you my van. It'll throw them off the track for a while."

Mick shook his head. "And get you into trouble."

"No way. I didn't know you were a fuckin draft resister. Or I would've turned you in right away."

"Me too," Daisy said, eyes glistening.

"We'll write something up for the DMV. A bill of sale." Jack pulled a pen from his pocket, "Daisy, you got some paper?"

He finished writing two copies, one sentence each, and they signed them. Jack glanced out the window. "Time for you to get going."

Mick gathered up his sleeping bag, backpack and other gear and threw it all into the Econoline. Daisy was packing too. He held her arm. "If you leave with me, you're aiding a fugitive. That's a felony."

She yanked it away. "I don't care. I can say I never knew."

"You'll do five years. Maybe more than me."

"I'm not losing you again."

"Finish your thesis. I'll be back."

She looked at him, squinting against the light. "You can't make me."

"I've never wanted to *make* you do anything. But now you have to."

He ached for her, ached not to leave her, golden-haired against the

235

sun, slender, tall, brave and beautiful. "I've loved you nearly all my life." He tugged her fingers from his shirt. "But now I can't even call you."

She squeezed his hands. "How soon?"

"How soon what?"

"How soon you'll come back?"

"Not till it's safe. Till they're not following you."

"*Please* let me go too—"

He pulled away. "You don't know where I went. And now you know who I am you don't care."

SOUTH OF SALINAS he turned west toward the coastal mountains, keeping to small roads, thinking about Daisy, running without a plan, trying to make one but there were too many variables. Were they watching the borders? Did all the cops have his photos? If he got caught, could Lou Graziano get him some kind of bail? Could he get to Mexico and from there to France? Would he be safe *there*?

It was late at night, the moon basking on the western horizon. The road was thin and misty, following the hills. Fear was making his chest hollow and his heart ache. If they pulled him over, should he run? Would they shoot?

The steering wheel yanked from his hands as the front right tire blew spinning the van onto the soft shoulder and over the edge. It lurched upside down and the roof crushed in, the steering wheel smashing his chest. With a clatter and tinkle of metal and glass and the hiss of leaking fuel it stopped rolling and lay still.

The pain was awful. He couldn't see, pinned in the broken seat, tried to think, holding his breath against the hot gasoline stink.

He shoved his fingers down the seat to where it had collapsed and held him, squeezed against the crushed-in door but it would not open. Gas *drip drip dripped* against the engine, spattering and seething. He rolled the other way, bent hard against the seat back till it broke, squirmed out the ripped passenger door and crawled across the gully and lay in a little stream.

Far-off rumblings became cars passing on the road above. Time had passed; it was bright day, the sun hot. He rolled over and drank from the stream. If only Daisy were here. But there was some reason she couldn't be.

One by one he moved his limbs. Everything hurt but nothing seemed broken. Above the crumpled Econoline rose a rocky slope of madrone and black oak: from the road above it neither he nor the van could be seen. He could lie here till he died.

Even if he could walk there was no way to escape but by hitching or on foot. Which made him so much easier to catch. Weak from hunger, beat up, how far could he get? To where? He crawled into the van, shoved clothes, another pair of running shoes, a sleeping bag, tarp and cook kit into his backpack but could not find his wallet.

He dug through the brush around the van but the wallet wasn't there. He crawled back into the van and checked everywhere but couldn't find it. He scrambled hand over hand up the slope to the road but the wallet had disappeared. He slid back down and stumbled up the arroyo.

By nightfall the valley leveled and the oak brush gave way to rows of orchards in the moonlight. Far away a dog was baying. The trees drooped with fragrant apricots; he ate them till sickened then camped in a sandy side arroyo with a tendril of stream down the middle. The night smelled of sage and hot dry earth; the stars were bright. He drifted in and out of sleep, awakening, shifting sore limbs, remembering and drifting again, each time telling himself that to return to Daisy was to implicate her.

"*Arriba! Arriba!*" someone was calling, harsh and imperious. "*Y no verde!*" Mick sat up in shocking pain then remembered. A red sun was rising from the purple hills. He crawled to the edge of the scrub and saw people milling in the orchard by two stake-sided trucks. A few had climbed ladders into the trees.

He slept all day in the sun and that night ate apricots till he could stand no more, then took more back to his camp in the arroyo. Wild pig and deer prints crisscrossed its hard-packed sand. If he cut a willow pole and fire-hardened the point, could he kill one?

With no car there was nowhere to go except a city.

Nowhere to go without money. No way to *live* without money.

At dawn he went down to the orchard. The foreman was short and broad-shouldered with a long-eared, big-nosed flat Mayan face. "What you know pick?"

"Apples, back home in Wisconsin. Every fall. I pick fast."

The foreman glanced at his crew, mostly men, a few women, all Mexican except for one stooped black man. "Eighteen cents a bucket. No damage, no green, no stem."

The low fruit was easy to pull by handfuls into the bucket slung over his arm, just a quick twist of the wrist and the apricot came free, the bucket growing heavier as it filled. When it was rounded at the top he grabbed another and filled it and ran with both down the aisle of trees to the pile of Del Monte packing crates where the foreman punched two holes in his card. "Too slow!"

After picking the low fruit he climbed the ladder more. *"Arriba! Arriba!"* the foreman yelled. *Higher! Higher!* The highest branches were full of golden fruit ripening in the sun, fat and easy to reach. For a weary moment his gaze wandered over the long lawns of treetops down to a gentle green valley of iridescent irrigated lettuce then a dry riverbed and dust-hazy tan gray hills beyond. It seemed so peaceful.

The day grew hotter, the air thick with tan dust that clogged the throat and dried out the lungs. At noon the foreman called, *"Almuerzo!"*, and the others sat under the trees eating tortillas with beans and drinking water from metal jugs. "You have no things to eat?" called an old man in a straw sombrero.

"Not hungry." Mick smiled, patted his stomach. "Apricots."

The old man filled a tortilla with beans and handed it to him. *"Vemos que no tienes nada para comer,"* he said. "We see you have no food," a woman translated. "So we give food to you till Saturday. Then is pay."

He looked in awe at the little circle of wiry weary peasants, dark-faced and rough-handed in their worn khakis and jeans and torn cotton shirts and ragged sandals. For an instant in the hot still air and chirring cicadas he felt admitted into a sacred tribe—a moment of completeness, connection and understanding, the epiphany that they and he were one. "*Gracias. Mille gracias.*"

The old man spoke fast and the woman translated. "He says already you are learning Spanish. It will be easy for you."

That night they gave him a dish of beans and rice and two tortillas. After payday Saturday he rode on the back of a flatbed into Gonzales with five others. It was safe; he looked as Mexican as they—dirty worn clothes, dusty shoes, sun-darkened skin. Like them he bought food at a farmers' market, shocked to see himself in a Rexall window: narrow-faced, his long hair tangled and dirty. *They'll arrest you just for looking like this.* He bought a razor and scissors in a hardware store and shaved and cut his hair in the stream's reflection and dyed it red while swallows chittered in nests dug in the arroyo walls.

For two weeks he picked with them, thinking of Daisy, imagining what she was doing, wanting to go back to her and making himself stop thinking it, then realized he was thinking it again. They moved from one orchard to the next; he came back to the arroyo every night, weary, back aching, sticky-fingered hands sore from the heavy bucket's handle, the fatigue of always running, always picking too fast, never stopping to relax.

The first day he'd done only seventy-two buckets, thirteen dollars for ten hours of hard work in the hot sun. By the end he'd been picking a hundred fifty buckets a day, almost as good as some of the Mexicans, over twenty-five dollars.

Apricot season was over. They were going south to the peach orchards, and he didn't dare go with them. He'd saved a hundred thirty dollars. He couldn't go back to Daisy, but didn't want to do anything else.

THE GREEN-BLACK Los Padres mountains loomed above the southwest horizon, far from Highway 101 and its dangers. He hiked all day and the next, the land rising from brushy hills and dry arroyos to undulant grassy hills then to steep timbered ridges. That night he camped under a rocky overhang in the foothills and next day climbed higher, deeper into wilderness. Following a stream up a wide piney valley he reached a meadow of multicolored flowers and as the sun was setting built a fire and spread out his poncho and sleeping bag and cooked rice with canned tuna.

The water trickling down the meadow was delicious, the grass soft and fragrant, the stars countless and brilliant. Yet in the darkness he had never been so lonely, thought of dying in the Sahara, of shipwrecked sailors who had floated alone for weeks on tiny rafts—how many had vanished for the few who survived? Or climbers lost in a storm, soldiers cut off by the enemy. An injured deer surrounded by wolves. The loneliness of dying.

The thought of Daisy made his chest hollow and his heart ache. He saw her years from now, in a warm middle-aged marriage with a pipe-smoking professor. Is that what she wanted? *No, she wants to be with you*...But no woman waits ten years. By then he'd be just a pleasant memory. He saw her writhing ecstatically beneath another man, how soon and easy that would happen.

After a week of hiking he climbed a ridge with a distant view of the sea. Below, at the bottom of a steep timbered valley he saw a golden meadow and a stone shed with a rusty galvanized roof and a dirt road with a telephone wire across it.

The door was open, the shed empty. It had a warm resiny smell. Bees buzzed in the sun; a hawk screeched. A path led downstream past gardens then rhododendrons and pines to a paved courtyard shaded by two huge oaks, their roots pushing up the stones.

A large brass bell hung from a redwood post. A stone building with vines circling its small windows sat behind a stone wall. Other stone buildings followed the stream in the shade of alders and rhododendrons. A slender muscled man in a blue work shirt and jeans stepped from the building. "This's private here."

"Sorry. I've been hiking for days. Didn't know where I was."

"This's Tassajara. We're a retreat of San Francisco Zen Center." The man was not unfriendly, just distant, thirty-five maybe, a flat face and sandy crew cut. "From here it's forty miles by road to Carmel."

His eyelids rose. "You want a glass of water before you go? You look pretty dusty and tired."

"I've done at least twenty miles today, all up and down."

"Come to the zendo. I'll get you something."

The zendo was a screened porch at the back of the building with five pine plank tables and benches. The man went into the kitchen and came out with tea, a clay water jug, a loaf of rough dark bread, a bowl of peaches.

"This is so good," Mick said, trying not to eat too fast.

"I'm Chuck," the man said, offered his hand.

"I'm, uh, John."

Chuck raised his eyebrows. "John who?"

Mick's mind wouldn't work. "John Dillingham."

"Where'd you come from?"

"Been hiking and hitching south from Tahoe."

Two young guys in orange robes came in, bowed toward them, took two peaches from the bowl and left, one easing the screen door shut so it wouldn't slap.

"Anything out there," Chuck said, "you're getting away from?"

"Everything. Haven't you?"

Chuck shrugged. "Lots of good reasons to be here."

Downstream three men in jeans and t-shirts were working on a log bridge. Further down two others were shingling a hut roof, the noise of their hammers softened by the stream's chatter. "Lot of work to be done here," Chuck said as if following Mick's thoughts. "It was built a hundred years ago by Chinese laborers as a hot springs spa. People came by train from San Francisco to Salinas, then over the mountains in a stage coach." He smiled as if remembering. "I'd love to see it, see them, as if it were now..."

The decision came before Mick considered it. "I'm a carpenter. Can repair anything."

Chuck nodded as if he'd known. "So stay a couple days? See if you like us, the meditation and study? We won't hurt you."

They let him stay in a stone hut among others on both sides of the creek, all built of granite slabs with pine plank doors, handmade pine windows and pine shake roofs. Below his hut the path crossed the stream on a split log and vanished into the forest.

Mick sat on the edge of his hard bunk staring through the tiny window at the fading day, wondering what Daisy was doing. It was insane to be here but he could think of no better choice. And this kind of loneliness was something he'd just have to get used to.

AT FOUR A.M. the wake-up bell rang. The day began at four-thirty with *zazen*, meditation, sitting for two hours cross-legged in the cold *zendo*, the meditation hall.

The *zendo* had large double doors, small windows along the side, and a high roof. Inside was dark and incense-thick. There were pillows down both sides for sitting and a raised altar at the far end. When dawn came it filtered weakly through the little windows and glimmered palely on the adzed rafters and down on the oak floor.

After *zazen* came morning service then a breakfast of rice and green tea. Then an hour of private study of Buddhist doctrines, the *dharma*. At eleven the Teacher, a long-whiskered little man with a round Japanese face, conducted the *dharma* talk, a mix of lecture, questions, parables and riddles. Then came the noon service, an afternoon of work, a wash in the hot springs then the cold stream, a bland meal, *zazen* again till nine then lights out. One did not speak or make noise from evening *zazen* to noon the next day, other times as little as possible.

One had to carry with both hands one's *okesa*, *rakusus*, and *oryoki*, three nesting bowls with white wiping cloths, at eye level in the *zendo* and at heart level elsewhere. There were similar details for the types of robes to wear and what underneath, what socks on which days, what shoes were acceptable.

Before bathing one did three standing bows at the altar then recited *gatha*, the bath chant, silently. One stepped over the *zendo* threshold with the foot closest to the hinge side, took two steps and bowed in *gassho*, palms clasped and fingers pointing upward, arms paralleling the floor, to show thankfulness and reverence.

But when you entered the area behind the altar you had to bow in *shashu*, centering the left thumb tip in the palm of that hand and making a fist around it. Then, keeping elbows away from the body and forearms parallel to the ground, one covered it with the right hand. *What happy horseshit*, Mick decided, imagining how Daisy would laugh.

To either make or listen to music was forbidden, or to move quickly or make excess noise, to drink alcohol or use drugs. Nor were pets allowed—no contact with the animal world. Pleasure in any form was discouraged. "These rules," the Teacher said, "aren't to hem you in but strengthen your search for freedom. Freedom from suffering. From yes and no." But they seemed just like the inane rules in Catholic Mass defining the priest's hand motions, how he opened the Bible and where he put it, intricate pointless doctrine to ward off outsiders, create a cult of complexity.

"Does that mean God?" Mick asked out of frustration.

The Teacher had caramel-colored spots on the backs of his hands and his cheeks, dim old watery eyes, a wide smile on small teeth, a nearly shorn white-fringed skull. "The being or non-being of God is a question that can't be answered. Anyone who's sure God exists *or* that there is no God—anyone who says they *know* this—they're confusing what they know with what they believe."

"So why this ritual?"

"Zen is neither a religion nor a philosophy. It's a way of life. By following its strictures you purify the search for yourself. If you want to understand what life is, you must first understand yourself."

But the quiet, hunched students all seemed imprisoned in a doctrine that promised to make them free, all inhabiting a non-sensory, passionless world. A time capsule of total idiocy buried at the bottom of the sea, more lonely than living in the mountains alone.

21

THE FATE OF AMERICA

"**B**UDDHA TELLS US that the secret of health for both mind and body is not to mourn for the past, or worry about the future, or anticipate troubles," Chuck said, "but to live in the present moment wisely and earnestly.

"I was an Air Force pilot in Japan," he continued. "That's how I got to know Buddhism. Then Vietnam, flying F-104s out of Danang. After that I worked in Bakersfield and kept reading everything on Buddhism, looking for answers to Nam and all the other things I couldn't understand."

"Did you find answers to Nam?"

"Everyone finds his own."

"What about the people dying there?"

"You learn all paths are the same." Chuck pointed. "Here's your compost heap."

It was a mound ten feet in diameter and three feet high enclosed in chicken wire staked to steel pipes driven into the ground. "As you can see it's full," Chuck said. "Pull the posts out letting the wire stay, and drive the posts into the ground over here, where we'll make a new compost heap and cover this one with hay and tarps to decompose."

The ground was rocky; after a few inches the three-quarter-inch pipe would drive no further, its top mushrooming under the sledge. One by one Mick dug the rocks out and threw them aside till the pipes sank two feet, solid.

By the old compost pile a jar hung from a pole, filled with bumbling buzzing flies and angry yellowjackets that could get in through a hole in the lid but not out. He unscrewed the jar's lid, let out the flies and yellowjackets, and dumped the dead ones.

"Don't do that!" a student named Timothy came running, tugging his orange gown up from his skinny sandals.

"What's this about the sacredness of life if you're killing them for no reason?"

"They lay eggs in the compost. People could get stung..."

Mick grinned, swinging the sledge. "Who was here first? You or them?"

Timothy smiled faintly. "That's true for all of us, isn't it?"

IN ANCIENT TIMES, said the Teacher, there was a young man named Siddhartha Gautama who left his wealthy, privileged existence and became a wandering ascetic, trying to understand the reasons for death and human suffering. After years of meditation, he concluded that suffering is caused by desire, and to suppress desire, to not *want* anything, leads to *Nirvana*.

Humans, the Teacher added, are subject to natural laws from which there is no escape or alteration; they are born and die and are reborn many times without being able to free themselves from this cycle. But by adhering to basic moral virtues such as honesty, charity, justice and temperance, they can be reborn in a higher existence. Ignoring these virtues, however, leads to *Naraka*, hot or cold hells, and rebirth in a lower existence.

"But how do you know?" Mick said.

"Because it makes sense," a student named Tony answered. "And that supreme joy, *Nirvana* or unconscious existence, is reached by the suppression of all passions and desires, in essence the total dissolution of oneself in the infinite."

As always Mick thought of Daisy, that he would never suppress the desire to be with her. "But didn't even Gautama—Buddha—condemn withdrawing from the world?"

Tall and slightly stooped, Tony had a long patient face, small chin and receding curly hair. "Out in the world there's so many ways to avoid seeing inside yourself—people, work, books, television, movies, radio, telephones, traffic...Daily pleasures, responsibilities and other distractions."

"Are you going back to the world?"

Tony clasped his knobby knees in pale slender hands. "I've been here four years. Next year I'll go back. But for the rest of my life, I will have had this, learned to know myself and what is real. What's under the surface of things, the distractions...The great truth connecting all things."

"You can do that with drugs, mountain climbing—"

Tony tut-tutted. "Drugs are too easy. We learn only from what's difficult."

Mick's back ached from sitting cross-legged. He stood rubbing and stretching it. "You see," Tony said, "there you are turning away. Not facing."

"I stood because my back hurts."

"Your back hurts because you don't want to face yourself."

Rubbing his back Mick grinned down at him. "Bullshit."

"It's true," Tony said. "To understand the interwoven complexity of the universe, its luminous infinite completeness, this path of clear light, we first must learn not to hide from ourselves. Discard all the projections we make on the world—what we love and hate, what makes us happy or sad, what we believe is good and bad—for these are all mirages, mirrors of our own internal confusion, born in what's happened to us in the past and our subconscious feelings. Only after diligent meditation can we perceive the world as it truly is, without illusion. Not shaded by what we desire or imagine it to be..."

He sat back, hands on knees. "That is Awakening. And when death does come we are ready, for we are already on the path of clear light."

"That's a kind of acid—"

"Acid?"

Mick grinned. "LSD. You can see without illusion, the path of clear light..."

Tony smiled. "You're making fun of me."

"You should try it, compare it to meditation."

"As I said, nothing comes easy."

"Think what you just said."

"I did."

Mick thought of Virgin Peak, the Sahara. "Sometimes we're most aware of ourselves in danger, in total effort."

"Maybe danger can force us to live perfectly. When anything less will kill us."

"How do we know this enlightened state isn't imaginary too?"

The question seemed to stun Tony. Mick thought how a good Christian would react: think up answers, treat it as a test of faith.

"If your enlightened state is imaginary, it isn't enlightened." Tony stood gathering his robes around him. "It's by submission to *dharma* that we free ourselves."

Feeling cheated somehow, Mick made the obligatory bow and left. To find out who we are, seek the meaning of life, was the most important task, but was doctrine how to get there? Wasn't it the same patent medicine served up by all faiths? Wasn't it better to find your way without the false, beguiling crutch of faith?

There were so many ways to lose your freedom. Religion, work, war, possessions. For each possession also possessed *you*. Humans spent most of their time in the pursuit and maintenance of possessions, worked at jobs they hated to have shiny cars and nice houses, then spent most of their free time maintaining them, fixing up the house, washing the car on weekends, mowing the lawns, all the other tasks that kept them from living.

That day in the fifth grade he'd been right not to wear the clown suit. He smiled at the silly Zen robe, socks and shoes, and tossed them on the floor under the window.

FREEDOM could never be simply discarding one system for another. To go from the American Christian worldview to a Zen monastery's was simply changing one's jailer. The acolytes weeding the garden or prostrating themselves on the path were not free, were even more regimented than Troy's Marines.

Zen said to live without attachments. If your brother dies it makes no difference. But that was still too painful. What mantra would free him of Troy's death? If the object was to live without attachments, without people you love, why live? Who would he be without Daisy?

It was nearly time for noon service, then lunch in the porch by the stream, the quiet chewing of humans above the gay clatter of water, the breeze perfumed with pine.

No matter how detached you were, if Vietnam didn't break your heart, you weren't alive. Maybe that's what Buddhism was: not being alive. Being prepared for death by being dead in life.

These arguments kept going round and round in his mind. Wasn't freedom the absence of things you *had* to do? Freedom was wandering, not following orders; it was loving, not celibacy.

The value of meditation was clear: to sit still, mind focused on nothing, not wandering or preoccupied with some daily issue. How to renew the soul. But you could also renew your soul with drugs. Face to face. See the universe for what it was: endless and timeless, and you a brief cell, this earth and galaxy just moments in the enormity of time. The cold endless night where we're all headed.

Tassajara was like Troy's description of Parris Island without the violence. The regimented schedule, primitive discomfort, a doctrinal system to dominate individuality and submit one to a rote existence— to prove what? That we can be trained to believe and defend almost anything?

Soon he had to decide: go to Mexico or back to Daisy.

THE FATE OF AMERICA, he had to accept, was beyond his grasp. No matter how much he loved his country he could no longer help it. Would it survive the war, the calculated slaughter of millions, the loss of faith in a nation that once had been good? The revolutions Jefferson had anticipated would never come—already the country was too old, too arthritic to change. What would it become?

He had to see himself no longer as an American but as a human being, an outsider, not part of the herd, one of the long tradition of loners who value their own and others' lives, and the joy and beauty of living. Who are their own saviors, their own governments. The individual first and foremost is a free person, and when the herd tells him to die or to kill others he must first ask why, and decide for himself if it is justified.

And how sad it was that we humans could do so much, be so much. There was no reason we had to hate, murder and destroy.

"MOST PEOPLE," the Teacher said, "are imprisoned inside their minds. Driven by expectations of how life should be. By fears and hopes and opinions about the world and what will happen. Dissatisfied with how things are, this *expectation-mind* hopes for something else, or fears or worries and seeks other mental distractions.

"Zen teaches us to see these mind poisons when they enter our thoughts or emotions. We learn to follow them back to where they came from, and understand the pain or hunger that bred them. By living in that pain and hunger until it no longer has any effect on us, we dismiss these poisons from our lives.

"*Suffering follows expectations, judgments and evil thoughts*, the Buddha taught us, *as a cart's wheels follow the oxen that draw it*. So you see, living in that *expectation-mind* prevents us from being in the real world, in the magnificent beauty of life, from reaching *Satori*, enlightenment."

If he could only believe this, Mick thought later, it wouldn't be so bad without Daisy. He was driving a spike upward into a rafter, nailing the rafter to the ridgepole, not paying attention; the hammer smashed his thumb and he walked around the room swearing at the agonizing pain.

From another ladder Chuck watched him. "When that happens it's a clue."

Mick waved his throbbing hand. "*What's* a goddamn clue?"

"You hurt yourself because you weren't doing what you were doing."

"Bullshit." Mick cradled his thumb against his chest. But it *was* true —he'd been thinking the same old question: *Did he dare go back?* He hadn't focused on the spike and hammer: it *was* a clue. "You're right," he said crossly.

"Life's like a *koan*. Always teaching us to pay attention."

That night with his throbbing thumb held high he understood that life *is* a *koan*, a paradox. *Always teaching us to pay attention*. Just like Kierkegaard had said, the central question is *what should we do in life*, what shall we believe? Most people seemed to live without ever deeply asking these questions or living by the answers. And like Buddhism, Kierkegaard wanted to shake people up, make them realize how flimsy and irrelevant their surface lives were, so they could perhaps find a deeper, more meaningful path.

But that didn't mean it was the only solution. Or that there *was* a solution.

And it was almost a truism that the cause of sorrow is desire. If he didn't love Daisy so much, he wouldn't be so unhappy. If you want or care for nothing, then there's nothing to sorrow for. But desire also brings joy: to make love, to eat and drink happily and well, to lie in the sun, play music, or run up a mountain—all these are joy. What the Buddhists were doing was trading away joy to avoid sorrow.

What did *he* believe in? For an instant the world seemed to shift with the significance of the question. Hadn't his entire life been leading to this? He believed in love not solitude, in the body not denial. In music, food, wine, laughter and transitory happiness, in the woods, fields, mountains, oceans and lakes, in the joys of the sun.

Enlightenment was simply the shining of light, clarification. You could seek it in denial of the body, physical suffering that pretends the body's irrelevant. But true enlightenment was fulfillment of love, the body, desires, knowing that once lost they can never be recovered. As his mother had told him after she'd died, one day when he stood by her grave: *Live in the flesh.*

He felt a moment of great awareness, satisfaction and peace. *This* is who you are and how you should live. True, the world is illusion but a universal heart throbs beneath it. Live as intensely as you can, take care of others, do no harm. What greater code?

It had been two months since he left Daisy.

"To be in a hurry," the Teacher told him, "is a great waste of time."

He was straddling a hut wall and nailing another rafter in place when Chuck came up to him. "Can I speak to you for a minute?"

This was unusual, in the silent part of the day. Mick followed Chuck downstream past his hut across the split log into the trees. "I went to town today," Chuck said. "Tom Sweeney, the sheriff, sees me and I stop to say hi and he asks me *have I seen this guy, he was in Salinas recently,* and shows me a photo of you."

"That's nuts. No reason they'd want *me.*"

"He says there's a nationwide search for you. They say you crossed state lines to start a riot, that you're in conspiracies against the government."

"Some guy who looks like me?"

"So I'm in shock," Chuck said, "I said we don't get many visitors this time of year. The sheriff was trying to act friendly and open-minded, but he doesn't like religious weirdoes like us, particularly not his own countrymen espousing an Asian cult. He says let him know if I see or hear of you, and I realized I hadn't lied, I just hadn't answered his question."

Mick took a breath. "Thanks."

"If he's asking *me,* he'll ask others when they go to town...I can't prevent people from going to town...So sooner or later, probably sooner, they'll come for you."

"I'll leave tonight. After *zazen.*"

Chuck watched him. "Where to?"

Mick shook his head, thinking of Daisy, Mexico, many places. "Don't know."

"In the barn at the top of the meadow there's an old Simca. It runs okay, the plates are good." He dug into his pocket. "Registration's in the glove box. Here's the key."

Mick slid open the barn's wooden doors letting in beams of sunlight. It was a green four-door sedan covered with dust. It started on the second turn; he drove it into the sunlight and wiped dust off the windshield. He looked at Chuck. "I can't bring it back."

"I know. If needed, I can say you stole it."

"Why are you helping me? Why not let it slide?"

Chuck grinned. "Zen doesn't teach inaction. For that too is a choice."

22

PRISON CAMP

HE LEFT THE SIMCA on Bolinas Mesa and walked silently downtown. Daisy's lights were out. Parked beside her Karmann Ghia was a two-tone '57 Chevy with Arizona plates.

For a while he watched her hut for possible surveillance, but nothing moved either near or far away. He edged along the boathouse onto the deck, watching, seeing nothing.

There was a sound inside, a woman. Gasping. Moaning.

Daisy was in there fucking the guy who drove that Arizona Chevy.

He sat in the shadows of the lagoon edge, behind the boathouse. He should go in and beat the guy up. But he'd been gone two months, so she was fucking someone. So what? She'd still want to see him, missed him.

But wasn't this what *had* to happen? He had no right to mess up her life. If she stayed with him she'd lose her PhD, all the years of research, could go to prison. If he loved her, didn't he owe her what was best for her? He had to leave, make it on his own. Mexico.

He glanced at the lagoon one last time, memorizing its odor of tidewater muck, grass, fish and mollusk and the damp smell of the deck's worn redwood boards, remembering the many times he'd sat there with her.

You never realize when you're happy that it won't last.

He walked past the boathouse up to the street, took a last glance back at the lagoon. On its silvery moonlit surface something moving. A small boat.

A canoe. It came closer, pulled up to the boathouse. Daisy got out and slid the paddle quietly between the thwarts. He went down to her, his heart singing, body shaking.

"Daisy!" he whispered. "Daisy, it's me."

She jumped in surprise then rushed into his arms, hair damp from the lagoon, her hands cold. For a long time they stood just holding each other. "At night I can't sleep," she said. "I go out in the lagoon and think of you. Wonder where you are and if you're coming back."

He touched her cheek. "Of course I was coming back. I'll always come back."

She held his hand against her cheek. "Don't you ever leave me again."

"I can't stand it without you. We have to get away."

"They're watching me."

"Who's in the house?"

"Bethany, my old roommate from Kent State. She was with me in Mississippi. And her boyfriend Nate." She pulled closer. "They don't know about you."

"I want to see Tara, before I go."

"Two weeks ago I went to see her. I couldn't stand it, being without you, had to see someone who knew you. I didn't call or anything, just knocked on her door one night. Troy's mom Ginnie was there and Tara and I talked a few minutes and I left. I don't think anybody saw me."

"How was she?"

"Better than last time. She's talking to her agent about a tour by herself with backup studio musicians. Ginnie's staying with her and they seem to be close. Healing each other."

He tried to imagine this woman he'd never seen, this mother of his dead brother, Tara talking with her, confiding in her. Maybe he'd never known Tara, or loved her enough?

"She's been off heroin for six and a half months," Daisy said.

"Because of Troy's mom?"

"And the helicopter crash. And because of a nurse she met back in Detroit, during the riots. They talk all the time on the phone. Tara calls her Joan of Arc. And Tara's going to do an album, just her and studio musicians. *Revolution*, she wants to call it but RCA doesn't. Did you know they censor all their groups' songs? All the record companies do."

"What name do they want?"

"*Redemption.* Can you imagine?"

A car was moving along the narrow road on the far side of the lagoon, its headlights twisting and turning against the forested hills and flashing out across the water. "How soon can you be ready?"

"Fifteen minutes. I already sent all my books and stuff to my mom's." She kissed his hand, the side of his neck, his cheek. "I wanted to be ready."

The thought overwhelmed him, her waiting for him to come back, quietly keeping the faith. "We'll take the Simca to Berkeley, you try to find Tara and meet her someplace...I'll be watching. Then you and I vanish."

"If you don't get caught in Berkeley."

"Just a few minutes. If we're careful I won't get caught—"

THE INTERNATIONAL House of Pancakes sat alongside the Eastshore Freeway in the roar, rumble, dust and exhaust of trucks gearing down for the on-ramp, tire-whirring cars, taxis, buses and clattering motorcycles. Its front parking lot was jammed with cars and pickups, semis packed like sardines along the back. Sitting in an orange booth with a tasteless coffee getting cold on the sticky formica, he worried was this too dangerous, too public with so few exits? But like Modoc Jack had said, *You got to act normal.*

But nothing was normal any more. He leaned back in the booth trying to watch the parking lot without seeming to. He'd bought a *Chronicle,* but the news was boring and distracting, Nixon the war criminal planning to visit China, more drug busts in the Mission...He could only think of one thing anyway and that was being caught and doing time and losing Daisy.

A back page headline caught his eye: *Four Climbers in New Himalayan Ascent*:

Four New Zealand climbers have reached the top of Nepal's Mount Lhotse by a never-before ascended northwest face..."It was a beaut little hike," said veteran Himalayan climber Skip McDonald...

The huge deadly northwest face of Lhotse, vertical miles of rock and ice, a climb no one could make. His heart raced to think of Skip, this fine, caring and cheery friend. That Skip had succeeded was a good omen: *maybe I too can make it...*"Good on you, Mate," Skip would say. "Good on you."

"They paved paradise," the radio was singing, *"and put up a parking lot."* The green Simca pulled into the lot with two people in front and one in back. Daisy got out and Tara and a woman in the back, maybe Troy's mom. Mick went out to them and held Tara, tousle-haired, still musky with sleep. "You silly," he whispered, "you've still got your slippers on. You look so good. I've missed you so—"

She kissed him on the cheek, the forehead, holding his head in her hands. "Daisy said there's no time...Here's Ginnie Barden, Troy's—Daniel's—Mom."

She was a wide-faced, worn woman in her early fifties, reddish hair going gray above a high forehead. They sat in the pearly aura of the pancake house fluorescents, Mick and Tara holding hands and looking into each other's eyes and telling each other the same things, remembering the same things, and Mick kept watching the clock. It had been forty-five minutes and he was risking their freedom too, just like his.

"The danger," he said, "is Daisy'n me together. They'll be expecting it."

"They won't be looking for a little old lady from Pasadena," Ginnie said.

"You're from Cleveland," Tara smiled.

"Who won't be looking?" Mick said.

"The J. Edgar Hoovers. Didya know, he's swishier than a water-melon, that guy?"

"Hoover?"

"When I worked the HoJo's in Cleveland, didya know, a girl had the same shift as me, she told me."

"Ahh she made it up," Tara said. "How would she know?"

"He did it with her brother. He was that way too."

"I thought the FBI arrests homosexuals..." Daisy said.

"They do," Mick said. "That explains it..."

"Anyway," Ginnie tugged at her placemat, palmed her hair. "I'm drivin' you two to Canada."

Mick almost laughed. "When?"

"Then I'll drive back here. I already brought my suitcase."

"She did," Tara said.

"Nobody'll suspect a middle-aged lady from Cleveland of having two terrorists in her trunk."

"If we're going to do that," Daisy said. "I better go pee."

"When you get back here," Mick said to Tara, "can you guys drive the Simca down to Tassajara? And leave it with Chuck?"

"Then I'm coming to Paris," she said, "soon as you get there..."

"YOU HAVE SMELLY FEET," Daisy said. "And don't you dare fart."

It was worse than Skull Cave, the Simca's trunk. Jammed together, the air stinking of gasoline from the Simca's leaky tank and exhaust from its bad muffler, the car's differential howling and its unbalanced tires hissing and the metal floor bouncing them up and down on every bump.

And not knowing where you were. Ginnie had stopped for gas in Ukiah at noon and again in Eureka after dark and then drove up a logging road so they could get out and stumble around and piss and eat something. It was near midnight when she pulled into a motel then drove to a room at the back of the building and a few minutes later came out and opened the trunk; as they shuffled quickly into the room Mick realized they were in Gasquet, an hour's drive from Earthsoul, and how strange and far ago that was.

By noon they had passed Portland. It was getting dark when Ginnie pulled onto a jouncy dirt road, bounced along it a few minutes, stopped and opened the trunk. Mick waited for Daisy to squeeze out, then followed. "My ears are ringing," Daisy said.

"That's the bells of freedom," Ginnie joked. "Not far now."

It was a damp country road, no lights, a salty smell of sea. "Where are we?"

"Northern Washington. A mile from the border. Over there's railroad tracks heading straight north. There's no lights and no fence. You should be able to just walk across."

Other side of the line, Mick thought. *Freedom.* He hugged Ginnie. "You saved us."

She squeezed him. "Send me a postcard from Paris. Always wanted to go there."

FLYING OVER THE POLE from Vancouver to Paris he couldn't sleep; leaving his country was a horrendous amputation. Even though he'd left it many times before, it was always to return, and now he couldn't.

But in another way he was free, out from under the threat of a decade in jail. The American government wouldn't attempt to extradite or snatch him in France, not with the French already sheltering thousands of AWOL American soldiers and draft resisters.

He would be free, free every day to breathe without fear, without hiding, without expecting every happy moment to be followed by capture.

He thought of other plane rides—back from Bali with two million deaths behind him, making love with Lily on the Air France 707 to Paris, another flight from Cairo with the Sinai dust in his throat and the countless deaths in his heart, the heady optimism of the trip to California to help Bobby and the sorrowed return, Troy's two flights to Danang and the single one home.

He would never cease missing Troy. Troy had been like rebar uniting them, a flash of lightning that made them see themselves and how perilously alone they were. Troy had given them hope, for seeing how powerfully he was smitten by sorrow and solitude, how could they not be grateful for their own fates?

He and Troy had started on the path together, riding the train to Florida but never got there. If Mick could some day return, if the sentence against him was ever dropped, he and Daisy and Tara could go to Florida and say goodbye to Troy on a beach under the palm trees, because maybe that's where he would be.

And go back to Bolinas too, the place where he and Daisy had finally come together, hopefully for good. To walk down the ravine to RCA Beach, on the far side of the country from Florida, and just sit there, watch the waves, figure out the secret to life.

"NOW THAT I'VE MET DAISY," Johann gave her a lascivious grin, "I understand why Mick wouldn't come here to Paris, after the oil spill."

"He was waiting for me to finish my PhD." Daisy smiled at Mick. "He's crazy."

"I first met Mick in Athens, the coup," Johann said. "Then we nearly die in the Sinai, then who do I see in Bolinas, that oil spill? Now here!"

"At the oil spill," Mick said, "was when you told me to come to Paris."

"And so you have!" Johann declared, his widespread arms embracing not only the little wooden table of wine, bread, grapes and cheese, but his whole tiny apartment six floors above a cobblestone street in the Eighteenth Arrondissement, its windows on the gleaming city extending from the Eiffel Tower past Notre Dame.

"But we agreed," Johann added, "that someday we'd drink Amstel by the Amstel and screw beautiful women till the river froze over... And sadly, now look at you—"

"*You're* the one," Mick laughed, "who always said that. When we were getting shot at in the Sinai."

Johann glanced out over the river. "Such a beautiful place, Paris. So full of human hope and beauty."

"Hitler tried to burn it down," Daisy said.

"I often wonder," Mick said, "what things would have been like if Jack had lived."

"Jack?"

"Kennedy. If they hadn't murdered him there would've been no war, both Vietnam and America would be united, our cities wouldn't have burned, three million deaths—"

"More than three million," Johann said.

"Only half the Holocaust," Daisy said.

"Every death," Johann said, "is a Holocaust."

"– and if they hadn't killed Bobby." It brought Mick near tears. "What a different world."

"We never get a good world," Johann said. "We must learn to survive in this evil one." He opened another wine bottle. "And we must accept that evil nearly always wins. And that doing good will not protect us from evil. And because good people will not do evil to win, and evil people will do *anything* to win, evil usually wins."

"What about Hitler?" Daisy said. "He was finally defeated."

"Evil had already won. For six years it turned the world into a cauldron of hatred, killed sixty million, destroyed the world's most beautiful cities, left another billion people injured or displaced...Now in Vietnam, too, evil has already won...The weapons makers and empire builders have kept it going almost a decade—billions of profits, millions of dead...Yes, Vietnam's already a great success for evil."

Though it was no longer possible to imagine the world as good, Mick thought, it might be possible to avoid the worst. And though the world of people and politics and media and war was but a mirror reflecting itself, there was a much deeper world behind it, a place of truth, beauty and infinite understanding. But as long as men were ready to enslave themselves in armies there would always be war.

"But," Johann said, changing subjects, "still no work being found?"

"She has a job already," Mick said. "The *Institut Pasteur*."

Johann's eyebrows rose. "Wow!" He looked at her, at Mick. "But no journalist jobs?"

"I'm working for a real estate company that finds apartments for Americans and Brits in Paris. Two thousand francs for every signed contract. I'm starting to enjoy capitalism."

"What about your friends, when you were here, the riots?"

"Monique and Thierry? They've moved to Montpellier, he's teaching at the university, she's busy writing articles and making children. Milton Greene, the guy who led the AWOL group, he got his Sorbonne PhD in biochemistry and is working in DNA research...And Gisèle, the Senate candidate, she's writing national legislation to make rape a crime...A first in France...She chaired the Stockholm Tribunal, you know."

"Pity, it made no difference." Johann leaned toward him. "Still, you know, *you* should write about it someday."

"About what?"

"These last years, the war, the protests, the drugs and sex and fun, the revolution that never happened."

Mick shook his head. "We'll never know, will we?" *If I were to write it,* he realized, *it would be for Troy.*

TARA put her feet up on the porch rail and leaned back in the rocker, her Dreadnought 12-string like a tiger across her lap, stroking it like a cat and the beautiful sounds coming out so delectable to the soul. That's why they called it the blues, the simplest three progressions, the one, four and five that could stand for life's every rhythm. And life *was* the blues, a mix of loving and losing, and until you accepted one you never got the other.

She fingered the C with her left pinkie on the high E three, didn't even know what chord it was, dropped into C then sliding into G7 down to G, and how lovely and simple, how perfectly beautiful the melody and words of a slave's daughter who couldn't read or write, sang it down and played it out on her old gut guitar till God stopped what He was doing just to listen, tears in His eyes,

Freight train, freight train, run so fast,
Please don't tell what train I'm on,
They won't know what route I've gone

Was anything more heart-achingly beautiful than music? How could you live without it? Without beauty? Of love, of forests and wild rivers and free animals and endless meadows and mountains—when it was gone you found you'd sold your soul for nothing.

"The best," Sybil had once said about Janis, "are always the first to crash and burn."

She wasn't going to crash and burn. No scag for 197 days. And counting. Wouldn't go back to it now. Even though it was the best lover she'd ever had, one that truly made her come, in every sense. But there'd be a man out there, tall and handsome with a big dick. A brilliant, caring, empathetic guy who was tough as nails. Just thinking about him made her hot.

Now that she had Ginnie living with her, scag was the past. She smiled to think of Ginnie fielding her calls and taking messages from her studio musicians and feeding Onya kitty treats and sitting down with Tara for hours to talk things out. It was Ginnie who'd convinced her to buy the place in the wilds of northern Marin, two hundred acres of fields and forests in Ignacio with a pink stucco farmhouse they'd repaint and a chicken house and a huge barn they'd soundproof and turn into a studio...she could have a dog again, a dog like Rusty...

And her friend Joan of Arc calling—or, *to be honest,* Tara reminded herself, *most of the time I'm calling her.* But it felt lovely to have a sister, someone closer to you than yourself.

Like Troy.

Luis used to say death is evil. It haunted him that life so wonderful should be stolen, given to us then snatched away. She wondered as she always did what he'd thought as the chopper went down, if he died fast or burned alive. How what he'd hated most had come for him so early, before he'd barely learned to live.

She had to live for them all now, Blade and Sybil and Luis and Tiny and Troy. She had to carry into the world the message they were trying to give it. You could say it was easy because they were all inside her and all she had to do was let them go, be the instrument on which they played, hearing Luis' searing solo at the end of *Little Red Rooster*, how it got down inside you and sawed your bones apart.

The guitarist's soaring music reaching out for God.

If God would only listen.

MICK AMBLED IN SUNLIGHT along a street of *boulangeries* and cafés and lovely carved stone buildings—Paris the great reservoir of the human spirit, the infinite and eternal till the next Hitler razed it, *the city of love for life*. And wasn't the love for life, caring for life, the prime component of existence?

Everything seemed to crowd in on him, the city's beauty, the vivacity of its people and architecture, the sense that life could be good, was *supposed* to be good, and we humans also. And in that sense, he realized for the first time, he'd been a good man, had done the right thing, had taken care of others, and tried to do the best he could. When you got down to it, he had tried to live by Christ's words.

But *If it feels good do it* was a higher moral law than *Do unto others*. Because *If it feels good* leads to joy and the power of the self, and fairness to others who also enjoy this life. As the spider on the ceiling in Cell 131 had told him, *If it feels good do it IS the path with heart*. And to do good was simply to lessen suffering, and to do evil was to increase it.

And the path with heart was easy to know. Like Castañeda said, *if it has a heart the path is good, if it doesn't it has no use*. Both went nowhere, but one was a joyful journey. And the other made you curse your life.

He had been given the great gift of this life and the loved ones and friends still living and those who had died. Gifted by Daisy and the child in her belly; what she and hopefully the children they would have were the deepest life, for how could anything else be as important as *making* life? And anything more evil than *taking* it?

And it was good to thank the Lord for this life even if there *wasn't* a Lord. He walked in the sun with the Seine on his left and the spires of Notre Dame before him, thinking even if there *is* a Lord, that Lord certainly doesn't care if you thank It. And even if there isn't any Lord it's still good to be grateful for this gift of the majesty and mystery of life.

It was Milton Greene's favorite café. In the Fifth, not far from the tourist-busy *Quartier Latin*, but on a back street by the Panthéon.

Milton stood when Mick twisted his way through the tables. "You're always early," Mick laughed as they hugged.

"You gettin a bit fat?" Milton poked Mick in the gut. "Daisy feeding you too well?"

"You should talk—Lamia's Moroccan cuisine. How's the baby?"

"Like you warned me, what your mom once said—all babies do is shit, eat, fuss and sleep."

"Your own damn fault."

Milton smiled. "And Daisy being so big, whose fault is that?"

Mick gripped Milton's wrist. "*Life* is what counts."

"Kids. A wife and kids." Milton signaled the waiter. "That's what counts."

"And that it's a beautiful day. I've been thinking, that if it feels good it *is* good."

Milton gave him a half grin. "You just figured that out?"

Mick ordered a double espresso. "And that I just escaped ten years in Leavenworth."

"Your brother?" Milton eyed him gently. "The MIA? You know where he went gone?"

Mick crimped his lips. "Near the Cambodian border."

Milton caressed his empty beer glass in both hands. "One of my new AWOLs says there's Americans in an NVA Cambodian prison camp near there." He shrugged. "No connection, I'm sure. Just wanted you to know." He gave Mick a look of infinite condolence.

"Where?"

"Place called Krabas Village, this AWOL guy tells me, in the Mimot District, of Kâmpóng Cham Province."

Mick felt his whole life shift. Against hope, he said, "What makes you think—"

"He says there was a Marine there, named Troy..."

The guts felt ripped out of Mick's body; he stood, sat, again. "I need to talk to this guy."

Milton shook his head. "I sent him to a safe house in Marly. But he never got there. Yesterday his body showed up in the Seine, all the way downriver to Mantes-la-Jolie." He shrugged. "Somebody's killing my guys; I don't know who."

"I do." Mick took a breath, tried to figure it out. "How do I get there?"

"Krabas Village? It's about ninety miles northeast of Phnom Penh. We fought our way there, part of our non-existent Cambodia invasion."

Mick sat back, thinking it through. "I can be in Bangkok in two days."

"You'll never get into Cambodia alive. Let alone back out."

Mick stood, wavering in stunned awareness, barely able to see, to think. Troy stood before him. "Don't try to find me, brother," Troy said. "You'll get killed."

Mick tossed coins on the table. "I have to tell Daisy."

"Tell her what?" Milton said.

"That I'm leaving for Cambodia."

THE END

EXCERPT FROM AMERICA, BOOK 1

BURN DOWN THE WORLD

IN THE FALL Troy left for the Air Force Academy and Tara for Berkeley. The Academy's discipline and detail came to Troy automatically, as if he'd always lived it. The rest of the world, the soft undisciplined entertainment-seekers, was insignificant, unreal. Pity we're training to risk our lives to save *them*. But that's what I signed on for.

The Academy was like the Boys' Home, driven by the need to dominate and denigrate. Troy hated the nastiness of the upper classmen who picked on the new ones, made them serfs because once *they* had been picked on, made serfs. "I can't see how it teaches anything military," he said.

"It inculcates numb obedience," a cadet named Throcker said.

"Obedience to your CO," another named Coulton added. "No matter who he is."

But is it always right, Troy wondered, to follow your CO? Suppose he's wrong and leads you into danger?

The principles of war. The science of killing. When you peeled off the image that's what the Academy really was: a place that taught young men how to manage steel machines in the sky to better kill and destroy people and places on the earth.

But he didn't want to kill, had to admit it. Killing a buck every fall hurt his soul but it was food for the family. Yanking a turkey's neck across a pine block and chopping through it was the same: feeding your loved ones. And the kid. The kid he and Tara had killed, who smiled at Troy from his playpen every day, and cooed to him at night.

To drop a steel tube of high explosives on people far down below, people you've never seen, didn't seem what Christ would want. It chilled his spine. He didn't want to kill, he wanted to reach the moon.

President Kennedy wanted to catch the Russians in space. That meant a man on the moon. But with what delivery system, what landing module? How to get fuel for the return? All impossible.

Some cadets didn't like Kennedy because he was a Democrat or because he was a Catholic, even though he was a real war hero not a coward like Nixon. But Troy defended Kennedy because he'd get us into space. It was all part of Kennedy's New Frontier.

After the moon Mars was next. By the time Troy was forty, in 1983, humans could be living on Mars. The Academy was the first step, because wherever NASA went the Air Force was going to be headed. "Test pilots," a professor told him, "NASA's going to use test pilots for astronauts."

I'm going to be a test pilot, Troy decided.

Soon he'd start flying lessons. Already he'd spent hours on the Link Trainer; every free half-hour running to the classroom off the Parade Loop to leap into the Link, knew the instruments by heart, the commands, could take off and land flawlessly.

Next would be glider school, the sailplanes with the student in the front and the instructor behind. Then you were in the T-28, with an 800-horse Wright that was slow to respond but had plenty of tail-end power. Then the T-37, a twin-engine jet they called The Screamer because of its small engine intakes, a low-down nasty airplane that could take you there and back just like combat.

But it's really hard, he wrote Dad. *This cult of blind obedience – I can see it in warfare, maybe, but not for learning? What are we learning? Not to think for ourselves? That's what they're inculcating and I'm not sure it's good. And there's too much pride in it, in this blindness – "I can be a better automaton than you" – Pride of the enslaved who will one day be enslavers.*

My personal slavemaster is a third-year cadet named Steward Metcalf. A pimple-faced guy from Concrete, Washington. For him I have to run silly errands, polish his boots and shoes, iron his uniform, do pushups and whatever else enters his otherwise vacant mind. "You're going to crash and burn," he told me first day, adding, "I'll be laughing as you go."

So it's a mix of fear and excitement, the worry I've made the wrong choice, that I should've gone to MIT like Mr. Cohen wanted. But I can make it here and I owe this to you. Ever since my earliest memory I've wanted to fly. Without you I never would have been here.

Tough it out, Dad wrote back. *Of course you can make it but don't kill yourself trying to be first. Whatever you do, wherever you go, remember: you're already fine the way you are.*

BERKELEY stunned Tara with its bright clarity of sun and sky glinting off white buildings and voluptuous tan hills. She was intoxicated by the cool, salty wind from the Bay, the warm night breeze down from the hills, the cafés and bistros alive with espresso and wine, the sidewalks thick with young intense people, the sense of easy freedom.

"San Francisco's even groovier," her roommate Juliet said, snapping her gum. "North Beach has all these coffee houses, Italian restaurants, poetry readings, cool bars full of beatnik artists – you can get an ounce for fifteen bucks –"

"An ounce?" Tara said, thinking of recipes.

"Grass, silly!"

"Oh." Tara nodded. That stuff that a junior named Liam had tried to get her to smoke. That made her cough. Would wreck your voice.

Juliet crackled her gum. "They let you into bars sometimes..." She tugged from her purse a California Driver's License coated in plastic, a dim photo. "Says I'm twenty-one'n a half. Randy over in Campbell, he'll make you one if you fuck him."

269

Here the sun wasn't like back east. It had a dry deep heat sinking into her shoulders as she sat cross-legged on the thick grass reading Goethe, *Du wandelst jetzt wohl still und mild,* chasing the words down one by one in the dictionary, conscious of the raw German and of the sun heating the back of her neck and the sweet crinkly fragrant grass and the dance of light and shadows on the golden hills.

Even classes were fun: there was a purpose to learning. Everything was brighter, more alive, more erotic, as if paradise were closer, beauty of place united with intensity of thought. As if things *could* be understood and it *was* possible to make the world better.

"This's like heaven," she told Juliet. "Not that I think there's such a place."

"Depends on your LOT."

"Your lot in life?"

"Your Life Orgasm Total – the higher it is the further up the wheel of Paradise you go."

TO TROY THE ROCKIES were stunning in their crystalline beauty and dry high air, their peaks snowy even in September, their stark sleek slopes of fir and pine, ragged rocky ridges and red sandstone pinnacles and canyons with icy trout-filled streams.

And there was cross country. The joy of running fleet-footed over the rough piney soil, breathing steady and relaxed, legs stretching out effortlessly, almost flying. For the first weeks the altitude had left him gasping after runs. But once he got in shape, whenever he had a few free hours he ran up the 13-mile Barr Trail to the top of 14,000-foot Pike's Peak, scorning the flabby tourists who had driven cars or taken the cog railway to the top, scorning the doughnut stands and souvenir shops, but entranced by the white-gold prairie so far below, the granite ridges and velvety forests, the sky so blue it was almost black. *Closer to the stars.*

And he liked the wide-streeted Colorado Springs downtown of red sandstone buildings, and to the east the magnificent emerald prairies that when the sun went down behind the Rockies turned the color of blood.

I know I can make it, he wrote Tara. *I love it but I'm afraid ... You should come visit. Colorado's a beautiful place.* When he wrote this he almost tore up the page but he'd already filled the other side and didn't want to rewrite. *I've given myself away,* he thought wryly, but didn't know how.

When he could he hid out in the library studying aeronautics texts. Far back in 1915, Robert Goddard had created both the multi-stage and the liquid-fueled rockets, but only now, 45 years later, were they being truly implemented. In 1919 Goddard had written *A Method of Reaching Extreme Altitudes,* full of brilliant ideas ignored for half a century. If you're going to succeed, Troy reminded himself, don't expect the credit.

All Goddard's life people had made fun of him. *The New York Times,* of course, had caustically dismissed his ideas. But while the Americans ridiculed him and the Army Air Corps ignored his designs, the Germans under Werner von Braun used them to create the V2 and other weapons of mass death. That was the problem with advancing the human mind: it could be used to help or to kill.

He was transfixed by Goddard's recollection of climbing a cherry tree in 1893 behind his childhood home, and having a sudden inspiration how to send a rocket to Mars. "I was a very different boy when I descended the tree from when I ascended," Goddard had written. "Existence at last seemed very purposive." And this was ten years before the Wright brothers' first flight.

If you have a task that fulfills you, Troy realized, existence *is* purposive.

By November he had talked his way into aircraft design, stunned by the beauty and simplicity of flight. *It's thrust and lift versus gravity,* he wrote Dad. *Everything comes down to that.*

A week later when Steward Metcalf was decapitated in a glider crash while on approach for the field east of the Academy, Troy felt guilty as though he'd killed him by wishing him gone. In December he broke the freshman indoor mile record at 4:19:32, a stunning time given the 7,200-foot altitude. The older cadets stopped harassing him and those in his class seemed to view him with respectful distance. It rarely occurred to him that he had no friends; perhaps that was what the Academy was all about.

TWO WEEKS BEFORE Christmas vacation, at an Oakland party full of blues and Motown, the air blue with weed smoke, Tara bumped into a tall black man in a lilac jacket, silver slacks and crimson cowboy boots. "Watch your big feet," she said.

"I'm too busy watchin you."

"Well cut it out."

He took her wrist as she pushed past. "Ain't you the one that sings?"

She pulled away. "Everybody sings."

"You the one. Tara O'Brien."

"So who are you?"

"Blade."

"Shit. Really?"

"Come in here." He nodded at a bedroom door. "I want to hear you sing."

It was a wide room with orange curtains and a kingsize bed in the middle and a wall of guitars. "Sly won't mind," Blade said, "we play one of his." He took down a worn Martin with a scratched top, sat on the bed. "What you wanna sing?"

The wall of gleaming guitars made her nervous and unsure. "*Black Cat Blues*? The way you do it?"

He led into it gently, the soft notes and the deep chords giving her a platform to throw her voice on, and she watched his eyes glisten and that made her sing even freer, brighter, till suddenly the room was full of people in rapt silence and she broke down for an instant in this communion with them and the core of song and life, caught herself and cleared her voice.

"Whoa," Blade shook his head. "You something, girl."

"Sing another one," someone said. "Yeah," others urged, and soon she no longer felt fear but lust, lust to pour life into them, the *fire* of life. To burn down the world with song.

IT FELT STRANGE to Troy to leave the Air Force Academy and be back in Nyack for Christmas. At once, he realized, he missed the Academy. The reassurance of its bright straight hallways, the pure discipline, how you greeted someone, how you lived. How you see yourself. What you demand of yourself. Demand of yourself without shirking or complaint. Because the military gives you the confidence, the power, to believe you can do so.

Even the posture – how you'd got used to your back being absolutely straight at all time, shoulders back, until any other bearing felt unreal. And the bitter dry December Rockies wind so much cleaner than this swamp-like, lowland chill.

The little house in Nyack felt out of place, and Mick and Dad foreign there, as if they too didn't belong. Which of course, he told himself, they didn't.

And Tara hovering there like a St. Elmo fire blazing at the tip of his wing. To divert him into death. To watch the ground reach up for you and not care.

Yet seeing her in the living room when he came in and dropped his duffle on the carpet she looked so lovely and kind he had to hold her, inhale her long ravelly hair incensed with tobacco – didn't matter – her heady scent. As if nothing had changed.

"How are you?" he gasped, stepping back.

She gave him a lovely smile, eyes flashing. "Good to see you."

"And you." He pulled away. "Where's Dad?"

"In the kitchen." She kissed him, hard. "Go see him."

He looked at her. "You're thin."

Dad was sitting in a wooden chair by the woodstove, in a blue plaid shirt and khaki wool pants, work boots unlaced; he turned and saw Troy and stood quickly, "Well where the hell *you* come from?" reaching out to embrace him and almost falling.

"It's okay, Dad." Troy took him in his arms and sat him back down.

He turned another chair backwards and sat facing Dad, his hand on Dad's wrist which felt cold and thin.

"Tara told me you were coming," Dad said. "I thought tomorrow."

"I'm here now." Troy looked at him closer. "How are you doing?"

"Doing fine." Dad shrugged. "Just old age."

Troy went to the door. "Tara! Mick!" he called, "get in here. I want to catch up with both of you."

CHRISTMAS EVE was somber despite everyone's attempts to have fun. The family gathered at Hal and Sylvia's small brick colonial tucked into a back street behind the 1776 House. Grampy in a chair by the fire with his whisky neat, Uncle Howard stuttering and glancing at the gold watch he kept tugging from his pocket, as if he had somewhere to go, Uncle Ted who had once fought off a black bear and now seemed old and stooped, lonely and disoriented after his wife Cordelia's sudden death from an aneurism last year. Even Uncle Phil's wife, Aunt Wilma, she of the small dangerous fists, seemed less intimidating.

Johnny sat in the background gazing at the fire as if it held some explanation for how and why everything had changed, but would not tell them. Troy thought of saying hi and decided *wait till later*, turned to look for Tara or Mick but couldn't see them.

Maybe it's just I'm older, Troy thought, remembering back to his and Mick's thirteenth birthday party, the first time he'd met most of this close-knit farm family now slowly being disjointed by time and the new suburban world devouring the land they had worked and loved. No, it's time, time itself, which destroys us all eventually.

He wanted to help them, fight for them, defend them. How?

And Dad – he owed him his life, his happiness, the Academy, everything. How to help him? Ever since Ma had died Dad had retreated further and further into himself, and the illness made it worse because Dad wouldn't admit it. For Dad, Troy realized, all that counted now was the happiness of his three children. Even me, he thought, suddenly near tears.

He went out on the rickety back deck where Tara stood looking at the dark, rambling sky. "At the farm we saw thousands of stars," she said. "Here there's nothing."

"That's civilization for you," he joked, wondering how she'd known it was he. He put an arm around her waist and pulled her close, her slender hard hip against his thigh.

She turned into him, hugged him hard, pulled back. "I can't wait to get out of here, back to Berkeley. This whole place drives me crazy. The whole deal."

"Dad?"

"Not him. But I feel I can't leave him."

"We all feel that. But we *are* leaving him." He smiled. "I told him I'd take a year off from the Academy and come back to be with him, and he said *If you do I'll shoot you.* I think he meant it."

She hugged him again and pulled away. "I'm sure he did."

He wanted to kiss her more, knew she'd let him, that she wanted him, but it wasn't possible, not here with the family gathered round, not possible now that he'd gone to the Academy and she was his sister again.

Everything we do to get free, he thought, only binds us tighter.

FROM THE STERN of the *S.S. Statendam* Mick watched the Statue of Liberty shrink into the darkening sea. The strangeness of this wild ocean, of leaving America, the cold salty wind and frothing waves, the lunge, rumble and roll of the ship, all gave him a sense of fearful solitude, ecstatic communion, and the rupture of an ancient chain.

He was leaving it all behind: Williams, the family after Christmas Eve, and all the subterranean sorrow invested there, Dad, Tara and Troy... Dad in weary pain, Troy's distance and rigid formality, Tara's craziness about music – as if that were going to be a way to live her life ... And all the time he'd hoped Berkeley would give her some sense.

Driving Coke trucks all summer and fall he'd saved nine hundred dollars. This round-trip voyage had cost two hundred forty for a tiny third class cabin with four bunks deep in the hull. He had six hundred sixty dollars to last four months in France.

Years ago, he and Troy had wandered the rails and begun a new life. It had been fun and lonely and very scary and there'd been a lot of pain at the end. Now he was on a new walkabout and it was going to be scary sometimes too. But he was older now, and what he felt, he realized, was elation.

How can one always be free? Was it possible? Being free made him think of Daisy, and his mind shied from the pain. Why had he not written her more often? And now, was he leaving her behind? He imagined her standing at the rail beside him, the wind in her hair, her gladdened eyes and wide smile, their unspoken, invincible together-ness. Why had he stopped writing her?

Because it was over, he told himself. Had to put it behind me.

In the semi-darkness laughing gulls rose and fell screaming over the ship's wake. The other passengers went in one by one and he was alone, palms on the wet rail, watching the darkening wake and sky. His ancestors had once passed here going the other way, excited, nervous, and solitary. Was he closing some circle?

Seeking the Holy Grail was the quest for the meaning of life. Tonight it was *here*, just beyond reach, beyond a wave's glistening crest, the starry horizon, ready to appear.

EXCERPT FROM FREEDOM, BOOK 2

DUMP JOHNSON

HUÉ WAS A TROPICAL PARIS, the loveliest city Troy had ever seen. Its ornate boulevards and wide French homes in expansive gardens and palm groves, its classic stone buildings, its bistros, sidewalk cafés, parks and open-air markets all seemed part of a civilized and stable union of east and west far wiser than either by itself.

Like the Seine, the Perfume River cut the city's middle, the ancient stone Citadel and its more ancient Imperial Palace and the Palace of Perfect Peace on one bank, and on the other bank a younger city with a French-designed capitol building, resplendent university, wide-lawned country club, and tree-shaded streets of red, orange, white and yellows roses, purple bougainvillea, lotus and orchids.

Along the many canals the straw-roofed huts clustered under papaya and mango trees with boughs spread over the water. Blue age-silvered sampans floated in their silver-gold reflections; on the streets and alleys the myriad bicycles clanged constantly, with baskets on the front or over the rear wheels, and ridden by lovely girls in white gowns or by grizzled old women selling oranges.

Statues of meditating Buddhas smiled like Mona Lisas over

yellow-robed barefoot monks holding out brass begging bowls on sidewalks where uniformed school children filed solemnly, each clutching the back of the shirt of the one ahead, shepherded by slender lovely teachers in *ao dais*. Old women with wide earrings and betel-nut teeth, their faces maps of many lives and places, chatted with him toothlessly and cackled at his pronunciations.

Even the birds' cries seemed familiar. People here seemed freer, as if the War were far away. Often he felt pointless guilt for being here while his platoon waded through paddies and humped through leafless forests stinking of Agent Orange that made them nauseous and gave them harsh headaches. Even after a week in Hué the ache had persisted in the middle of his forehead, a chemical tartness on his tongue.

His Vietnamese was still rudimentary but people could understand, were shocked he'd tried to speak it. And each day he was getting better. How could you win their hearts and minds if you didn't speak their language?

In a shady street a girl was trying to start a Vespa, her sandaled heel angrily banging the starter, her yellow straw hat sideways. It puttered helplessly and died; she thumped her fist on the handlebar. "Can I help to you?" he said in Vietnamese.

She glanced up shocked then faced away, an impassive perfect face with almond slanted eyes and thin deep lips, little ski-jump nose and long neck down into a willowy body with high small breasts under a pale pink blouse, slender arms and long fingers. She shook her head not looking at him. "It's your *carburateur*," he said, the French word. "It's under water."

She giggled, then looked away and wouldn't speak or acknowledge he was there. He knelt beside her and turned off the key. "Give it some minutes." He popped open the engine compartment and wiped the carburetor down with the tail of his shirt and blew it dry. He shut the clutch and started the engine. "To not go fast."

"I'm late –"

"Hurrying makes you later."

She gave him a foreign glance as if surprised by some species of insect that had shown a hint of vestigial intelligence, then twisted the throttle and spun away, her yellow hat vanishing in the crowd.

He stood on a bridge over a canal remembering the curve of her back and her slim buttocks, her long rangy arms and wind-trailing ebony hair, how she leaned the Vespa into a corner like a jockey on a fast horse. A sampan full of long green stalks slid under the bridge, the man's dark bony knees apart, the leaves of his conical hat visible from above, his long slender pole trailing drops along the water.

The Vespa had only gone a few streets. He walked toward the last sound he'd heard, past thick-trunked massive trees and high stucco walls with little front gardens and two-story houses behind them. She was pushing the Vespa, head down, forcing it. "I'm glad I came back," he said in French.

"You didn't fix it very good," she said in English.

"WE'RE GOING TO DUMP Lyndon Johnson," Al Lowenstein said. "With a student movement. Based *on* the campuses. To stop him from running next year."

"I don't think anybody can stop Lyndon," Bobby Kennedy said. "The War's still approved by fifty-nine percent of Americans. Sure, there's Wayne Morse and Bill Fulbright and Gene McCarthy and a few other senators speaking out. But who's listening? Come on, Al, you don't depose a sitting president within his own party."

"Even Martin Luther King has *finally* come out against the War. Says it's immoral, and risks revolution at home. These young black men who don't get a fair shake here then face death over there supposedly for freedoms they don't have at home – it's true."

They sat on gilded couches in the vast, corniced library of oriental rugs and oak herringbone floors in Lowenstein's apartment on Central Park West. Al made his pitch, pacing, leading with his Yale lawyer's logic to an irrefutable conclusion: the antiwar movement had the strength and the energy to depose a sitting president. But it needed an alternative candidate.

Bobby had been Senator for over two years. He had hardened

against the War but didn't know how to stop it. "If you decide to," Al said, "you can do it."

"Me?" Bobby chuckled. "I couldn't touch Lyndon next year. If I had any thoughts of running it'd have to be in seventy-two. *If* I had such thoughts."

"In the meantime," Al said softly, "how many thousand American boys are going to die who wouldn't if you won in sixty-eight? How many million Indochinese?"

"Al," Bobby snapped, "don't throw that shit at me."

AT SIX A.M. the alarm rang, the girl beside Mick mumbling. Furious he'd set it so early, he reset it for six-fifteen and fell asleep. An instant later it buzzed. He forced himself awake thinking if he was late Ephraim would make him do something dangerous, out on a beam with no tie-in.

Barefooting round roaches he washed his face and brushed his teeth in the tub, not bothering to shave, doused his dirty underwear and the armpit of yesterday's blue work shirt with deodorant, asked the girl to leave the key under the doormat and raced to the subway.

He hung to the strap half-seeing the ads for secretarial schools, life insurance and breath mints, the downturned faces of the other passengers wasting their precious lives by marching clockwork from one hive to another. And he too. *Termites, rats in a cage* – is that what Sabrina had meant? Where *was* she?

Life so short even if you lived to old age. And he could die now – anyone could – any second. A quick slip off a beam and twenty stories down. *This amazing mystery of consciousness*, how crazy to squander it. And a major way of squandering was mindless labor, lugging concrete all day, setting bolts into steel to create more air-conditioned boxes for people to get trapped in. *Why* was he doing this?

Most of the other people traveling this subway seemed resigned to squandering their lives. He imagined them sitting all day at their desks then going home to watch television. They complained about having to work but went shopping for things they didn't need and so had to keep working. *Half-lives*, the walking dead.

But the antiwar effort was wasting time too, the constant meetings chewing over the same issues till the more reluctant groups came aboard, the constant need to grow through unity by bringing in more people, diluting the message to include all.

The problem was he was alone while others had a fabric to their lives, nice apartments and friends. He was a failure: didn't have relationships, structure and meaning. Just like Cousin Johnny – caustic and indifferent, vaunting solitude because it was all he had? Was there more than one kind of heroin?

Peter and Lois, Seth and Miranda, other couples he knew had all found each other, sexually alive, casual nakedness and breakfasts together – when would he stop refusing love, running away? He envisioned a girl, long dark hair, slender face and body, a fine and sensitive awareness, someone with whom meaning could be discovered. Somebody like Daisy Moran had been, once.

Yet the girls he met he wanted to leave once they'd made love. Till then he'd feel full of interest and charm, wanting them with the deep unpurged hunger of a monk. Then he'd find himself beside a sticky disheveled stranger, conscious of her emanations and distasteful odors, her moles and imperfections. The breasts that only minutes ago had so excited him now seemed ungainly, or the nipples too large or too dark. Her lovely soft-haired pubis and the deep hot slit within her now seemed less interesting. He wanted to be alone but the intimacy he'd been so hungry to create was now fraught with duties of affection and respect.

He'd pace the floor naked, get dressed, not wanting to hurt her, castigating himself for lacking tenderness. He'd always be alone, too immature for deep, enduring love. "I have to be at work in four hours," he'd say, or pretending some suddenly remembered task, kissed her unwillingly and descended into the damp echoing midnight filling his lungs with the fetid reek of freedom.

The next night he wanted her again, or another. He'd meet her in a bar or playing guitar or on the street. If she smoked grass with him she'd sleep with him – grass a little sin to loosen the feelings, excite the body, open the thighs to greater sins and excitements. With grass she lowered her guard, was intimate already in another way, and its sensuality made her want to fuck. Priming the pump, lubricating the piston of love.

"Damn you," Rachel said, "you dance the best, take the best drugs, climb the nastiest mountains, fuck the hardest, fight out there in the night alone..." she smiled, looking down at him, his prick in her hand. "And you have the body of Michelangelo's David. So of course we *want* you. And you're hot because we can't really have you, not like we want. Your damn freedom enslaves us –"

Sex throbbed in him with the steady heavy thrum of an electric guitar and he had to purge it as the guitarist does with every song. The girls with spread thighs and aching breasts, slippery in their own lust and sweat, their hair in his lips and their nipples supple hard as he plunged into their volcano of life. Then the dream unsatisfied, the grail lost, he awakened in a stranger's arms.

But a day or two without sex and he'd burn inside. In political meetings or in the streets and bars he ached for every lissome girl. All the supposed raptures of religion, he now understood, were claimed by those who feared or hated sex. Religious passion was nothing more than ersatz sex, a blowup doll for the soul.

And sex was a good religion, built on the naked flesh of girls and women, on lovely salacious pleasure and deep aching joy. The lovely moment when a girl slid off her clothes – slender and silvery in streetlight through the window, kissing her fragrant body and sinking into her slim velvet heat, her cries and moans as she drove her body against his – was the deepest, loveliest, most fulfilling joy he knew. The closest you could get to God, why so many people said *Jesus* or *Oh God* when they came. And the deep glow inside afterwards, as if closer to the hearth of life, the eternal fire. Door to the spirit world, the body's pulse, the love of mystery and adventure.

Each girl a new country, some long-legged, narrow-bellied and too deep to reach completely, some wilder with a thick red bush, others blonde, distracted and sylphlike. Each unique and infinite, the taste and texture of her hair, and scent of crotch and skin and underarms, the softness behind her ear and the roughness of her soles, the way her breasts hung and how she bit her lip or moaned or swore, her undisclosed thoughts and reservations, a half-candid laugh or flash of anger – how was the great city of the world seen through her windows? What was it like inside her skin?

This most essential act for life, Rachel had once said. A perfect Darwinism: the greater the urge for sex the more likely the species survives. Why then did we so shame and denigrate it? As Miranda had said long ago, one dusty afternoon in Mick's dentist's office in Williamstown – why do they *hate* it? Why do they *fear* it? When it's so much *fun*?

Why fear and shun it when it was one of life's deepest joys, brought happiness, serenity and health? There seemed no answer other than a rote Freudian: it's only by controlling lust that we've evolved. Or that humans take more joy in pain than pleasure.

One night late on Second Avenue the woman of his dreams came toward him – tall, slender, dark-haired, pretty, but weeping. Instantly he wanted her to know her, comfort her. Her weeping made her more approachable, vulnerable, making him ache to talk with her, hold her, love her. "Hey," he halted in mid-street. "You okay?"

She tossed her head and kept going, an unmanned vessel heedless of shores. He walked with her for two blocks, begged her to talk, trying to show he'd give her more than she'd lost. But in her total absorption in her own pain he did not exist but for the furious heart-broken shake of her head signifying he was another pretender, another predator so far below the man for whom she sorrowed as to be unworthy of response.

THE GIRL WITH THE VESPA was named Su Li. She was a teacher in Bach Dang, a quarter of Hué between the northeast wall of the Citadel and the river, and lived with her mother and two younger brothers in a two-room house with a storefront where her mother sold rice, dried fish, vegetables, Coca Cola, coconut candy and anything else she

283

could find. Su Li's father was dead and her income as a teacher was the major support for her family.

At first she had almost refused to speak. When her Vespa had broken down again he had cleaned the carburetor again and told her to empty the gas tank. "*Nu-oc*," he said, then in English, "You have water in your gas tank. You have to empty it and fill it with good petrol."

She nodded tugging aside a wisp of sable hair, watched him without expression as he tipped the Vespa and let the gas run iridescent into the mud, then walked silently beside him as he pushed it to a godown where an old man sold gas out of five-gallon tins. Refilled it ran perfectly.

She faced him, distant, nearly hostile. "*Cam on*" – Thanks.

He held the handlebar. "I should go with you, make sure it doesn't stop again."

"No." A sideways shake of the head, cold utter refusal.

He gripped the handlebar, afraid, indecisive, then dared: "Have tea with me?"

She lifted her chin in a brief laugh as if he'd asked something foolish and illicit. Emboldened he added, "If you don't, the scooter won't run."

She cocked her head sideways, not understanding.

"*Si vous n'avez pas tra avec moi, la machine ne va pas –*"

She giggled, slim fingers over her lips, eyes suddenly black. Fearing to do it he took the key from the ignition and put it in his pocket, nodded at a café tilting on rotten posts over the Perfume River. "*Hai tra?*" – two teas?

She scanned the roofs of shacks and shanties and the low white clouds and piercing blue sky, him. "You are officer?"

"Second lieutenant."

"Oh-kay," she smiled, face bright as the sun.

He felt outlandish in the little café with its tiny tables and tipsy stools, the thin-whiskered old men tipping faces into their cups, the proprietor's wife staring at him with undisguised hate then grinning gold teeth when he caught her glance. His pistol felt ungainly on his belt, his uniform too hot, the girl across from him more beautiful than a lotus, than the sky itself, and more remote. He was trembling – why? *I can have ten of you in a whorehouse for a hundred bucks*, he told her silently but that didn't change his excitement, his fear she'd walk away and he'd never see her again.

At first he talked foolishly of wanting peace, seeing as he spoke the napalmed bodies and phosphorized villages, realized he was being an idiot. Her long fingers laced round her cup, her small breasts beneath her pink blouse, her full lips like some flower about to open, the arc of dimple on each cheek as she smiled – he was stunned by them all. Again she flitted from somber hostility to a kind of teasing grace, as if trying out attitudes with him to find the right one, sometimes bantering in Vietnamese he couldn't follow then translating in school-girl English with here and there a word of French, "We have *bonne chance*, that you Americans save us from Communists."

It's not that simple, he wanted to say. *I'd be a Communist too if I was a peasant here, a factory worker*, shocking himself with the thought.

His tea reflected a fighter group crossing the blue sky, their roar eclipsing her words. In her simple cotton blouse and black trousers she seemed proof of all he'd lost, never had. Insanely he wanted to ask her *will you marry me*, knowing in some deep place if they did marry he'd never regret it. He resettled the pistol on his belt. She rose. "I go now," held out her hand. *"Tam biet"* – Goodbye.

Suddenly nothing seemed more important than not losing her. His mind scrambled for ideas. "I must go with you, if Vespa is lazy again."

Slender as bamboo she seemed taller than she was. "If you go my house, Communists make trouble my family."

He tried not to tower over her. "Please, come with me to finest dinner in Hué," aware of speaking pidgin, easy to understand. "Tonight, tomorrow?"

Again she looked away, as if calculating a sum. She looked into his eyes with that distant nearly hostile gaze. "Where?"

He didn't know, had never eaten here, knew only C-rations gulped down between patrols. "Where is best place in Hué?"

She grinned at his innocence. "Tomorrow, six in night? We meet here? Then we go Chez Henri – you like French food?"

He felt she was slipping away but had no room to argue. "Please come. Please don't stay away."

She smiled pure white teeth. "If I say, I do."

"IT'S PISSING ON YOUR COUNTRY," Al Murillo said as they sat eating lunch on an I-beam thirty-six stories up, "to turn in your draft card."

"If the War was right I'd be the first to fight," Mick answered. "But I won't kill people for no reason."

Murillo balled up a tinfoil wrapper and dropped it into the void. "What kinda freedom you think these Vietnamese will have, them Communists win?"

"Al, are *you* ready to die for their freedom? If you're a grunt with a girl and a '57 Chevy waiting for you back home, are you willing to die in a mudhole, your chest or balls or head blown apart? When it's a lie and you know it?"

Murillo spit. "When you put it like that –"

Looking down on gray Manhattan it occurred to Mick his country had become the specter of itself, *I Want to Hold Your Hand* replaced by *Eve of Destruction* – a new dark vision of *Amerika* where automatons goose-step to mindless verities and steel bombers unleash fiery death on distant peasants. But what if we'd always been this way? Though too young, too much a product of it, or too damn dumb, to realize?

"You and me riskin our lives," Al Murillo swung one leg over the girder and sat sideways. "On these skyscrapers, to push them up into the blue, huh?"

"Yeah?" Mick waited.

"You start with a piece of land then these architects plan how to squeeze the last bit of space onto each floor, push higher till the damn things bend in the wind like bamboo, huh? And the bankers change the zoning so you can go even higher and make more money squeezing more and more people into less and less space, huh?"

Murillo adjusted his seat on the cold girder. "Well, it's you and me riskin death so the big guys can make money. So I think, how is that different than this War, huh?"

ON JUDGEMENT DAY Mick woke early, took two tabs of acid and lay beside Rachel waiting for it to hit but it didn't. He'd had nightmares again of Troy wounded, of himself hunted in Bali. Rain hammered the window-panes and sloshed down the downspout. Rachel fumbled for her watch in her clothes on the floor. "Hey it's eight-forty."

In the Lex train going downtown he couldn't tell if he was stoned or not. The weird advertisements, the drum and shriek of wheels, the gently rocking passengers, were clearly hallucinations. But there was no disconnect between what he thought and did: he wasn't stoned. *Damn.* He tried to think how to raise his blood pressure.

The doctor sat at his metal Selective Service desk scorning petitions of malady from a line of supplicants. Implacable and lethal, he had literal power of life or death over his cringing naked subjects. He said you were 4-F and you were out on the street, free forever. He said you were 1-A and you climbed on a bus to Fort Benning and in three months could leave your brains and guts on some Vietnamese hill.

He scanned Mick's file, took his blood pressure. "You don't have hypertension."

"It says right there –"

"*I* said you don't have it. You're headed to Vietnam." He stuffed Mick's file back in its folder, cocked a thumb at the induction room. "Get in line."

Mick stood in a line of young men in a dark corridor, all naked, feet cold, soles dirty, clasping their folders before them like fig leaves. Not sure why, he stepped into the john. It had two stalls, one with no door. Holding his breath against the smell of shit he waited for the one with the door, locked it and scanned his file. Everything was there.

Terrified at what he was doing he ripped the first three pages to small pieces then the rest, then the folder too, flushed and flushed again till all were gone. Sure that abject terror would show in his face, he stepped into the corridor and joined the line going the other way of young men who had been rejected and had their files turned in.

Wouldn't the Selective Service know it was gone? Or would its absence simply make him invisible? When they checked on the draft status of Resistance leaders wouldn't they see it was missing? With shaking knees and a hollow stomach he dressed and stepped dizzily out the heavy door into bright midmorning sun.

"IF YOU'RE NOT WORKING," Thierry Gascon's voice crackled across the undersea cable, "why not come to Paris and work on Gisèle's campaign?"

"I can't hear you," Mick said.

"There – is that better?"

"You don't have to yell!"

"If you have no work on skyscrapers in winter, and you've decided not to join the War..."

After two years teaching at Williams, Thierry had returned to Paris to teach medieval lit at the Sorbonne. Gisèle Halimi was running for the French Senate, a brilliant and beautiful Socialist lawyer, a friend of Sartre and de Beauvoir. A defender of the poor and oppressed, she had represented Algerian revolutionaries in military courts and had become notorious and widely praised for exposing the Army's torture programs, while, however, the atrocities perpretrated by the Algerian revolutionaries went unreported.

Mick had saved good money from steelworking all summer and fall. Al Lowenstein wanted him to work full time for the antiwar movement, live on what he'd saved.

Or he could take some time off from the meetings, rallies, phone banks, all the intensity.

Plus he'd just torn up his draft file. If they came after him, he'd be a lot harder to find in Paris.

"Election's next March," Thierry said. "Gisèle could win. Imagine, the first woman senator in France..."

ABOUT THE AUTHOR

MIKE BOND is the author of nearly a dozen best-selling novels, a war and human rights journalist, ecologist, international energy expert and award-winning poet. He has been called *"the master of the existential thriller"* (BBC), *"one of America's best thriller writers"* (Culture Buzz), *"a nature writer of the caliber of Matthiessen"* (WordDreams), and *"one of the 21st century's most exciting authors"* (Washington Times).

He has covered wars, revolutions, terrorism, military dictatorships and death squads in the Middle East, Latin America, Asia and Africa, and environmental issues including elephant poaching, habitat loss, wilderness survival, whales, wolves and many other endangered species.

His novels place the reader in intense experiences in the world's most perilous places, in dangerous liaisons, political and corporate conspiracies, wars and revolutions, making *"readers sweat with [their] relentless pace"* (Kirkus) "in that fatalistic margin where life and death are one and the existential reality leaves one caring only to survive." (Sunday Oregonian).

He has climbed mountains on every continent and trekked more than 50,000 miles in the Himalayas, Mongolia, Russia, Europe, New Zealand, North and South America, and Africa.

Website for Mike Bond: mikebondbooks.com

For film, translation or publication rights,
or for interviews contact:
Meryl Moss Media
meryl@merylmossmedia.com or 203-226-0199

ALSO BY MIKE BOND

FREEDOM

From the war-shattered jungles of Vietnam to America's burning cities, near-death in Tibet, peace marches, the battle of Hué and the battle of the Pentagon, wild drugs, rock concerts, free love, CIA coups in Indonesia and Greece, the Six Days' War, and Bobby Kennedy's last campaign and assassination. *Freedom* puts you in the Sixties as if it were now.

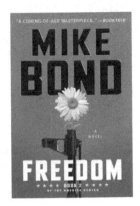

AMERICA

America is the first of Mike Bond's seven-volume historical novel series, capturing the victories and heartbreaks of the last 70 years and of our nation's most profound upheavals since the Civil War – a time that defined the end of the 20th Century and where we are today. Through the wild, joyous, heartbroken and visionary lives of four young people and many others, the Sixties come alive again. *"An extraordinary and deftly crafted novel."* – MIDWEST BOOK REVIEW

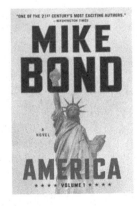

GOODBYE PARIS

Special Forces veteran Pono Hawkins races from Tahiti to France when a terrorist he'd thought was dead has a nuclear weapon to destroy Paris. Joining allies from US and French intelligence, Pono faces impossible odds to save the most beautiful city on earth. Alive with covert action and insider details from the war against terrorism, Goodbye Paris is a hallmark Mike Bond thriller: tense, exciting, and full of real places, and that will keep you up all night. *"A rip-roaring page-turner."* – CULTURE BUZZ

SNOW

Three hunters find a crashed plane filled with cocaine in the Montana wilderness. Two steal the cocaine and are soon hunted by the Mexican cartel, the DEA, Las Vegas killers, and the police of several states. From the frozen peaks of Montana to the heights of Wall Street, the Denver slums and million-dollar Vegas tables, Snow is an electric portrait of today's America, the invisible line between good and evil, and what people will do in their frantic search for love and freedom. *"Action-packed adventure."* – DENVER POST

ASSASSINS

From its terrifying start in the night skies over Afghanistan to its stunning end in the Paris terrorist attacks, Assassins is an insider's thriller of the last 30 years of war between Islam and the West. A US commando, an Afghani warlord, a French woman doctor, a Russian major, a top CIA operator, and a British woman journalist fight for their lives and loves in the deadly 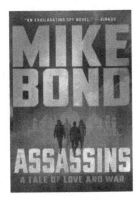 streets and lethal deserts of the Middle East. *"An epic spy story."* – HONOLULU STAR-ADVERTISER

KILLING MAINE

Surfer and Special Forces veteran Pono Hawkins quits sunny Hawaii for Maine's brutal winter to help a former SF buddy beat a murder rap and fight the state's rampant political corruption. *"A gripping tale of murders, manhunts and other crimes set amidst today's dirty politics and corporate graft, an unforgettable hero facing enormous dangers as he tries to save a friend, protect the women he loves,*  *and defend a beautiful, endangered place."* – FIRST PRIZE FOR FICTION, NEW ENGLAND BOOK FESTIVAL

SAVING PARADISE

When Special Forces veteran Pono Hawkins finds a beautiful journalist drowned off Waikiki, he is caught in a web of murder and political corruption. Hunting her killers, he soon finds them hunting him, and blamed for her death. A relentless thriller of politics, sex, and murder, *"an action-packed, must read novel ... taking readers behind the alluring façade of Hawaii's pristine beaches and tourist traps into a festering underworld of murder, intrigue and corruption."* – WASHINGTON TIMES

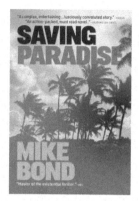

THE LAST SAVANNA

An intense memoir of humanity's ancient heartland, its people, wildlife, deserts and jungles, and the deep, abiding power of love. *"One of the best books yet on Africa, a stunning tale of love and loss amid a magnificent wilderness and its myriad animals, and a deadly manhunt through savage jungles, steep mountains and fierce deserts as an SAS commando tries to save the elephants, the woman he loves and the soul of Africa itself."* – FIRST PRIZE FOR FICTION, LOS ANGELES BOOK FESTIVAL

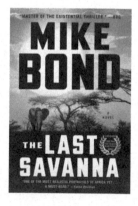

HOLY WAR

Based on the author's experiences in Middle East conflicts, Holy War is the story of the battle of Beirut, of implacable hatreds and frantic love affairs, of explosions, betrayals, assassinations, snipers and ambushes. An American spy, a French commando, a Hezbollah terrorist and a Palestinian woman guerrilla all cross paths on the deadly streets and fierce deserts of the Middle East. *"A profound tale of war... Impossible to stop reading."* – BRITISH ARMED FORCES BROADCASTING

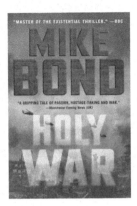

HOUSE OF JAGUAR

A stunning thriller of CIA operations in Latin America, guerrilla wars, drug flights, military dictatorships, and genocides, based on the author's experiences as as one of the last foreign journalists left alive in Guatemala after over 150 journalists had been killed by Army death squads. *"An extraordinary story that speaks from and to the heart. And a terrifying description of one man's battle against the CIA and Latin American death squads."* – BBC

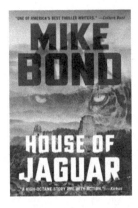

TIBETAN CROSS

An exciting international manhunt and stunning love story. An American climber in the Himalayas stumbles on a shipment of nuclear weapons headed into Tibet for use against China. Pursued by spy agencies and other killers across Asia, Africa, Europe and the US, he is captured then rescued by a beautiful woman with whom he forms a deadly liaison. They escape, are captured and escape again, death always at their heels.

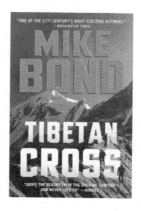

"Grips the reader from the opening chapter and never lets go." – MIAMI HERALD

THE DRUM THAT BEATS WITHIN US

The tradition of the poet warrior endures throughout human history, from our Stone Age ancestors to the Bible's King David, the Vikings of Iceland, Japan's Samurai, the Shambhala teachings of Tibet, the ancient Greeks and medieval knights. Initially published by Lawrence Ferlinghetti in City Lights Books, Mike Bond has won multiple prizes for his poetry and prose. *"Passionately felt emotional connections, particularly to Western landscapes and Native American culture."* – KIRKUS